FROM THE PAGES OF *THE COUNTRY OF THE POINTED FIRS AND SELECTED SHORT FICTION*

We were standing where there was a fine view of the harbor and its long stretches of shore all covered by the great army of the pointed firs, darkly cloaked and standing as if they waited to embark. As we looked far seaward among the outer islands, the trees seemed to march seaward still, going steadily over the heights and down to the water's edge. (from *The Country of the Pointed Firs*, page 29)

Her hospitality was something exquisite; she had the gift which so many women lack, of being able to make themselves and their houses belong entirely to a guest's pleasure,—that charming surrender for the moment of themselves and whatever belongs to them.

(from *The Country of the Pointed Firs*, page 43)

In the life of each of us, I said to myself, there is a place remote and islanded, and given to endless regret or secret happiness.

(from *The Country of the Pointed Firs*, page 73)

"You can never tell beforehand how it's goin' to be, and 't ain't worth while to wear a day all out before it comes."

(from *The Country of the Pointed Firs*, page 76)

The ease that belongs to simplicity is charming enough to make up for whatever a simple life may lack, and the gifts of peace are not for those who live in the thick of battle.

(from *The Country of the Pointed Firs*, page 111)

So we die before our own eyes; so we see some chapters of our lives come to their natural end.

(from *The Country of the Pointed Firs*, page 112)

One can never be so certain of good New England weather as in the days when a long easterly storm has blown away the warm late-summer mists, and cooled the air so that however bright the sunshine is by day, the nights come nearer and nearer to frostiness.

(from "The Queen's Twin," page 123)

So the day did not begin very well, and I began to recognize that it was one of the days when nothing could be done without company.

(from "A Dunnet Shepherdess," page 141)

"I can't think of anything I should like so much as to find that heron's nest."

(from "A White Heron," page 202)

To be leaders of society in the town of Dulham was as satisfactory to Miss Dobin and Miss Lucinda Dobin as if Dulham were London itself.

(from "The Dulham Ladies," page 207)

"When you remember, in years to come, that I came here to see the old school-house, remember that I said: Wish for the best things, and work hard to win them; try to be good men and women, for the honor of the school and the town, and the noble young country that gave you birth; be kind at home and generous abroad. Remember that I, an old man who had seen much of life, begged you to be brave and good."

(from "A Native of Winby," page 253)

"I can forgive a person, but when I'm done with 'em, I'm done."

(from "The Guests of Mrs. Timms," page 341)

Being a New Englander, it is natural that I should first speak about the weather.

(from "The White Rose Road," page 349)

Andrea Bourne

THE COUNTRY OF THE POINTED FIRS

AND SELECTED SHORT FICTION

SARAH ORNE JEWETT

With an Introduction and Notes by Ted Olson

GEORGE STADE
CONSULTING EDITORIAL DIRECTOR

BARNES & NOBLE CLASSICS
NEW YORK

BARNES & NOBLE CLASSICS
NEW YORK

Published by Barnes & Noble Books
122 Fifth Avenue
New York, NY 10011

www.barnesandnoble.com/classics

The Country of the Pointed Firs was first published in 1896.
See For Further Reading (p. 383) for detailed information on the original publication of all texts in this edition.

Published in 2005 by Barnes & Noble Classics with new Introduction, Notes, Biography, Chronology, Inspired By, Comments & Questions, and For Further Reading.

The Country of the Pointed Firs and Selected Short Fiction
ISBN 1-59308-262-2
LC Control Number 2004112691

Produced and published in conjunction with:
Fine Creative Media, Inc.
322 Eighth Avenue
New York, NY 10001
Michael J. Fine, President and Publisher

Printed in the United States of America

QM

1 3 5 7 9 10 8 6 4 2

FIRST PRINTING

SARAH ORNE JEWETT

Sarah Orne Jewett was born on September 3, 1849, in South Berwick, Maine. Her family lived in a comfortable house next door to her paternal grandparents. From an early age her educated family and especially her father instilled in her a love of literature, and she read widely. Sarah's father, a country doctor, took her in his horse-drawn carriage to see patients, often as an alternative to attending a village school; she also frequently failed to attend school because of recurring bouts of rheumatism. On their trips together Sarah's father taught her to carefully observe the Maine countryside and coastal towns and the country folk who lived there. Sarah's travels with her father and the time she spent listening to the local sailors who swapped stories in her grandfather's general store fed her talent for storytelling; by age eighteen Sarah had published her first piece of fiction, "Jenny Garrow's Lovers (1868)," under the pen name A. C. Eliot. Having received an inheritance from her grandfather, she was free to pursue a writer's life without financial worries.

William Dean Howells, then editor of the acclaimed *Atlantic Monthly*, accepted the story "Mr. Bruce" in 1869, thereby launching Jewett's career. While in her imagination and writing Jewett may have remained loyal to her native state, her literary circle stretched far beyond the borders of South Berwick and included some of the most distinguished authors of the era. Through Howells, and later her lifelong friend Annie Fields, Jewett came to know such figures as Mark Twain, Matthew Arnold, Harriet Beecher Stowe, Alfred Tennyson, Henry James, and Charles Dickens.

In 1873 the *Atlantic Monthly* published "The Shore House," a sketch about life in the fictional Maine town of Deephaven, which resembled South Berwick. (The magazine first published most of the short works that Jewett later published in book form.) With this sketch Jewett began to find her voice as a "local color" writer—that is, one who focuses on the unique qualities of a particular region and its people. With Howell's editorial guidance, these sketches and others were later collected in Jewett's first book, *Deephaven* (1877).

Jewett was greatly saddened by her father's death in 1878 and eventually dedicated two books to him: *Country By-Ways* (1881), a book of nonfiction sketches, and *A Country Doctor* (1884), a novel whose main character is based on her father. By the mid-1880s Jewett was producing the work for which she is best known. In 1886 she published *A White Heron and Other Stories*, a book of short fiction. The title story is one of the most anthologized in America. Her short story collections from this fruitful time include *The King of Folly Island, and Other People* (1888) and *A Native of Winby, and Other Tales* (1893).

Jewett's quiet life in South Berwick was often interrupted by travels in America and abroad. She frequently divided her time between her own home and Fields's residences in Boston and Manchester-by-the-Sea on the Massachusetts coast. She made four major journeys to Europe with Fields, as well as numerous excursions to visit friends in the New England area.

When her masterpiece, *The Country of the Pointed Firs*, was serialized in the *Atlantic Monthly* and then published in book form by Houghton Mifflin in 1896, Jewett was at the height of her literary powers. Glowing reviews from the likes of Henry James and Rudyard Kipling and excellent book sales helped cement her reputation as a leading author of the time. In 1900 Jewett received an honorary doctorate from Bowdoin College—the first the institution had ever given to a woman.

A carriage accident on her birthday in 1902 left Jewett too physically incapacitated to write, thus effectively ending her literary career. She did, however, maintain her numerous friendships; in her final years she became a mentor to the promising young writer Willa Cather, who was inspired by Jewett's writing. In 1909 Sarah Orne Jewett was partly paralyzed by a stroke but still expressed good spirits and humor in her letters. She died of a second stroke on June 24 in South Berwick.

TABLE OF CONTENTS

THE WORLD OF SARAH ORNE JEWETT AND *THE COUNTRY OF THE POINTED FIRS*

1849 Sarah Orne Jewett is born on September 3 in South Berwick, Maine. The second of three daughters, she will spend most of her childhood in the spacious family house adjacent to her paternal grandparents' home.

1850 Nathaniel Hawthorne's *The Scarlet Letter* appears. The Fugitive Slave Law is enacted.

1851 *Moby-Dick*, by Herman Melville, is published.

1852 *Uncle Tom's Cabin*, by Harriet Beecher Stowe, is published.

1854 *Walden*, by Henry David Thoreau, is published.

1855 Caroline Augusta, Jewett's sister, is born. Walt Whitman's slim first edition of *Leaves of Grass* is published.

1861 After attending a village school irregularly (because of rheumatism, which she suffers from girlhood), Jewett enters Berwick Academy. The American Civil War begins.

1862 Harriet Beecher Stowe's book *The Pearl of Orr's Island*—a local color work that later inspires Jewett's writing—is published.

1863 Abraham Lincoln signs the Emancipation Proclamation.

1865 Jewett graduates from Berwick Academy and ends her formal education. She considers pursuing a career in medicine but decides against it because of frail health. She begins to write short fiction. The Civil War ends. President Lincoln is assassinated. Whitman's *Drum-Taps*, a book of Civil War poetry, is published.

1868 Jewett's first story to be accepted for publication, "Jenny Garrow's Lovers," appears in the *Flag of Our Union* under the pen name A. C. Eliot. Jewett travels to Cincinnati, where she stays with relatives for several months. She frequently travels to Boston and New York. Louisa May Alcott publishes *Little Women.*

1869 Following the rejection of several other stories, Jewett's story "Mr. Bruce" is accepted by the *Atlantic Monthly* and published under the name A. C. Eliot. The Union Pacific Railroad is completed, linking the east and west coasts of the United States. Mark Twain's *The Innocents Abroad* is published.

early 1870s William Dean Howells, editor of the *Atlantic Monthly*, introduces Jewett to a number of Boston-area literati.

1873 "The Shore House," the first of a number of sketches set in the fictional town of Deephaven, Maine, is published in the *Atlantic Monthly*. During this period she forms lasting bonds with her Cambridge and Boston friends.

1875 She travels to Philadelphia, Chicago, and Wisconsin.

1876 Mark Twain's *The Adventures of Tom Sawyer* is published. Alexander Graham Bell invents the telephone.

1877 With Howell's editorial guidance, Jewett refines and publishes her first book, *Deephaven*, a collection of previously published sketches and other writings.

1878 Jewett is deeply saddened by the death of her father. *Play Days*, a book of children's stories, is published.

1880 Jewett develops a lifelong friendship with Boston literary figure Annie Fields (1834–1915), the wife of *Atlantic Monthly* publisher and editor James T. Fields.

1881 Fields's husband dies. Jewett and Fields will spend part of each year together until Jewett's death. They will travel widely in the United States and Europe and will meet many prominent American and European writers, including Mark Twain, Henry James, John Greenleaf Whittier, Harriet Beecher Stowe, Alfred Tennyson, Rudyard Kipling, and Charles Dickens. *Country By-Ways*, a book of nonfiction sketches dedicated to Jewett's father, is published.

1882 Jewett and Fields sail for Europe, the first of four major trips they will take to the continent.

1884 Jewett's first novel, *A Country Doctor*, whose main character is based on her father, is published. Mark Twain's *Adventures of Huckleberry Finn* appears.

1885 Jewett's second novel, *A Marsh Island*, is published in book form.

1886 Jewett publishes *A White Heron, and Other Stories*, a collection of short fiction that includes the popular satiric story "The Dulham Ladies."

1888 *The King of Folly Island, and Other People*, one of Jewett's finest short-story collections, is published.

1890 A novel for younger readers, *Betty Leicester*, is published. William James's *Principles of Psychology* is published.

1892 Jewett and Fields make a second trip to Europe. Jewett's autobiographical essay "Looking Back on Girlhood" is published in the magazine *Youth's Companion*.

1893 *A Native of Winby, and Other Tales* is published.

1895 *The Life of Nancy* is published.

1896 Jewett and Fields take a cruise through the Caribbean. Jewett's masterpiece, *The Country of the Pointed Firs*, is serialized in the *Atlantic Monthly* and then published in book form by Houghton Mifflin. The reviews are overwhelmingly positive, and the book earns the admiration of such writers as Henry James and Rudyard Kipling.

1898 Jewett and Fields travel to Europe a third time.

1899 *The Queen's Twin, and Other Stories* is published. It contains two stories that take place in Dunnet Landing, the fictional town of *The Country of the Pointed Firs*.

1900 Jewett and Fields make a fourth visit to Europe. The *Atlantic Monthly* publishes "The Foreigner," another Dunnet Landing story and one that some consider Jewett's best story.

1901 Jewett is the first woman to receive an honorary Doctor of Letters degree from Bowdoin College in Maine. *The Tory Lover*, the final major volume of her work published during her lifetime, is published following its serialization in the *Atlantic Monthly*.

1902 A carriage accident on her birthday injures Jewett's neck and causes a concussion. She suffers from pain, memory loss, and other symptoms, and for the rest of her life her literary abilities are limited, though she maintains correspondences with friends and visits with them as much as her health allows. William James's *The Varieties of Religious Experience* is published.

1908 When Jewett visits Fields in Boston, the two are introduced to writer Willa Cather. Jewett and Cather become friends, and Jewett inspires Cather to write honestly about the ways of the American prairie, where the younger woman was raised.

1909 In March, while visiting Annie Fields in Boston, Jewett is partially paralyzed by a stroke; she dies in her Berwick home of a second stroke on June 24. She is buried in the Portland Street Cemetery in South Berwick.

1910 The *Atlantic Monthly* publishes "William's Wedding," the last of the Dunnet Landing stories.

INTRODUCTION

Sarah Orne Jewett was born on September 3, 1849, in the small town of South Berwick, Maine. Located in southern Maine near the Atlantic Ocean and not far from that state's border with New Hampshire, South Berwick by the last half of the nineteenth century had already amassed a fascinating history, which inspired Jewett throughout her life. Founded in the 1620s when English emigrants bartered with indigenous peoples for land between the Salmon Falls River and Great Works River, South Berwick was settled primarily by comparatively well-to-do people who in general were not seeking to escape the Old World to attain religious freedom in the New World, but rather were interested in improving their own business prospects. Hence, the community around South Berwick did not share the strongly Puritanical character of many New England towns (such as those in eastern Massachusetts).

The author's formal baptismal name was Theodora Sarah Orne Jewett, though she rarely used her first name when an adult. Her parents were Dr. Theodore Herman Jewett, a physician, and Caroline Frances Perry, whose own father, Dr. William Perry, had been a physician. The second of three children—all daughters—born to Caroline and Theodore Jewett, Sarah Orne Jewett entered an independent elementary school in 1855, though she was frequently ill as a youth and often missed classes; she showed talent in writing but was otherwise an unexceptional student. In 1861, Jewett's parents enrolled young Sarah in another private school, Berwick Academy, which proved to be her final stint in formal education. Graduating from Berwick Academy in 1865, she considered training to become a doctor, then chose not to pursue that goal because of frail health—she was a lifelong sufferer of intermittent rheumatism. About this time, she received an inheritance from her grandfather that freed her from having to pursue a conventional career or having to get married for economic security.

Years later, Sarah Orne Jewett confessed to an interviewer that her most essential learning experiences when young came while she accompanied her father on his service calls in and around South Berwick: "The best of my education was received in my father's buggy and the places to which it carried me. . . . Now, as I write my sketches of country life, I remember again and again the wise things he said, and the sights he made me see" (Cary, *Sarah Orne Jewett Letters*, p. 21; see "For Further Reading"). Strongly influenced by her father's scientifically trained eye and mind, young Sarah learned how to "read" the natural landscape and how to evaluate the behavior of humans living within that landscape.

Dr. Jewett also introduced his daughter to the world of literature, including European classics by such authors as Cervantes, Fielding, and Sterne. On her own, Sarah discovered works by authors from a number of literary traditions—initially, Austen, George Eliot, Emerson, and Thackeray, and, eventually, Zola, Balzac, Flaubert, George Sand, Tolstoy, and Turgenev. According to scholar Josephine Donovan, who investigated Sarah Orne Jewett's unpublished diaries, Jewett by 1869 was reading writings by various female authors of the American "local color" school (*Sara Orne Jewett*, p. 9). "Local color" writing—a literary subgenre that dominated the most prestigious periodicals published in the United States between the end of the Civil War and the beginning of the twentieth century—comprised short stories and nonfiction sketches that attempted to depict the lives of people possessing distinctive regional identities. Local color works tended to feature representations of character types from various American regions (though such representations were often replete with stereotypes); other local color stylistic qualities included romanticized regional settings and literary interpretations of regional dialectical speech. While many local color works did not succeed either as aesthetically memorable creative writing or as ethnographically accurate accounts of specific American regional cultures, several authors associated with this subgenre wrote material of lasting interest, and at least four of those authors caught Jewett's attention during this period, including Elizabeth Stuart Phelps, Rebecca Harding Davis, Louisa May Alcott, and

Harriet Beecher Stowe. During the mid-1860s, Jewett had read Stowe's 1862 book, *The Pearl of Orr's Island*, an early local color classic that portrays life along the coast of Maine with empathy and considerable accuracy. Jewett continued to value Stowe's book into the 1870s, as it inspired the younger author to attempt to depict—with a commitment to the accurate representation of that region and its culture—the rhythms of everyday life in her section of coastal Maine. While the local color movement in American literature would produce many nonfiction sketches, short stories, and novels that were arguably less than successful at capturing in prose the essence of American regions and their cultures, Jewett's work convincingly transcends the usual limitations of the genre by virtue of her direct yet graceful prose style and her intimate familiarity with her subjects—the people and places she had known all her life—which she renders believable through a knowing selection of salient details.

In addition to having physicians in her family lineage, Jewett descended from people who owed their livelihoods to the sea—such as her paternal grandfather Theodore Furber Jewett, a captain of whaling ships. Sarah Orne Jewett grew up profoundly aware of the historical ties between the sea and the human communities situated adjacent to it. As a small New England coastal town, South Berwick was both picturesque and stagnant during the mid-nineteenth century, owing to the steadily declining role of Maine in the national economy. This decline was a result of several factors: the collapse of the whaling industry; the shifting of the center of American shipping from the coast of Maine southward to New York City; Maine's slow recovery from the Embargo Act of 1807, which mandated the freezing of all shipping trade between the United States and England and between the United States and France; and the concurrent western expansion of the United States.

These historical forces may have stunted economic growth along the coast of Maine, yet they also spawned the cultural conditions portrayed in Jewett's writings. Only rarely would Jewett set her fiction outside her native section of Maine, though it was not for lack of travel to other places. By the age of twenty, Jewett had frequently visited Boston; Newport, Rhode Island; and New York City, and she had spent several months in Cincinnati visiting her maternal uncle, a newspaper editorial writer, and his family. By age thirty, Jewett had visited Philadelphia and Chicago, and in 1882 she took her first of four trips to Europe. Jewett's early fascination with the people and places of coastal Maine led her to focus her fiction on that region's wealth of traditional culture. Most of her short stories and novels—set in an environment relatively unchanged by industrialization—contained vivid descriptions of people maintaining traditional lives that relied upon the natural by-products of the land and the sea. The unnamed narrator of Jewett's *The Country of the Pointed Firs*, a woman from the city who is nonetheless an astute observer of small-town culture, describes in considerable detail the occupational folk-ways practiced by the people she meets during a protracted stay in the fictional town of Dunnet Landing, located on the coast of Maine. For example, the narrator's friend Almira Todd maintains an herb garden and brews "old-fashioned spruce beer" for local customers. Also, while visiting Almira's birthplace on Green Island, the narrator witnesses that the Todd family depends upon small-scale agriculture (practiced by Almira Todd's mother) and herring fishing (a job of Almira's brother William Todd).

Jewett's representation of Maine in her fictional works does not fully reflect that she was well aware her childhood home place had been dramatically changed by economic and social forces wrought by the post–Civil War prosperity. By the late 1870s, while Jewett was gaining national attention through her publications, South Berwick was, as the author stated in a letter, "growing and flourishing in a way that breaks my heart" (Blanchard, *Sarah Orne Jewett: Her World and Her Work*, p. 43). The changes in South Berwick were the result of several factors: the reduced role of the sea-related trades in a rapidly industrializing nation; dramatic postwar population growth in the United States, which led to a rise in tourism and second-home development along the Maine coast; the construction of new houses that were architecturally incompatible with the town's older buildings; and the cutting down of trees and the plowing up of fields to accommodate that growth. In 1894, Jewett looked back on the changes in Maine since the Civil War, and lamented that

> tradition and time-honored custom were to be swept away together by the irresistible current. Character and architecture seemed to lose

> individuality and distinction. The new riches of the country were seldom very well spent in those days; the money that the tourist or summer citizen left behind him was apt to be used to sweep away the quaint houses, the roadside thicket, the shady woodland, that had lured him first. . . . It will remain for later generations to make amends for the sad use of riches after the war, for our injury of what we inherited, for the irreparable loss of certain ancient buildings which would have been twice as interesting in the next century as we are just beginning to be wise enough to think them in this (quoted in Blanchard, p. 82).

That in her fiction Jewett tended to overlook—and to condemn in her letters and diaries—this "progress" suggests that the author possessed a powerful psychological connection to her own childhood—manifested in her fascination with preindustrial Maine and its traditional culture. According to biographer Paula Blanchard, Jewett retained her sense of wonder well into her adulthood:

> The sense of seeing everyone and everything with a fresh eye, the playfulness, the absolute honesty and lack of pretense that we associate with the characteristic Jewett style, all belong to her childhood self and are typical of the voice heard in the earliest available letters and diaries. Simplicity is the very essence of the Jewett persona; and while she matured intellectually and deepened emotionally in the normal course of events, her ability always to remain surprised by the world around her was inseparable from her ability to re-create it (Blanchard, p. 45).

One possible biographical explanation for Jewett's idealization of her childhood world during her early adulthood is that her beloved father was ill through much of the 1870s (he died in 1878). In all probability, her memory of her father was integrally associated with the less chaotic (if economically marginal) prewar era when "poor but proud" rural Maine folk—from her romanticized perspective—maintained a hardscrabble yet affirming existence in an ongoing communion with the land and with the sea. Such an attitude, of course, reflected the literary and philosophical influence of early-nineteenth-century English Romantics as reinterpreted by mid-nineteenth-century New England Transcendentalists. Certainly, some of Jewett's work (most memorably in *The Country of the Pointed Firs*) evinces a mystical bond between humans and nature—a bond that Jewett herself deeply felt. In an undated letter written after a nighttime walk through South Berwick, Jewett confessed that she had witnessed

> a great grey cloud in the west but all the rest of the sky was clear and it was very beautiful—When one goes out of doors and wanders about alone at such a time, how wonderfully one becomes part of nature—like an atom of quicksilver against a great mass—I hardly keep my separate consciousness but go on and on until the mood has spent itself (Blanchard, p. 187).

Jewett's first published work of fiction, the short story "Jenny Garrow's Lovers," appeared under a pseudonym in the January 18, 1868, edition of the widely distributed weekly periodical *Flag of Our Union*. Jewett had previously composed poems, several of which had been published in the local Berwick paper, again under pseudonyms, and a few of her poems appeared in print after "Jenny Garrow's Lovers" brought her work to a readership outside South Berwick (Jewett's poetry was posthumously collected in a 1916 book entitled *Verses*).

Although she later disowned "Jenny Garrow's Lovers," Jewett gravitated to fiction as her primary genre of literary expression. The next year brought her first publication in a major national periodical—the short story "Mr. Bruce," which appeared in the December 1869 issue of the *Atlantic Monthly*. Sending new stories to the editors of leading literary magazines and journals, Jewett by the mid-1870s had developed a circle of supporters who would prove crucial to her career, including the editors of the *Atlantic Monthly*, James T. Fields and William Dean Howells.

Howells—who was a leading promoter of the Emersonian vision for a distinctly American literature—played a major role in the evolution of Jewett's fiction by encouraging her to accentuate in her work her own uniquely American experience. From Howells's mentorship, Jewett wrote a variety of pieces that either were overtly autobiographical sketches or were fictional narratives modeled on her own experience of growing up in Maine. Most of her writings reflect the mood of optimism that infused New England society after the Civil War. Affiliated with Congregationalist and Episcopalian churches as a child, Jewett as an adult rejected the more pessimistic Calvinistic religious stances associated with rural and small-town New England in favor of a positivistic humanism influenced by her strong interest in Swedenborgian doctrine (popularized for Jewett's generation by Harvard professor Theophilus Parsons), which advocated belief in the cosmic interplay between seemingly diametrically opposed entities (body/soul, material/spiritual, life/death, etc.).

Before long, Jewett's short stories and nonfiction sketches—virtually all depicting rural Maine social life—were appearing in the *Atlantic Monthly* as well as in *Harper's* and *Scribner's*. By 1877, encouraged by Howells, Jewett revised some of her sketches published in the *Atlantic Monthly* and mixed them with unpublished writings to create her first book, *Deephaven*. Lacking thematic unity yet balancing insightful realism and unsentimental empathy toward its characters, *Deephaven* sold comparatively well nationally and drew the attention of prominent authors across the United States. Ultimately, however, Jewett's growing success as an author led to her feeling alienated from neighbors and friends in South Berwick. Hence, the 1870s were increasingly lonely for Jewett. She refused to marry, feeling repulsed at the limitations that the institution imposed upon women of her era. And though she greatly valued relationships with other women (in the idealized and intimate yet nonsexual way of many late-nineteenth-century upper-middle-class New England women, according to the speculation of biographer Paula Blanchard), Jewett could find few female companions, beyond her beloved sisters, in South Berwick. During the last half of that decade, she traveled frequently from Maine to visit new friends in other states, which only increased her frustration with her hometown's seeming insularity.

Jewett's mood brightened by the early 1880s when she developed a friendship with Annie Adams Fields, the wife of former publisher and *Atlantic Monthly* editor James T. Fields. Jewett had met Annie Fields sometime in the mid-1870s, at one of many social functions they mutually attended, yet it would be several years before they became friends. In her role as wife to James Fields, Annie hosted innumerable social events for the New England literary establishment, both at the Fields's house on Charles Street in Boston and at their summer residence in the small community of Manchester-by-the-Sea, located north of Boston along the Massachusetts coast. At one Boston literary gathering in 1879, Jewett—who was then an initiate in New England literary circles—impressed Annie Fields, and the latter subsequently invited Jewett to spend a few days in Manchester the following summer. The friendship between the two women deepened after James Fields's death from a heart attack in the spring of 1881; later that year, knowing that Annie Fields was still deeply grieving, Jewett traveled to Boston to look after her friend. Indeed, both women were taking care of each other, since Jewett had been suffering from a recent bout of rheumatism. Thus began one of the most renowned of the so-called "Boston marriages," which were rather common domestic arrangements among late-nineteenth-century New England women, in which two women would choose to live together—constantly or frequently—in mutually symbiotic partnerships. Over the next three decades, Jewett regularly visited Annie at the elder woman's two residences, and the two women often traveled together to various U.S. destinations and to Europe on four separate occasions.

In the early 1880s, while having found fulfilling companionship with Annie, Jewett felt profound sadness at the recent loss of her father. In fact, she dedicated two books to him: her 1881 collection compiling nonfiction sketches of the Maine coast, *Country By-Ways*, and her 1884 novel, *A Country Doctor* (essentially a fictionalized portrait of her father). These books were therapeutic, helping the author convert grief to inspiration. Indeed, while Annie remained a pillar of support for Jewett during her successful years as an author as well as during her last years of illness and injury, the memory of Theodore Herman Jewett continued to serve as a catalyst for Sarah Orne Jewett's creativity during the decade of her greatest productivity and achievement: 1886–1896. Her printed dedication in the earlier of the aforementioned two books suggests the depth of Dr. Jewett's impact upon her: "My dear father; my dear friend; the best and wisest man I ever knew; who taught me many lessons and showed me many things as we went together along the country by-ways." Inevitably, the author's evocations of Maine in her finest nonfiction sketches, short stories, and novels were largely drawn from the well of her memory, which had been filled during a childhood spent traveling around South Berwick with her father, the country doctor. Adoration for Dr. Jewett likely contributed to Sarah Orne Jewett's avoidance of relationships—particularly a marital relationship—with men. Not surprisingly, her fictional depictions of male-female marriage relationships were less passionate and less psychologically and spiritually transformational than her representations of female-female friendships.

In the mid-1880s, Jewett began to produce the works she is remembered for today, though she had already attained considerable financial success through the publication of her work in prestigious literary magazines and in books issued by major publishers (James R. Osgood and Company and, later, Houghton Mifflin and Company, and, for one book, G. P. Putnam's Sons). Her published works through 1885 were *Deephaven* (1877); a book for children, *Play Days* (1878); *Country By-Ways* (1881); two short-story collections, *Old Friends and New* (1879) and *The Mate of the Daylight, and Friends Ashore* (1884); and the novels *A Country Doctor* (1884) and *A Marsh Island* (1885) (the latter had been originally serialized in the *Atlantic Monthly*).

In 1886, Jewett's publisher, Houghton Mifflin, issued her collection of short fiction *A White Heron, and Other Stories*; the title story from that book remains not only Jewett's best-known work of short fiction but also among the most anthologized short stories by any nineteenth-century American author. Also featuring the popular Jewett story "The Dulham Ladies," *A White Heron, and Other Stories* constituted a major advance for Jewett, as the finest stories in that collection marked her emergence as arguably the most skilled among writers of American regional local color fiction. Subtler and more carefully crafted than her earlier work, those 1886 short stories and several later ones by Jewett—along with her classic novel *The Country of the Pointed Firs*, a book published in 1896 after being serialized in the *Atlantic Monthly*—would secure for the author a central position in American literary history as an important transitional figure who transcended the limitations of the local color movement by producing literary work that both chronicled and universalized one American region and its human culture.

Not all of her works published between *A White Heron, and Other Stories* and *The Country of the Pointed Firs* were among Jewett's most noteworthy efforts, however. Two books intended for younger readers—*The Story of the Normans* (1887; her only book published by G. P. Putnam's Sons), an impressionistic account of the Norman invasion, and the novel *Betty Leicester: A Story for Girls* (1890)—are seldom read today. Nevertheless, the latter book foreshadows *The Country of the Pointed Firs* in that both novels chronicle the interactions between "outsider" protagonists and rural Maine folk, with both "insiders" and "outsiders" mutually benefiting from the experience. (*Betty Leicester* was followed in 1894 by a sequel, *Betty Leicester's English Christmas: A New Chapter of an Old Story.*)

Between *The Story of the Normans* and *The Country of the Pointed Firs*, Jewett published four new collections of short stories: *The King of Folly Island, and Other People* (1888), *Strangers and Wayfarers* (1890), *A Native of Winby, and Other Tales* (1893), and *The Life of Nancy* (1895). These collections contain some of her most memorable efforts in the short-story form, from "The Courting of Sister Wisby" (1888), which humorously critiques the institution of marriage; to "A Winter Courtship" (1890), which portrays the social expectations of an older couple planning their marriage; to "The Flight of Betsey Lane" (1893), which explores the independence from society of a character unconcerned with class or money. Also included in those four collections are some of Jewett's most enduring nonfiction sketches—such as "The White Rose Road" (1890), which assesses the environmental degradation of her native section of Maine—as well as some short stories of primarily historical rather than purely literary interest. Among the latter stories are the 1893 "Decoration Day" (a favorite of Jewett herself but little read in recent years), which depicts a Civil War commemoration ceremony attended by veterans of that war, and "A Native of Winby" (1893), which chronicles a fictional United States senator's return to visit his hometown and his encounter with a woman he had courted in the past. Other memorable short stories from this phase of Jewett's career include "The Passing of Sister Barsett" (1893), which concerns a nurse's disgust at the callousness of relatives who fail to show proper respect to a dying elderly woman; "The Hiltons' Holiday" (1895), which portrays the aspirations of Maine girls who seek to develop imaginations in a hostile rural environment; and "The Guests of Mrs. Timms" (1895), an exploration of the subtlety of class distinctions among late-nineteenth-century New England women.

By 1896 Jewett had produced a diverse body of work, with her greatest aesthetic achievement having been in the short story; she had emerged as one of the most respected American authors, praised by critics and fellow writers (from John Greenleaf Whittier to Henry James) and passionately appreciated by female readers who valued Jewett's keen insight into the hearts and minds of women (her fictional characterizations of men were generally less compelling). Jewett's next work, *The Country of the Pointed Firs*, revealed that she could sustain an imaginative narrative beyond the necessarily limited scope of the short story form. That novel garnered emphatically positive responses from readers and critics as well as from such fellow authors as Rudyard Kipling, who wrote in a letter to Jewett: "I maintain (and will maintain with outcries if necessary) that that is the realest New England book ever given us" (Blanchard, p. 304).

Interestingly, Jewett herself was less sure regarding the worth of that work, and for some years afterward she insisted that she preferred her earlier novel, *A Marsh Island*, which today is seldom read. Jewett was exhausted after completing *The Country of the Pointed Firs*, and three years would pass before the appearance of her next book. *The Queen's Twin, and Other Stories* (1899) contains two pieces of short fiction (the title story and "A Dunnet Shepherdess") set in the fictional town—Dunnet Landing—that was featured in *The Country of the Pointed Firs*, suggesting that that novel had made a deeper impression in Jewett's psyche than the author could admit at the time. During this period, Jewett wrote two other Dunnet Landing stories, "The Foreigner" and "William's Wedding." "The Queen's Twin" and "A Dunnet Shepherdess" were originally published in the *Atlantic Monthly* in 1899; "The Foreigner" (which some Jewett scholars consider as one of her finest short stories) appeared in that same periodical in 1900; while "William's Wedding" was published there posthumously in 1910. The editors of *The Best Stories of Sarah Orne Jewett* (published by Houghton Mifflin in 1925) incorporated all of those Dunnet Landing stories except for

"The Foreigner" into the original text of *The Country of the Pointed Firs* without Jewett's direction or approval. In the present edition, the four later Dunnet Landing stories are printed in a separate section to reflect the fact that Jewett in all likelihood intended those stories to stand apart from the original text of *The Country of the Pointed Firs* as individualized narrative statements.

The final major volume of Jewett's work published during her lifetime, *The Tory Lover*, appeared in 1901, though that historical novel had been previously serialized in the *Atlantic Monthly*. Set in both England and Maine during the Revolutionary War, *The Tory Lover* depicts the plights of protagonists—English settlers in the New World—whose loyalties shift from supporting the king to sympathizing with the colonialist cause. While judged by several of Jewett's literary friends, including Henry James, as being of less value as imaginative literature than *The Country of the Pointed Firs*, *The Tory Lover* was personally significant to Jewett because in writing it the author psychologically wove together many strands of her ancestral and regional identities. Shortly after the novel's publication, Jewett conveyed in a letter: "I cannot believe that so much of my heart was put into it without some life staying there—I could not have died until I got it done!" (Blanchard, p. 348). While *The Tory Lover* was neither a critical success nor a popular best-seller, the year 1901 nonetheless brought Jewett a measure of professional recognition when she received an honorary Doctor of Letters degree from Maine's Bowdoin College, which was the first such degree ever bestowed upon a woman by an all-male academic institution in the United States.

On the day she turned fifty-three years of age, September 3, 1902, while on a horse-drawn carriage ride with her sister and a friend, Jewett was injured after the horse fell, hurling the author onto the ground. Jewett's wounds (including neck injuries and a concussion) were serious, and she never fully recovered. Certainly, her productivity as an author diminished after the accident. During the remaining years of her life, Jewett would produce just one more book, *An Empty Purse* (1905), which contained a single short story. Over the next several years, her health remained precarious—she suffered from chronic physical discomfort caused by rheumatism as well as by emotional factors (specifically, Annie Fields's 1902 stroke and the

1904 death of Jewett's friend Sarah Whitman). While Jewett did not write much fiction during this period, by 1907 she had regained some of her strength, though her primary commitment to writing involved sending letters to friends and acquaintances (many of these documents were collected in a 1911 volume of Jewett's letters edited by Annie Fields). One of Jewett's newest correspondents was the younger author Willa Cather, whom Jewett befriended during the final year of her life (after Jewett's death, Cather would publicly credit Jewett for her mentorship and would continue to promote Jewett's work). In March 1909, while visiting Annie Fields in Boston, Jewett suffered a stroke. Moved back the next month by train to South Berwick, she died on June 24, 1909, in her home.

Sarah Orne Jewett's most enduring contributions to the canon of American literature were *The Country of the Pointed Firs* and a dozen or so short stories—most if not all of which, arguably, are included in this Barnes & Noble Classics edition. Needless to say, the author's standing among literary critics has grown steadily through the years. Only a few pieces of criticism on Jewett's literary output appeared during her lifetime—notably, two essays published in the *Atlantic Monthly*: "Miss Jewett" (1894), by Horace E. Scudder, and "The Art of Miss Jewett" (1904), by Charles Miner Thompson. A revelatory source of information on Jewett's life and literary career published before the author's death was her own 1892 essay "Looking Back on Girlhood," which originally appeared in the nationally popular magazine *Youth's Companion*. In a 1903 edition of the British literary magazine *Academy and Literature*, critic Edward Garnett wrote prophetically regarding the value of *The Country of the Pointed Firs* and regarding the inevitable embrace of that book by future generations: "So delicate is the artistic lesson of this little masterpiece that it will probably be left for generations of readers less hurried than ours to assimilate" (Cary, *Appreciation of Sarah Orne Jewett*, p. 25).

After Jewett's death, critics and scholars began the process of assessing the author's overall literary achievement. An August 1909 piece in the *Atlantic Monthly* by M. A. De Wolfe Howe featured an appreciation of Jewett and her work. In a 1913 essay in the *Yale Review*, Edward M. Chapman critically evaluated Jewett's entire oeuvre. Likely the most influential appraisal of Jewett was from Willa Cather, who, in her preface to the aforementioned 1925 selected edition of Jewett's fiction, stated that *The Country of the Pointed Firs* was one of the few true classics of American literature. As Cather proposed in that preface:

> If I were asked to name three American books which have the possibility of a long, long life, I would say at once, *The Scarlet Letter*, *Huckleberry Finn*, and *The Country of the Pointed Firs*. I can think of no others that confront time and change so serenely. The latter book seems to me fairly to shine with the reflection of its long, joyous future. It is so tightly yet so lightly built, so little encumbered with heavy materialism that deteriorates and grows old-fashioned. I like to think with what pleasure, with what a sense of rich discovery, the young student of American literature in far distant years to come will take up this book and say, "A masterpiece!" as proudly as if he himself had made it (Cather, p. xviii).

That 1925 edition attracted many new readers to Jewett's fiction, and interest in the author's work continued to grow among scholars. Francis Otto Matthiessen, in a 1929 biography of Jewett, wrote: "She has withstood the onslaught of time, and is secure within her limits" (*Sarah Orne Jewett*, p. 145). In a 1940 study of New England literature, Van Wyck Brooks stated that he believed Jewett was one of the finest fiction writers in the history of that region: "No one since Hawthorne had pictured this New England world with such exquisite freshness of feeling" (*New England: Indian Summer, 1865–1915*, p. 353). Carlos Baker, in a 1948 survey of American literary history, asserted that Jewett had "the most distinguished career among all the writers of regional fiction. [She] developed her gifts more rapidly, maintained them at a higher level, and employed them with greater dexterity and control than did any of her predecessors in the field" (quoted in Spiller, *Literary History of the United States*, p. 845). According to the 1955 textbook *American Heritage: An Anthology and Interpretive Survey of Our Literature*: "It was Miss Jewett's *The Country of the Pointed Firs* which brought the local color novel to its highest degree of artistic perfection in nineteenth century America" (Howard et al., p. 316).

All those comments, however positive they seemed in their overtones, inadvertently limited Jewett's literary reputation. By suggesting that *The Country of the Pointed Firs* and Jewett's various short stories were primarily successful within the boundaries of the generally disrespected literary genre of local color writing and within New England regional literature, those scholars underestimated the impact of Jewett's achievement. In a more balanced, contemporary perspective on the author's work, biographer Paula Blanchard criticized Jewett for her lack of objectivity about her own work (which Blanchard thought had weakened many of Jewett's writings); similarly, Blanchard chastised the author for catering to "the modest expectations of the periodical reader" (Blanchard, p. 337). Nonetheless, the biographer praised Jewett's best work as being increasingly relevant today, since "thematically Jewett's stories form a coherent whole, expressing concerns about spiritual alienation, social fragmentation, commercial exploitation, and the failure of the national memory" (Blanchard, pp. 337–338).

Jewett has significantly influenced the literary efforts of numerous authors. Kate Chopin, Mary E. Wilkins Freeman, and Mary Noailles Murfree all cited Jewett's fictional works—especially "A White Heron" and *The Country of the Pointed Firs*—as excellent models of imaginative regional writing that had inspired them at some stage in their careers. Willa Cather dedicated her 1913 novel *O Pioneers!* to Jewett, stating in her dedication that "I tried to tell the story of the people [in *O Pioneers!*] as truthfully and simply as if I were telling it to her [Jewett] by word of mouth." Jewett's works were distinguishable by her distinctive literary style, created, according to Cather, out of a "very personal quality of perception, a vivid and intensely personal experience of life" (Donovan, p. 137). Interestingly, Jewett's unique perception—a transcendent, minimalist vision—was originally fostered by her father, who not only encouraged his daughter to write but also provided advice as to how she might do so more effectively. As Jewett wrote in an 1871 diary entry: "Father said this one day[:] 'A story should be managed so that it should *suggest* interesting things to the *reader* instead of the author's doing all the thinking for him, and setting it before him in black and white. The best compliment is for the reader to say "Why didn't he put in this or that[?]"' " (Donovan, p. 4; Jewett's italics). In addition to suggesting that his daughter write in an understated way, Dr. Jewett encouraged the aspiring author to interpret the world realistically rather than sentimentally. Elsewhere in her diary, Jewett wrote: "My dear father used to say to me very often, 'Tell things *just as they are!*' " (Donovan, p. 5; Jewett's italics).

Some recent critics have suggested that Jewett did not heed her father's latter point. In *The Country of the Pointed Firs* and in some short stories, these critics believe, Jewett indulged in nostalgia. According to critic Susan Allen Toth, "Most writers on Jewett agree that the world of Dunnet Landing, recorded in *The Country of the Pointed Firs*, is one of nostalgic charm, quiet appeal, warmth, and community. Yet it is also a decaying world, since its guardians are all old[,] and no generation waits to take their place" (*Regionalism and the Female Imagination: A Collection of Essays*, p. 25). Yet, the nostalgic representation of a well-ordered rural culture in an American region is precisely part of the appeal of Jewett's work to American readers in urban, modern times. Indeed, *The Country of the Pointed Firs* explored a world that exhibited little of the vitality rampant in the United States during the post–Civil War prosperity.

It might be said that Jewett loved the past (though her vision of history was often romanticized) and feared the future (Jewett was well aware that Maine was becoming economically and politically marginal compared to more prosperous states). Jewett's conservatism was perhaps partly a result of her psychological desire to maintain her social standing in a largely rural region. The plight of the unnamed narrator in *The Country of the Pointed Firs* echoed Jewett's own insider/outsider status in South Berwick. That narrator, a writer like Jewett, was visiting the fictional village of Dunnet Landing in the hope of finding the peace of mind to write and to be spiritually transformed in a cultural environment unencumbered by divisive, class-based snobbery. Both Jewett and her alter ego sought escape from the strictures of Victorian society by consciously seeking acceptance within a traditional rural culture. These two women—the creator and her fictional personae—form bonds of friendship with other females in order to better express their natural selves within a natural rather than manmade environment; this was an act of rebellion that permitted the women to escape from the social straitjacket constructed for them by the Victorian male hierarchy.

Jewett's effort to experience the range of human life in and around her hometown of South Berwick, Maine, and to record that life in fictional works resulted in the author becoming an important literary figure in American letters and one of the more acclaimed female writers in all of American literature prior to the twentieth century. Certainly, Jewett immortalized her native place, and her memory is permanently implanted in that landscape. Her childhood home—a stately colonial-style house in which she lived until 1887—is today the South Berwick Public Library, while her equally impressive later residence—the Jewett House, a Georgian mansion built in 1774 and owned by members of the Jewett family since 1819—has been preserved as an historic building by the organization long called the Society for the Preservation of New England Antiquities and now known as Historic New England. Perhaps most significantly, nearly a century after her death, Jewett's literary achievement continues to influence not only the cultural life of her hometown, but also that of her home state and of her nation.

Ted Olson holds a Ph.D. in English (1997) from the University of Mississippi. Presently Associate Professor at East Tennessee State University in Johnson City, Tennessee, Olson is the author of *Blue Ridge Folklife* (University Press of Mississippi, 1998); the editor of a poetry collection by the late Kentucky author James Still, *From the Mountain, From the Valley: New and Collected Poems* (University Press of Kentucky, 2001); the editor of *CrossRoads: A Southern Culture Annual* (Mercer University Press, 2004); the coeditor (with Charles K. Wolfe) of *The Bristol Sessions: Writings About the Big Bang of Country Music* (McFarland, 2005); the music section editor and associate editor for the *Encyclopedia of Appalachia* (University of Tennessee Press, 2006); the author of *So Far: Poems* (Creeker Press, 1994); and a contributing author to *Hiking Trails of the Smokies* (Great Smoky Mountains Natural History Association, 1994, revised edition, 2001). Additionally, Olson is the author of many articles, essays, encyclopedia entries, reviews, oral histories, poems, and creative nonfiction pieces published in a wide variety of books and periodicals. For more than twenty-five years he has performed American, British, and Irish folk songs and ballads at a wide variety of educational and entertainment venues.

THE COUNTRY OF THE POINTED FIRS

To Alice Greenwood Howe

CONTENTS

CONTENTS

1.

The Return.

There was something about the coast town of Dunnet[1] which made it seem more attractive than other maritime villages of eastern Maine. Perhaps it was the simple fact of acquaintance with that neighborhood which made it so attaching, and gave such interest to the rocky shore and dark woods, and the few houses which seemed to be securely wedged and tree-nailed in among the ledges by the Landing. These houses made the most of their seaward view, and there was a gayety and determined floweriness in their bits of garden ground; the small-paned high windows in the peaks of their steep gables were like knowing eyes that watched the harbor and the far sea-line beyond, or looked northward all along the shore and its background of spruces and balsam firs. When one really knows a village like this and its surroundings, it is like becoming acquainted with a single person. The process of falling in love at first sight is as final as it is swift in such a case, but the growth of true friendship may be a lifelong affair.

After a first brief visit made two or three summers before in the course of a yachting cruise, a lover of Dunnet Landing returned to find the unchanged shores of the pointed firs, the same quaintness of the village with its elaborate conventionalities; all that mixture of remoteness, and childish certainty of being the centre of civilization of which her affectionate dreams had told. One evening in June, a single passenger landed upon the steamboat wharf. The tide was high, there was a fine crowd of spectators, and the younger portion of the company followed her with subdued excitement up the narrow street of the salt-aired, white-clapboarded little town.

2.

Mrs. Todd.

LATER, THERE WAS ONLY one fault to find with this choice of a summer lodging-place, and that was its complete lack of seclusion. At first the tiny house of Mrs. Almira Todd, which stood with its end to the street, appeared to be retired and sheltered enough from the busy world, behind its bushy bit of a green garden, in which all the blooming things, two or three gay hollyhocks and some London-pride, were pushed back against the gray-shingled wall. It was a queer little garden and puzzling to a stranger, the few flowers being put at a disadvantage by so much greenery; but the discovery was soon made that Mrs. Todd was an ardent lover of herbs, both wild and tame, and the sea-breezes blew into the low end-window of the house laden with not only sweet-brier and sweet-mary, but balm and sage and borage and mint, wormwood and southernwood. If Mrs. Todd had occasion to step into the far corner of her herb plot, she trod heavily upon thyme, and made its fragrant presence known with all the rest. Being a very large person, her full skirts brushed and bent almost every slender stalk that her feet missed. You could always tell when she was stepping about there, even when you were half awake in the morning, and learned to know, in the course of a few weeks' experience, in exactly which corner of the garden she might be.

At one side of this herb plot were other growths of a rustic pharmacopœia, great treasures and rarities among the commoner herbs. There were some strange and pungent odors that roused a dim sense and remembrance of something in the forgotten past. Some of these might once have belonged to sacred and mystic rites, and have had some occult knowledge handed with them down the centuries; but now they pertained only to humble compounds brewed at intervals with molasses or vinegar or spirits in a small caldron on Mrs. Todd's kitchen stove. They were dispensed to suffering neighbors, who usually came at night as if by stealth, bringing their own ancient-looking vials to be filled. One nostrum was called the

Indian remedy, and its price was but fifteen cents; the whispered directions could be heard as customers passed the windows. With most remedies the purchaser was allowed to depart unadmonished from the kitchen, Mrs. Todd being a wise saver of steps; but with certain vials she gave cautions, standing in the doorway, and there were other doses which had to be accompanied on their healing way as far as the gate, while she muttered long chapters of directions, and kept up an air of secrecy and importance to the last. It may not have been only the common ails of humanity with which she tried to cope; it seemed sometimes as if love and hate and jealousy and adverse winds at sea might also find their proper remedies among the curious wild-looking plants in Mrs. Todd's garden.

The village doctor and this learned herbalist were upon the best of terms. The good man may have counted upon the unfavorable effect of certain potions which he should find his opportunity in counteracting; at any rate, he now and then stopped and exchanged greetings with Mrs. Todd over the picket fence. The conversation became at once professional after the briefest preliminaries, and he would stand twirling a sweet-scented sprig in his fingers, and make suggestive jokes, perhaps about her faith in a too persistent course of thoroughwort elixir, in which my landlady professed such firm belief as sometimes to endanger the life and usefulness of worthy neighbors.

To arrive at this quietest of seaside villages late in June, when the busy herb-gathering season was just beginning, was also to arrive in the early prime of Mrs. Todd's activity in the brewing of old-fashioned spruce beer. This cooling and refreshing drink had been brought to wonderful perfection through a long series of experiments; it had won immense local fame, and the supplies for its manufacture were always giving out and having to be replenished. For various reasons, the seclusion and uninterrupted days which had been looked forward to proved to be very rare in this otherwise delightful corner of the world. My hostess and I had made our shrewd business agreement on the basis of a simple cold luncheon at noon, and liberal restitution in the matter of hot suppers, to provide for which the lodger might sometimes be seen hurrying down the road, late in the day, with cunner line* in hand. It was soon found that this

---

*String of fish.

arrangement made large allowance for Mrs. Todd's slow herb-gathering progresses through woods and pastures. The spruce-beer customers were pretty steady in hot weather, and there were many demands for different soothing syrups and elixirs with which the unwise curiosity of my early residence had made me acquainted. Knowing Mrs. Todd to be a widow, who had little beside this slender business and the income from one hungry lodger to maintain her, one's energies and even interest were quickly bestowed, until it became a matter of course that she should go afield every pleasant day, and that the lodger should answer all peremptory knocks at the side door.

In taking an occasional wisdom-giving stroll in Mrs. Todd's company, and in acting as business partner during her frequent absences, I found the July days fly fast, and it was not until I felt myself confronted with too great pride and pleasure in the display, one night, of two dollars and twenty-seven cents which I had taken in during the day, that I remembered a long piece of writing, sadly belated now, which I was bound to do. To have been patted kindly on the shoulder and called "darlin'," to have been offered a surprise of early mushrooms for supper, to have had all the glory of making two dollars and twenty-seven cents in a single day, and then to renounce it all and withdraw from these pleasant successes, needed much resolution. Literary employments are so vexed with uncertainties at best, and it was not until the voice of conscience sounded louder in my ears than the sea on the nearest pebble beach that I said unkind words of withdrawal to Mrs. Todd. She only became more wistfully affectionate than ever in her expressions, and looked as disappointed as I expected when I frankly told her that I could no longer enjoy the pleasure of what we called "seein' folks." I felt that I was cruel to a whole neighborhood in curtailing her liberty in this most important season for harvesting the different wild herbs that were so much counted upon to ease their winter ails.

"Well, dear," she said sorrowfully, "I've took great advantage o' your bein' here. I ain't had such a season for years, but I have never had nobody I could so trust. All you lack is a few qualities, but with time you'd gain judgment an' experience, an' be very able in the business. I'd stand right here an' say it to anybody."

Mrs. Todd and I were not separated or estranged by the change in our business relations; on the contrary, a deeper intimacy seemed to begin. I do not know what herb of the night it was that used sometimes to send out a penetrating odor late in the evening, after the dew had fallen, and the moon was high, and the cool air came up from the sea. Then Mrs. Todd would feel that she must talk to somebody, and I was only too glad to listen. We both fell under the spell, and she either stood outside the window, or made an errand to my sitting-room, and told, it might be very commonplace news of the day, or, as happened one misty summer night, all that lay deepest in her heart. It was in this way that I came to know that she had loved one who was far above her.

"No, dear, him I speak of could never think of me," she said. "When we was young together his mother didn't favor the match, an' done everything she could to part us; and folks thought we both married well, but 't wa'n't what either one of us wanted most; an' now we're left alone again, an' might have had each other all the time. He was above bein' a seafarin' man, an' prospered more than most; he come of a high family, an' my lot was plain an' hard-workin'. I ain't seen him for some years; he's forgot our youthful feelin's, I expect, but a woman's heart is different; them feelin's comes back when you think you've done with 'em, as sure as spring comes with the year. An' I've always had ways of hearin' about him."

She stood in the centre of a braided rug, and its rings of black and gray seemed to circle about her feet in the dim light. Her height and massiveness in the low room gave her the look of a huge sibyl, while the strange fragrance of the mysterious herb blew in from the little garden.

3.

The Schoolhouse.

For some days after this, Mrs. Todd's customers came and went past my windows, and, haying-time being nearly over, strangers began to arrive from the inland country, such was her widespread reputation. Sometimes I saw a pale young creature like a white windflower left over into midsummer, upon whose face consumption had set its bright and wistful mark; but oftener two stout, hard-worked women from the farms came together, and detailed their symptoms to Mrs. Todd in loud and cheerful voices, combining the satisfactions of a friendly gossip with the medical opportunity. They seemed to give much from their own store of therapeutic learning. I became aware of the school in which my landlady had strengthened her natural gift; but hers was always the governing mind, and the final command, "Take of hy'sop one handful" (or whatever herb it was), was received in respectful silence. One afternoon, when I had listened,—it was impossible not to listen, with cottonless ears,—and then laughed and listened again, with an idle pen in my hand, during a particularly spirited and personal conversation, I reached for my hat, and, taking blotting-book and all under my arm, I resolutely fled further temptation, and walked out past the fragrant green garden and up the dusty road. The way went straight uphill, and presently I stopped and turned to look back.

The tide was in, the wide harbor was surrounded by its dark woods, and the small wooden houses stood as near as they could get to the landing. Mrs. Todd's was the last house on the way inland. The gray ledges of the rocky shore were well covered with sod in most places, and the pasture bayberry and wild roses grew thick among them. I could see the higher inland country and the scattered farms. On the brink of the hill stood a little white schoolhouse, much wind-blown and weather-beaten, which was a landmark to seagoing folk; from its door there was a most beautiful view of sea and shore. The summer vacation now prevailed, and after finding the door unfastened, and taking a long look through one of the seaward windows, and reflecting afterward for some time in a shady place near by among the bayberry bushes, I returned to the chief place of business in the village, and, to the amusement of two of the selectmen, brothers and autocrats of Dunnet Landing, I hired the schoolhouse for the rest of the vacation for fifty cents a week.

Selfish as it may appear, the retired situation seemed to possess great advantages, and I spent many days there quite undisturbed, with the sea-breeze blowing through the small, high windows and swaying the heavy outside shutters to and fro. I hung my hat and luncheon-basket on an entry nail as if I were a small scholar, but I sat at the teacher's desk as if I were that great authority, with all the timid empty benches in rows before me. Now and then an idle sheep came and stood for a long time looking in at the door. At sundown I went back, feeling most businesslike, down toward the village again, and usually met the flavor, not of the herb garden, but of Mrs. Todd's hot supper, halfway up the hill. On the nights when there were evening meetings or other public exercises that demanded her presence we had tea very early, and I was welcomed back as if from a long absence.

Once or twice I feigned excuses for staying at home, while Mrs. Todd made distant excursions, and came home late, with both hands full and a heavily laden apron. This was in pennyroyal time, and when the rare lobelia was in its prime and the elecampane was coming on. One day she appeared at the schoolhouse itself, partly out of amused curiosity about my industries; but she explained that there was no tansy in the neighborhood with such snap to it as some that grew about the schoolhouse lot. Being scuffed down all the spring made it grow so much the better, like some folks that had it hard in their youth, and were bound to make the most of themselves before they died.

4.

At the Schoolhouse Window.

ONE DAY I REACHED the schoolhouse very late, owing to attendance upon the funeral of an acquaintance and neighbor, with whose sad decline in health I had been familiar, and whose last days both the doctor and Mrs. Todd had tried in vain to ease. The services had taken place at one o'clock, and now, at quarter past two, I stood at the schoolhouse window, looking down at the procession as it went along the lower road close to the shore. It was a walking funeral, and even at that distance I could recognize most of the mourners as they went their solemn way. Mrs. Begg had been very much respected, and there was a large company of friends following to her grave. She had been brought up on one of the neighboring farms, and each of the few times that I had seen her she professed great dissatisfaction with town life. The people lived too close together for her liking, at the Landing, and she could not get used to the constant sound of the sea. She had lived to lament three seafaring husbands, and her house was decorated with West Indian curiosities, specimens of conch shells and fine coral which they had brought home from their voyages in lumber-laden ships. Mrs. Todd had told me all our neighbor's history. They had been girls together, and, to use her own phrase, had "both seen trouble till they knew the best and worst on 't." I could see the sorrowful, large figure of Mrs. Todd as I stood at the window. She made a break in the procession by walking slowly and keeping the after-part of it back. She held a handkerchief to her eyes, and I knew, with a pang of sympathy, that hers was not affected grief.

Beside her, after much difficulty, I recognized the one strange and unrelated person in all the company, an old man who had always been mysterious to me. I could see his thin, bending figure. He wore a narrow, long-tailed coat and walked with a stick, and had the same "cant to leeward" as the wind-bent trees on the height above.

This was Captain Littlepage, whom I had seen only once or twice before, sitting pale and old behind a closed window; never out of doors until now. Mrs. Todd always shook her head gravely when I asked a question, and said that he wasn't what he had been once, and seemed to class him with her other secrets. He might have belonged with a simple which grew in a certain slug-haunted corner of the garden, whose use she could never be betrayed into telling me, though I saw her cutting the tops by moonlight once, as if it were a charm, and not a medicine, like the great fading bloodroot leaves.

I could see that she was trying to keep pace with the old captain's lighter steps. He looked like an aged grasshopper of some strange human variety. Behind this pair was a short, impatient, little person, who kept the captain's house, and gave it what Mrs. Todd and others believed to be no proper sort of care. She was usually called "that Mari' Harris" in subdued conversation between intimates, but they treated her with anxious civility when they met her face to face.

The bay-sheltered islands and the great sea beyond stretched away to the far horizon southward and eastward; the little procession in the foreground looked futile and helpless on the edge of the rocky shore. It was a glorious day early in July, with a clear, high sky; there were no clouds, there was no noise of the sea. The song sparrows sang and sang, as if with joyous knowledge of immortality, and contempt for those who could so pettily concern themselves with death. I stood watching until the funeral procession had crept round a shoulder of the slope below and disappeared from the great landscape as if it had gone into a cave.

An hour later I was busy at my work. Now and then a bee blundered in and took me for an enemy; but there was a useful stick upon the teacher's desk, and I rapped to call the bees to order as if they were unruly scholars, or waved them away from their riots over the ink, which I had bought at the Landing store, and discovered too late to be scented with bergamot, as if to refresh the labors of anxious scribes. One anxious scribe felt very dull that day; a sheep-bell tinkled near by, and called her wandering wits after it. The sentences failed to catch these lovely summer cadences. For the first time I began to wish for a companion and for news from the outer world, which had been, half unconsciously, forgotten. Watching the funeral gave one a sort of pain. I began to wonder if I ought not to have walked with the rest, instead of hurrying away at the end of the services. Perhaps the Sunday gown I had put on for the occasion was making this disastrous change of feeling, but I had now made myself and my friends remember that I did not really belong to Dunnet Landing.

I sighed, and turned to the half-written page again.

5.

Captain Littlepage.

It was a long time after this; an hour was very long in that coast town where nothing stole away the shortest minute. I had lost myself completely in work, when I heard footsteps outside. There was a steep footpath between the upper and the lower road, which I climbed to shorten the way, as the children had taught me, but I believed that Mrs. Todd would find it inaccessible, unless she had occasion to seek me in great haste. I wrote on, feeling like a besieged miser of time, while the footsteps came nearer, and the sheep-bell tinkled away in haste as if some one had shaken a stick in its wearer's face. Then I looked, and saw Captain Littlepage passing the nearest window; the next moment he tapped politely at the door.

"Come in, sir," I said, rising to meet him; and he entered, bowing with much courtesy. I stepped down from the desk and offered him a chair by the window, where he seated himself at once, being sadly spent by his climb. I returned to my fixed seat behind the teacher's desk, which gave him the lower place of a scholar.

"You ought to have the place of honor, Captain Littlepage," I said.

"A happy, rural seat of various views,"

he quoted, as he gazed out into the sunshine and up the long wooded shore. Then he glanced at me, and looked all about him as pleased as a child.

"My quotation was from Paradise Lost: the greatest of poems, I suppose you know?" and I nodded. "There's nothing that ranks, to my mind, with Paradise Lost; it's all lofty, all lofty," he continued. "Shakespeare was a great poet; he copied life, but you have to put up with a great deal of low talk."

I now remembered that Mrs. Todd had told me one day that Captain Littlepage had overset his mind with too much reading; she had also made dark reference to his having "spells" of some unexplainable nature. I could not help wondering what errand had brought him out in search of me. There was something quite charming in his appearance: it was a face thin and delicate with refinement, but worn into appealing lines, as if he had suffered from loneliness and misapprehension. He looked, with his careful precision of dress, as if he were the object of cherishing care on the part of elderly unmarried sisters, but I knew Mari' Harris to be a very commonplace, inelegant person, who would have no such standards; it was plain that the captain was his own attentive valet. He sat looking at me expectantly. I could not help thinking that, with his queer head and length of thinness, he was made to hop along the road of life rather than to walk. The captain was very grave indeed, and I bade my inward spirit keep close to discretion.

"Poor Mrs. Begg has gone," I ventured to say. I still wore my Sunday gown by way of showing respect.

"She has gone," said the captain,—"very easy at the last, I was informed; she slipped away as if she were glad of the opportunity."

I thought of the Countess of Carberry,[2] and felt that history repeated itself.

"She was one of the old stock," continued Captain Littlepage, with touching sincerity. "She was very much looked up to in this town, and will be missed."

I wondered, as I looked at him, if he had sprung from a line of ministers; he had the refinement of look and air of command which are the heritage of the old ecclesiastical families of New England. But as Darwin says in his autobiography, "there is no such king as a sea-captain; he is greater even than a king or a schoolmaster!"

Captain Littlepage moved his chair out of the wake of the sunshine, and still sat looking at me. I began to be very eager to know upon what errand he had come.

"It may be found out some o' these days," he said earnestly. "We may know it all, the next step; where Mrs. Begg is now, for instance. Certainty, not conjecture, is what we all desire."

"I suppose we shall know it all some day," said I.

"We shall know it while yet below," insisted the captain, with a flush of impatience on his thin cheeks. "We have not looked for truth in the right direction. I know what I speak of; those who have laughed at me little know how much reason my ideas are based upon." He waved his hand toward the village below. "In that handful of houses they fancy that they comprehend the universe."

I smiled, and waited for him to go on.

"I am an old man, as you can see," he continued, "and I have been a shipmaster the greater part of my life,—forty-three years in all. You may not think it, but I am above eighty years of age."

He did not look so old, and I hastened to say so.

"You must have left the sea a good many years ago, then, Captain Littlepage?" I said.

"I should have been serviceable at least five or six years more," he answered. "My acquaintance with certain—my experience upon a certain occasion, I might say, gave rise to prejudice. I do not mind telling you that I chanced to learn of one of the greatest discoveries that man has ever made."

Now we were approaching dangerous ground, but a sudden sense of his sufferings at the hands of the ignorant came to my help, and I asked to hear more with all the deference I really felt. A swallow flew into the schoolhouse at this moment as if a kingbird were after it, and beat itself against the walls for a minute, and escaped again to the open air; but Captain Littlepage took no notice whatever of the flurry.

"I had a valuable cargo of general merchandise from the London docks to Fort Churchill, a station of the old company on Hudson's Bay," said the captain earnestly. "We were delayed in lading, and baffled by head winds and a heavy tumbling sea all the way north-about and across. Then the fog kept us off the coast; and when I made port at last, it was too late to delay in those northern waters with such a vessel and such a crew as I had. They cared for nothing, and idled me into a fit of sickness; but my first mate was a good, excellent man, with no more idea of being frozen in there until spring than I had, so we made what speed we could to get clear of Hudson's Bay and off the coast. I owned an eighth of the vessel, and he owned a sixteenth of her. She was a full-rigged ship, called the Minerva, but she was getting old and leaky. I meant it should be my last v'y'ge in her, and so it proved. She had been an excellent vessel in her day. Of the cowards aboard her I can't say so much."

"Then you were wrecked?" I asked, as he made a long pause.

"I wa'n't caught astern o' the lighter by any fault of mine," said the captain gloomily. "We left Fort Churchill and run out into the

Bay with a light pair o' heels; but I had been vexed to death with their red-tape rigging at the company's office, and chilled with stayin' on deck an' tryin' to hurry up things, and when we were well out o' sight o' land, headin' for Hudson's Straits, I had a bad turn o' some sort o' fever, and had to stay below. The days were getting short, and we made good runs, all well on board but me, and the crew done their work by dint of hard driving."

I began to find this unexpected narrative a little dull. Captain Littlepage spoke with a kind of slow correctness that lacked the longshore high flavor to which I had grown used; but I listened respectfully while he explained the winds having become contrary, and talked on in a dreary sort of way about his voyage, the bad weather, and the disadvantages he was under in the lightness of his ship, which bounced about like a chip in a bucket, and would not answer the rudder or properly respond to the most careful setting of sails.

"So there we were blowin' along anyways," he complained; but looking at me at this moment, and seeing that my thoughts were unkindly wandering, he ceased to speak.

"It was a hard life at sea in those days, I am sure," said I, with redoubled interest.

"It was a dog's life," said the poor old gentleman, quite reassured, "but it made men of those who followed it. I see a change for the worse even in our own town here; full of loafers now, small and poor as 't is, who once would have followed the sea, every lazy soul of 'em. There is no occupation so fit for just that class o' men who never get beyond the fo'cas'le. I view it, in addition, that a community narrows down and grows dreadful ignorant when it is shut up to its own affairs, and gets no knowledge of the outside world except from a cheap, unprincipled newspaper. In the old days, a good part o' the best men here knew a hundred ports and something of the way folks lived in them. They saw the world for themselves, and like's not their wives and children saw it with them. They may not have had the best of knowledge to carry with 'em sight-seein', but they were some acquainted with foreign lands an' their laws, an' could see outside the battle for town clerk here in Dunnet; they got some sense o' proportion. Yes, they lived more dignified, and their houses were better within an' without. Shipping's a terrible loss to this part o' New England from a social point o' view, ma'am."

"I have thought of that myself," I returned, with my interest quite awakened. "It accounts for the change in a great many things,—the sad disappearance of sea-captains,—doesn't it?"

"A shipmaster was apt to get the habit of reading," said my companion, brightening still more, and taking on a most touching air of unreserve. "A captain is not expected to be familiar with his crew, and for company's sake in dull days and nights he turns to his book. Most of us old shipmasters came to know 'most everything about something; one would take to readin' on farming topics, and some were great on medicine,—but Lord help their poor crews!—or some were all for history, and now and then there'd be one like me that gave his time to the poets. I was well acquainted with a shipmaster that was all for bees an' bee-keepin'; and if you met him in port and went aboard, he'd sit and talk a terrible while about their havin' so much information, and the money that could be made out of keepin' 'em. He was one of the smartest captains that ever sailed the seas, but they used to call the Newcastle, a great bark he commanded for many years, Tuttle's beehive. There was old Cap'n Jameson: he had notions of Solomon's Temple, and made a very handsome little model of the same, right from the Scripture measurements, same's other sailors make little ships and design new tricks of rigging and all that. No, there's nothing to take the place of shipping in a place like ours. These bicycles offend me dreadfully; they don't afford no real opportunities of experience such as a man gained on a voyage. No: when folks left home in the old days they left it to some purpose, and when they got home they stayed there and had some pride in it. There's no large-minded way of thinking now: the worst have got to be best and rule everything; we're all turned upside down and going back year by year."

"Oh no, Captain Littlepage, I hope not," said I, trying to soothe his feelings.

There was a silence in the schoolhouse, but we could hear the noise of the water on a beach below. It sounded like the strange warning wave that gives notice of the turn of the tide. A late golden robin, with the most joyful and eager of voices, was singing close by in a thicket of wild roses.

6.

The Waiting Place.

"How DID YOU MANAGE with the rest of that rough voyage on the Minerva?" I asked.

"I shall be glad to explain to you," said Captain Littlepage, forgetting his grievances for the moment. "If I had a map at hand I could explain better. We were driven to and fro 'way up toward what we used to call Parry's Discoveries,[3] and lost our bearings. It was thick and foggy, and at last I lost my ship; she drove on a rock, and we managed to get ashore on what I took to be a barren island, the few of us that were left alive. When she first struck, the sea was somewhat calmer than it had been, and most of the crew, against orders, manned the long-boat and put off in a hurry, and were never heard of more. Our own boat upset, but the carpenter kept himself and me above water, and we drifted in. I had no strength to call upon after my recent fever, and laid down to die; but he found the tracks of a man and dog the second day, and got along the shore to one of those far missionary stations that the Moravians support. They were very poor themselves, and in distress; 't was a useless place. There were but few Esquimaux left in that region. There we remained for some time, and I became acquainted with strange events."

The captain lifted his head and gave me a questioning glance. I could not help noticing that the dulled look in his eyes had gone, and there was instead a clear intentness that made them seem dark and piercing.

"There was a supply ship expected, and the pastor, an excellent Christian man, made no doubt that we should get passage in her. He was hoping that orders would come to break up the station; but everything was uncertain, and we got on the best we could for a while. We fished, and helped the people in other ways; there was no other way of paying our debts. I was taken to the pastor's house until I got better; but they were crowded, and I felt myself in the way, and made excuse to join with an old seaman, a Scotchman, who had built him a warm cabin, and had room in it for another. He was looked upon with regard, and had stood by the pastor in some troubles with the people. He had been on one of those English exploring parties that found one end of the road to the north pole, but never could find the other. We lived like dogs in a kennel, or so you'd thought if you had seen the hut from the outside; but the main thing was to keep warm; there were piles of birdskins to lie on, and he'd made him a good bunk, and there was another for me. 'T was dreadful dreary waitin' there; we begun to think the supply steamer was lost, and my poor ship broke up and strewed herself all along the shore. We got to watching on the headlands; my men and me knew the people were short of supplies and had to pinch themselves. It ought to read in the Bible, 'Man cannot live by fish alone,' if they'd told the truth of things; 't aint bread that wears the worst on you! First part of the time, old Gaffett, that I lived with, seemed speechless, and I didn't know what to make of him, nor he of me, I dare say; but as we got acquainted, I found he'd been through more disasters than I had, and had troubles that wa'n't going to let him live a great while. It used to ease his mind to talk to an understanding person, so we used to sit and talk together all day, if it rained or blew so that we couldn't get out. I'd got a bad blow on the back of my head at the time we came ashore, and it pained me at times, and my strength was broken, anyway; I've never been so able since."

Captain Littlepage fell into a reverie.

"Then I had the good of my reading," he explained presently. "I had no books; the pastor spoke but little English, and all his books were foreign; but I used to say over all I could remember. The old poets little knew what comfort they could be to a man. I was well acquainted with the works of Milton, but up there it did seem to me as if Shakespeare was the king; he has his sea terms very accurate, and some beautiful passages were calming to the mind. I could say them over until I shed tears; there was nothing beautiful to me in that place but the stars above and those passages of verse.

"Gaffett was always brooding and brooding, and talking to himself; he was afraid he should never get away, and it preyed upon his mind. He thought when I got home I could interest the scientific men in his discovery: but they're all taken up with their own notions;

some didn't even take pains to answer the letters I wrote. You observe that I said this crippled man Gaffett had been shipped on a voyage of discovery. I now tell you that the ship was lost on its return, and only Gaffett and two officers were saved off the Greenland coast, and he had knowledge later that those men never got back to England; the brig they shipped on was run down in the night. So no other living soul had the facts, and he gave them to me. There is a strange sort of a country 'way up north beyond the ice, and strange folks living in it. Gaffett believed it was the next world to this."

"What do you mean, Captain Littlepage?" I exclaimed. The old man was bending forward and whispering; he looked over his shoulder before he spoke the last sentence.

"To hear old Gaffett tell about it was something awful," he said, going on with his story quite steadily after the moment of excitement had passed. "'T was first a tale of dogs and sledges, and cold and wind and snow. Then they begun to find the ice grow rotten; they had been frozen in, and got into a current flowing north, far up beyond Fox Channel, and they took to their boats when the ship got crushed, and this warm current took them out of sight of the ice, and into a great open sea; and they still followed it due north, just the very way they had planned to go. Then they struck a coast that wasn't laid down or charted, but the cliffs were such that no boat could land until they found a bay and struck across under sail to the other side where the shore looked lower; they were scant of provisions and out of water, but they got sight of something that looked like a great town. 'For God's sake, Gaffett!' said I, the first time he told me. 'You don't mean a town two degrees farther north than ships had ever been?' for he'd got their course marked on an old chart that he'd pieced out at the top; but he insisted upon it, and told it over and over again, to be sure I had it straight to carry to those who would be interested. There was no snow and ice, he said, after they had sailed some days with that warm current, which seemed to come right from under the ice that they'd been pinched up in and had been crossing on foot for weeks."

"But what about the town?" I asked. "Did they get to the town?"

"They did," said the captain, "and found inhabitants; 't was an awful condition of things. It appeared, as near as Gaffett could express it, like a place where there was neither living nor dead. They could see the place when they were approaching it by sea pretty near like any town, and thick with habitations; but all at once they lost sight of it altogether, and when they got close inshore they could see the shapes of folks, but they never could get near them,—all blowing gray figures that would pass along alone, or sometimes gathered in companies as if they were watching. The men were frightened at first, but the shapes never came near them,—it was as if they blew back; and at last they all got bold and went ashore, and found birds' eggs and sea fowl, like any wild northern spot where creatures were tame and folks had never been, and there was good water. Gaffett said that he and another man came near one o' the fog-shaped men that was going along slow with the look of a pack on his back, among the rocks, an' they chased him; but, Lord! he flittered away out o' sight like a leaf the wind takes with it, or a piece of cobweb. They would make as if they talked together, but there was no sound of voices, and 'they acted as if they didn't see us, but only felt us coming towards them,' says Gaffett one day, trying to tell the particulars. They couldn't see the town when they were ashore. One day the captain and the doctor were gone till night up across the high land where the town had seemed to be, and they came back at night beat out and white as ashes, and wrote and wrote all next day in their notebooks, and whispered together full of excitement, and they were sharp-spoken with the men when they offered to ask any questions.

"Then there came a day," said Captain Littlepage, leaning toward me with a strange look in his eyes, and whispering quickly. "The men all swore they wouldn't stay any longer; the man on watch early in the morning gave the alarm, and they all put off in the boat and got a little way out to sea. Those folks, or whatever they were, come about 'em like bats; all at once they raised incessant armies* and come as if to drive 'em back to sea. They stood thick at the edge o' the water like the ridges o' grim war; no thought o' flight, none of retreat.† Sometimes a standing fight, then soaring on main wing

*Reference to John Milton's *Paradise Lost* (1667), book 6.
†Reference to *Paradise Lost*, book 6.

tormented all the air.* And when they'd got the boat out o' reach o' danger, Gaffett said they looked back, and there was the town again, standing up just as they'd seen it first, comin' on the coast. Say what you might, they all believed 't was a kind of waiting-place between this world an' the next."

The captain had sprung to his feet in his excitement, and made excited gestures, but he still whispered huskily.

"Sit down, sir," I said as quietly as I could, and he sank into his chair quite spent.

"Gaffett thought the officers were hurrying home to report and to fit out a new expedition when they were all lost. At the time, the men got orders not to talk over what they had seen," the old man explained presently in a more natural tone.

"Weren't they all starving, and wasn't it a mirage or something of that sort?" I ventured to ask. But he looked at me blankly.

"Gaffett had got so that his mind ran on nothing else," he went on. "The ship's surgeon let fall an opinion to the captain, one day, that 't was some condition o' the light and the magnetic currents that let them see those folks. 'T wa'n't a right-feeling part of the world, anyway; they had to battle with the compass to make it serve, an' everything seemed to go wrong. Gaffett had worked it out in his own mind that they was all common ghosts, but the conditions were unusual favorable for seeing them. He was always talking about the Ge'graphical Society, but he never took proper steps, as I view it now, and stayed right there at the mission. He was a good deal crippled, and thought they'd confine him in some jail of a hospital. He said he was waiting to find the right men to tell, somebody bound north. Once in a while they stopped there to leave a mail or something. He was set in his notions, and let two or three proper explorin' expeditions go by him because he didn't like their looks; but when I was there he had got restless, fearin' he might be taken away or something. He had all his directions written out straight as a string to give the right ones. I wanted him to trust 'em to me, so I might have something to show, but he wouldn't. I suppose he's dead now. I wrote to him, an' I done all I could. 'T will be a great exploit some o' these days."

---

*Reference to Milton's *Paradise Lost*, book 6.

I assented absent-mindedly, thinking more just then of my companion's alert, determined look and the seafaring, ready aspect that had come to his face; but at this moment there fell a sudden change, and the old, pathetic, scholarly look returned. Behind me hung a map of North America, and I saw, as I turned a little, that his eyes were fixed upon the northernmost regions and their careful recent outlines with a look of bewilderment.

7.

The Outer Island.

Gaffett with his good bunk and the bird-skins, the story of the wreck of the Minerva, the human-shaped creatures of fog and cobweb, the great words of Milton with which he described their onslaught upon the crew, all this moving tale had such an air of truth that I could not argue with Captain Littlepage. The old man looked away from the map as if it had vaguely troubled him, and regarded me appealingly.

"We were just speaking of"—and he stopped. I saw that he had suddenly forgotten his subject.

"There were a great many persons at the funeral," I hastened to say.

"Oh yes," the captain answered, with satisfaction. "All showed respect who could. The sad circumstances had for a moment slipped my mind. Yes, Mrs. Begg will be very much missed. She was a capital manager for her husband when he was at sea. Oh yes, shipping is a very great loss." And he sighed heavily. "There was hardly a man of any standing who didn't interest himself in some way in navigation. It always gave credit to a town. I call it low-water mark now here in Dunnet."

He rose with dignity to take leave, and asked me to stop at his house some day, when he would show me some outlandish things that he had brought home from sea. I was familiar with the subject of the decadence of shipping interests in all its affecting branches, having been already some time in Dunnet, and I felt sure that Captain Littlepage's mind had now returned to a safe level.

As we came down the hill toward the village our ways divided, and when I had seen the old captain well started on a smooth piece of sidewalk which would lead him to his own door, we parted, the best of friends. "Step in some afternoon," he said, as affectionately as if I were a fellow-shipmaster wrecked on the lee shore of age like himself. I turned toward home, and presently met Mrs. Todd coming toward me with an anxious expression.

"I see you sleevin' the old gentleman down the hill," she suggested.

"Yes. I've had a very interesting afternoon with him," I answered; and her face brightened.

"Oh, then he's all right. I was afraid 't was one o' his flighty spells, an' Mari' Harris wouldn't"—

"Yes," I returned, smiling, "he has been telling me some old stories, but we talked about Mrs. Begg and the funeral beside, and Paradise Lost."

"I expect he got tellin' of you some o' his great narratives," she answered, looking at me shrewdly. "Funerals always sets him goin'. Some o' them tales hangs together toler'ble well," she added, with a sharper look than before. "An' he's been a great reader all his seafarin' days. Some thinks he overdid, and affected his head, but for a man o' his years he's amazin' now when he's at his best. Oh, he used to be a beautiful man!"

We were standing where there was a fine view of the harbor and its long stretches of shore all covered by the great army of the pointed firs, darkly cloaked and standing as if they waited to embark. As we looked far seaward among the outer islands, the trees seemed to march seaward still, going steadily over the heights and down to the water's edge.

It had been growing gray and cloudy, like the first evening of autumn, and a shadow had fallen on the darkening shore. Suddenly, as we looked, a gleam of golden sunshine struck the outer islands, and one of them shone out clear in the light, and revealed itself in a compelling way to our eyes. Mrs. Todd was looking off across the bay with a face full of affection and interest. The sunburst upon that outermost island made it seem like a sudden revelation of the world beyond this which some believe to be so near.

"That's where mother lives," said Mrs. Todd. "Can't we see it plain? I was brought up out there on Green Island. I know every rock an' bush on it."

"Your mother!" I exclaimed, with great interest.

"Yes, dear, cert'in; I've got her yet, old's I be. She's one of them spry, light-footed little women; always was, an' lighthearted, too," answered Mrs. Todd, with satisfaction. "She's seen all the trouble folks can see, without it's her last sickness; an' she's got a word of courage for everybody. Life ain't spoilt her a mite. She's eighty-six an' I'm sixty-seven, and I've seen the time I've felt a good sight the oldest. 'Land sakes alive!' says she, last time I was out to see her. 'How you do lurch about steppin' into a bo't!' I laughed so I liked to have gone right over into the water; an' we pushed off, an' left her laughin' there on the shore."

The light had faded as we watched. Mrs. Todd had mounted a gray rock, and stood there grand and architectural, like a *caryatide.* Presently she stepped down, and we continued our way homeward.

"You an' me, we'll take a bo't an' go out some day and see mother," she promised me. "'T would please her very much, an' there's one or two sca'ce herbs grows better on the island than anywheres else. I ain't seen their like nowheres here on the main."

"Now I'm goin' right down to get us each a mug o' my beer," she announced as we entered the house, "an' I believe I'll sneak in a little mite o' camomile. Goin' to the funeral an' all, I feel to have had a very wearin' afternoon."

I heard her going down into the cool little cellar, and then there was considerable delay. When she returned, mug in hand, I noticed the taste of camomile, in spite of my protest; but its flavor was disguised by some other herb that I did not know, and she stood over me until I drank it all and said that I liked it.

"I don't give that to everybody," said Mrs. Todd kindly; and I felt for a moment as if it were part of a spell and incantation, and as if my enchantress would now begin to look like the cobweb shapes of the arctic town. Nothing happened but a quiet evening and some delightful plans that we made about going to Green Island, and on the morrow there was the clear sunshine and blue sky of another day.

8.

Green Island.

ONE MORNING, VERY EARLY, I heard Mrs. Todd in the garden outside my window. By the unusual loudness of her remarks to a passer-by, and the notes of a familiar hymn which she sang as she worked among the herbs, and which came as if directed purposely to the sleepy ears of my consciousness, I knew that she wished I would wake up and come and speak to her.

In a few minutes she responded to a morning voice from behind the blinds. "I expect you're goin' up to your schoolhouse to pass all this pleasant day; yes, I expect you're goin' to be dreadful busy," she said despairingly.

"Perhaps not," said I. "Why, what's going to be the matter with you, Mrs. Todd?" For I supposed that she was tempted by the fine weather to take one of her favorite expeditions along the shore pastures to gather herbs and simples, and would like to have me keep the house.

"No, I don't want to go nowhere by land," she answered gayly,—"no, not by land; but I don't know's we shall have a better day all the rest of the summer to go out to Green Island an' see mother. I waked up early thinkin' of her. The wind's light northeast,—'t will take us right straight out; an' this time o' year it's liable to change round southwest an' fetch us home pretty, 'long late in the afternoon. Yes, it's goin' to be a good day."

"Speak to the captain and the Bowden boy, if you see anybody going by toward the landing," said I. "We'll take the big boat."

"Oh, my sakes! now you let me do things my way," said Mrs. Todd scornfully. "No, dear, we won't take no big bo't. I'll just git a handy dory, an' Johnny Bowden an' me, we'll man her ourselves. I don't want no abler bo't than a good dory, an' a nice light breeze ain't goin' to make no sea; an' Johnny's my cousin's son,—mother'll like to have him come; an' he'll be down to the herrin' weirs all the time we're there, anyway; we don't want to carry no men folks havin' to be considered every minute an' takin' up all our time. No, you let me do; we'll just slip out an' see mother by ourselves. I guess what breakfast you'll want's about ready now."

I had become well acquainted with Mrs. Todd as landlady, herb-gatherer, and rustic philosopher; we had been discreet fellow-passengers once or twice when I had sailed up the coast to a larger town than Dunnet Landing to do some shopping; but I was yet to become acquainted with her as a mariner. An hour later we pushed off from the landing in the desired dory. The tide was just on the turn, beginning to fall, and several friends and acquaintances stood along the side of the dilapidated wharf and cheered us by their words and evident interest. Johnny Bowden and I were both rowing in haste to get out where we could catch the breeze and put up the small sail which lay clumsily furled along the gunwale. Mrs. Todd sat aft, a stern and unbending lawgiver.

"You better let her drift; we'll get there 'bout as quick; the tide 'll take her right out from under these old buildin's; there's plenty wind outside."

"Your bo't ain't trimmed proper, Mis' Todd!" exclaimed a voice from shore. "You're lo'ded so the bo't'll drag; you can't git her before the wind, ma'am. You set 'midships, Mis' Todd, an' let the boy hold the sheet 'n' steer after he gits the sail up; you won't never git out to Green Island that way. She's lo'ded bad, your bo't is,—she's heavy behind's she is now!"

Mrs. Todd turned with some difficulty and regarded the anxious adviser, my right oar flew out of water, and we seemed about to capsize. "That you, Asa? Good-mornin'," she said politely. "I al'ays liked the starn seat best. When'd you git back from up country?"

This allusion to Asa's origin was not lost upon the rest of the company. We were some little distance from shore, but we could hear a chuckle of laughter, and Asa, a person who was too ready with his criticism and advice on every possible subject, turned and walked indignantly away.

When we caught the wind we were soon on our seaward course, and only stopped to underrun a trawl, for the floats of which Mrs. Todd looked earnestly, explaining that her mother might not be prepared for three extra to dinner; it was her brother's trawl, and she meant to just run her eye along for the right sort of a little haddock. I leaned over the boat's side with great interest and excitement, while she skillfully handled the long line of hooks, and made scornful remarks upon worthless, bait-consuming creatures of the sea as she reviewed them and left them on the trawl or shook them off into the waves. At last we came to what she pronounced a proper haddock, and having taken him on board and ended his life resolutely, we went our way.

As we sailed along I listened to an increasingly delightful commentary upon the islands, some of them barren rocks, or at best giving sparse pasturage for sheep in the early summer. On one of these an eager little flock ran to the water's edge and bleated at us so affectingly that I would willingly have stopped; but Mrs. Todd steered away from the rocks, and scolded at the sheep's mean owner, an acquaintance of hers, who grudged the little salt and still less care which the patient creatures needed. The hot midsummer sun makes prisons of these small islands that are a paradise in early June, with their cool springs and short thick-growing grass. On a larger island, farther out to sea, my entertaining companion showed me with glee the small houses of two farmers who shared the island between them, and declared that for three generations the people had not spoken to each other even in times of sickness or death or birth. "When the news come that the war was over, one of 'em knew it a week, and never stepped across his wall to tell the others," she said. "There, they enjoy it: they've got to have somethin' to interest 'em in such a place; 't is a good deal more tryin' to be tied to folks you don't like than 't is to be alone. Each of 'em tells the neighbors their wrongs; plenty likes to hear and tell again; them as fetch a bone'll carry one, an' so they keep the fight a-goin'. I must say I like variety myself; some folks washes Monday an' irons Tuesday the whole year round, even if the circus is goin' by!"

A long time before we landed at Green Island we could see the small white house, standing high like a beacon, where Mrs. Todd was born and where her mother lived, on a green slope above the water, with dark spruce woods still higher. There were crops in the fields, which we presently distinguished from one another. Mrs. Todd examined them while we were still far at sea. "Mother's late potatoes looks backward; ain't had rain enough so far," she pronounced her opinion. "They look weedier than what they call Front Street down to Cowper Centre. I expect brother William is so occupied with his herrin' weirs an' servin' out bait to the schooners that he don't think once a day of the land."

"What's the flag for, up above the spruces there behind the house?" I inquired, with eagerness.

"Oh, that's the sign for herrin'," she explained kindly, while Johnny Bowden regarded me with contemptuous surprise. "When they get enough for schooners they raise that flag; an' when 't is a poor catch in the weir pocket they just fly a little signal down by the shore, an' then the small bo'ts comes and get enough an' over for their trawls. There, look! there she is: mother sees us; she's wavin' somethin' out o' the fore door! She'll be to the landin'-place quick's we are."

I looked, and could see a tiny flutter in the doorway, but a quicker signal had made its way from the heart on shore to the heart on the sea.

"How do you suppose she knows it's me?" said Mrs. Todd, with a tender smile on her broad face. "There, you never get over bein' a child long's you have a mother to go to. Look at the chimney, now; she's gone right in an' brightened up the fire. Well, there, I'm glad mother's well; you'll enjoy seein' her very much."

Mrs. Todd leaned back into her proper position, and the boat trimmed again. She took a firmer grasp of the sheet, and gave an impatient look up at the gaff and the leech of the little sail, and twitched the sheet as if she urged the wind like a horse. There came at once a fresh gust, and we seemed to have doubled our speed. Soon we were near enough to see a tiny figure with handkerchiefed head come down across the field and stand waiting for us at the cove above a curve of pebble beach.

Presently the dory grated on the pebbles, and Johnny Bowden, who had been kept in abeyance during the voyage, sprang out and used manful exertions to haul us up with the next wave, so that Mrs. Todd could make a dry landing.

"You done that very well," she said, mounting to her feet, and coming ashore somewhat stiffly, but with great dignity, refusing our outstretched hands, and returning to possess herself of a bag which had lain at her feet.

"Well, mother, here I be!" she announced with indifference; but they stood and beamed in each other's faces.

"Lookin' pretty well for an old lady, ain't she?" said Mrs. Todd's mother, turning away from her daughter to speak to me. She was a delightful little person herself, with bright eyes and an affectionate air of expectation like a child on a holiday. You felt as if Mrs. Blackett were an old and dear friend before you let go her cordial hand. We all started together up the hill.

"Now don't you haste too fast, mother," said Mrs. Todd warningly; "'t is a far reach o' risin' ground to the fore door, and you won't set an' get your breath when you're once there, but go trotting about. Now don't you go a mite faster than we proceed with this bag an' basket. Johnny, there, 'll fetch up the haddock. I just made one stop to underrun William's trawl till I come to jes' such a fish's I thought you'd want to make one o' your nice chowders of. I've brought an onion with me that was layin' about on the window-sill at home."

"That's just what I was wantin'," said the hostess. "I give a sigh when you spoke o' chowder, knowin' my onions was out. William forgot to replenish us last time he was to the Landin'. Don't you haste so yourself, Almiry, up this risin' ground. I hear you commencin' to wheeze a'ready."

This mild revenge seemed to afford great pleasure to both giver and receiver. They laughed a little, and looked at each other affectionately, and then at me. Mrs. Todd considerately paused, and faced about to regard the wide sea view. I was glad to stop, being more out of breath than either of my companions, and I prolonged the halt by asking the names of the neighboring islands. There was a fine breeze blowing, which we felt more there on the high land than when we were running before it in the dory.

"Why, this ain't that kitten I saw when I was out last, the one that I said didn't appear likely?" exclaimed Mrs. Todd as we went our way.

"That's the one, Almiry," said her mother. "She always had a likely look to me, an' she's right after her business. I never see such a mouser for one of her age. If 't wan't for William, I never should have housed that other dronin' old thing so long; but he sets by her on account of her havin' a bob tail. I don't deem it advisable to maintain cats just on account of their havin' bob tails; they're like all other curiosities, good for them that wants to see 'em twice. This kitten catches mice for both, an' keeps me respectable as I ain't been for a year. She's a real understandin' little help, this kitten is. I picked her from among five Miss Augusta Pennell had over to Burnt Island," said the old woman, trudging along with the kitten close at her skirts. "Augusta, she says to me, 'Why, Mis' Blackett, you've took the homeliest;' an' says I, 'I've got the smartest; I'm satisfied.' "

"I'd trust nobody sooner 'n you to pick out a kitten, mother," said the daughter handsomely, and we went on in peace and harmony.

The house was just before us now, on a green level that looked as if a huge hand had scooped it out of the long green field we had been ascending. A little way above, the dark spruce woods began to climb the top of the hill and cover the seaward slopes of the island. There was just room for the small farm and the forest; we looked down at the fish-house and its rough sheds, and the weirs stretching far out into the water. As we looked upward, the tops of the firs came sharp against the blue sky. There was a great stretch of rough pasture-land round the shoulder of the island to the eastward, and here were all the thick-scattered gray rocks that kept their places, and the gray backs of many sheep that forever wandered and fed on the thin sweet pasturage that fringed the ledges and made soft hollows and strips of green turf like growing velvet. I could see the rich green of bayberry bushes here and there, where the rocks made room. The air was very sweet; one could not help wishing to be a citizen of such a complete and tiny continent and home of fisherfolk.

The house was broad and clean, with a roof that looked heavy on its low walls. It was one of the houses that seem firm-rooted in the ground, as if they were two-thirds below the surface, like icebergs. The front door stood hospitably open in expectation of company, and an orderly vine grew at each side; but our path led to the kitchen door at the house-end, and there grew a mass of gay flowers and greenery, as if they had been swept together by some diligent garden broom into a tangled heap: there were portulacas all along under the lower step and straggling off into the grass, and clustering mallows that crept as near as they dared, like poor relations. I saw the bright eyes and brainless little heads of two half-grown chickens who were snuggled down among the mallows as if they had been chased away from the door more than once, and expected to be again.

"It seems kind o' formal comin' in this way," said Mrs. Todd impulsively, as we passed the flowers and came to the front doorstep; but she was mindful of the proprieties, and walked before us into the best room on the left.

"Why, mother, if you haven't gone an' turned the carpet!" she exclaimed, with something in her voice that spoke of awe and admiration. "When'd you get to it? I s'pose Mis' Addicks come over an' helped you, from White Island Landing?"

"No, she didn't," answered the old woman, standing proudly erect, and making the most of a great moment. "I done it all myself with William's help. He had a spare day, an' took right holt with me; an' 't was all well beat on the grass, an' turned, an' put down again afore we went to bed. I ripped an' sewed over two o' them long breadths. I ain't had such a good night's sleep for two years."

"There, what do you think o' havin' such a mother as that for eighty-six year old?" said Mrs. Todd, standing before us like a large figure of Victory.

As for the mother, she took on a sudden look of youth; you felt as if she promised a great future, and was beginning, not ending, her summers and their happy toils.

"My, my!" exclaimed Mrs. Todd. "I couldn't ha' done it myself, I've got to own it."

"I was much pleased to have it off my mind," said Mrs. Blackett, humbly; "the more so because along at the first of the next week I wasn't very well. I suppose it may have been the change of weather."

Mrs. Todd could not resist a significant glance at me, but, with charming sympathy, she forbore to point the lesson or to connect this illness with its apparent cause. She loomed larger than ever in the little old-fashioned best room, with its few pieces of good furniture and pictures of national interest. The green paper curtains were stamped with conventional landscapes of a foreign order,—castles on inaccessible crags, and lovely lakes with steep wooded shores; under-foot the treasured carpet was covered thick with home-made rugs. There were empty glass lamps and crystallized bouquets of grass and some fine shells on the narrow mantelpiece.

"I was married in this room," said Mrs. Todd unexpectedly; and I heard her give a sigh after she had spoken, as if she could not help the touch of regret that would forever come with all her thoughts of happiness.

"We stood right there between the windows," she added, "and the minister stood here. William wouldn't come in. He was always odd about seein' folks, just's he is now. I run to meet 'em from a child, an' William, he'd take an' run away."

"I've been the gainer," said the old mother cheerfully. "William has been son an' daughter both since you was married off the island. He's been 'most too satisfied to stop at home 'long o' his old mother, but I always tell 'em I'm the gainer."

We were all moving toward the kitchen as if by common instinct. The best room was too suggestive of serious occasions, and the shades were all pulled down to shut out the summer light and air. It was indeed a tribute to Society to find a room set apart for her behests out there on so apparently neighborless and remote an island. Afternoon visits and evening festivals must be few in such a bleak situation at certain seasons of the year, but Mrs. Blackett was of those who do not live to themselves, and who have long since passed the line that divides mere self-concern from a valued share in whatever Society can give and take. There were those of her neighbors who never had taken the trouble to furnish a best room, but Mrs. Blackett was one who knew the uses of a parlor.

"Yes, do come right out into the old kitchen; I shan't make any stranger of you," she invited us pleasantly, after we had been properly received in the room appointed to formality. "I expect Almiry, here, 'll be driftin' out 'mongst the pasture-weeds quick's she can find a good excuse. 'T is hot now. You'd better content yourselves till you get nice an' rested, an' 'long after dinner the sea-breeze'll spring up, an' then you can take your walks, an' go up an' see the prospect from the big ledge. Almiry'll want to show off everything there is. Then I'll get you a good cup o' tea before you start to go home. The days are plenty long now."

While we were talking in the best room the selected fish had been mysteriously brought up from the shore, and lay all cleaned and ready in an earthen crock on the table.

"I think William might have just stopped an' said a word," remarked Mrs. Todd, pouting with high affront as she caught sight of it. "He's friendly enough when he comes ashore, an' was remarkable social the last time, for him."

"He ain't disposed to be very social with the ladies," explained William's mother, with a delightful glance at me, as if she counted upon my friendship and tolerance. "He's very particular, and he's all in his old fishin'-clothes to-day. He'll want me to tell him everything you said and done, after you've gone. William has very deep affections. He'll want to see you, Almiry. Yes, I guess he'll be in by an' by."

"I'll search for him by 'n' by, if he don't," proclaimed Mrs. Todd, with an air of unalterable resolution. "I know all of his burrows down 'long the shore. I'll catch him by hand 'fore he knows it. I've got some business with William, anyway. I brought forty-two cents with me that was due him for them last lobsters he brought in."

"You can leave it with me," suggested the little old mother, who was already stepping about among her pots and pans in the pantry, and preparing to make the chowder.

I became possessed of a sudden unwonted curiosity in regard to William, and felt that half the pleasure of my visit would be lost if I could not make his interesting acquaintance.

9.

William.

Mrs. Todd had taken the onion out of her basket and laid it down upon the kitchen table. "There's Johnny Bowden come with us, you know," she reminded her mother. "He'll be hungry enough to eat his size."

"I've got new doughnuts, dear," said the little old lady. "You don't often catch William 'n' me out o' provisions. I expect you might have chose a somewhat larger fish, but I'll try an' make it do. I shall have to have a few extra potatoes, but there's a field full out there, an' the hoe's leanin' against the well-house, in 'mongst the climbin'-beans." She smiled, and gave her daughter a commanding nod.

"Land sakes alive! Le' 's blow the horn for William," insisted Mrs. Todd, with some excitement. "He needn't break his spirit so far's to come in. He'll know you need him for something particular, an' then we can call to him as he comes up the path. I won't put him to no pain."

Mrs. Blackett's old face, for the first time, wore a look of trouble, and I found it necessary to counteract the teasing spirit of Almira. It was too pleasant to stay indoors altogether, even in such rewarding companionship; besides, I might meet William; and, straying out presently, I found the hoe by the well-house and an old splint basket at the woodshed door, and also found my way down to the field where there was a great square patch of rough, weedy potato-tops and tall ragweed. One corner was already dug, and I chose a fat-looking hill where the tops were well withered. There is all the pleasure that one can have in gold-digging in finding one's hopes satisfied in the riches of a good hill of potatoes. I longed to go on; but it did not seem frugal to dig any longer after my basket was full, and at last I took my hoe by the middle and lifted the basket to go back up the hill. I was sure that Mrs. Blackett must be waiting impatiently to slice the potatoes into the chowder, layer after layer, with the fish.

"You let me take holt o' that basket, ma'am," said a pleasant, anxious voice behind me.

I turned, startled in the silence of the wide field, and saw an elderly man, bent in the shoulders as fishermen often are, gray-headed and clean-shaven, and with a timid air. It was William. He looked just like his mother, and I had been imagining that he was large and stout like his sister, Almira Todd; and, strange to say, my fancy had led me to picture him not far from thirty and a little loutish. It was necessary instead to pay William the respect due to age.

I accustomed myself to plain facts on the instant, and we said good-morning like old friends. The basket was really heavy, and I put the hoe through its handle and offered him one end; then we moved easily toward the house together, speaking of the fine weather and of mackerel which were reported to be striking in all about the bay. William had been out since three o'clock, and had taken an extra fare of fish. I could feel that Mrs. Todd's eyes were upon us as we approached the house, and although I fell behind in the narrow path, and let William take the basket alone and precede me at some little distance the rest of the way, I could plainly hear her greet him.

"Got round to comin' in, didn't you?" she inquired, with amusement. "Well, now, that's clever. Didn't know's I should see you today, William, an' I wanted to settle an account."

I felt somewhat disturbed and responsible, but when I joined them they were on most simple and friendly terms. It became evident that, with William, it was the first step that cost, and that, having once joined in social interests, he was able to pursue them with more or less pleasure. He was about sixty, and not young-looking for his years, yet so undying is the spirit of youth, and bashfulness has such a power of survival, that I felt all the time as if one must try to make the occasion easy for some one who was young and new to the affairs of social life. He asked politely if I would like to go up to the great ledge while dinner was getting ready; so, not without a deep sense of pleasure, and a delighted look of surprise from the two hostesses, we started, William and I, as if both of us felt much younger than we looked. Such was the innocence and simplicity of the moment that when I heard Mrs. Todd laughing behind us in the kitchen I laughed too, but William did not even blush. I think he was a little deaf, and he stepped along before me most businesslike and intent upon his errand.

We went from the upper edge of the field above the house into a smooth, brown path among the dark spruces. The hot sun brought out the fragrance of the pitchy bark, and the shade was pleasant as we climbed the hill. William stopped once or twice to show me a great wasps'-nest close by, or some fishhawks'-nests below in a bit of swamp. He picked a few sprigs of late-blooming linnæa as we came out upon an open bit of pasture at the top of the island, and gave them to me without speaking, but he knew as well as I that one could not say half he wished about linnæa. Through this piece of rough pasture ran a huge shape of stone like the great backbone of an enormous creature. At the end, near the woods, we could climb up on it and walk along to the highest point; there above the circle of pointed firs we could look down over all the island, and could see the ocean that circled this and a hundred other bits of island-ground, the mainland shore and all the far horizons. It gave a sudden sense of space, for nothing stopped the eye or hedged one in,—that sense of liberty in space and time which great prospects always give.

"There ain't no such view in the world, I expect," said William proudly, and I hastened to speak my heartfelt tribute of praise; it was impossible not to feel as if an untraveled boy had spoken, and yet one loved to have him value his native heath.

10.

Where Pennyroyal Grew.

We were a little late to dinner, but Mrs. Blackett and Mrs. Todd were lenient, and we all took our places after William had paused to wash his hands, like a pious Brahmin, at the well, and put on a neat blue coat which he took from a peg behind the kitchen door. Then he resolutely asked a blessing in words that I could not hear, and we ate the chowder and were thankful. The kitten went round and round the table, quite erect, and, holding on by her fierce young claws, she stopped to mew with pathos at each elbow, or darted off to the open door when a song sparrow forgot himself and lit in the grass too near. William did not talk much, but his sister Todd occupied the time and told all the news there was to tell of Dunnet Landing and its coasts, while the old mother listened with delight. Her hospitality was something exquisite; she had the gift which so many women lack, of being able to make themselves and their houses belong entirely to a guest's pleasure,—that charming surrender for the moment of themselves and whatever belongs to them, so that they make a part of one's own life that can never be forgotten. Tact is after all a kind of mind-reading, and my hostess held the golden gift. Sympathy is of the mind as well as the heart, and Mrs. Blackett's world and mine were one from the moment we met. Besides, she had that final, that highest gift of heaven, a perfect self-forgetfulness. Sometimes, as I watched her eager, sweet old face, I wondered why she had been set to shine on this lonely island of the northern coast. It must have been to keep the balance true, and make up to all her scattered and depending neighbors for other things which they may have lacked.

When we had finished clearing away the old blue plates, and the kitten had taken care of her share of the fresh haddock, just as we were putting back the kitchen chairs in their places, Mrs. Todd said briskly that she must go up into the pasture now to gather the desired herbs.

"You can stop here an' rest, or you can accompany me," she announced. "Mother ought to have her nap, and when we come back she an' William'll sing for you. She admires music," said Mrs. Todd, turning to speak to her mother.

But Mrs. Blackett tried to say that she couldn't sing as she used, and perhaps William wouldn't feel like it. She looked tired, the good old soul, or I should have liked to sit in the peaceful little house while she slept; I had had much pleasant experience of pastures already in her daughter's company. But it seemed best to go with Mrs. Todd, and off we went.

Mrs. Todd carried the gingham bag which she had brought from home, and a small heavy burden in the bottom made it hang straight and slender from her hand. The way was steep, and she soon grew breathless, so that we sat down to rest awhile on a convenient large stone among the bayberry.

"There, I wanted you to see this,—'t is mother's picture," said Mrs. Todd; " 't was taken once when she was up to Portland, soon after she was married. That's me," she added, opening another worn case, and displaying the full face of the cheerful child she looked like still in spite of being past sixty. "And here's William an' father together. I take after father, large and heavy, an' William is like mother's folks, short an' thin. He ought to have made something o' himself, bein' a man an' so like mother; but though he's been very steady to work, an' kept up the farm, an' done his fishin' too right along, he never had mother's snap an' power o' seein' things just as they be. He's got excellent judgment, too," meditated William's sister, but she could not arrive at any satisfactory decision upon what she evidently thought his failure in life. "I think it is well to see any one so happy an' makin' the most of life just as it falls to hand," she said as she began to put the daguerreotypes away again; but I reached out my hand to see her mother's once more, a most flower-like face of a lovely young woman in quaint dress. There was in the eyes a look of anticipation and joy, a far-off look that sought the horizon; one often sees it in seafaring families, inherited by girls and boys alike from men who spend their lives at sea, and are always watching for distant sails or the first loom of the land. At sea there is nothing to be seen close by, and this has its counterpart in a sailor's character, in the large and brave and patient traits that are developed, the hopeful pleasantness that one loves so in a seafarer.

When the family pictures were wrapped again in a big handkerchief, we set forward in a narrow footpath and made our way to a lonely place that faced northward, where there was more pasturage and fewer bushes, and we went down to the edge of short grass above some rocky cliffs where the deep sea broke with a great noise, though the wind was down and the water looked quiet a little way from shore. Among the grass grew such pennyroyal as the rest of the world could not provide. There was a fine fragrance in the air as we gathered it sprig by sprig and stepped along carefully, and Mrs. Todd pressed her aromatic nosegay between her hands and offered it to me again and again.

"There's nothin' like it," she said; "oh no, there's no such pennyr'yal as this in the State of Maine. It's the right pattern of the plant, and all the rest I ever see is but an imitation. Don't it do you good?" And I answered with enthusiasm.

"There, dear, I never showed nobody else but mother where to find this place; 't is kind of sainted to me. Nathan, my husband, an' I used to love this place when we was courtin', and"—she hesitated, and then spoke softly—"when he was lost, 't was just off shore tryin' to get in by the short channel out there between Squaw Islands, right in sight o' this headland where we'd set an' made our plans all summer long."

I had never heard her speak of her husband before, but I felt that we were friends now since she had brought me to this place.

"'T was but a dream with us," Mrs. Todd said. "I knew it when he was gone. I knew it"—and she whispered as if she were at confession—"I knew it afore he started to go to sea. My heart was gone out o' my keepin' before I ever saw Nathan; but he loved me well, and he made me real happy, and he died before he ever knew what he'd had to know if we'd lived long together. 'T is very strange about love. No, Nathan never found out, but my heart was troubled when I knew him first. There's more women likes to be loved than there is of those that loves. I spent some happy hours right here. I always liked Nathan, and he never knew. But this pennyr'yal always reminded me, as I'd sit and gather it and hear him talkin'—it always would remind me of—the other one."

She looked away from me, and presently rose and went on by herself. There was something lonely and solitary about her great determined shape. She might have been Antigone alone on the Theban plain.* It is not often given in a noisy world to come to the places of great grief and silence. An absolute, archaic grief possessed this countrywoman; she seemed like a renewal of some historic soul, with her sorrows and the remoteness of a daily life busied with rustic simplicities and the scents of primeval herbs.

I was not incompetent at herb-gathering, and after a while, when I had sat long enough waking myself to new thoughts, and reading a page of remembrance with new pleasure, I gathered some bunches, as I was bound to do, and at last we met again higher up the shore, in the plain every-day world we had left behind when we went down to the pennyroyal plot. As we walked together along the high edge of the field we saw a hundred sails about the bay and farther seaward; it was mid-afternoon or after, and the day was coming to an end.

"Yes, they're all makin' towards the shore,—the small craft an' the lobster smacks an' all," said my companion. "We must spend a little time with mother now, just to have our tea, an' then put for home."

"No matter if we lose the wind at sundown; I can row in with Johnny," said I; and Mrs. Todd nodded reassuringly and kept to her steady plod, not quickening her gait even when we saw William come round the corner of the house as if to look for us, and wave his hand and disappear.

"Why, William's right on deck; I didn't know's we should see any more of him!" exclaimed Mrs. Todd. "Now mother'll put the kettle right on; she's got a good fire goin'." I too could see the blue smoke thicken, and then we both walked a little faster, while Mrs. Todd groped in her full bag of herbs to find the daguerreotypes and be ready to put them in their places.

---

*Reference to a scene in Sophocles' play *Antigone* in which Antigone buries her brother's slain body in defiance of an edict from King Creon to leave the body on the Theban field.

II.

The Old Singers.

William was sitting on the side door step, and the old mother was busy making her tea; she gave into my hand an old flowered-glass tea-caddy.

"William thought you'd like to see this, when he was settin' the table. My father brought it to my mother from the island of Tobago; an' here's a pair of beautiful mugs that came with it." She opened the glass door of a little cupboard beside the chimney. "These I call my best things, dear," she said. "You'd laugh to see how we enjoy 'em Sunday nights in winter: we have a real company tea 'stead o' livin' right along just the same, an' I make somethin' good for a s'prise an' put on some o' my preserves, an' we get a-talkin' together an' have real pleasant times."

Mrs. Todd laughed indulgently, and looked to see what I thought of such childishness.

"I wish I could be here some Sunday evening," said I.

"William an' me'll be talkin' about you an' thinkin' o' this nice day," said Mrs. Blackett affectionately, and she glanced at William, and he looked up bravely and nodded. I began to discover that he and his sister could not speak their deeper feelings before each other.

"Now I want you an' mother to sing," said Mrs. Todd abruptly, with an air of command, and I gave William much sympathy in his evident distress.

"After I've had my cup o' tea, dear," answered the old hostess cheerfully; and so we sat down and took our cups and made merry while they lasted. It was impossible not to wish to stay on forever at Green Island, and I could not help saying so.

"I'm very happy here, both winter an' summer," said old Mrs. Blackett. "William an' I never wish for any other home, do we, William? I'm glad you find it pleasant; I wish you'd come an' stay, dear, whenever you feel inclined. But here's Almiry; I always think Providence was kind to plot an' have her husband leave her a good house where she really belonged. She'd been very restless if she'd had to continue here on Green Island. You wanted more scope, didn't you, Almiry, an' to live in a large place where more things grew? Sometimes folks wonders that we don't live together; perhaps we shall some time," and a shadow of sadness and apprehension flitted across her face. "The time o' sickness an' failin' has got to come to all. But Almiry's got an herb that's good for everything." She smiled as she spoke, and looked bright again.

"There's some herb that's good for everybody, except for them that thinks they're sick when they ain't," announced Mrs. Todd, with a truly professional air of finality. "Come, William, let's have Sweet Home, an' then mother'll sing Cupid an' the Bee for us."

Then followed a most charming surprise. William mastered his timidity and began to sing. His voice was a little faint and frail, like the family daguerreotypes, but it was a tenor voice, and perfectly true and sweet. I have never heard Home, Sweet Home sung as touchingly and seriously as he sang it; he seemed to make it quite new; and when he paused for a moment at the end of the first line and began the next, the old mother joined him and they sang together, she missing only the higher notes, where he seemed to lend his voice to hers for the moment and carry on her very note and air. It was the silent man's real and only means of expression, and one could have listened forever, and have asked for more and more songs of old Scotch and English inheritance and the best that have lived from the ballad music of the war. Mrs. Todd kept time visibly, and sometimes audibly, with her ample foot. I saw the tears in her eyes sometimes, when I could see beyond the tears in mine. But at last the songs ended and the time came to say good-by; it was the end of a great pleasure.

Mrs. Blackett, the dear old lady, opened the door of her bedroom while Mrs. Todd was tying up the herb bag, and William had gone down to get the boat ready and to blow the horn for Johnny Bowden, who had joined a roving boat party who were off the shore lobstering.

I went to the door of the bedroom, and thought how pleasant it looked, with its pink-and-white patchwork quilt and the brown unpainted paneling of its woodwork.

"Come right in, dear," she said. "I want you to set down in my old quilted rockin'-chair there by the window; you'll say it's the prettiest view in the house. I set there a good deal to rest me and when I want to read."

There was a worn red Bible on the lightstand, and Mrs. Blackett's heavy silver-bowed glasses; her thimble was on the narrow window-ledge, and folded carefully on the table was a thick striped-cotton shirt that she was making for her son. Those dear old fingers and their loving stitches, that heart which had made the most of everything that needed love! Here was the real home, the heart of the old house on Green Island! I sat in the rocking-chair, and felt that it was a place of peace, the little brown bedroom, and the quiet outlook upon field and sea and sky.

I looked up, and we understood each other without speaking. "I shall like to think o' your settin' here to-day," said Mrs. Blackett. "I want you to come again. It has been so pleasant for William."

The wind served us all the way home, and did not fall or let the sail slacken until we were close to the shore. We had a generous freight of lobsters in the boat, and new potatoes which William had put aboard, and what Mrs. Todd proudly called a full "kag" of prime number one salted mackerel; and when we landed we had to make business arrangements to have these conveyed to her house in a wheelbarrow.

I never shall forget the day at Green Island. The town of Dunnet Landing seemed large and noisy and oppressive as we came ashore. Such is the power of contrast; for the village was so still that I could hear the shy whippoorwills singing that night as I lay awake in my downstairs bedroom, and the scent of Mrs. Todd's herb garden under the window blew in again and again with every gentle rising of the sea-breeze.

12.

A Strange Sail.

EXCEPT FOR A FEW stray guests, islanders or from the inland country, to whom Mrs. Todd offered the hospitalities of a single meal, we were quite by ourselves all summer; and when there were signs of invasion, late in July, and a certain Mrs. Fosdick appeared like a strange sail on the far horizon, I suffered much from apprehension. I had been living in the quaint little house with as much comfort and unconsciousness as if it were a larger body, or a double shell, in whose simple convolutions Mrs. Todd and I had secreted ourselves, until some wandering hermit crab of a visitor marked the little spare room for her own. Perhaps now and then a castaway on a lonely desert island dreads the thought of being rescued. I heard of Mrs. Fosdick for the first time with a selfish sense of objection; but after all, I was still vacation-tenant of the schoolhouse, where I could always be alone, and it was impossible not to sympathize with Mrs. Todd, who, in spite of some preliminary grumbling, was really delighted with the prospect of entertaining an old friend.

For nearly a month we received occasional news of Mrs. Fosdick, who seemed to be making a royal progress from house to house in the inland neighborhood, after the fashion of Queen Elizabeth. One Sunday after another came and went, disappointing Mrs. Todd in the hope of seeing her guest at church and fixing the day for the great visit to begin; but Mrs. Fosdick was not ready to commit herself to a date. An assurance of "some time this week" was not sufficiently definite from a free-footed housekeeper's point of view, and Mrs. Todd put aside all herb-gathering plans, and went through the various stages of expectation, provocation, and despair. At last she was ready to believe that Mrs. Fosdick must have forgotten her promise and returned to her home, which was vaguely said to be over Thomaston way. But one evening, just as the supper-table was cleared and "readied up," and Mrs. Todd had put her large apron over her head and stepped forth for an evening stroll in the garden, the unexpected happened. She heard the sound of wheels, and gave an excited cry to me, as I sat by the window, that Mrs. Fosdick was coming right up the street.

"She may not be considerate, but she's dreadful good company," said Mrs. Todd hastily, coming back a few steps from the neighborhood of the gate. "No, she ain't a mite considerate, but there's a small lobster left over from your tea; yes, it's a real mercy there's a lobster. Susan Fosdick might just as well have passed the compliment o' comin' an hour ago."

"Perhaps she has had her supper," I ventured to suggest, sharing the housekeeper's anxiety, and meekly conscious of an inconsiderate appetite for my own supper after a long expedition up the bay. There were so few emergencies of any sort at Dunnet Landing that this one appeared overwhelming.

"No, she's rode 'way over from Nahum Brayton's place. I expect they were busy on the farm, and couldn't spare the horse in proper season. You just sly out an' set the teakittle on again, dear, an' drop in a good han'ful o' chips; the fire 's all alive. I'll take her right up to lay off her things, an' she'll be occupied with explanations an' gettin' her bunnit off, so you'll have plenty o' time. She's one I shouldn't like to have find me unprepared."

Mrs. Fosdick was already at the gate, and Mrs. Todd now turned with an air of complete surprise and delight to welcome her.

"Why, Susan Fosdick," I heard her exclaim in a fine unhindered voice, as if she were calling across a field, "I come near giving of you up! I was afraid you'd gone an' 'portioned out my visit to somebody else. I s'pose you've been to supper?"

"Lor', no, I ain't, Almiry Todd," said Mrs. Fosdick cheerfully, as she turned, laden with bags and bundles, from making her adieux to the boy driver. "I ain't had a mite o' supper, dear. I've been lottin' all the way on a cup o' that best tea o' yourn,—some o' that Oolong you keep in the little chist. I don't want none o' your useful herbs."

"I keep that tea for ministers' folks," gayly responded Mrs. Todd. "Come right along in, Susan Fosdick. I declare if you ain't the same old sixpence!"

As they came up the walk together, laughing like girls, I fled, full of cares, to the kitchen, to brighten the fire and be sure that the lobster, sole dependence of a late supper, was well out of reach of the cat. There proved to be fine reserves of wild raspberries and bread and butter, so that I regained my composure, and waited impatiently for my own share of this illustrious visit to begin. There was an instant sense of high festivity in the evening air from the moment when our guest had so frankly demanded the Oolong tea.

The great moment arrived. I was formally presented at the stairfoot, and the two friends passed on to the kitchen, where I soon heard a hospitable clink of crockery and the brisk stirring of a teacup. I sat in my high-backed rocking-chair by the window in the front room with an unreasonable feeling of being left out, like the child who stood at the gate in Hans Andersen's story. Mrs. Fosdick did not look, at first sight, like a person of great social gifts. She was a serious-looking little bit of an old woman, with a birdlike nod of the head. I had often been told that she was the "best hand in the world to make a visit,"—as if to visit were the highest of vocations; that everybody wished for her, while few could get her; and I saw that Mrs. Todd felt a comfortable sense of distinction in being favored with the company of this eminent person who "knew just how." It was certainly true that Mrs. Fosdick gave both her hostess and me a warm feeling of enjoyment and expectation, as if she had the power of social suggestion to all neighboring minds.

The two friends did not reappear for at least an hour. I could hear their busy voices, loud and low by turns, as they ranged from public to confidential topics. At last Mrs. Todd kindly remembered me and returned, giving my door a ceremonious knock before she stepped in, with the small visitor in her wake. She reached behind her and took Mrs. Fosdick's hand as if she were young and bashful, and gave her a gentle pull forward.

"There, I don't know whether you're goin' to take to each other or not; no, nobody can't tell whether you'll suit each other, but I expect you'll get along some way, both having seen the world," said our affectionate hostess. "You can inform Mis' Fosdick how we found the folks out to Green Island the other day. She's always been well acquainted with mother. I'll slip out now an' put away the supper things an' set my bread to rise, if you'll both excuse me. You can come out an' keep me company when you get ready, either or both." And Mrs. Todd, large and amiable, disappeared and left us.

Being furnished not only with a subject of conversation, but with a safe refuge in the kitchen in case of incompatibility, Mrs. Fosdick and I sat down, prepared to make the best of each other. I soon discovered that she, like many of the elder women of that coast, had spent a part of her life at sea, and was full of a good traveler's curiosity and enlightenment. By the time we thought it discreet to join our hostess we were already sincere friends.

You may speak of a visit's setting in as well as a tide's, and it was impossible, as Mrs. Todd whispered to me, not to be pleased at the way this visit was setting in; a new impulse and refreshing of the social currents and seldom visited bays of memory appeared to have begun. Mrs. Fosdick had been the mother of a large family of sons and daughters,—sailors and sailors' wives,—and most of them had died before her. I soon grew more or less acquainted with the histories of all their fortunes and misfortunes, and subjects of an intimate nature were no more withheld from my ears than if I had been a shell on the mantelpiece. Mrs. Fosdick was not without a touch of dignity and elegance; she was fashionable in her dress, but it was a curiously well-preserved provincial fashion of some years back. In a wider sphere one might have called her a woman of the world, with her unexpected bits of modern knowledge, but Mrs. Todd's wisdom was an intimation of truth itself. She might belong to any age, like an idyl of Theocritus; but while she always understood Mrs. Fosdick, that entertaining pilgrim could not always understand Mrs. Todd.

That very first evening my friends plunged into a borderless sea of reminiscences and personal news. Mrs. Fosdick had been staying with a family who owned the farm where she was born, and she had visited every sunny knoll and shady field corner; but when she said that it might be for the last time, I detected in her tone something expectant of the contradiction which Mrs. Todd promptly offered.

"Almiry," said Mrs. Fosdick, with sadness, "you may say what you like, but I am one of nine brothers and sisters brought up on the old place, and we're all dead but me."

"Your sister Dailey ain't gone, is she? Why, no, Louisa ain't gone!" exclaimed Mrs. Todd, with surprise. "Why, I never heard of that occurrence!"

"Yes 'm; she passed away last October, in Lynn. She had made her distant home in Vermont State, but she was making a visit to her youngest daughter. Louisa was the only one of my family whose funeral I wasn't able to attend, but 't was a mere accident. All the rest of us were settled right about home. I thought it was very slack of 'em in Lynn not to fetch her to the old place; but when I came to hear about it, I learned that they'd recently put up a very elegant monument, and my sister Dailey was always great for show. She'd just been out to see the monument the week before she was taken down, and admired it so much that they felt sure of her wishes."

"So she's really gone, and the funeral was up to Lynn!" repeated Mrs. Todd, as if to impress the sad fact upon her mind.

"She was some years younger than we be, too. I recollect the first day she ever came to school; 't was that first year mother sent me inshore to stay with aunt Topham's folks and get my schooling. You fetched little Louisa to school one Monday mornin' in a pink dress an' her long curls, and she set between you an' me, and got cryin' after a while, so the teacher sent us home with her at recess."

"She was scared of seeing so many children about her; there was only her and me and brother John at home then; the older boys were to sea with father, an' the rest of us wa'n't born," explained Mrs. Fosdick. "That next fall we all went to sea together. Mother was uncertain till the last minute, as one may say. The ship was waiting orders, but the baby that then was, was born just in time, and there was a long spell of extra bad weather, so mother got about again before they had to sail, an' we all went. I remember my clothes were all left ashore in the east chamber in a basket where mother 'd took them out o' my chist o' drawers an' left 'em ready to carry aboard. She didn't have nothing aboard, of her own, that she wanted to cut up for me, so when my dress wore out she just put me into a spare suit o' John's, jacket and trousers. I wasn't but eight years old an' he was most seven and large of his age. Quick as we made a port she went right ashore an' fitted me out pretty, but we was bound for the East Indies and didn't put in anywhere for a good while. So I had quite a spell o' freedom. Mother made my new skirt long because I was growing, and I poked about the deck after that, real discouraged, feeling the hem at my heels every minute, and as if youth was past and gone. I liked the trousers best; I used to climb the riggin' with 'em and frighten mother till she said an' vowed she'd never take me to sea again."

I thought by the polite absent-minded smile on Mrs. Todd's face this was no new story.

"Little Louisa was a beautiful child; yes, I always thought Louisa was very pretty," Mrs. Todd said. "She was a dear little girl in those days. She favored your mother; the rest of you took after your father's folks."

"We did certain," agreed Mrs. Fosdick, rocking steadily. "There, it does seem so pleasant to talk with an old acquaintance that knows what you know. I see so many of these new folks nowadays, that seem to have neither past nor future. Conversation 's got to have some root in the past, or else you've got to explain every remark you make, an' it wears a person out."

Mrs. Todd gave a funny little laugh. "Yes 'm, old friends is always best, 'less you can catch a new one that's fit to make an old one out of," she said, and we gave an affectionate glance at each other which Mrs. Fosdick could not have understood, being the latest comer to the house.

13.

Poor Joanna.

One evening my ears caught a mysterious allusion which Mrs. Todd made to Shell-heap Island. It was a chilly night of cold northeasterly rain, and I made a fire for the first time in the Franklin stove in my room, and begged my two housemates to come in and keep me company. The weather had convinced Mrs. Todd that it was time to make a supply of cough-drops, and she had been bringing forth herbs from dark and dry hiding-places, until now the pungent dust and odor of them had resolved themselves into one mighty flavor of spearmint that came from a simmering caldron of syrup in the kitchen. She called it done, and well done, and had ostentatiously left it to cool, and taken her knitting-work because Mrs. Fosdick was busy with hers. They sat in the two rocking-chairs, the small woman and the large one, but now and then I could see that Mrs. Todd's thoughts remained with the cough-drops. The time of gathering herbs was nearly over, but the time of syrups and cordials had begun.

The heat of the open fire made us a little drowsy, but something in the way Mrs. Todd spoke of Shell-heap Island waked my interest. I waited to see if she would say any more, and then took a roundabout way back to the subject by saying what was first in my mind: that I wished the Green Island family were there to spend the evening with us,—Mrs. Todd's mother and her brother William.

Mrs. Todd smiled, and drummed on the arm of the rocking-chair. "Might scare William to death," she warned me; and Mrs. Fosdick mentioned her intention of going out to Green Island to stay two or three days, if this wind didn't make too much sea.

"Where is Shell-heap Island?" I ventured to ask, seizing the opportunity.

"Bears nor'east somewheres about three miles from Green Island; right off-shore, I should call it about eight miles out," said Mrs. Todd. "You never was there, dear; 't is off the thoroughfares, and a very bad place to land at best."

"I should think 't was," agreed Mrs. Fosdick, smoothing down her black silk apron. " 'T is a place worth visitin' when you once get there. Some o' the old folks was kind o' fearful about it. 'T was 'counted a great place in old Indian times; you can pick up their stone tools 'most any time if you hunt about. There's a beautiful spring 'o water, too. Yes, I remember when they used to tell queer stories about Shell-heap Island. Some said 't was a great bangeing-place* for the Indians, and an old chief resided there once that ruled the winds; and others said they'd always heard that once the Indians come down from up country an' left a captive there without any bo't, an' 't was too far to swim across to Black Island, so called, an' he lived there till he perished."

"I've heard say he walked the island after that, and sharp-sighted folks could see him an' lose him like one o' them citizens Cap'n Littlepage was acquainted with up to the north pole," announced Mrs. Todd grimly. "Anyway, there was Indians,—you can see their shell-heap that named the island; and I've heard myself that 't was one o' their cannibal places, but I never could believe it. There never was no cannibals on the coast 'o Maine. All the Indians o' these regions are tame-looking folks."

"Sakes alive, yes!" exclaimed Mrs. Fosdick. "Ought to see them painted savages I've seen when I was young out in the South Sea Islands! That was the time for folks to travel, 'way back in the old whalin' days!"

"Whalin' must have been dull for a lady, hardly ever makin' a lively port, and not takin' in any mixed cargoes," said Mrs. Todd. "I never desired to go a whalin' v'y'ge myself."

"I used to return feelin' very slack an' behind the times, 't is true," explained Mrs. Fosdick, "but 't was excitin', an' we always done extra well, and felt rich when we did get ashore. I liked the variety. There, how times have changed; how few seafarin' families there are left! What a lot o' queer folks there used to be about here, anyway, when we was young, Almiry. Everybody's just like everybody else, now; nobody to laugh about, and nobody to cry about."

---

*In the rural speech of nineteenth-century New England, being idle or lazy.

It seemed to me that there were peculiarities of character in the region of Dunnet Landing yet, but I did not like to interrupt.

"Yes," said Mrs. Todd after a moment of meditation, "there was certain a good many curiosities of human natur' in this neighborhood years ago. There was more energy then, and in some the energy took a singular turn. In these days the young folks is all copy-cats, 'fraid to death they won't be all just alike; as for the old folks, they pray for the advantage o' bein' a little different."

"I ain't heard of a copy-cat this great many years," said Mrs. Fosdick, laughing; "'t was a favorite term o' my grandmother's. No, I wa'n't thinking o' those things, but of them strange straying creatur's that used to rove the country. You don't see them now, or the ones that used to hive away in their own houses with some strange notion or other."

I thought again of Captain Littlepage, but my companions were not reminded of his name; and there was brother William at Green Island, whom we all three knew.

"I was talking o' poor Joanna the other day. I hadn't thought of her for a great while," said Mrs. Fosdick abruptly. "Mis' Brayton an' I recalled her as we sat together sewing. She was one o' your peculiar persons, wa'n't she? Speaking of such persons," she turned to explain to me, "there was a sort of a nun or hermit person lived out there for years all alone on Shell-heap Island. Miss Joanna Todd, her name was,—a cousin o' Almiry's late husband."

I expressed my interest, but as I glanced at Mrs. Todd I saw that she was confused by sudden affectionate feeling and unmistakable desire for reticence.

"I never want to hear Joanna laughed about," she said anxiously.

"Nor I," answered Mrs. Fosdick reassuringly. "She was crossed in love,—that was all the matter to begin with; but as I look back, I can see that Joanna was one doomed from the first to fall into a melancholy. She retired from the world for good an' all, though she was a well-off woman. All she wanted was to get away from folks; she thought she wasn't fit to live with anybody, and wanted to be free. Shell-heap Island come to her from her father, and first thing folks knew she'd gone off out there to live, and left word she didn't want no company. 'T was a bad place to get to, unless the wind an' tide were just right; 't was hard work to make a landing."

"What time of year was this?" I asked.

"Very late in the summer," said Mrs. Fosdick. "No, I never could laugh at Joanna, as some did. She set everything by the young man, an' they were going to marry in about a month, when he got bewitched with a girl 'way up the bay, and married her, and went off to Massachusetts. He wasn't well thought of,—there were those who thought Joanna's money was what had tempted him; but she'd given him her whole heart, an' she wa'n't so young as she had been. All her hopes were built on marryin', an' havin' a real home and somebody to look to; she acted just like a bird when its nest is spoilt. The day after she heard the news she was in dreadful woe, but the next she came to herself very quiet, and took the horse and wagon, and drove fourteen miles to the lawyer's, and signed a paper givin' her half of the farm to her brother. They never had got along very well together, but he didn't want to sign it, till she acted so distressed that he gave in. Edward Todd's wife was a good woman, who felt very bad indeed, and used every argument with Joanna; but Joanna took a poor old boat that had been her father's and lo'ded in a few things, and off she put all alone, with a good land breeze, right out to sea. Edward Todd ran down to the beach, an' stood there cryin' like a boy to see her go, but she was out o' hearin'. She never stepped foot on the mainland again long as she lived."

"How large an island is it? How did she manage in winter?" I asked.

"Perhaps thirty acres, rocks and all," answered Mrs. Todd, taking up the story gravely. "There can't be much of it that the salt spray don't fly over in storms. No, 't is a dreadful small place to make a world of; it has a different look from any of the other islands, but there's a sheltered cove on the south side, with mud-flats across one end of it at low water where there's excellent clams, and the big shell-heap keeps some o' the wind off a little house her father took the trouble to build when he was a young man. They said there was an old house built o' logs there before that, with a kind of natural cellar in the rock under it. He used to stay out there days to a time, and anchor a little sloop he had, and dig clams to fill it, and sail up to Portland. They said the dealers always gave him an extra price, the clams were so noted. Joanna used to go out and stay with him. They were always great companions, so she knew just what 't was out there. There was a few sheep that belonged to her brother an' her, but she bargained for him to come and get them on the edge o' cold weather. Yes, she desired him to come for the sheep; an' his wife thought perhaps Joanna'd return, but he said no, an' lo'ded the bo't with warm things an' what he thought she'd need through the winter. He come home with the sheep an' left the other things by the house, but she never so much as looked out o' the window. She done it for a penance. She must have wanted to see Edward by that time."

Mrs. Fosdick was fidgeting with eagerness to speak.

"Some thought the first cold snap would set her ashore, but she always remained," concluded Mrs. Todd soberly.

"Talk about the men not having any curiosity!" exclaimed Mrs. Fosdick scornfully. "Why, the waters round Shell-heap Island were white with sails all that fall. 'T was never called no great of a fishin'-ground before. Many of 'em made excuse to go ashore to get water at the spring; but at last she spoke to a bo't-load, very dignified and calm, and said that she'd like it better if they'd make a practice of getting water to Black Island or somewheres else and leave her alone, except in case of accident or trouble. But there was one man who had always set everything by her from a boy. He'd have married her if the other hadn't come about an' spoilt his chance, and he used to get close to the island, before light, on his way out fishin', and throw a little bundle 'way up the green slope front o' the house. His sister told me she happened to see, the first time, what a pretty choice he made o' useful things that a woman would feel lost without. He stood off fishin', and could see them in the grass all day, though sometimes she'd come out and walk right by them. There was other bo'ts near, out after mackerel. But early next morning his present was gone. He didn't presume too much, but once he took her a nice firkin* o' things he got up to Portland, and when spring come he landed her a hen and chickens in a nice little coop. There was a good many old friends had Joanna on their minds."

"Yes," said Mrs. Todd, losing her sad reserve in the growing sympathy of these reminiscences. "How everybody used to notice whether there was smoke out of the chimney! The Black Island

---

*A small vessel or cask.

folks could see her with their spy-glass, and if they'd ever missed getting some sign o' life they'd have sent notice to her folks. But after the first year or two Joanna was more and more forgotten as an every-day charge. Folks lived very simple in those days, you know," she continued, as Mrs. Fosdick's knitting was taking much thought at the moment. "I expect there was always plenty of driftwood thrown up, and a poor failin' patch of spruces covered all the north side of the island, so she always had something to burn. She was very fond of workin' in the garden ashore, and that first summer she began to till the little field out there, and raised a nice parcel o' potatoes. She could fish, o' course, and there was all her clams an' lobsters. You can always live well in any wild place by the sea when you'd starve to death up country, except 't was berry time. Joanna had berries out there, blackberries at least, and there was a few herbs in case she needed them. Mullein in great quantities and a plant o' wormwood I remember seeing once when I stayed there, long before she fled out to Shell-heap. Yes, I recall the wormwood, which is always a planted herb, so there must have been folks there before the Todds' day. A growin' bush makes the best gravestone; I expect that wormwood always stood for somebody's solemn monument. Catnip, too, is a very endurin' herb about an old place."

"But what I want to know is what she did for other things," interrupted Mrs. Fosdick. "Almiry, what did she do for clothin' when she needed to replenish, or risin' for her bread, or the piece-bag that no woman can live long without?"

"Or company," suggested Mrs. Todd. "Joanna was one that loved her friends. There must have been a terrible sight o' long winter evenin's that first year."

"There was her hens," suggested Mrs. Fosdick, after reviewing the melancholy situation. "She never wanted the sheep after that first season. There wa'n't no proper pasture for sheep after the June grass was past, and she ascertained the fact and couldn't bear to see them suffer; but the chickens done well. I remember sailin' by one spring afternoon, an' seein' the coops out front o' the house in the sun. How long was it before you went out with the minister? You were the first ones that ever really got ashore to see Joanna."

I had been reflecting upon a state of society which admitted such personal freedom and a voluntary hermitage. There was something mediæval in the behavior of poor Joanna Todd under a disappointment of the heart. The two women had drawn closer together, and were talking on, quite unconscious of a listener.

"Poor Joanna!" said Mrs. Todd again, and sadly shook her head as if there were things one could not speak about.

"I called her a great fool," declared Mrs. Fosdick, with spirit, "but I pitied her then, and I pity her far more now. Some other minister would have been a great help to her,—one that preached self-forgetfulness and doin' for others to cure our own ills; but Parson Dimmick was a vague person, well meanin', but very numb in his feelin's. I don't suppose at that troubled time Joanna could think of any way to mend her troubles except to run off and hide."

"Mother used to say she didn't see how Joanna lived without having nobody to do for, getting her own meals and tending her own poor self day in an' day out," said Mrs. Todd sorrowfully.

"There was the hens," repeated Mrs. Fosdick kindly. "I expect she soon came to makin' folks o' them. No, I never went to work to blame Joanna, as some did. She was full o' feeling, and her troubles hurt her more than she could bear. I see it all now as I couldn't when I was young."

"I suppose in old times they had their shut-up convents for just such folks," said Mrs. Todd, as if she and her friend had disagreed about Joanna once, and were now in happy harmony. She seemed to speak with new openness and freedom. "Oh yes, I was only too pleased when the Reverend Mr. Dimmick invited me to go out with him. He hadn't been very long in the place when Joanna left home and friends. 'T was one day that next summer after she went, and I had been married early in the spring. He felt that he ought to go out and visit her. She was a member of the church, and might wish to have him consider her spiritual state. I wa'n't so sure o' that, but I always liked Joanna, and I'd come to be her cousin by marriage. Nathan an' I had conversed about goin' out to pay her a visit, but he got his chance to sail sooner 'n he expected. He always thought everything of her, and last time he come home, knowing nothing of her change, he brought her a beautiful coral pin from a port he'd touched at somewheres up the Mediterranean. So I wrapped the little box in a nice piece of paper and put it in my pocket, and picked her a bunch of fresh lemon balm, and off we started."

Mrs. Fosdick laughed. "I remember hearin' about your trials on the v'y'ge," she said.

"Why, yes," continued Mrs. Todd in her company manner. "I picked her the balm, an' we started. Why, yes, Susan, the minister liked to have cost me my life that day. He would fasten the sheet, though I advised against it. He said the rope was rough an' cut his hand. There was a fresh breeze, an' he went on talking rather high flown, an' I felt some interested. All of a sudden there come up a gust, and he give a screech and stood right up and called for help, 'way out there to sea. I knocked him right over into the bottom o' the bo't, getting by to catch hold of the sheet an' untie it. He wasn't but a little man; I helped him right up after the squall passed, and made a handsome apology to him, but he did act kind o' offended."

"I do think they ought not to settle them landlocked folks in parishes where they're liable to be on the water," insisted Mrs. Fosdick. "Think of the families in our parish that was scattered all about the bay, and what a sight o' sails you used to see, in Mr. Dimmick's day, standing across to the mainland on a pleasant Sunday morning, filled with church-going folks, all sure to want him some time or other! You couldn't find no doctor that would stand up in the boat and screech if a flaw struck her."

"Old Dr. Bennett had a beautiful sailboat, didn't he?" responded Mrs. Todd. "And how well he used to brave the weather! Mother always said that in time o' trouble that tall white sail used to look like an angel's wing comin' over the sea to them that was in pain. Well, there's a difference in gifts. Mr. Dimmick was not without light."

"'T was light o' the moon, then," snapped Mrs. Fosdick; "he was pompous enough, but I never could remember a single word he said. There, go on, Mis' Todd; I forget a great deal about that day you went to see poor Joanna."

"I felt she saw us coming, and knew us a great way off; yes, I seemed to feel it within me," said our friend, laying down her knitting. "I kept my seat, and took the bo't inshore without saying a word; there was a short channel that I was sure Mr. Dimmick wasn't acquainted with, and the tide was very low. She never came out to warn us off nor anything, and I thought, as I hauled the bo't up on a wave and let the Reverend Mr. Dimmick step out, that it was somethin' gained to be safe ashore. There was a little smoke out o' the chimney o' Joanna's house, and it did look sort of homelike and pleasant with wild mornin'-glory vines trained up; an' there was a plot o' flowers under the front window, portulacas and things. I believe she'd made a garden once, when she was stopping there with her father, and some things must have seeded in. It looked as if she might have gone over to the other side of the island. 'T was neat and pretty all about the house, and a lovely day in July. We walked up from the beach together very sedate, and I felt for poor Nathan's little pin to see if 't was safe in my dress pocket. All of a sudden Joanna come right to the fore door and stood there, not sayin' a word."

14.

The Hermitage.

My companions and I had been so intent upon the subject of the conversation that we had not heard any one open the gate, but at this moment, above the noise of the rain, we heard a loud knocking. We were all startled as we sat by the fire, and Mrs. Todd rose hastily and went to answer the call, leaving her rocking-chair in violent motion. Mrs. Fosdick and I heard an anxious voice at the door speaking of a sick child, and Mrs. Todd's kind, motherly voice inviting the messenger in: then we waited in silence. There was a sound of heavy dropping of rain from the eaves, and the distant roar and undertone of the sea. My thoughts flew back to the lonely woman on her outer island; what separation from humankind she must have felt, what terror and sadness, even in a summer storm like this!

"You send right after the doctor if she ain't better in half an hour," said Mrs. Todd to her worried customer as they parted; and I felt a warm sense of comfort in the evident resources of even so small a neighborhood, but for the poor hermit Joanna there was no neighbor on a winter night.

"How did she look?" demanded Mrs. Fosdick, without preface, as our large hostess returned to the little room with a mist about her from standing long in the wet doorway, and the sudden draught of her coming beat out the smoke and flame from the Franklin stove. "How did poor Joanna look?"

"She was the same as ever, except I thought she looked smaller," answered Mrs. Todd after thinking a moment; perhaps it was only a last considering thought about her patient. "Yes, she was just the same, and looked very nice, Joanna did. I had been married since she left home, an' she treated me like her own folks. I expected she'd look strange, with her hair turned gray in a night or somethin', but she wore a pretty gingham dress I'd often seen her wear before she went away; she must have kept it nice for best in the afternoons. She always had beautiful, quiet manners. I remember she waited till we were close to her, and then kissed me real affectionate, and inquired for Nathan before she shook hands with the minister, and then she invited us both in. 'T was the same little house her father had built him when he was a bachelor, with one livin'-room, and a little mite of a bedroom out of it where she slept, but 't was neat as a ship's cabin. There was some old chairs, an' a seat made of a long box that might have held boat tackle an' things to lock up in his fishin' days, and a good enough stove so anybody could cook and keep warm in cold weather. I went over once from home and stayed 'most a week with Joanna when we was girls, and those young happy days rose up before me. Her father was busy all day fishin' or clammin'; he was one o' the pleasantest men in the world, but Joanna's mother had the grim streak, and never knew what 't was to be happy. The first minute my eyes fell upon Joanna's face that day I saw how she had grown to look like Mis' Todd. 'T was the mother right over again."

"Oh dear me!" said Mrs. Fosdick.

"Joanna had done one thing very pretty. There was a little piece o' swamp on the island where good rushes grew plenty, and she'd gathered 'em, and braided some beautiful mats for the floor and a thick cushion for the long bunk. She'd showed a good deal of invention; you see there was a nice chance to pick up pieces o' wood and boards that drove ashore, and she'd made good use o' what she found. There wasn't no clock, but she had a few dishes on a shelf, and flowers set about in shells fixed to the walls, so it did look sort of homelike, though so lonely and poor. I couldn't keep the tears out o' my eyes, I felt so sad. I said to myself, I must get mother to come over an' see Joanna; the love in mother's heart would warm her, an' she might be able to advise."

"Oh no, Joanna was dreadful stern," said Mrs. Fosdick.

"We were all settin' down very proper, but Joanna would keep stealin' glances at me as if she was glad I come. She had but little to say; she was real polite an' gentle, and yet forbiddin'. The minister found it hard," confessed Mrs. Todd; "he got embarrassed, an' when he put on his authority and asked her if she felt to enjoy religion in her present situation, an' she replied that she must be excused from answerin', I thought I should fly. She might have made it easier for him; after all, he was the minister and had taken some trouble to come out, though 't was kind of cold an' unfeelin' the way he inquired.

I thought he might have seen the little old Bible a-layin' on the shelf close by him, an' I wished he knew enough to just lay his hand on it an' read somethin' kind an' fatherly 'stead of accusin' her, an' then given poor Joanna his blessin' with the hope she might be led to comfort. He did offer prayer, but 't was all about hearin' the voice o' God out o' the whirlwind; and I thought while he was goin' on that anybody that had spent the long cold winter all alone out on Shell-heap Island knew a good deal more about those things than he did. I got so provoked I opened my eyes and stared right at him.

"She didn't take no notice, she kep' a nice respectful manner towards him, and when there come a pause she asked if he had any interest about the old Indian remains, and took down some queer stone gouges and hammers off of one of her shelves and showed them to him same's if he was a boy. He remarked that he'd like to walk over an' see the shell-heap; so she went right to the door and pointed him the way. I see then that she'd made her some kind o' sandal-shoes out o' the fine rushes to wear on her feet; she stepped light an' nice in 'em as shoes."

Mrs. Fosdick leaned back in her rocking-chair and gave a heavy sigh.

"I didn't move at first, but I'd held out just as long as I could," said Mrs. Todd, whose voice trembled a little. "When Joanna returned from the door, an' I could see that man's stupid back departin' among the wild rose bushes, I just ran to her an' caught her in my arms. I wasn't so big as I be now, and she was older than me, but I hugged her tight, just as if she was a child. 'Oh, Joanna dear,' I says, 'won't you come ashore an' live 'long o' me at the Landin', or go over to Green Island to mother's when winter comes? Nobody shall trouble you, an' mother finds it hard bein' alone. I can't bear to leave you here'—and I burst right out crying. I'd had my own trials, young as I was, an' she knew it. Oh, I did entreat her; yes, I entreated Joanna."

"What did she say then?" asked Mrs. Fosdick, much moved.

"She looked the same way, sad an' remote through it all," said Mrs. Todd mournfully. "She took hold of my hand, and we sat down close together; 't was as if she turned round an' made a child of me. 'I haven't got no right to live with folks no more,' she said. 'You must never ask me again, Almiry: I've done the only thing I could do, and I've made my choice. I feel a great comfort in your kindness, but I don't deserve it. I have committed the unpardonable sin; you don't understand,' says she humbly. 'I was in great wrath and trouble, and my thoughts was so wicked towards God that I can't expect ever to be forgiven. I have come to know what it is to have patience, but I have lost my hope. You must tell those that ask how 't is with me,' she said, 'an' tell them I want to be alone.' I couldn't speak; no, there wa'n't anything I could say, she seemed so above everything common. I was a good deal younger then than I be now, and I got Nathan's little coral pin out o' my pocket and put it into her hand; and when she saw it and I told her where it come from, her face did really light up for a minute, sort of bright an' pleasant. 'Nathan an' I was always good friends; I'm glad he don't think hard of me,' says she. 'I want you to have it, Almiry, an' wear it for love o' both o' us,' and she handed it back to me. 'You give my love to Nathan,—he's a dear good man,' she said; 'an' tell your mother, if I should be sick she mustn't wish I could get well, but I want her to be the one to come.' Then she seemed to have said all she wanted to, as if she was done with the world, and we sat there a few minutes longer together. It was real sweet and quiet except for a good many birds and the sea rollin' up on the beach; but at last she rose, an' I did too, and she kissed me and held my hand in hers a minute, as if to say good-by; then she turned and went right away out o' the door and disappeared.

"The minister come back pretty soon, and I told him I was all ready, and we started down to the bo't. He had picked up some round stones and things and was carrying them in his pocket-handkerchief; an' he sat down amidships without making any question, and let me take the rudder an' work the bo't, an' made no remarks for some time, until we sort of eased it off speaking of the weather, an' subjects that arose as we skirted Black Island, where two or three families lived belongin' to the parish. He preached next Sabbath as usual, somethin' high soundin' about the creation, and I couldn't help thinkin' he might never get no further; he seemed to know no remedies, but he had a great use of words."

Mrs. Fosdick sighed again. "Hearin' you tell about Joanna brings the time right back as if 't was yesterday," she said. "Yes, she was one o' them poor things that talked about the great sin; we don't seem to hear nothing about the unpardonable sin now, but you may say 't was not uncommon then."

"I expect that if it had been in these days, such a person would be plagued to death with idle folks," continued Mrs. Todd, after a long pause. "As it was, nobody trespassed on her; all the folks about the bay respected her an' her feelings; but as time wore on, after you left here, one after another ventured to make occasion to put somethin' ashore for her if they went that way. I know mother used to go to see her sometimes, and send William over now and then with something fresh an' nice from the farm. There is a point on the sheltered side where you can lay a boat close to shore an' land anything safe on the turf out o' reach o' the water. There were one or two others, old folks, that she would see, and now an' then she'd hail a passin' boat an' ask for somethin'; and mother got her to promise that she would make some sign to the Black Island folks if she wanted help. I never saw her myself to speak to after that day."

"I expect nowadays, if such a thing happened, she'd have gone out West to her uncle's folks or up to Massachusetts and had a change, an' come home good as new. The world's bigger an' freer than it used to be," urged Mrs. Fosdick.

"No," said her friend. "'T is like bad eyesight, the mind of such a person: if your eyes don't see right there may be a remedy, but there's no kind of glasses to remedy the mind. No, Joanna was Joanna, and there she lays on her island where she lived and did her poor penance. She told mother the day she was dyin' that she always used to want to be fetched inshore when it come to the last; but she'd thought it over, and desired to be laid on the island, if 't was thought right. So the funeral was out there, a Saturday afternoon in September. 'T was a pretty day, and there wa'n't hardly a boat on the coast within twenty miles that didn't head for Shell-heap cram-full o' folks, an' all real respectful, same's if she'd always stayed ashore and held her friends. Some went out o' mere curiosity, I don't doubt,—there's always such to every funeral; but most had real feelin', and went purpose to show it. She'd got most o' the wild sparrows as tame as could be, livin' out there so long among 'em, and one flew right in and lit on the coffin an' begun to sing while Mr. Dimmick was speakin'. He was put out by it, an' acted as if he didn't know whether to stop or go on. I may have been prejudiced, but I wa'n't the only one thought the poor little bird done the best of the two."

"What became o' the man that treated her so, did you ever hear?" asked Mrs. Fosdick. "I know he lived up to Massachusetts for a while. Somebody who came from the same place told me that he was in trade there an' doin' very well, but that was years ago."

"I never heard anything more than that; he went to the war in one o' the early rigiments. No, I never heard any more of him," answered Mrs. Todd. "Joanna was another sort of person, and perhaps he showed good judgment in marryin' somebody else, if only he'd behaved straight-forward and manly. He was a shifty-eyed, coaxin' sort of man, that got what he wanted out o' folks, an' only gave when he wanted to buy, made friends easy and lost 'em without knowin' the difference. She'd had a piece o' work tryin' to make him walk accordin' to her right ideas, but she'd have had too much variety ever to fall into a melancholy. Some is meant to be the Joannas in this world, an' 't was her poor lot."

15.

On Shell-heap Island.

SOME TIME AFTER MRS. Fosdick's visit was over and we had returned to our former quietness, I was out sailing alone with Captain Bowden in his large boat. We were taking the crooked northeasterly channel seaward, and were well out from shore while it was still early in the afternoon. I found myself presently among some unfamiliar islands, and suddenly remembered the story of poor Joanna. There is something in the fact of a hermitage that cannot fail to touch the imagination; the recluses are a sad kindred, but they are never commonplace. Mrs. Todd had truly said that Joanna was like one of the saints in the desert; the loneliness of sorrow will forever keep alive their sad succession.

"Where is Shell-heap Island!" I asked eagerly.

"You see Shell-heap now, layin' 'way out beyond Black Island there," answered the captain, pointing with outstretched arm as he stood, and holding the rudder with his knee.

"I should like very much to go there," said I, and the captain, without comment, changed his course a little more to the eastward and let the reef out of his mainsail.

"I don't know's we can make an easy landin' for ye," he remarked doubtfully. "May get your feet wet; bad place to land. Trouble is I ought to have brought a tag-boat; but they clutch on to the water so, an' I do love to sail free. This gre't boat gets easy bothered with anything trailin'. 'T ain't breakin' much on the meetin'-house ledges; guess I can fetch in to Shell-heap."

"How long is it since Miss Joanna Todd died?" I asked, partly by way of explanation.

"Twenty-two years come September," answered the captain, after reflection. "She died the same year my oldest boy was born, an' the town house was burnt over to the Port. I didn't know but you merely wanted to hunt for some o' them Indian relics. Long 's you want to see where Joanna lived—No, 't ain't breakin' over the ledges; we'll manage to fetch across the shoals somehow, 't is such a distance to go 'way round, and tide 's a-risin'," he ended hopefully, and we sailed steadily on, the captain speechless with intent watching of a difficult course, until the small island with its low whitish promontory lay in full view before us under the bright afternoon sun.

The month was August, and I had seen the color of the islands change from the fresh green of June to a sunburnt brown that made them look like stone, except where the dark green of the spruces and fir balsam kept the tint that even winter storms might deepen, but not fade. The few wind-bent trees on Shell-heap Island were mostly dead and gray, but there were some low-growing bushes, and a stripe of light green ran along just above the shore, which I knew to be wild morning-glories. As we came close I could see the high stone walls of a small square field, though there were no sheep left to assail it; and below, there was a little harbor-like cove where Captain Bowden was boldly running the great boat in to seek a landing-place. There was a crooked channel of deep water which led close up against the shore.

"There, you hold fast for'ard there, an' wait for her to lift on the wave. You'll make a good landin' if you're smart; right on the port-hand side!" the captain called excitedly; and I, standing ready with high ambition, seized my chance and leaped over to the grassy bank.

"I'm beat if I ain't aground after all!" mourned the captain despondently.

But I could reach the bowsprit, and he pushed with the boat-hook, while the wind veered round a little as if on purpose and helped with the sail; so presently the boat was free and began to drift out from shore.

"Used to call this p'int Joanna's wharf privilege, but 't has worn away in the weather since her time. I thought one or two bumps wouldn't hurt us none,—paint's got to be renewed, anyway,—but I never thought she'd tetch. I figured on shyin' by," the captain apologized. "She's too gre't a boat to handle well in here; but I used to sort of shy by in Joanna's day, an' cast a little somethin' ashore—some apples or a couple o' pears if I had 'em—on the grass, where she'd be sure to see."

I stood watching while Captain Bowden cleverly found his way back to deeper water. "You needn't make no haste," he called to me; "I'll keep within call. Joanna lays right up there in the far corner o' the field. There used to be a path led to the place. I always knew her well. I was out here to the funeral."

I found the path; it was touching to discover that this lonely spot was not without its pilgrims. Later generations will know less and less of Joanna herself, but there are paths trodden to the shrines of solitude the world over,—the world cannot forget them, try as it may; the feet of the young find them out because of curiosity and dim foreboding, while the old bring hearts full of remembrance. This plain anchorite had been one of those whom sorrow made too lonely to brave the sight of men, too timid to front the simple world she knew, yet valiant enough to live alone with her poor insistent human nature and the calms and passions of the sea and sky.

The birds were flying all about the field; they fluttered up out of the grass at my feet as I walked along, so tame that I liked to think they kept some happy tradition from summer to summer of the safety of nests and good fellowship of mankind. Poor Joanna's house was gone except the stones of its foundations, and there was little trace of her flower garden except a single faded sprig of much-enduring French pinks, which a great bee and a yellow butterfly were befriending together. I drank at the spring, and thought that now and then some one would follow me from the busy, hard-worked, and simple-thoughted countryside of the mainland, which lay dim and dreamlike in the August haze, as Joanna must have watched it many a day. There was the world, and here was she with eternity well begun. In the life of each of us, I said to myself, there is a place remote and islanded, and given to endless regret or secret happiness; we are each the uncompanioned hermit and recluse of an hour or a day; we understand our fellows of the cell to whatever age of history they may belong.

But as I stood alone on the island, in the sea-breeze, suddenly there came a sound of distant voices; gay voices and laughter from a pleasure-boat that was going seaward full of boys and girls. I knew, as if she had told me, that poor Joanna must have heard the like on many and many a summer afternoon, and must have welcomed the good cheer in spite of hopelessness and winter weather, and all the sorrow and disappointment in the world.

16.

The Great Expedition.

Mrs. Todd never by any chance gave warning over night of her great projects and adventures by sea and land. She first came to an understanding with the primal forces of nature, and never trusted to any preliminary promise of good weather, but examined the day for herself in its infancy. Then, if the stars were propitious, and the wind blew from a quarter of good inheritance whence no surprises of sea-turns or southwest sultriness might be feared, long before I was fairly awake I used to hear a rustle and knocking like a great mouse in the walls, and an impatient tread on the steep garret stairs that led to Mrs. Todd's chief place of storage. She went and came as if she had already started on her expedition with utmost haste and kept returning for something that was forgotten. When I appeared in quest of my breakfast, she would be absent-minded and sparing of speech, as if I had displeased her, and she was now, by main force of principle, holding herself back from altercation and strife of tongues.

These signs of a change became familiar to me in the course of time, and Mrs. Todd hardly noticed some plain proofs of divination one August morning when I said, without preface, that I had just seen the Beggs' best chaise go by, and that we should have to take the grocery. Mrs. Todd was alert in a moment.

"There! I might have known!" she exclaimed. "It's the 15th of August, when he goes and gets his money. He heired an annuity from an uncle o' his on his mother's side. I understood the uncle said none o' Sam Begg's wife's folks should make free with it, so after Sam's gone it'll all be past an' spent, like last summer. That's what Sam prospers on now, if you can call it prosperin'. Yes, I might have known. 'T is the 15th o' August with him, an' he gener'ly stops to dinner with a cousin's widow on the way home. Feb'uary an' August is the times. Takes him 'bout all day to go an' come."

I heard this explanation with interest. The tone of Mrs. Todd's voice was complaining at the last.

"I like the grocery just as well as the chaise," I hastened to say, referring to a long-bodied high wagon with a canopy-top, like an attenuated four-posted bedstead on wheels, in which we sometimes journeyed. "We can put things in behind—roots and flowers and raspberries, or anything you are going after—much better than if we had the chaise."

Mrs. Todd looked stony and unwilling. "I counted upon the chaise," she said, turning her back to me, and roughly pushing back all the quiet tumblers on the cupboard shelf as if they had been impertinent. "Yes, I desired the chaise for once. I ain't goin' berryin' nor to fetch home no more wilted vegetation this year. Season 's about past, except for a poor few o' late things," she added in a milder tone. "I'm goin' up country. No, I ain't intendin' to go berryin'. I've been plottin' for it the past fortnight and hopin' for a good day."

"Would you like to have me go too?" I asked frankly, but not without a humble fear that I might have mistaken the purpose of this latest plan.

"Oh certain, dear!" answered my friend affectionately. "Oh no, I never thought o' any one else for comp'ny, if it's convenient for you, long's poor mother ain't come. I ain't nothin' like so handy with a conveyance as I be with a good bo't. Comes o' my early bringing-up. I expect we've got to make that great high wagon do. The tires want settin' and 't is all loose-jointed, so I can hear it shackle the other side o' the ridge. We'll put the basket in front. I ain't goin' to have it bouncin' an' twirlin' all the way. Why, I've been makin' some nice hearts and rounds to carry."

These were signs of high festivity, and my interest deepened moment by moment.

"I'll go down to the Beggs' and get the horse just as soon as I finish my breakfast," said I. "Then we can start whenever you are ready."

Mrs. Todd looked cloudy again. "I don't know but you look nice enough to go just as you be," she suggested doubtfully. "No, you wouldn't want to wear that pretty blue dress o' yourn 'way up country. 'T ain't dusty now, but it may be comin' home. No, I expect you'd rather not wear that and the other hat."

"Oh yes. I shouldn't think of wearing these clothes," said I, with sudden illumination. "Why, if we're going up country and are likely to see some of your friends, I'll put on my blue dress, and you must wear your watch; I am not going at all if you mean to wear the big hat."

"Now you're behavin' pretty," responded Mrs. Todd, with a gay toss of her head and a cheerful smile, as she came across the room, bringing a saucerful of wild raspberries, a pretty piece of salvage from supper-time. "I was cast down when I see you come to breakfast. I didn't think 't was just what you'd select to wear to the reunion, where you're goin' to meet everybody."

"What reunion do you mean?" I asked, not without amazement. "Not the Bowden Family's? I thought that was going to take place in September."

"To-day's the day. They sent word the middle o' the week. I thought you might have heard of it. Yes, they changed the day. I been thinkin' we'd talk it over, but you never can tell beforehand how it's goin' to be, and 't ain't worth while to wear a day all out before it comes." Mrs. Todd gave no place to the pleasures of anticipation, but she spoke like the oracle that she was. "I wish mother was here to go," she continued sadly. "I did look for her last night, and I couldn't keep back the tears when the dark really fell and she wa'n't here, she does so enjoy a great occasion. If William had a mite o' snap an' ambition, he'd take the lead at such a time. Mother likes variety, and there ain't but a few nice opportunities 'round here, an' them she has to miss 'less she contrives to get ashore to me. I do re'lly hate to go to the reunion without mother, an' 't is a beautiful day; everybody'll be asking where she is. Once she'd have got here anyway. Poor mother 's beginnin' to feel her age."

"Why, there 's your mother now!" I exclaimed with joy, I was so glad to see the dear old soul again. "I hear her voice at the gate." But Mrs. Todd was out of the door before me.

There, sure enough, stood Mrs. Blackett, who must have left Green Island before daylight. She had climbed the steep road from the water-side so eagerly that she was out of breath, and was standing by the garden fence to rest. She held an old-fashioned brown wicker cap-basket in her hand, as if visiting were a thing of every day, and looked up at us as pleased and triumphant as a child.

"Oh, what a poor, plain garden! Hardly a flower in it except your bush o' balm!" she said. "But you do keep your garden neat, Almiry.

Are you both well, an' goin' up country with me?" She came a step or two closer to meet us, with quaint politeness and quite as delightful as if she were at home. She dropped a quick little curtsey before Mrs. Todd.

"There, mother, what a girl you be! I am so pleased! I was just bewailin' you," said the daughter, with unwonted feeling. "I was just bewailin' you, I was so disappointed, an' I kep' myself awake a good piece o' the night scoldin' poor William. I watched for the boat till I was ready to shed tears yisterday, and when 't was comin' dark I kep' making errands out to the gate an' down the road to see if you wa'n't in the doldrums somewhere down the bay."

"There was a head wind, as you know," said Mrs. Blackett, giving me the cap-basket, and holding my hand affectionately as we walked up the clean-swept path to the door. "I was partly ready to come, but dear William said I should be all tired out and might get cold, havin' to beat all the way in. So we give it up, and set down and spent the evenin' together. It was a little rough and windy outside, and I guess 't was better judgment; we went to bed very early and made a good start just at daylight. It's been a lovely mornin' on the water. William thought he'd better fetch across beyond Bird Rocks, rowin' the greater part o' the way; then we sailed from there right over to the Landin', makin' only one tack. William'll be in again for me to-morrow, so I can come back here an' rest me over night, an' go to meetin' to-morrow, and have a nice, good visit."

"She was just havin' her breakfast," said Mrs. Todd, who had listened eagerly to the long explanation without a word of disapproval, while her face shone more and more with joy. "You just sit right down an' have a cup of tea and rest you while we make our preparations. Oh, I am so gratified to think you've come! Yes, she was just havin' her breakfast, and we were speakin' of you. Where's William?"

"He went right back; he said he expected some schooners in about noon after bait, but he'll come an' have his dinner with us to-morrow, unless it rains; then next day. I laid his best things out all ready," explained Mrs. Blackett, a little anxiously. "This wind will serve him nice all the way home. Yes, I will take a cup of tea, dear,—a cup of tea is always good; and then I'll rest a minute and be all ready to start."

"I do feel condemned for havin' such hard thoughts o' William," openly confessed Mrs. Todd. She stood before us so large and serious that we both laughed and could not find it in our hearts to convict so rueful a culprit. "He shall have a good dinner to-morrow, if it can be got, and I shall be real glad to see William," the confession ended handsomely, while Mrs. Blackett smiled approval and made haste to praise the tea. Then I hurried away to make sure of the grocery wagon. Whatever might be the good of the reunion, I was going to have the pleasure and delight of a day in Mrs. Blackett's company, not to speak of Mrs. Todd's.

The early morning breeze was still blowing, and the warm, sunshiny air was of some ethereal northern sort, with a cool freshness as if it came over new-fallen snow. The world was filled with a fragrance of fir-balsam and the faintest flavor of seaweed from the ledges, bare and brown at low tide in the little harbor. It was so still and so early that the village was but half awake. I could hear no voices but those of the birds, small and great,—the constant song sparrows, the clink of a yellow-hammer over in the woods, and the far conversation of some deliberate crows. I saw William Blackett's escaping sail already far from land, and Captain Littlepage was sitting behind his closed window as I passed by, watching for some one who never came. I tried to speak to him, but he did not see me. There was a patient look on the old man's face, as if the world were a great mistake and he had nobody with whom to speak his own language or find companionship.

17.

A Country Road.

WHATEVER DOUBTS AND ANXIETIES I may have had about the inconvenience of the Beggs' high wagon for a person of Mrs. Blackett's age and shortness, they were happily overcome by the aid of a chair and her own valiant spirit. Mrs. Todd bestowed great care upon seating us as if we were taking passage by boat, but she finally pronounced that we were properly trimmed. When we had gone only a little way up the hill she remembered that she had left the house door wide open, though the large key was safe in her pocket. I offered to run back, but my offer was met with lofty scorn, and we lightly dismissed the matter from our minds, until two or three miles further on we met the doctor, and Mrs. Todd asked him to stop and ask her nearest neighbor to step over and close the door if the dust seemed to blow in the afternoon.

"She'll be there in her kitchen; she'll hear you the minute you call; 't wont give you no delay," said Mrs. Todd to the doctor. "Yes, Mis' Dennett's right there, with the windows all open. It isn't as if my fore door opened right on the road, anyway." At which proof of composure Mrs. Blackett smiled wisely at me.

The doctor seemed delighted to see our guest; they were evidently the warmest friends, and I saw a look of affectionate confidence in their eyes. The good man left his carriage to speak to us, but as he took Mrs. Blackett's hand he held it a moment, and, as if merely from force of habit, felt her pulse as they talked; then to my delight he gave the firm old wrist a commending pat.

"You're wearing well: good for another ten years at this rate," he assured her cheerfully, and she smiled back. "I like to keep a strict account of my old stand-bys," and he turned to me. "Don't you let Mrs. Todd overdo to-day,—old folks like her are apt to be thoughtless;" and then we all laughed, and, parting, went our ways gayly.

"I suppose he puts up with your rivalry the same as ever?" asked Mrs. Blackett. "You and he are as friendly as ever, I see, Almiry," and Almira sagely nodded.

"He's got too many long routes now to stop to 'tend to all his door patients," she said, "especially them that takes pleasure in talkin' themselves over. The doctor and me have got to be kind of partners; he's gone a good deal, far an' wide. Looked tired, didn't he? I shall have to advise with him an' get him off for a good rest. He'll take the big boat from Rockland an' go off up to Boston an' mouse round among the other doctors, once in two or three years, and come home fresh as a boy. I guess they think consider'ble of him up there." Mrs. Todd shook the reins and reached determinedly for the whip, as if she were compelling public opinion.

Whatever energy and spirit the white horse had to begin with were soon exhausted by the steep hills and his discernment of a long expedition ahead. We toiled slowly along. Mrs. Blackett and I sat together, and Mrs. Todd sat alone in front with much majesty and the large basket of provisions. Part of the way the road was shaded by thick woods, but we also passed one farmhouse after another on the high uplands, which we all three regarded with deep interest, the house itself and the barns and garden-spots and poultry all having to suffer an inspection of the shrewdest sort. This was a highway quite new to me; in fact, most of my journeys with Mrs. Todd had been made afoot and between the roads, in open pasture-lands. My friends stopped several times for brief dooryard visits, and made so many promises of stopping again on the way home that I began to wonder how long the expedition would last. I had often noticed how warmly Mrs. Todd was greeted by her friends, but it was hardly to be compared to the feeling now shown toward Mrs. Blackett. A look of delight came to the faces of those who recognized the plain, dear old figure beside me; one revelation after another was made of the constant interest and intercourse that had linked the far island and these scattered farms into a golden chain of love and dependence.

"Now, we mustn't stop again if we can help it," insisted Mrs. Todd at last. "You'll get tired, mother, and you'll think the less o' reunions. We can visit along here any day. There, if they ain't frying doughnuts in this next house, too! These are new folks, you know, from over St. George way; they took this old Talcot farm last year. 'T is the best water on the road, and the checkrein's come undone—yes, we'd best delay a little and water the horse."

We stopped, and seeing a party of pleasure-seekers in holiday attire, the thin, anxious mistress of the farmhouse came out with wistful sympathy to hear what news we might have to give. Mrs. Blackett first spied her at the half-closed door, and asked with such cheerful directness if we were trespassing that, after a few words, she went back to her kitchen and reappeared with a plateful of doughnuts.

"Entertainment for man and beast," announced Mrs. Todd with satisfaction. "Why, we've perceived there was new doughnuts all along the road, but you're the first that has treated us."

Our new acquaintance flushed with pleasure, but said nothing.

"They're very nice; you've had good luck with 'em," pronounced Mrs. Todd. "Yes, we've observed there was doughnuts all the way along; if one house is frying all the rest is; 't is so with a great many things."

"I don't suppose likely you're goin' up to the Bowden reunion?" asked the hostess as the white horse lifted his head and we were saying good-by.

"Why, yes," said Mrs. Blackett and Mrs. Todd and I, all together.

"I am connected with the family. Yes, I expect to be there this afternoon. I've been lookin' forward to it," she told us eagerly.

"We shall see you there. Come and sit with us if it's convenient," said dear Mrs. Blackett, and we drove away.

"I wonder who she was before she was married?" said Mrs. Todd, who was usually unerring in matters of genealogy. "She must have been one of that remote branch that lived down beyond Thomaston. We can find out this afternoon. I expect that the families'll march together, or be sorted out some way. I'm willing to own a relation that has such proper ideas of doughnuts."

"I seem to see the family looks," said Mrs. Blackett. "I wish we'd asked her name. She's a stranger, and I want to help make it pleasant for all such."

"She resembles Cousin Pa'lina Bowden about the forehead," said Mrs. Todd with decision.

We had just passed a piece of woodland that shaded the road, and come out to some open fields beyond, when Mrs. Todd suddenly reined in the horse as if somebody had stood on the roadside and stopped her. She even gave that quick reassuring nod of her head which was usually made to answer for a bow, but I discovered that she was looking eagerly at a tall ash-tree that grew just inside the field fence.

"I thought 't was goin' to do well," she said complacently as we went on again. "Last time I was up this way that tree was kind of drooping and discouraged. Grown trees act that way sometimes, same 's folks; then they'll put right to it and strike their roots off into new ground and start all over again with real good courage. Ash-trees is very likely to have poor spells; they ain't got the resolution of other trees."

I listened hopefully for more; it was this peculiar wisdom that made one value Mrs. Todd's pleasant company.

"There's sometimes a good hearty tree growin' right out of the bare rock, out o' some crack that just holds the roots;" she went on to say, "right on the pitch o' one o' them bare stony hills where you can't seem to see a wheel-barrowful o' good earth in a place, but that tree'll keep a green top in the driest summer. You lay your ear down to the ground an' you'll hear a little stream runnin'. Every such tree has got its own livin' spring; there's folks made to match 'em."

I could not help turning to look at Mrs. Blackett, close beside me. Her hands were clasped placidly in their thin black woolen gloves, and she was looking at the flowery wayside as we went slowly along, with a pleased, expectant smile. I do not think she had heard a word about the trees.

"I just saw a nice plant o' elecampane growin' back there," she said presently to her daughter.

"I haven't got my mind on herbs today," responded Mrs. Todd, in the most matter-of-fact way. "I'm bent on seeing folks," and she shook the reins again.

I for one had no wish to hurry, it was so pleasant in the shady roads. The woods stood close to the road on the right; on the left were narrow fields and pastures where there were as many acres of spruces and pines as there were acres of bay and juniper and huckleberry, with a little turf between. When I thought we were in the heart of the inland country, we reached the top of a hill, and suddenly there lay spread out before us a wonderful great view of well-cleared fields that swept down to the wide water of a bay. Beyond this were distant shores like another country in the midday haze which half hid the hills beyond, and the far-away pale blue mountains on the northern horizon. There was a schooner with all sails set coming down the bay from a white village that was sprinkled on the shore, and there were many sailboats flitting about. It was a noble landscape, and my eyes, which had grown used to the narrow inspection of a shaded roadside, could hardly take it in.

"Why, it's the upper bay," said Mrs. Todd. "You can see 'way over into the town of Fessenden. Those farms 'way over there are all in Fessenden. Mother used to have a sister that lived up that shore. If we started as early 's we could on a summer mornin', we couldn't get to her place from Green Island till late afternoon, even with a fair, steady breeze, and you had to strike the time just right so as to fetch up 'long o' the tide and land near the flood. 'T was ticklish business, an' we didn't visit back an' forth as much as mother desired. You have to go 'way down the co'st to Cold Spring Light an' round that long point,—up here's what they call the Back Shore."

"No, we were 'most always separated, my dear sister and me, after the first year she was married," said Mrs. Blackett. "We had our little families an' plenty o' cares. We were always lookin' forward to the time we could see each other more. Now and then she'd get out to the island for a few days while her husband 'd go fishin'; and once he stopped with her an' two children, and made him some flakes right there and cured all his fish for winter. We did have a beautiful time together, sister an' me; she used to look back to it long 's she lived."

"I do love to look over there where she used to live," Mrs. Blackett went on as we began to go down the hill. "It seems as if she must still be there, though she's long been gone. She loved their farm,—she didn't see how I got so used to our island; but somehow I was always happy from the first."

"Yes, it's very dull to me up among those slow farms," declared Mrs. Todd. "The snow troubles 'em in winter. They're all besieged by winter, as you may say; 't is far better by the shore than up among such places. I never thought I should like to live up country."

"Why, just see the carriages ahead of us on the next rise!" exclaimed Mrs. Blackett. "There's going to be a great gathering, don't you believe there is, Almiry? It hasn't seemed up to now as if anybody was going but us. An' 't is such a beautiful day, with yesterday cool and pleasant to work an' get ready, I shouldn't wonder if everybody was there, even the slow ones like Phebe Ann Brock."

Mrs. Blackett's eyes were bright with excitement, and even Mrs. Todd showed remarkable enthusiasm. She hurried the horse and caught up with the holiday-makers ahead. "There's all the Dep'fords goin', six in the wagon," she told us joyfully; "an' Mis' Alva Tilley's folks are now risin' the hill in their new carryall."

Mrs. Blackett pulled at the neat bow of her black bonnet-strings, and tied them again with careful precision. "I believe your bonnet 's on a little bit sideways, dear," she advised Mrs. Todd as if she were a child; but Mrs. Todd was too much occupied to pay proper heed. We began to feel a new sense of gayety and of taking part in the great occasion as we joined the little train.

18.

The Bowden Reunion.

It is very rare in country life, where high days and holidays are few, that any occasion of general interest proves to be less than great. Such is the hidden fire of enthusiasm in the New England nature that, once given an outlet, it shines forth with almost volcanic light and heat. In quiet neighborhoods such inward force does not waste itself upon those petty excitements of every day that belong to cities, but when, at long intervals, the altars to patriotism, to friendship, to the ties of kindred, are reared in our familiar fields, then the fires glow, the flames come up as if from the inexhaustible burning heart of the earth; the primal fires break through the granite dust in which our souls are set. Each heart is warm and every face shines with the ancient light. Such a day as this has transfiguring powers, and easily makes friends of those who have been cold-hearted, and gives to those who are dumb their chance to speak, and lends some beauty to the plainest face.

"Oh, I expect I shall meet friends to-day that I haven't seen in a long while," said Mrs. Blackett with deep satisfaction. "'T will bring out a good many of the old folks, 't is such a lovely day. I'm always glad not to have them disappointed."

"I guess likely the best of 'em 'll be there," answered Mrs. Todd with gentle humor, stealing a glance at me. "There 's one thing certain: there 's nothing takes in this whole neighborhood like anything related to the Bowdens. Yes, I do feel that when you call upon the Bowdens you may expect most families to rise up between the Landing and the far end of the Back Cove. Those that aren't kin by blood are kin by marriage."

"There used to be an old story goin' about when I was a girl," said Mrs. Blackett, with much amusement. "There was a great many more Bowdens then than there are now, and the folks was all setting in meeting a dreadful hot Sunday afternoon, and a scatter-witted little bound girl came running to the meetin'-house door all out o' breath from somewheres in the neighborhood. 'Mis' Bowden, Mis'

Bowden!' says she. 'Your baby 's in a fit!' They used to tell that the whole congregation was up on its feet in a minute and right out into the aisles. All the Mis' Bowdens was setting right out for home; the minister stood there in the pulpit trying' to keep sober, an' all at once he burst right out laughin'. He was a very nice man, they said, and he said he'd better give 'em the benediction, and they could hear the sermon next Sunday, so he kept it over. My mother was there, and she thought certain 't was me."

"None of our family was ever subject to fits," interrupted Mrs. Todd severely. "No, we never had fits, none of us, and 't was lucky we didn't 'way out there to Green Island. Now these folks right in front: dear sakes knows the bunches o' soothing catnip an' yarrow I've had to favor old Mis' Evins with dryin'! You can see it right in their expressions, all them Evins folks. There, just you look up to the crossroads, mother," she suddenly exclaimed. "See all the teams ahead of us. And oh, look down on the bay; yes, look down on the bay! See what a sight o' boats, all headin' for the Bowden place cove!"

"Oh, ain't it beautiful!" said Mrs. Blackett, with all the delight of a girl. She stood up in the high wagon to see everything, and when she sat down again she took fast hold of my hand.

"Hadn't you better urge the horse a little, Almiry?" she asked. "He's had it easy as we came along, and he can rest when we get there. The others are some little ways ahead, and I don't want to lose a minute."

We watched the boats drop their sails one by one in the cove as we drove along the high land. The old Bowden house stood, low-storied and broad-roofed, in its green fields as if it were a motherly brown hen waiting for the flock that came straying toward it from every direction. The first Bowden settler had made his home there, and it was still the Bowden farm; five generations of sailors and farmers and soldiers had been its children. And presently Mrs. Blackett showed me the stone-walled burying-ground that stood like a little fort on a knoll overlooking the bay, but, as she said, there were plenty of scattered Bowdens who were not laid there,—some lost at sea, and some out West, and some who died in the war; most of the home graves were those of women.

We could see now that there were different footpaths from along shore and across country. In all these there were straggling processions walking in single file, like old illustrations of the Pilgrim's Progress. There was a crowd about the house as if huge bees were swarming in the lilac bushes. Beyond the fields and cove a higher point of land ran out into the bay, covered with woods which must have kept away much of the northwest wind in winter. Now there was a pleasant look of shade and shelter there for the great family meeting.

We hurried on our way, beginning to feel as if we were very late, and it was a great satisfaction at last to turn out of the stony high-road into a green lane shaded with old apple-trees. Mrs. Todd encouraged the horse until he fairly pranced with gayety as we drove round to the front of the house on the soft turf. There was an instant cry of rejoicing, and two or three persons ran toward us from the busy group.

"Why, dear Mis' Blackett!—here's Mis' Blackett!" I heard them say, as if it were pleasure enough for one day to have a sight of her. Mrs. Todd turned to me with a lovely look of triumph and self-forgetfulness. An elderly man who wore the look of a prosperous sea-captain put up both arms and lifted Mrs. Blackett down from the high wagon like a child, and kissed her with hearty affection. "I was master afraid she wouldn't be here," he said, looking at Mrs. Todd with a face like a happy sunburnt schoolboy, while everybody crowded round to give their welcome.

"Mother 's always the queen," said Mrs. Todd. "Yes, they'll all make everything of mother; she'll have a lovely time to-day. I wouldn't have had her miss it, and there won't be a thing she'll ever regret, except to mourn because William wa'n't here."

Mrs. Blackett having been properly escorted to the house, Mrs. Todd received her own full share of honor, and some of the men, with a simple kindness that was the soul of chivalry, waited upon us and our baskets and led away the white horse. I already knew some of Mrs. Todd's friends and kindred, and felt like an adopted Bowden in this happy moment. It seemed to be enough for any one to have arrived by the same conveyance as Mrs. Blackett, who presently had her court inside the house, while Mrs. Todd, large, hospitable, and preeminent, was the centre of a rapidly increasing crowd about the lilac bushes. Small companies were continually coming up the long green slope from the water, and nearly all the boats had come to shore. I counted three or four that were baffled by the light breeze, but before long all the Bowdens, small and great, seemed to have assembled, and we started to go up to the grove across the field.

Out of the chattering crowd of noisy children, and large-waisted women whose best black dresses fell straight to the ground in generous folds, and sunburnt men who looked as serious as if it were town-meeting day, there suddenly came silence and order. I saw the straight, soldierly little figure of a man who bore a fine resemblance to Mrs. Blackett, and who appeared to marshal us with perfect ease. He was imperative enough, but with a grand military sort of courtesy, and bore himself with solemn dignity of importance. We were sorted out according to some clear design of his own, and stood as speechless as a troop to await his orders. Even the children were ready to march together, a pretty flock, and at the last moment Mrs. Blackett and a few distinguished companions, the ministers and those who were very old, came out of the house together and took their places. We ranked by fours, and even then we made a long procession.

There was a wide path mowed for us across the field, and, as we moved along, the birds flew up out of the thick second crop of clover, and the bees hummed as if it still were June. There was a flashing of white gulls over the water where the fleet of boats rode the low waves together in the cove, swaying their small masts as if they kept time to our steps. The plash of the water could be heard faintly, yet still be heard; we might have been a company of ancient Greeks going to celebrate a victory, or to worship the god of harvests in the grove above. It was strangely moving to see this and to make part of it. The sky, the sea, have watched poor humanity at its rites so long; we were no more a New England family celebrating its own existence and simple progress; we carried the tokens and inheritance of all such households from which this had descended, and were only the latest of our line. We possessed the instincts of a far, forgotten childhood; I found myself thinking that we ought to be carrying green branches and singing as we went. So we came to the thick shaded grove still silent, and were set in our places by the straight trees that swayed together and let sunshine through here and there like a single golden leaf that flickered down, vanishing in the cool shade.

The grove was so large that the great family looked far smaller than it had in the open field; there was a thick growth of dark pines and firs with an occasional maple or oak that gave a gleam of color like a bright window in the great roof. On three sides we could see the water, shining behind the tree-trunks, and feel the cool salt breeze that began to come up with the tide just as the day reached its highest point of heat. We could see the green sunlit field we had just crossed as if we looked out at it from a dark room, and the old house and its lilacs standing placidly in the sun, and the great barn with a stockade of carriages from which two or three care-taking men who had lingered were coming across the field together. Mrs. Todd had taken off her warm gloves and looked the picture of content.

"There!" she exclaimed. "I've always meant to have you see this place, but I never looked for such a beautiful opportunity—weather an' occasion both made to match. Yes, it suits me: I don't ask no more. I want to know if you saw mother walkin' at the head! It choked me right up to see mother at the head, walkin' with the ministers," and Mrs. Todd turned away to hide the feelings she could not instantly control.

"Who was the marshal?" I hastened to ask. "Was he an old soldier?"

"Don't he do well?" answered Mrs. Todd with satisfaction.

"He don't often have such a chance to show off his gifts," said Mrs. Caplin, a friend from the Landing who had joined us. "That's Sant Bowden; he always takes the lead, such days. Good for nothing else most o' his time; trouble is, he"—

I turned with interest to hear the worst. Mrs. Caplin's tone was both zealous and impressive.

"Stim'lates," she explained scornfully.

"No, Santin never was in the war," said Mrs. Todd with lofty indifference. "It was a cause of real distress to him. He kep' enlistin', and traveled far an' wide about here, an' even took the bo't and went to Boston to volunteer; but he ain't a sound man, an' they wouldn't have him. They say he knows all their tactics, an' can tell all about the battle o' Waterloo well 's he can Bunker Hill. I told him once the country 'd lost a great general, an' I meant it, too."

"I expect you're near right," said Mrs. Caplin, a little crestfallen and apologetic.

"I be right," insisted Mrs. Todd with much amiability. "'T was most too bad to cramp him down to his peaceful trade, but he's a most excellent shoemaker at his best, an' he always says it's a trade that gives him time to think an' plan his manœuvres. Over to the Port they always invite him to march Decoration Day, same as the rest, an' he does look noble; he comes of soldier stock."

I had been noticing with great interest the curiously French type of face which prevailed in this rustic company. I had said to myself before that Mrs. Blackett was plainly of French descent, in both her appearance and her charming gifts, but this is not surprising when one has learned how large a proportion of the early settlers on this northern coast of New England were of Huguenot blood, and that it is the Norman Englishman, not the Saxon, who goes adventuring to a new world.

"They used to say in old times," said Mrs. Todd modestly, "that our family came of very high folks in France, and one of 'em was a great general in some o' the old wars. I sometimes think that Santin's ability has come 'way down from then. 'T ain't nothin' he's ever acquired; 't was born in him. I don't know 's he ever saw a fine parade, or met with those that studied up such things. He's figured it all out an' got his papers so he knows how to aim a cannon right for William's fish-house five miles out on Green Island, or up there on Burnt Island where the signal is. He had it all over to me one day, an' I tried hard to appear interested. His life 's all in it, but he will have those poor gloomy spells come over him now an' then, an' then he has to drink."

Mrs. Caplin gave a heavy sigh.

"There 's a great many such strayaway folks, just as there is plants," continued Mrs. Todd, who was nothing if not botanical. "I know of just one sprig of laurel that grows over back here in a wild spot, an' I never could hear of no other on this coast. I had a large bunch brought me once from Massachusetts way, so I know it. This piece grows in an open spot where you'd think 't would do well, but it's sort o' poor-lookin'. I've visited it time an' again, just to notice its poor blooms. 'T is a real Sant Bowden, out of its own place."

Mrs. Caplin looked bewildered and blank. "Well, all I know is, last year he worked out some kind of a plan so 's to parade the county conference in platoons, and got 'em all flustered up tryin' to sense his ideas of a holler square," she burst forth, "They was holler enough anyway after ridin' 'way down from up country into the salt air, and they'd been treated to a sermon on faith an' works from old Fayther Harlow that never knows when to cease. 'T wa'n't no time for tactics then,—they wa'n't a-thinkin' of the church military. Sant, he couldn't do nothin' with 'em. All he thinks of, when he sees a crowd, is how to march 'em. 'T is all very well when he don't 'tempt too much. He never did act like other folks."

"Ain't I just been maintainin' that he ain't like 'em?" urged Mrs. Todd decidedly. "Strange folks has got to have strange ways, for what I see."

"Somebody observed once that you could pick out the likeness of 'most every sort of a foreigner when you looked about you in our parish," said Sister Caplin, her face brightening with sudden illumination. "I didn't see the bearin' of it then quite so plain. I always did think Mari' Harris resembled a Chinee."

"Mari' Harris was pretty as a child, I remember," said the pleasant voice of Mrs. Blackett, who, after receiving the affectionate greetings of nearly the whole company, came to join us,—to see, as she insisted, that we were out of mischief.

"Yes, Mari' was one o' them pretty little lambs that make dreadful homely old sheep," replied Mrs. Todd with energy. "Cap'n Littlepage never 'd look so disconsolate if she was any sort of a proper person to direct things. She might divert him; yes, she might divert the old gentleman, an' let him think he had his own way, 'stead o' arguing everything down to the bare bone. 'T wouldn't hurt her to sit down an' hear his great stories once in a while."

"The stories are very interesting," I ventured to say.

"Yes, you always catch yourself a-thinkin' what if they was all true, and he had the right of it," answered Mrs. Todd. "He's a good sight better company, though dreamy, than such sordid creatur's as Mari' Harris."

"Live and let live," said dear old Mrs. Blackett gently. "I haven't seen the captain for a good while, now that I ain't so constant to meetin'," she added wistfully. "We always have known each other."

"Why, if it is a good pleasant day to-morrow, I'll get William to call an' invite the capt'in to dinner. William'll be in early so's to pass up the street without meetin' anybody."

"There, they're callin' out it's time to set the tables," said Mrs. Caplin, with great excitement.

"Here's Cousin Sarah Jane Blackett! Well, I am pleased, certain!" exclaimed Mrs. Todd, with unaffected delight; and these kindred spirits met and parted with the promise of a good talk later on. After this there was no more time for conversation until we were seated in order at the long tables.

"I'm one that always dreads seeing some o' the folks that I don't like, at such a time as this," announced Mrs. Todd privately to me after a season of reflection. We were just waiting for the feast to begin. "You wouldn't think such a great creatur' 's I be could feel all over pins an' needles. I remember, the day I promised to Nathan, how it come over me, just 's I was feelin' happy 's I could, that I'd got to have an own cousin o' his for my near relation all the rest o' my life, an' it seemed as if die I should. Poor Nathan saw somethin' had crossed me,—he had very nice feelings,—and when he asked me what 't was, I told him. 'I never could like her myself,' said he. 'You sha'n't be bothered, dear,' he says; an' 't was one o' the things that made me set a good deal by Nathan, he didn't make a habit of always opposin', like some men. 'Yes,' says I, 'but think o' Thanks-givin' times an' funerals; she's our relation, an' we've got to own her.' Young folks don't think o' those things. There she goes now, do let's pray her by!" said Mrs. Todd, with an alarming transition from general opinions to particular animosities. "I hate her just the same as I always did; but she's got on a real pretty dress. I do try to remember that she's Nathan's cousin. Oh dear, well; she's gone by after all, an' ain't seen me. I expected she'd come pleasantin' round just to show off an' say afterwards she was acquainted."

This was so different from Mrs. Todd's usual largeness of mind that I had a moment's uneasiness; but the cloud passed quickly over her spirit, and was gone with the offender.

There never was a more generous out-of-door feast along the coast than the Bowden family set forth that day. To call it a picnic would make it seem trivial. The great tables were edged with pretty oak-leaf trimming, which the boys and girls made. We brought flowers from the fence-thickets of the great field; and out of the disorder of flowers and provisions suddenly appeared as orderly a scheme for the feast as the marshal had shaped for the procession. I began to respect the Bowdens for their inheritance of good taste and skill and a certain pleasing gift of formality. Something made them do all these things in a finer way than most country people would have done them. As I looked up and down the tables there was a good cheer, a grave soberness that shone with pleasure, a humble dignity of bearing. There were some who should have sat below the salt for lack of this good breeding; but they were not many. So, I said to myself, their ancestors may have sat in the great hall of some old French house in the Middle Ages, when battles and sieges and processions and feasts were familiar things. The ministers and Mrs. Blackett, with a few of their rank and age, were put in places of honor, and for once that I looked any other way I looked twice at Mrs. Blackett's face, serene and mindful of privilege and responsibility, the mistress by simple fitness of this great day.

Mrs. Todd looked up at the roof of green trees, and then carefully surveyed the company. "I see 'em better now they're all settin' down," she said with satisfaction. "There's old Mr. Gilbraith and his sister. I wish they were settin' with us; they're not among folks they can parley with, an' they look disappointed."

As the feast went on, the spirits of my companion steadily rose. The excitement of an unexpectedly great occasion was a subtle stimulant to her disposition, and I could see that sometimes when Mrs. Todd had seemed limited and heavily domestic, she had simply grown sluggish for lack of proper surroundings. She was not so much reminiscent now as expectant, and as alert and gay as a girl. We who were her neighbors were full of gayety, which was but the reflected light from her beaming countenance. It was not the first time that I was full of wonder at the waste of human ability in this world, as a botanist wonders at the wastefulness of nature, the thousand seeds that die, the unused provision of every sort. The reserve force of society grows more and more amazing to one's thought. More than one face among the Bowdens showed that only opportunity and stimulus were lacking,—a narrow set of circumstances had caged a fine able character and held it captive. One sees exactly the same types in a country gathering as in the most brilliant city company. You are safe to be understood if the spirit of your speech is the same for one neighbor as for the other.

19.

The Feast's End.

THE FEAST WAS A noble feast, as has already been said. There was an elegant ingenuity displayed in the form of pies which delighted my heart. Once acknowledge that an American pie is far to be preferred to its humble ancestor, the English tart, and it is joyful to be reassured at a Bowden reunion that invention has not yet failed. Beside a delightful variety of material, the decorations went beyond all my former experience; dates and names were wrought in lines of pastry and frosting on the tops. There was even more elaborate reading matter on an excellent early-apple pie which we began to share and eat, precept upon precept. Mrs. Todd helped me generously to the whole word *Bowden*, and consumed *Reunion* herself, save an undecipherable fragment; but the most renowned essay in cookery on the tables was a model of the old Bowden house made of durable gingerbread, with all the windows and doors in the right places, and sprigs of genuine lilac set at the front. It must have been baked in sections, in one of the last of the great brick ovens, and fastened together on the morning of the day. There was a general sigh when this fell into ruin at the feast's end, and it was shared by a great part of the assembly, not without seriousness, and as if it were a pledge and token of loyalty. I met the maker of the gingerbread house, which had called up lively remembrances of a childish story. She had the gleaming eye of an enthusiast and a look of high ideals.

"I could just as well have made it all of frosted cake," she said, "but 't wouldn't have been the right shade; the old house, as you observe, was never painted, and I concluded that plain gingerbread would represent it best. It wasn't all I expected it would be," she said sadly, as many an artist had said before her of his work.

There were speeches by the ministers; and there proved to be a historian among the Bowdens, who gave some fine anecdotes of the family history; and then appeared a poetess, whom Mrs. Todd regarded with wistful compassion and indulgence, and when the long faded garland of verses came to an appealing end, she turned to me with words of praise.

"Sounded pretty," said the generous listener. "Yes, I thought she did very well. We went to school together, an' Mary Anna had a very hard time; trouble was, her mother thought she'd given birth to a genius, an' Mary Anna's come to believe it herself. There, I don't know what we should have done without her; there ain't nobody else that can write poetry between here and 'way up towards Rockland; it adds a great deal at such a time. When she speaks o' those that are gone, she feels it all, and so does everybody else, but she harps too much. I'd laid half of that away for next time, if I was Mary Anna. There comes mother to speak to her, an' old Mr. Gilbraith's sister; now she'll be heartened right up. Mother'll say just the right thing."

The leave-takings were as affecting as the meetings of these old friends had been. There were enough young persons at the reunion, but it is the old who really value such opportunities; as for the young, it is the habit of every day to meet their comrades,—the time of separation has not come. To see the joy with which these elder kinsfolk and acquaintances had looked in one another's faces, and the lingering touch of their friendly hands; to see these affectionate meetings and then the reluctant partings, gave one a new idea of the isolation in which it was possible to live in that after all thinly settled region. They did not expect to see one another again very soon; the steady, hard work on the farms, the difficulty of getting from place to place, especially in winter when boats were laid up, gave double value to any occasion which could bring a large number of families together. Even funerals in this country of the pointed firs were not without their social advantages and satisfactions. I heard the words "next summer" repeated many times, though summer was still ours and all the leaves were green.

The boats began to put out from shore, and the wagons to drive away. Mrs. Blackett took me into the old house when we came back from the grove: it was her father's birthplace and early home, and she had spent much of her own childhood there with her grandmother. She spoke of those days as if they had but lately passed; in fact, I could imagine that the house looked almost exactly the same to her. I could see the brown rafters of the unfinished roof as I looked up the steep staircase, though the best room was as handsome with its good wainscoting and touch of ornament on the cornice as any old room of its day in a town.

Some of the guests who came from a distance were still sitting in the best room when we went in to take leave of the master and mistress of the house. We all said eagerly what a pleasant day it had been, and how swiftly the time had passed. Perhaps it is the great national anniversaries which our country has lately kept, and the soldiers' meetings that take place everywhere, which have made reunions of every sort the fashion. This one, at least, had been very interesting. I fancied that old feuds had been overlooked, and the old saying that blood is thicker than water had again proved itself true, though from the variety of names one argued a certain adulteration of the Bowden traits and belongings. Clannishness is an instinct of the heart,—it is more than a birthright, or a custom; and lesser rights were forgotten in the claim to a common inheritance.

We were among the very last to return to our proper lives and lodgings. I came near to feeling like a true Bowden, and parted from certain new friends as if they were old friends; we were rich with the treasure of a new remembrance.

At last we were in the high wagon again; the old white horse had been well fed in the Bowden barn, and we drove away and soon began to climb the long hill toward the wooded ridge. The road was new to me, as roads always are, going back. Most of our companions had been full of anxious thoughts of home,—of the cows, or of young children likely to fall into disaster,—but we had no reasons for haste, and drove slowly along, talking and resting by the way. Mrs. Todd said once that she really hoped her front door had been shut on account of the dust blowing in, but added that nothing made any weight on her mind except not to forget to turn a few late mullein leaves that were drying on a newspaper in the little loft. Mrs. Blackett and I gave our word of honor that we would remind her of this heavy responsibility. The way seemed short, we had so much to talk about. We climbed hills where we could see the great bay and the islands, and then went down into shady valleys where the air began to feel like evening, cool and damp with a fragrance of wet ferns. Mrs. Todd alighted once or twice, refusing all assistance in securing some boughs of a rare shrub which she valued for its bark, though she proved incommunicative as to her reasons. We passed the house where we had been so kindly entertained with doughnuts earlier in the day, and found it closed and deserted, which was a disappointment.

"They must have stopped to tea somewheres and thought they'd finish up the day," said Mrs. Todd. "Those that enjoyed it best'll want to get right home so 's to think it over."

"I didn't see the woman there after all, did you?" asked Mrs. Blackett as the horse stopped to drink at the trough.

"Oh yes, I spoke with her," answered Mrs. Todd, with but scant interest or approval. "She ain't a member o' our family."

"I thought you said she resembled Cousin Pa'lina Bowden about the forehead," suggested Mrs. Blackett.

"Well, she don't," answered Mrs. Todd impatiently. "I ain't one that's ord'narily mistaken about family likenesses, and she didn't seem to meet with friends, so I went square up to her. 'I expect you're a Bowden by your looks,' says I. 'Yes, I take it you're one o' the Bowdens.' 'Lor', no,' says she. 'Dennett was my maiden name, but I married a Bowden for my first husband. I thought I'd come an' just see what was a-goin' on'!"

Mrs. Blackett laughed heartily. "I'm goin' to remember to tell William o' that," she said. "There, Almiry, the only thing that's troubled me all this day is to think how William would have enjoyed it. I do so wish William had been there."

"I sort of wish he had, myself," said Mrs. Todd frankly.

"There wa'n't many old folks there, somehow," said Mrs. Blackett, with a touch of sadness in her voice. "There ain't so many to come as there used to be, I'm aware, but I expected to see more."

"I thought they turned out pretty well, when you come to think of it; why, everybody was sayin' so an' feelin' gratified," answered Mrs. Todd hastily with pleasing unconsciousness; then I saw the quick color flash into her cheek, and presently she made some excuse to turn and steal an anxious look at her mother. Mrs. Blackett was smiling and thinking about her happy day, though she began to look a little tired. Neither of my companions was troubled by her burden of years. I hoped in my heart that I might be like them as I lived on into age, and then smiled to think that I too was no longer very young. So we always keep the same hearts, though our outer framework fails and shows the touch of time.

"'T was pretty when they sang the hymn, wasn't it?" asked Mrs. Blackett at supper-time, with real enthusiasm. "There was such a plenty o' men's voices; where I sat it did sound beautiful. I had to stop and listen when they came to the last verse."

I saw that Mrs. Todd's broad shoulders began to shake. "There was good singers there; yes, there was excellent singers," she agreed heartily, putting down her teacup, "but I chanced to drift alongside Mis' Peter Bowden o' Great Bay, an' I couldn't help thinkin' if she was as far out o' town as she was out o' tune, she wouldn't get back in a day."

20.

Along Shore.

One day as I went along the shore beyond the old wharves and the newer, high-stepped fabric of the steamer landing, I saw that all the boats were beached, and the slack water period of the early afternoon prevailed. Nothing was going on, not even the most leisurely of occupations, like baiting trawls or mending nets, or repairing lobster pots; the very boats seemed to be taking an afternoon nap in the sun. I could hardly discover a distant sail as I looked seaward, except a weather-beaten lobster smack, which seemed to have been taken for a plaything by the light airs that blew about the bay. It drifted and turned about so aimlessly in the wide reach off Burnt Island, that I suspected there was nobody at the wheel, or that she might have parted her rusty anchor chain while all the crew were asleep.

I watched her for a minute or two; she was the old Miranda, owned by some of the Caplins, and I knew her by an odd shaped patch of newish duck that was set into the peak of her dingy mainsail. Her vagaries offered such an exciting subject for conversation that my heart rejoiced at the sound of a hoarse voice behind me. At that moment, before I had time to answer, I saw something large and shapeless flung from the Miranda's deck that splashed the water high against her black side, and my companion gave a satisfied chuckle. The old lobster smack's sail caught the breeze again at this moment, and she moved off down the bay. Turning, I found old Elijah Tilley, who had come softly out of his dark fish house, as if it were a burrow.

"Boy got kind o'drowsy steerin' of her; Monroe he hove him right overboard; 'wake now fast enough," explained Mr. Tilley, and we laughed together.

I was delighted, for my part, that the vicissitudes and dangers of the Miranda, in a rocky channel, should have given me this opportunity to make acquaintance with an old fisherman to whom I had never spoken. At first he had seemed to be one of those evasive and uncomfortable persons who are so suspicious of you that they make you almost suspicious of yourself. Mr. Elijah Tilley appeared to regard a stranger with scornful indifference. You might see him standing on the pebble beach or in a fishhouse doorway, but when you came nearer he was gone. He was one of the small company of elderly, gaunt-shaped great fishermen whom I used to like to see leading up a deep-laden boat by the head, as if it were a horse, from the water's edge to the steep slope of the pebble beach. There were four of these large old men at the Landing, who were the survivors of an earlier and more vigorous generation. There was an alliance and understanding between them, so close that it was apparently speechless. They gave much time to watching one another's boats go out or come in; they lent a ready hand at tending one another's lobster traps in rough weather; they helped to clean the fish, or to sliver porgies for the trawls, as if they were in close partnership; and when a boat came in from deep-sea fishing they were never far out of the way, and hastened to help carry it ashore, two by two, splashing alongside, or holding its steady head, as if it were a willful sea colt. As a matter of fact no boat could help being steady and waywise under their instant direction and companionship. Abel's boat and Jonathan Bowden's boat were as distinct and experienced personalities as the men themselves, and as inexpressive. Arguments and opinions were unknown to the conversation of these ancient friends; you would as soon have expected to hear small talk in a company of elephants as to hear old Mr. Bowden or Elijah Tilley and their two mates waste breath upon any form of trivial gossip. They made brief statements to one another from time to time. As you came to know them you wondered more and more that they should talk at all. Speech seemed to be a light and elegant accomplishment, and their unexpected acquaintance with its arts made them of new value to the listener. You felt almost as if a landmark pine should suddenly address you in regard to the weather, or a lofty-minded old camel make a remark as you stood respectfully near him under the circus tent.

I often wondered a great deal about the inner life and thought of these self-contained old fishermen; their minds seemed to be fixed upon nature and the elements rather than upon any contrivances of man, like politics or theology. My friend, Captain Bowden, who was the nephew of the eldest of this group, regarded them with deference;

but he did not belong to their secret companionship, though he was neither young nor talkative.

"They've gone together ever since they were boys, they know most everything about the sea amon'st them," he told me once. "They was always just as you see 'em now since the memory of man."

These ancient seafarers had houses and lands not outwardly different from other Dunnet Landing dwellings, and two of them were fathers of families, but their true dwelling places were the sea, and the stony beach that edged its familiar shore, and the fishhouses, where much salt brine from the mackerel kits had soaked the very timbers into a state of brown permanence and petrifaction. It had also affected the old fishermen's hard complexions, until one fancied that when Death claimed them it could only be with the aid, not of any slender modern dart, but the good serviceable harpoon of a seventeenth century woodcut.

Elijah Tilley was such an evasive, discouraged-looking person, heavy-headed, and stooping so that one could never look him in the face, that even after his friendly exclamation about Monroe Pennell, the lobster smack's skipper, and the sleepy boy, I did not venture at once to speak again. Mr. Tilley was carrying a small haddock in one hand, and presently shifted it to the other hand lest it might touch my skirt. I knew that my company was accepted, and we walked together a little way.

"You mean to have a good supper," I ventured to say, by way of friendliness.

"Goin' to have this 'ere haddock an' some o' my good baked potatoes; must eat to live," responded my companion with great pleasantness and open approval. I found that I had suddenly left the forbidding coast and come into a smooth little harbor of friendship.

"You ain't never been up to my place," said the old man. "Folks don't come now as they used to; no, 't ain't no use to ask folks now. My poor dear she was a great hand to draw young company."

I remembered that Mrs. Todd had once said that this old fisherman had been sore stricken and unconsoled at the death of his wife.

"I should like very much to come," said I. "Perhaps you are going to be at home later on?"

Mr. Tilley agreed, by a sober nod, and went his way bent-shouldered and with a rolling gait. There was a new patch high on the shoulder of his old waistcoat, which corresponded to the renewing of the Miranda's mainsail down the bay, and I wondered if his own fingers, clumsy with much deep-sea fishing, had set it in.

"Was there a good catch to-day?" I asked, stopping a moment. "I didn't happen to be on the shore when the boats came in."

"No; all come in pretty light," answered Mr. Tilley. "Addicks an' Bowden they done the best; Abel an' me we had but a slim fare. We went out 'arly, but not so 'arly as sometimes; looked like a poor mornin'. I got nine haddick, all small, and seven fish; the rest on 'em got more fish than haddick. Well, I don't expect they feel like bitin' every day; we l'arn to humor 'em a little, an' let 'em have their way 'bout it. These plaguey dog-fish kind of worry 'em." Mr. Tilley pronounced the last sentence with much sympathy, as if he looked upon himself as a true friend of all the haddock and codfish that lived on the fishing grounds, and so we parted.

Later in the afternoon I went along the beach again until I came to the foot of Mr. Tilley's land, and found his rough track across the cobble-stones and rocks to the field edge, where there was a heavy piece of old wreck timber, like a ship's bone, full of treenails. From this a little footpath, narrow with one man's treading, led up across the small green field that made Mr. Tilley's whole estate, except a straggling pasture that tilted on edge up the steep hillside beyond the house and road. I could hear the tinkle-tankle of a cow-bell somewhere among the spruces by which the pasture was being walked over and forested from every side; it was likely to be called the wood lot before long, but the field was unmolested. I could not see a bush or a brier anywhere within its walls, and hardly a stray pebble showed itself. This was most surprising in that country of firm ledges, and scattered stones which all the walls that industry could devise had hardly begun to clear away off the land. In the narrow field I noticed some stout stakes, apparently planted at random in the grass and among the hills of potatoes, but carefully painted yellow and white to match the house, a neat sharp-edged little dwelling, which looked strangely modern for its owner. I should have much sooner believed that the smart young wholesale egg merchant of the Landing was its occupant than Mr. Tilley, since a man's house is really but his larger body, and expresses in a way his nature and character.

I went up the field, following the smooth little path to the side door. As for using the front door, that was a matter of great ceremony; the long grass grew close against the high stone step, and a snowberry bush leaned over it, top-heavy with the weight of a morning-glory vine that had managed to take what the fishermen might call a half hitch about the door-knob. Elijah Tilley came to the side door to receive me; he was knitting a blue yarn stocking without looking on, and was warmly dressed for the season in a thick blue flannel shirt with white crockery buttons, a faded waistcoat and trousers heavily patched at the knees. These were not his fishing clothes. There was something delightful in the grasp of his hand, warm and clean, as if it never touched anything but the comfortable woolen yarn, instead of cold sea water and slippery fish.

"What are the painted stakes for, down in the field?" I hastened to ask, and he came out a step or two along the path to see; and looked at the stakes as if his attention were called to them for the first time.

"Folks laughed at me when I first bought this place an' come here to live," he explained. "They said 't wa'n't no kind of a field privilege at all; no place to raise anything, all full o' stones. I was aware 't was good land, an' I worked some on it—odd times when I didn't have nothin' else on hand—till I cleared them loose stones all out. You never see a prettier piece than 't is now; now did ye? Well, as for them painted marks, them 's my buoys. I struck on to some heavy rocks that didn't show none, but a plow 'd be liable to ground on 'em, an' so I ketched holt an' buoyed 'em same 's you see. They don't trouble me no more 'n if they wa'n't there."

"You haven't been to sea for nothing," I said laughing.

"One trade helps another," said Elijah with an amiable smile. "Come right in an' set down. Come in an' rest ye," he exclaimed, and led the way into his comfortable kitchen. The sunshine poured in at the two further windows, and a cat was curled up sound asleep on the table that stood between them. There was a new-looking light oilcloth of a tiled pattern on the floor, and a crockery teapot, large for a household of only one person, stood on the bright stove. I ventured to say that somebody must be a very good housekeeper.

"That's me," acknowledged the old fisherman with frankness. "There ain't nobody here but me. I try to keep things looking right, same 's poor dear left 'em. You set down here in this chair, then you can look off an' see the water. None on 'em thought I was goin' to get along alone, no way, but I wa'n't goin' to have my house turned upsi' down an' all changed about; no, not to please nobody. I was the only one knew just how she liked to have things set, poor dear, an' I said I was goin' to make shift, and I have made shift. I'd rather tough it out alone." And he sighed heavily, as if to sigh were his familiar consolation.

We were both silent for a minute; the old man looked out of the window, as if he had forgotten I was there.

"You must miss her very much?" I said at last.

"I do miss her," he answered, and sighed again. "Folks all kep' repeatin' that time would ease me, but I can't find it does. No, I miss her just the same every day."

"How long is it since she died?" I asked.

"Eight year now, come the first of October. It don't seem near so long. I've got a sister that comes and stops 'long o' me a little spell, spring an' fall, an' odd times if I send after her. I ain't near so good a hand to sew as I be to knit, and she's very quick to set everything to rights. She's a married woman with a family; her son's folks lives at home, an' I can't make no great claim on her time. But it makes me a kind' o good excuse, when I do send, to help her a little; she ain't none too well off. Poor dear always liked her, and we used to contrive our ways together. 'T is full as easy to be alone. I set here an' think it all over, an' think considerable when the weather's bad to go outside. I get so some days it feels as if poor dear might step right back into this kitchen. I keep a watchin' them doors as if she might step in to ary one. Yes, ma'am, I keep a-lookin' off an' droppin' o' my stitches; that's just how it seems. I can't git over losin' of her no way nor no how. Yes, ma'am, that's just how it seems to me."

I did not say anything, and he did not look up.

"I git feelin' so sometimes I have to lay everything by an' go out door. She was a sweet pretty creatur' long 's she lived," the old man added mournfully. "There's that little rockin' chair o' her'n, I set an' notice it an' think how strange 't is a creatur' like her should be gone an' that chair be here right in its old place."

"I wish I had known her; Mrs. Todd told me about your wife one day," I said.

"You'd have liked to come and see her; all the folks did," said poor Elijah. "She'd been so pleased to hear everything and see somebody new that took such an int'rest. She had a kind o' gift to make it pleasant for folks. I guess likely Almiry Todd told you she was a pretty woman, especially in her young days; late years, too, she kep' her looks and come to be so pleasant lookin'. There, 't ain't so much matter, I shall be done afore a great while. No; I sha'n't trouble the fish a great sight more."

The old widower sat with his head bowed over his knitting, as if he were hastily shortening the very thread of time. The minutes went slowly by. He stopped his work and clasped his hands firmly together. I saw he had forgotten his guest, and I kept the afternoon watch with him. At last he looked up as if but a moment had passed of his continual loneliness.

"Yes, ma'am, I'm one that has seen trouble," he said, and began to knit again.

The visible tribute of his careful housekeeping, and the clean bright room which had once enshrined his wife, and now enshrined her memory, was very moving to me; he had no thought for any one else or for any other place. I began to see her myself in her home,—a delicate-looking, faded little woman, who leaned upon his rough strength and affectionate heart, who was always watching for his boat out of this very window, and who always opened the door and welcomed him when he came home.

"I used to laugh at her, poor dear," said Elijah, as if he read my thought. "I used to make light of her timid notions. She used to be fearful when I was out in bad weather or baffled about gittin' ashore. She used to say the time seemed long to her, but I've found out all about it now. I used to be dreadful thoughtless when I was a young man and the fish was bitin' well. I'd stay out late some o' them days, an' I expect she'd watch an' watch an' lose heart a-waitin'. My heart alive! what a supper she'd git, an' be right there watchin' from the door, with somethin' over her head if 't was cold, waitin' to hear all about it as I come up the field. Lord, how I think o' all them little things!"

"This was what she called the best room; in this way," he said presently, laying his knitting on the table, and leading the way across the front entry and unlocking a door, which he threw open with an air of pride. The best room seemed to me a much sadder and more empty place than the kitchen; its conventionalities lacked the simple perfection of the humbler room and failed on the side of poor ambition; it was only when one remembered what patient saving, and what high respect for society in the abstract go to such furnishing that the little parlor was interesting at all. I could imagine the great day of certain purchases, the bewildering shops of the next large town, the aspiring anxious woman, the clumsy sea-tanned man in his best clothes, so eager to be pleased, but at ease only when they were safe back in the sail-boat again, going down the bay with their precious freight, the hoarded money all spent and nothing to think of but tiller and sail. I looked at the unworn carpet, the glass vases on the mantelpiece with their prim bunches of bleached swamp grass and dusty marsh rosemary, and I could read the history of Mrs. Tilley's best room from its very beginning.

"You see for yourself what beautiful rugs she could make; now I'm going to show you her best tea things she thought so much of," said the master of the house, opening the door of a shallow cupboard. "That's real chiny, all of it on those two shelves," he told me proudly. "I bought it all myself, when we was first married, in the port of Bordeaux. There never was one single piece of it broke until— Well, I used to say, long as she lived, there never was a piece broke, but long at the last I noticed she'd look kind o' distressed, an' I thought 't was 'count o' me boastin'. When they asked if they should use it when the folks was here to supper, time o' her funeral, I knew she'd want to have everything nice, and I said 'certain.' Some o' the women they come runnin' to me an' called me, while they was takin' of the chiny down, an' showed me there was one o' the cups broke an' the pieces wropped in paper and pushed way back here, corner o' the shelf. They didn't want me to go an' think they done it. Poor dear! I had to put right out o' the house when I see that. I knowed in one minute how 't was. We'd got so used to sayin' 't was all there just 's I fetched it home, an' so when she broke that cup somehow or 'nother she couldn't frame no words to come an' tell me. She couldn't think 't would vex me, 't was her own hurt pride. I guess there wa'n't no other secret ever lay between us."

The French cups with their gay sprigs of pink and blue, the best tumblers, an old flowered bowl and tea caddy, and a japanned waiter or two adorned the shelves. These, with a few daguerreotypes in a little square pile, had the closet to themselves, and I was conscious of much pleasure in seeing them. One is shown over many a house in these days where the interest may be more complex, but not more definite.

"Those were her best things, poor dear," said Elijah as he locked the door again. "She told me that last summer before she was taken away that she couldn't think o' anything more she wanted, there was everything in the house, an' all her rooms was furnished pretty. I was goin' over to the Port, an' inquired for errands. I used to ask her to say what she wanted, cost or no cost—she was a very reasonable woman, an' 't was the place where she done all but her extra shopping. It kind o' chilled me up when she spoke so satisfied."

"You don't go out fishing after Christmas?" I asked, as we came back to the bright kitchen.

"No; I take stiddy to my knitting after January sets in," said the old seafarer. " 'T ain't worth while, fish make off into deeper water an' you can't stand no such perishin' for the sake o' what you get. I leave out a few traps in sheltered coves an' do a little lobsterin' on fair days. The young fellows braves it out, some on 'em; but, for me, I lay in my winter's yarn an' set here where 't is warm, an' knit an' take my comfort. Mother learnt me once when I was a lad; she was a beautiful knitter herself. I was laid up with a bad knee, an' she said 't would take up my time an' help her; we was a large family. They'll buy all the folks can do down here to Addicks' store. They say our Dunnet stockin's is gettin' to be celebrated up to Boston,—good quality o' wool an' even knittin' or somethin'. I've always been called a pretty hand to do nettin', but seines is master cheap to what they used to be when they was all hand worked. I change off to nettin' long towards spring, and I piece up my trawls and lines and get my fishin' stuff to rights. Lobster pots they require attention, but I make 'em up in spring weather when it's warm there in the barn. No; I ain't one o' them that likes to set an' do nothin'."

"You see the rugs, poor dear did them; she wa'n't very partial to knittin'," old Elijah went on, after he had counted his stitches. "Our rugs is beginnin' to show wear, but I can't master none o' them womanish tricks. My sister, she tinkers 'em up. She said last time she was here that she guessed they'd last my time."

"The old ones are always the prettiest," I said.

"You ain't referrin' to the braided ones now?" answered Mr. Tilley. "You see ours is braided for the most part, an' their good looks is all in the beginnin'. Poor dear used to say they made an easier floor. I go shufflin' round the house same's if 't was a bo't, and I always used to be stubbin' up the corners o' the hooked kind. Her an' me was always havin' our jokes together same's a boy an' girl. Outsiders never'd know nothin' about it to see us. She had nice manners with all, but to me there was nobody so entertainin'. She'd take off anybody's natural talk winter evenin's when we set here alone, so you'd think 't was them a-speakin'. There, there!"

I saw that he had dropped a stitch again, and was snarling the blue yarn round his clumsy fingers. He handled it and threw it off at arm's length as if it were a cod line; and frowned impatiently, but I saw a tear shining on his cheek.

I said that I must be going, it was growing late, and asked if I might come again, and if he would take me out to the fishing grounds some day.

"Yes, come any time you want to," said my host, "'t ain't so pleasant as when poor dear was here. Oh, I didn't want to lose her an' she didn't want to go, but it had to be. Such things ain't for us to say; there's no yes an' no to it."

"You find Almiry Todd one o' the best o' women?" said Mr. Tilley as we parted. He was standing in the doorway and I had started off down the narrow green field. "No, there ain't a better hearted woman in the State o' Maine. I've known her from a girl. She's had the best o' mothers. You tell her I'm liable to fetch her up a couple or three nice good mackerel early to-morrow," he said. "Now don't let it slip your mind. Poor dear, she always thought a sight o' Almiry, and she used to remind me there was nobody to fish for her; but I don't rec'lect it as I ought to. I see you drop a line yourself very handy now an' then."

We laughed together like the best of friends, and I spoke again about the fishing grounds, and confessed that I had no fancy for a southerly breeze and a ground swell.

"Nor me neither," said the old fisherman. "Nobody likes 'em, say what they may. Poor dear was disobliged by the mere sight of a bo't. Almiry's got the best o' mothers, I expect you know; Mis' Blackett out to Green Island; and we was always plannin' to go out when summer come; but there, I couldn't pick no day's weather that seemed to suit her just right. I never set out to worry her neither, 't wa'n't no kind o' use; she was so pleasant we couldn't have no fret nor trouble. 'T was never 'you dear an' you darlin'' afore folks, an' 'you divil' behind the door!"

As I looked back from the lower end of the field I saw him still standing, a lonely figure in the doorway. "Poor dear," I repeated to myself half aloud; "I wonder where she is and what she knows of the little world she left. I wonder what she has been doing these eight years!"

I gave the message about the mackerel to Mrs. Todd.

"Been visitin' with 'Lijah?" she asked with interest. "I expect you had kind of a dull session; he ain't the talkin' kind; dwellin' so much long o' fish seems to make 'em lose the gift o' speech." But when I told her that Mr. Tilley had been talking to me that day, she interrupted me quickly.

"Then 't was all about his wife, an' he can't say nothin' too pleasant neither. She was modest with strangers, but there ain't one o' her old friends can ever make up her loss. For me, I don't want to go there no more. There's some folks you miss and some folks you don't, when they're gone, but there ain't hardly a day I don't think o' dear Sarah Tilley. She was always right there; yes, you knew just where to find her like a plain flower. 'Lijah's worthy enough; I do esteem 'Lijah, but he's a ploddin' man."

21.

The Backward View.

AT LAST IT WAS the time of late summer, when the house was cool and damp in the morning, and all the light seemed to come through green leaves; but at the first step out of doors the sunshine always laid a warm hand on my shoulder, and the clear, high sky seemed to lift quickly as I looked at it. There was no autumnal mist on the coast, nor any August fog; instead of these, the sea, the sky, all the long shore line and the inland hills, with every bush of bay and every fir-top, gained a deeper color and a sharper clearness. There was something shining in the air, and a kind of lustre on the water and the pasture grass,—a northern look that, except at this moment of the year, one must go far to seek. The sunshine of a northern summer was coming to its lovely end.

The days were few then at Dunnet Landing, and I let each of them slip away unwillingly as a miser spends his coins. I wished to have one of my first weeks back again, with those long hours when nothing happened except the growth of herbs and the course of the sun. Once I had not even known where to go for a walk; now there were many delightful things to be done and done again, as if I were in London. I felt hurried and full of pleasant engagements, and the days flew by like a handful of flowers flung to the sea wind.

At last I had to say good-by to all my Dunnet Landing friends, and my homelike place in the little house, and return to the world in which I feared to find myself a foreigner. There may be restrictions to such a summer's happiness, but the ease that belongs to simplicity is charming enough to make up for whatever a simple life may lack, and the gifts of peace are not for those who live in the thick of battle.

I was to take the small unpunctual steamer that went down the bay in the afternoon, and I sat for a while by my window looking out on the green herb garden, with regret for company. Mrs. Todd had hardly spoken all day except in the briefest and most disapproving way; it was as if we were on the edge of a quarrel. It seemed impossible to take my departure with anything like composure. At last I heard a footstep, and looked up to find that Mrs. Todd was standing at the door.

"I've seen to everything now," she told me in an unusually loud and business-like voice. "Your trunks are on the w'arf by this time. Cap'n Bowden he come and took 'em down himself, an' is going to see that they're safe aboard. Yes, I've seen to all your 'rangements," she repeated in a gentler tone. "These things I've left on the kitchen table you'll want to carry by hand; the basket needn't be returned. I guess I shall walk over towards the Port now an' inquire how old Mis' Edward Caplin is."

I glanced at my friend's face, and saw a look that touched me to the heart. I had been sorry enough before to go away.

"I guess you'll excuse me if I ain't down there to stand round on the w'arf and see you go," she said, still trying to be gruff. "Yes, I ought to go over and inquire for Mis' Edward Caplin; it's her third shock, and if mother gets in on Sunday she'll want to know just how the old lady is." With this last word Mrs. Todd turned and left me as if with sudden thought of something she had forgotten, so that I felt sure she was coming back, but presently I heard her go out of the kitchen door and walk down the path toward the gate. I could not part so; I ran after her to say good-by, but she shook her head and waved her hand without looking back when she heard my hurrying steps, and so went away down the street.

When I went in again the little house had suddenly grown lonely, and my room looked empty as it had the day I came. I and all my belongings had died out of it, and I knew how it would seem when Mrs. Todd came back and found her lodger gone. So we die before our own eyes; so we see some chapters of our lives come to their natural end.

I found the little packages on the kitchen table. There was a quaint West Indian basket which I knew its owner had valued, and which I had once admired; there was an affecting provision laid beside it for my seafaring supper, with a neatly tied bunch of southernwood and a twig of bay, and a little old leather box which held the coral pin that Nathan Todd brought home to give to poor Joanna.

There was still an hour to wait, and I went up to the hill just above the schoolhouse and sat there thinking of things, and looking off to sea, and watching for the boat to come in sight. I could see Green Island, small and darkly wooded at that distance; below me were the houses of the village with their apple-trees and bits of garden ground. Presently, as I looked at the pastures beyond, I caught a last glimpse of Mrs. Todd herself, walking slowly in the footpath that led along, following the shore toward the Port. At such a distance one can feel the large, positive qualities that control a character. Close at hand, Mrs. Todd seemed able and warm-hearted and quite absorbed in her bustling industries, but her distant figure looked mateless and appealing, with something about it that was strangely self-possessed and mysterious. Now and then she stooped to pick something,—it might have been her favorite pennyroyal,—and at last I lost sight of her as she slowly crossed an open space on one of the higher points of land, and disappeared again behind a dark clump of juniper and the pointed firs.

As I came away on the little coastwise steamer, there was an old sea running which made the surf leap high on all the rocky shores. I stood on deck, looking back, and watched the busy gulls agree and turn, and sway together down the long slopes of air, then separate hastily and plunge into the waves. The tide was setting in, and plenty of small fish were coming with it, unconscious of the silver flashing of the great birds overhead and the quickness of their fierce beaks. The sea was full of life and spirit, the tops of the waves flew back as if they were winged like the gulls themselves, and like them had the freedom of the wind. Out in the main channel we passed a bent-shouldered old fisherman bound for the evening round among his lobster traps. He was toiling along with short oars, and the dory tossed and sank and tossed again with the steamer's waves. I saw that it was old Elijah Tilley, and though we had so long been strangers we had come to be warm friends, and I wished that he had waited for one of his mates, it was such hard work to row along shore through rough seas and tend the traps alone. As we passed I waved my hand and tried to call to him, and he looked up and answered my farewells by a solemn nod. The little town, with the tall masts of its disabled schooners in the inner bay, stood high above the flat sea for a few minutes, then it sank back into the uniformity of the coast, and became indistinguishable from the other towns that looked as if they were crumbled on the furzy-green stoniness of the shore.

The small outer islands of the bay were covered among the ledges with turf that looked as fresh as the early grass; there had been some days of rain the week before, and the darker green of the sweet-fern was scattered on all the pasture heights. It looked like the beginning of summer ashore, though the sheep, round and warm in their winter wool, betrayed the season of the year as they went feeding along the slopes in the low afternoon sunshine. Presently the wind began to blow, and we struck out seaward to double the long sheltering headland of the cape, and when I looked back again, the islands and the headland had run together and Dunnet Landing and all its coasts were lost to sight.

FOUR DUNNET LANDING STORIES

CONTENTS

THE QUEEN'S TWIN

I

THE COAST OF MAINE was in former years brought so near to foreign shores by its busy fleet of ships that among the older men and women one still finds a surprising proportion of travelers. Each seaward-stretching headland with its high-set houses, each island of a single farm, has sent its spies to view many a Land of Eshcol;* one may see plain, contented old faces at the windows, whose eyes have looked at far-away ports and known the splendors of the Eastern world. They shame the easy voyager of the North Atlantic and the Mediterranean; they have rounded the Cape of Good Hope and braved the angry seas of Cape Horn in small wooden ships; they have brought up their hardy boys and girls on narrow decks; they were among the last of the Northmen's children[4] to go adventuring to unknown shores. More than this one cannot give to a young State for its enlightenment; the sea captains and the captains' wives of Maine knew something of the wide world, and never mistook their native parishes for the whole instead of a part thereof; they knew not only Thomaston and Castine and Portland, but London and Bristol and Bordeaux, and the strange-mannered harbors of the China Sea.

One September day, when I was nearly at the end of a summer spent in a village called Dunnet Landing, on the Maine coast, my friend Mrs. Todd, in whose house I lived, came home from a long, solitary stroll in the wild pastures, with an eager look as if she were just starting on a hopeful quest instead of returning. She brought a little basket with blackberries enough for supper, and held it towards me so that I could see that there were also some late and surprising raspberries sprinkled on top, but she made no comment upon her wayfaring. I could tell plainly that she had something very important to say.

---

*Reference to the Bible, Numbers 13.

"You haven't brought home a leaf of anything," I ventured to this practiced herb-gatherer. "You were saying yesterday that the witch hazel might be in bloom."

"I dare say, dear," she answered in a lofty manner; "I ain't goin' to say it wasn't; I ain't much concerned either way 'bout the facts o' witch hazel. Truth is, I've been off visitin'; there's an old Indian foot-path leadin' over towards the Back Shore through the great heron swamp that anybody can't travel over all summer. You have to seize your time some day just now, while the low ground's summer-dried as it is today, and before the fall rains set in. I never thought of it till I was out o' sight o' home, and I says to myself, 'To-day's the day, certain!' and stepped along smart as I could. Yes, I've been visitin'. I did get into one spot that was wet underfoot before I noticed; you wait till I get me a pair o' dry woolen stockings, in case of cold, and I'll come an' tell ye."

Mrs. Todd disappeared. I could see that something had deeply interested her. She might have fallen in with either the sea-serpent* or the lost tribes of Israel, such was her air of mystery and satisfaction. She had been away since just before mid-morning, and as I sat waiting by my window I saw the last red glow of autumn sun-shine flare along the gray rocks of the shore and leave them cold again, and touch the far sails of some coast-wise schooners so that they stood like golden houses on the sea.

I was left to wonder longer than I liked. Mrs. Todd was making an evening fire and putting things in train for supper; presently she returned, still looking warm and cheerful after her long walk.

"There's a beautiful view from a hill over where I've been," she told me; "yes, there's a beautiful prospect of land and sea. You wouldn't discern the hill from any distance, but 't is the pretty situation of it that counts. I sat there a long spell, and I did wish for you. No, I didn't know a word about goin' when I set out this morning" (as if I had openly reproached her!); "I only felt one o' them travelin' fits comin' on, an' I ketched up my little basket; I didn't know but I

---

*Reference to the Bible, Isaiah 27:1.

might turn and come back time for dinner. I thought it wise to set out your luncheon for you in case I didn't. Hope you had all you wanted; yes, I hope you had enough."

"Oh, yes, indeed," said I. My landlady was always peculiarly bountiful in her supplies when she left me to fare for myself, as if she made a sort of peace-offering or affectionate apology.

"You know that hill with the old house right over top, over beyond the heron swamp? You'll excuse me for explainin'," Mrs. Todd began, "but you ain't so apt to strike inland as you be to go right along shore. You know that hill; there's a path leadin' right over to it that you have to look sharp to find nowadays; it belonged to the up-country Indians when they had to make a carry to the landing here to get to the out' islands. I've heard the old folks say that there used to be a place across a ledge where they'd worn a deep track with their moccasin feet, but I never could find it. 'T is so overgrown in some places that you keep losin' the path in the bushes and findin' it as you can; but it runs pretty straight considerin' the lay o' the land, and I keep my eye on the sun and the moss that grows one side o' the tree trunks. Some brook's been choked up and the swamp's bigger than it used to be. Yes; I did get in deep enough, one place!"

I showed the solicitude that I felt. Mrs. Todd was no longer young, and in spite of her strong, great frame and spirited behavior, I knew that certain ills were apt to seize upon her, and would end some day by leaving her lame and ailing.

"Don't you go to worryin' about me," she insisted, "settin' still's the only way the Evil One'll ever get the upper hand o' me. Keep me movin' enough, an' I'm twenty year old summer an' winter both. I don't know why 't is, but I've never happened to mention the one I've been to see. I don't know why I never happened to speak the name of Abby Martin, for I often give her a thought, but 't is a dreadful out-o'-the-way place where she lives, and I haven't seen her myself for three or four years. She's a real good interesting woman, and we're well acquainted; she's nigher mother's age than mine, but she's very young feeling. She made me a nice cup o' tea, and I don't know but I should have stopped all night if I could have got word to you not to worry."

Then there was a serious silence before Mrs. Todd spoke again to make a formal announcement.

"She is the Queen's Twin," and Mrs. Todd looked steadily to see how I might bear the great surprise.

"The Queen's Twin?" I repeated.

"Yes, she's come to feel a real interest in the Queen, and anybody can see how natural 't is. They were born the very same day, and you would be astonished to see what a number o' other things have corresponded.* She was speaking o' some o' the facts to me to-day, an' you'd think she'd never done nothing but read history. I see how earnest she was about it as I never did before. I've often and often heard her allude to the facts, but now she's got to be old and the hurry's over with her work, she's come to live a good deal in her thoughts, as folks often do, and I tell you 't is a sight o' company for her. If you want to hear about Queen Victoria, why Mis' Abby Martin'll tell you everything. And the prospect from that hill I spoke of is as beautiful as anything in this world; 't is worth while your goin' over to see her just for that."

"When can you go again?" I demanded eagerly.

"I should say to-morrow," answered Mrs. Todd; "yes, I should say to-morrow; but I expect 't would be better to take one day to rest, in between. I considered that question as I was comin' home, but I hurried so that there wa'n't much time to think. It's a dreadful long way to go with a horse; you have to go 'most as far as the old Bowden place an' turn off to the left, a master long, rough road, and then you have to turn right round as soon as you get there if you mean to get home before nine o'clock at night. But to strike across country from here, there's plenty o' time in the shortest day, and you can have a good hour or two's visit beside; 't ain't but a very few miles, and it's pretty all the way along. There used to be a few good families over there, but they've died and scattered, so now she's far from neighbors. There, she really cried, she was so glad to see anybody comin'. You'll be amused to hear her talk about the Queen, but I thought twice or three times as I set there 't was about all the company she'd got."

---

*Queen Victoria was born on May 24, 1819, was declared queen of the British Empire in 1837, and died in 1901.

"Could we go day after to-morrow?" I asked eagerly.

"'T would suit me exactly," said Mrs. Todd.

II

ONE CAN NEVER BE so certain of good New England weather as in the days when a long easterly storm has blown away the warm late-summer mists, and cooled the air so that however bright the sunshine is by day, the nights come nearer and nearer to frostiness. There was a cold freshness in the morning air when Mrs. Todd and I locked the house-door behind us; we took the key of the fields into our own hands that day, and put out across country as one puts out to sea. When we reached the top of the ridge behind the town it seemed as if we had anxiously passed the harbor bar and were comfortably in open sea at last.

"There, now!" proclaimed Mrs. Todd, taking a long breath, "now I do feel safe. It's just the weather, that's liable to bring somebody to spend the day; I've had a feeling of Mis' Elder Caplin from North Point bein' close upon me ever since I waked up this morning', an' I didn't want to be hampered with our present plans. She's a great hand to visit; she'll be spendin' the day somewhere from now till Thanksgivin', but there's plenty o' places at the Landin' where she goes, an' if I ain't there she'll just select another. I thought mother might be in, too, 't is so pleasant; but I run up the road to look off this mornin' before you was awake, and there was no sign o' the boat. If they hadn't started by that time they wouldn't start, just as the tide is now; besides, I see a lot o' mackerel-men headin' Green Island way, and they'll detain William. No, we're safe now, an' if mother should be comin' in to-morrow we'll have all this to tell her. She an' Mis' Abby Martin's very old friends."

We were walking down the long pasture slopes towards the dark woods and thickets of the low ground. They stretched away northward like an unbroken wilderness; the early mists still dulled much of the color and made the uplands beyond look like a very far-off country.

"It ain't so far as it looks from here," said my companion reassuringly, "but we've got no time to spare either," and she hurried on, leading the way with a fine sort of spirit in her step; and presently we struck into the old Indian footpath, which could be plainly seen across the long-unploughed turf of the pastures, and followed it among the thick, low-growing spruces. There the ground was smooth and brown under foot, and the thin-stemmed trees held a dark and shadowy roof overhead. We walked a long way without speaking; sometimes we had to push aside the branches, and sometimes we walked in a broad aisle where the trees were larger. It was a solitary woods, birdless and beastless; there was not even a rabbit to be seen, or a crow high in air to break the silence.

"I don't believe the Queen ever saw such a lonesome trail as this," said Mrs. Todd, as if she followed the thoughts that were in my mind. Our visit to Mrs. Abby Martin seemed in some strange way to concern the high affairs of royalty. I had just been thinking of English landscapes, and of the solemn hills of Scotland with their lonely cottages and stone-walled sheepfolds, and the wandering flocks on high cloudy pastures. I had often been struck by the quick interest and familiar allusion to certain members of the royal house which one found in distant neighborhoods of New England; whether some old instincts of personal loyalty had survived all changes of time and national vicissitudes, or whether it is only that the Queen's own character and disposition have won friends for her so far away, it is impossible to tell. But to hear of a twin sister was the most surprising proof of intimacy of all, and I must confess that there was something remarkably exciting to the imagination in my morning walk. To think of being presented at Court in the usual way was for the moment quite commonplace.

III

MRS. TODD WAS SWINGING her basket to and fro like a schoolgirl as she walked, and at this moment it slipped from her hand and rolled lightly along the ground as if there were nothing in it. I picked it up and gave it to her, whereupon she lifted the cover and looked in with anxiety.

"'T is only a few little things, but I don't want to lose 'em," she explained humbly. "'T was lucky you took the other basket if I was goin' to roll it round. Mis' Abby Martin complained o' lacking some pretty pink silk to finish one o' her little frames, an' I thought I'd carry her some, and I had a bunch o' gold thread that had been in a box o' mine this twenty year. I never was one to do much fancy work, but we're all liable to be swept away by fashion. And then there's a small packet o' very choice herbs that I gave a good deal of attention to; they'll smarten her up and give her the best of appetites, come spring. She was tellin' me that spring weather is very wiltin' an' tryin' to her, and she was beginnin' to dread it already. Mother's just the same way; if I could prevail on mother to take some o' these remedies in good season 't would make a world o' difference, but she gets all down hill before I have a chance to hear of it, and then William comes in to tell me, sighin' and bewailin', how feeble mother is. 'Why can't you remember 'bout them good herbs that I never let her be without?' I say to him—he does provoke me so; and then off he goes, sulky enough, down to his boat. Next thing I know, she comes in to go to meetin', wantin' to speak to everybody and feelin' like a girl. Mis' Martin's case is very much the same; but she's nobody to watch her. William's kind o' slow-molded; but there, any William's better than none when you get to be Mis' Martin's age."

"Hadn't she any children?" I asked.

"Quite a number," replied Mrs. Todd grandly, "but some are gone and the rest are married and settled. She never was a great hand to go about visitin'. I don't know but Mis' Martin might be called a little peculiar. Even her own folks has to make company of her; she never slips in and lives right along with the rest as if 't was at home, even in her own children's houses. I heard one o' her sons' wives say once she'd much rather have the Queen to spend the day if she could choose between the two, but I never thought Abby was so difficult as that. I used to love to have her come; she may have been sort o' ceremonious, but very pleasant and sprightly if you had sense enough to treat her her own way. I always think she'd know just how to live with great folks, and feel easier 'long of them an' their ways. Her son's wife's a great driver with farm-work, boards a great tableful o' men in hayin' time, an' feels right in her element. I don't say but she's a good woman an' smart, but sort o' rough. Anybody that's gentle-mannered an' precise like Mis' Martin would be a sort o' restraint.

"There's all sorts o' folks in the country, same's there is in the city," concluded Mrs. Todd gravely, and I as gravely agreed. The thick woods were behind us now, and the sun was shining clear overhead, the morning mists were gone, and a faint blue haze softened the distance; as we climbed the hill where we were to see the view, it seemed like a summer day. There was an old house on the height, facing southward—a mere forsaken shell of an old house, with empty windows that looked like blind eyes. The frost-bitten grass grew close about it like brown fur, and there was a single crooked bough of lilac holding its green leaves close by the door.

"We'll just have a good piece of bread-an'-butter now," said the commander of the expedition, "and then we'll hang up the basket on some peg inside the house out o' the way o' the sheep, and have a han'some entertainment as we're comin' back. She'll be all through her little dinner when we get there, Mis' Martin will; but she'll want to make us some tea, an' we must have our visit an' be startin' back pretty soon after two. I don't want to cross all that low ground again after it's begun to grow chilly. An' it looks to me as if the clouds might begin to gather late in the afternoon."

Before us lay a splendid world of sea and shore. The autumn colors already brightened the landscape; and here and there at the edge of a dark tract of pointed firs stood a row of bright swamp-maples like scarlet flowers. The blue sea and the great tide inlets were untroubled by the lightest winds.

"Poor land, this is!" sighed Mrs. Todd as we sat down to rest on the worn doorstep. "I've known three good hard-workin' families that come here full o' hope an' pride and tried to make something o' this farm, but it beat 'em all. There's one small field that's excellent for potatoes if you let half of it rest every year; but the land's always hungry. Now, you see them little peakéd-topped spruces an' fir balsams comin' up over the hill all green an' hearty; they've got it all their own way! Seems sometimes as if wild Natur' got jealous over a certain spot, and wanted to do just as she'd a mind to. You'll see here; she'll do her own ploughin' an' harrowin' with frost an' wet, an' plant just what she wants and wait for her own crops. Man can't do nothin' with it, try as he may, I tell you those little trees means business!"

I looked down the slope, and felt as if we ourselves were likely to be surrounded and overcome if we lingered too long. There was a vigor of growth, a persistence and savagery about the sturdy little trees that put weak human nature at complete defiance. One felt a sudden pity for the men and women who had been worsted after a long fight in that lonely place; one felt a sudden fear of the unconquerable, immediate forces of Nature, as in the irresistible moment of a thunderstorm.

"I can recollect the time when folks were shy o' these woods we just come through," said Mrs. Todd seriously. "The men-folks themselves never'd venture into 'em alone; if their cattle got strayed they'd collect whoever they could get, and start off all together. They said a person was liable to get bewildered in there alone, and in old times folks had been lost. I expect there was considerable fear left over from the old Indian times, and the poor days o' witchcraft; anyway, I've seen bold men act kind o' timid. Some women o' the Asa Bowden family went out one afternoon berryin' when I was a girl, and got lost and was out all night; they found 'em middle o' the mornin' next day, not half a mile from home, scared most to death, an' sayin' they'd heard wolves and other beasts sufficient for a caravan. Poor creatur's! They'd strayed at last into a kind of low place amongst some alders, an' one of 'em was so overset she never got over it, an' went off in a sort o' slow decline. 'T was like them victims that drowns in a foot o' water; but their minds did suffer dreadful. Some folks is born afraid of the woods and all wild places, but I must say they've always been like home to me."

I glanced at the resolute, confident face of my companion. Life was very strong in her, as if some force of Nature were personified in this simple-hearted woman and gave her cousinship to the ancient deities. She might have walked the primeval fields of Sicily; her strong gingham skirts might at that very moment bend the slender stalks of asphodel and be fragrant with trodden thyme, instead of the brown wind-brushed grass of New England and frost-bitten goldenrod. She was a great soul, was Mrs. Todd, and I her humble follower, as we went our way to visit the Queen's Twin, leaving the bright view of the sea behind us, and descending to a lower countryside through the dry pastures and fields.

The farms all wore a look of gathering age, though the settlement was, after all, so young. The fences were already fragile, and it seemed as if the first impulse of agriculture had soon spent itself without hope of renewal. The better houses were always those that had some hold upon the riches of the sea; a house that could not harbor a fishing-boat in some neighboring inlet was far from being sure of every-day comforts. The land alone was not enough to live upon in that stony region; it belonged by right to the forest, and to the forest it fast returned. From the top of the hill where we had been sitting we had seen prosperity in the dim distance, where the land was good and the sun shone upon fat barns, and where warm-looking houses with three or four chimneys apiece stood high on their solid ridge above the bay.

As we drew nearer to Mrs. Martin's it was sad to see what poor bushy fields, what thin and empty dwelling-places had been left by those who had chosen this disappointing part of the northern country for their home. We crossed the last field and came into a narrow rainwashed road, and Mrs. Todd looked eager and expectant and said that we were almost at our journey's end. "I do hope Mis' Martin'll ask you into her best room where she keeps all the Queen's pictures. Yes, I think likely she will ask you; but 't ain't everybody she deems worthy to visit 'em, I can tell you," said Mrs. Todd warningly. "She's been collectin' 'em an' cuttin' 'em out o' newspapers an' magazines time out o' mind, and if she heard of anybody sailin' for an English port she'd contrive to get a little money to 'em and ask to have the last likeness there was. She's most covered her best-room wall now; she keeps that room shut up sacred as a meetin'-house! 'I won't say but I have my favorites amongst 'em,' she told me t' other day, 'but they're all beautiful to me as they can be!' And she's made some kind o' pretty little frames for 'em all—you know there's always a new fashion o' frames comin' round; first 't was shell-work, and then 't was pine-cones, and bead-work's had its day, and now she's much concerned with perforated cardboard worked with silk. I tell you that best room's a sight to see! But you mustn't look for anything elegant," continued Mrs. Todd, after a moment's reflection. "Mis' Martin's always been in very poor, strugglin' circumstances. She had ambition for her children, though they took right after their father an' had little for themselves; she wa'n't over an' above well married, however kind she may see fit to speak. She's been patient an' hard-workin' all her life, and always high above makin' mean complaints of other folks. I expect all this business about the Queen has buoyed her over many a shoal place in life. Yes, you might say that Abby'd been a slave, but there ain't any slave but has some freedom."

IV

PRESENTLY I SAW A low gray house standing on a grassy bank close to the road. The door was at the side, facing us, and a tangle of snowberry bushes and cinnamon roses grew to the level of the window-sills. On the doorstep stood a bent-shouldered, little old woman; there was an air of welcome and of unmistakable dignity about her.

"She sees us coming," exclaimed Mrs. Todd in an excited whisper. "There, I told her I might be over this way again if the weather held good, and if I came I'd bring you. She said right off she'd take great pleasure in havin' a visit from you; I was surprised, she's usually so retirin'."

Even this reassurance did not quell a faint apprehension on our part; there was something distinctly formal in the occasion, and one felt that consciousness of inadequacy which is never easy for the humblest pride to bear. On the way I had torn my dress in an unexpected encounter with a little thorn-bush, and I could not imagine how it felt to be going to Court and forgetting one's feathers or her Court train.

The Queen's Twin was oblivious of such trifles; she stood waiting with a calm look until we came near enough to take her kind hand. She was a beautiful old woman, with clear eyes and a lovely quietness and genuineness of manner; there was not a trace of anything pretentious about her, or high-flown, as Mrs. Todd would say comprehensively. Beauty in age is rare enough in women who have spent their lives in the hard work of a farmhouse; but autumn-like and withered as this woman may have looked, her features had kept, or rather gained, a great refinement. She led us into her old kitchen and gave us seats, and took one of the little straight-backed chairs herself and sat a short distance away, as if she were giving audience to an ambassador. It seemed as if we should all be standing; you could not help feeling that the habits of her life were more ceremonious, but that for the moment she assumed the simplicities of the occasion.

Mrs. Todd was always Mrs. Todd, too great and self-possessed a soul for any occasion to ruffle. I admired her calmness, and presently the slow current of neighborhood talk carried one easily along; we spoke of the weather and the small adventures of the way, and then, as if I were after all not a stranger, our hostess turned almost affectionately to speak to me.

"The weather will be growing dark in London now. I expect that you've been in London, dear?" she said.

"Oh, yes," I answered. "Only last year."

"It is a great many years since I was there, along in the forties," said Mrs. Martin. "'T was the only voyage I ever made; most of my neighbors have been great travelers. My brother was master of a vessel, and his wife usually sailed with him; but that year she had a young child more frail than the others, and she dreaded the care of it at sea. It happened that my brother got a chance for my husband to go as super-cargo, being a good accountant, and came one day to urge him to take it; he was very ill-disposed to the sea, but he had met with losses, and I saw my own opportunity and persuaded them both to let me go too. In those days they didn't object to a woman's being aboard to wash and mend, the voyages were sometimes very long. And that was the way I come to see the Queen."

Mrs. Martin was looking straight in my eyes to see if I showed any genuine interest in the most interesting person in the world.

"Oh, I am very glad you saw the Queen," I hastened to say. "Mrs. Todd has told me that you and she were born the very same day."

"We were indeed, dear!" said Mrs. Martin, and she leaned back comfortably and smiled as she had not smiled before. Mrs. Todd gave a satisfied nod and glance, as if to say that things were going on as well as possible in this anxious moment.

"Yes," said Mrs. Martin again, drawing her chair a little nearer, "'t was a very remarkable thing; we were born the same day, and at exactly the same hour, after you allowed for all the difference in time. My father figured it out sea-fashion. Her Royal Majesty and I opened our eyes upon this world together; say what you may 't is a bond between us."

Mrs. Todd assented with an air of triumph, and untied her hat-strings and threw them back over her shoulders with a gallant air.

"And I married a man by the name of Albert, just the same as she did, and all by chance, for I didn't get the news that she had an Albert too till a fortnight afterward; news was slower coming then than it is now. My first baby was a girl, and I called her Victoria after my mate; but the next one was a boy, and my husband wanted the right to name him, and took his own name and his brother Edward's and pretty soon I saw in the paper that the little Prince o' Wales had been christened just the same. After that I made excuse to wait till I knew what she'd named her children. I didn't want to break the chain, so I had an Alfred, and my darling Alice that I lost long before she lost hers, and there I stopped. If I'd only had a dear daughter to stay at home with me, same's her youngest one, I should have been so thankful! But if only one of us could have a little Beatrice, I'm glad 't was the Queen; we've both seen trouble, but she's had the most care."

I asked Mrs. Martin if she lived alone all the year, and was told that she did except for a visit now and then from one of her grandchildren, "the only one that really likes to come an' stay quiet 'long o' grandma. She always says quick as she's through her schoolin' she's goin' to live with me all the time, but she's very pretty an' has taking ways," said Mrs. Martin, looking both proud and wistful, "so I can tell nothing at all about it! Yes, I've been alone most o' the time since my Albert was taken away, and that's a great many years; he had a long time o' failing and sickness first." (Mrs. Todd's foot gave an impatient scuff on the floor.) "An' I've always lived right here. I ain't like the Queen's Majesty, for this is the only palace I've got," said the dear old thing, smiling again. "I'm glad of it too, I don't like changing about, an' our stations in life are set very different. I don't require what the Queen does, but sometimes I've thought 't was left to me to do the plain things she don't have time for. I expect she's a beautiful housekeeper, nobody couldn't have done better in her high place, and she's been as good a mother as she's been a queen."

"I guess she has, Abby," agreed Mrs. Todd instantly. "How was it you happened to get such a good look at her? I meant to ask you again when I was here t' other day."

"Our ship was layin' in the Thames, right there above Wapping. We was dischargin' cargo, and under orders to clear as quick as we could for Bordeaux to take on an excellent freight o' French goods," explained Mrs. Martin eagerly. "I heard that the Queen was goin' to a great review of her army, and would drive out o' her Buckin'ham Palace about ten o'clock in the mornin', and I ran aft to Albert, my husband, and brother Horace where they was standin' together by the hatchway, and told 'em they must one of 'em take me. They laughed, I was in such a hurry, and said they couldn't go; and I found they meant it and got sort of impatient when I began to talk, and I was 'most broken-hearted; 't was all the reason I had for makin' that hard voyage. Albert couldn't help often reproachin' me, for he did so resent the sea, an' I'd known how 't would be before we sailed; but I'd minded nothing all the way till then, and I just crep' back to my cabin an' begun to cry. They was disappointed about their ship's cook, an' I'd cooked for fo'c's'le* an' cabin myself all the way over; 't was dreadful hard work, specially in rough weather; we'd had head winds an' a six weeks' voyage. They'd acted sort of ashamed o' me when I pled so to go ashore, an' that hurt my feelin's most of all. But Albert come below pretty soon; I'd never given way so in my life, an' he begun to act frightened, and treated me gentle just as he did when we was goin' to be married, an' when I got over sobbin' he went on deck and saw Horace an' talked it over what they could do; they really had their duty to the vessel, and couldn't be spared that day. Horace was real good when he understood everything, and he come an' told me I'd more than worked my passage an' was goin' to do just as I liked now we was in port. He'd engaged a cook, too, that was comin' aboard that mornin', and he was goin' to send the ship's carpenter with me—a nice fellow from up Thomaston way; he'd gone to put on his ashore clothes as quick's he could. So then I got ready, and we started off in the small boat and rowed up river. I was afraid we were too late, but the tide was setting up very strong, and we landed an' left the boat to a keeper, and I run all the way up those great streets and across a park. 'T was a great day, with sights o' folks

---

*Variant of the nautical term *forecastle*, for a structure at the bow of a merchant ship where the crew is housed.

everywhere, but 't was just as if they was nothin' but wax images to me. I kep' askin' my way an' runnin' on, with the carpenter comin' after as best he could, and just as I worked to the front o' the crowd by the palace, the gates was flung open and out she came; all prancin' horses and shinin' gold, and in a beautiful carriage there she sat; 't was a moment o' heaven to me. I saw her plain, and she looked right at me so pleasant and happy, just as if she knew there was somethin' different between us from other folks."

There was a moment when the Queen's Twin could not go on and neither of her listeners could ask a question.

"Prince Albert was sitting right beside her in the carriage," she continued. "Oh, he was a beautiful man! Yes, dear, I saw 'em both together just as I see you now, and then she was gone out o' sight in another minute, and the common crowd was all spread over the place pushin' an' cheerin'. 'T was some kind o' holiday, an' the carpenter and I got separated, an' then I found him again after I didn't think I should, an' he was all for makin' a day of it, and goin' to show me all the sights; he'd been in London before, but I didn't want nothin' else, an' we went back through the streets down to the waterside an' took the boat. I remember I mended an old coat o' my Albert's as good as I could, sittin' on the quarter-deck in the sun all that afternoon, and 't was all as if I was livin' in a lovely dream. I don't know how to explain it, but there hasn't been no friend I've felt so near to me ever since."

One could not say much—only listen. Mrs. Todd put in a discerning question now and then, and Mrs. Martin's eyes shone brighter and brighter as she talked. What a lovely gift of imagination and true affection was in this fond old heart! I looked about the plain New England kitchen, with its wood-smoked walls and homely braided rugs on the worn floor, and all its simple furnishings. The loud-ticking clock seemed to encourage us to speak; at the other side of the room was an early newspaper portrait of Her Majesty the Queen of Great Britain and Ireland. On a shelf below were some flowers in a little dish, as if they were put before a shrine.

"If I could have had more to read, I should have known 'most everything about her," said Mrs. Martin wistfully. "I've made the most of what I did have, and thought it over and over till it came clear. I sometimes seem to have her all my own, as if we'd lived right together. I've often walked out into the woods alone and told her what my troubles was, and it always seemed as if she told me 't was all right, an' we must have patience. I've got her beautiful book about the Highlands;* 't was dear Mis' Todd here that found out about her printing it and got a copy for me, and it's been a treasure to my heart, just as if 't was written right to me. I always read it Sundays now, for my Sunday treat. Before that I used to have to imagine a good deal, but when I come to read her book, I knew what I expected was all true. We do think alike about so many things," said the Queen's Twin with affectionate certainty. "You see, there is something between us, being born just at the same time; 't is what they call a birthright. She's had great tasks put upon her, being the Queen, an' mine has been the humble lot; but she's done the best she could, nobody can say to the contrary, and there's something between us; she's been the great lesson I've had to live by. She's been everything to me. An' when she had her Jubilee, oh, how my heart was with her."†

"There, 't wouldn't play the part in her life it has in mine," said Mrs. Martin generously, in answer to something one of her listeners had said. "Sometimes I think, now she's older, she might like to know about us. When I think how few old friends anybody has left at our age, I suppose it may be just the same with her as it is with me; perhaps she would like to know how we came into life together. But I've had a great advantage in seeing her, an' I can always fancy her goin' on, while she don't know nothin' yet about me, except she may feel my love stayin' her heart sometimes an' not know just where it comes from. An' I dream about our being together out in some pretty fields, young as ever we was, and holdin' hands as we walk along. I'd like to know if she ever has that dream too. I used to have days when I made believe she did know, an' was comin' to see

---

*A book attributed to Queen Victoria, entitled *Leaves from the Journal of Our Life in the Highlands, from 1848 to 1861* (1868), was edited (with a preface) by Arthur Helps. That book was followed by *More Leaves from the Journal of a Life in the Highlands, from 1862 to 1882* (1884).

†The "Jubilee" celebration marking fifty years of Victoria's reign as queen was held in 1887.

me," confessed the speaker shyly, with a little flush on her cheeks; "and I'd plan what I could have nice for supper, and I wasn't goin' to let anybody know she was here havin' a good rest, except I'd wish you, Almira Todd, or dear Mis' Blackett would happen in, for you'd know just how to talk with her. You see, she likes to be up in Scotland, right out in the wild country, better than she does anywhere else."

"I'd really love to take her out to see mother at Green Island," said Mrs. Todd with a sudden impulse.

"Oh, yes! I should love to have you," exclaimed Mrs. Martin, and then she began to speak in a lower tone. "One day I got thinkin' so about my dear Queen" she said, "an' livin' so in my thoughts, that I went to work an' got all ready for her, just as if she was really comin'. I never told this to a livin' soul before, but I feel you'll understand. I put my best fine sheets and blankets I spun an' wove myself on the bed, and I picked some pretty flowers and put 'em all round the house, an' I worked as hard an' happy as I could all day, and had as nice a supper ready as I could get, sort of telling myself a story all the time. She was comin' an' I was goin' to see her again, an' I kep' it up until nightfall; an' when I see the dark an' it come to me I was all alone, the dream left me, an' I sat down on the doorstep an' felt all foolish an' tired. An', if you'll believe it, I heard steps comin', an' an old cousin o' mine come wanderin' along, one I was apt to be shy of. She wasn't all there, as folks used to say, but harmless enough and a kind of poor old talking body. And I went right to meet her when I first heard her call, 'stead o' hidin' as I sometimes did, an' she come in dreadful willin', an' we sat down to supper together; 't was a supper I should have had no heart to eat alone."

"I don't believe she ever had such a splendid time in her life as she did then. I heard her tell all about it afterwards," exclaimed Mrs. Todd compassionately. "There, now I hear all this it seems just as if the Queen might have known and couldn't come herself, so she sent that poor old creatur' that was always in need!"

Mrs. Martin looked timidly at Mrs. Todd and then at me. "'T was childish o' me to go an' get supper," she confessed.

"I guess you wa'n't the first one to do that," said Mrs. Todd. "No, I guess you wa'n't the first one who got supper that way, Abby," and then for a moment she could say no more.

Mrs. Todd and Mrs. Martin had moved their chairs a little so that they faced each other, and I, at one side, could see them both.

"No, you never told me o' that before, Abby," said Mrs. Todd gently. "Don't it show that for folks that have any fancy in 'em, such beautiful dreams is the real part o' life? But to most folks the common things that happens outside 'em is all in all."

Mrs. Martin did not appear to understand at first, strange to say, when the secret of her heart was put into words; then a glow of pleasure and comprehension shone upon her face. "Why, I believe you're right, Almira!" she said, and turned to me.

"Wouldn't you like to look at my pictures of the Queen?" she asked, and we rose and went into the best room.

V

THE MID-DAY VISIT SEEMED very short; September hours are brief to match the shortening days. The great subject was dismissed for a while after our visit to the Queen's pictures, and my companions spoke much of lesser persons until we drank the cup of tea which Mrs. Todd had foreseen. I happily remembered that the Queen herself is said to like a proper cup of tea, and this at once seemed to make her Majesty kindly join so remote and reverent a company. Mrs. Martin's thin cheeks took on a pretty color like a girl's. "Somehow I always have thought of her when I make it extra good," she said. "I've got a real china cup that belonged to my grandmother, and I believe I shall call it hers now."

"Why don't you?" responded Mrs. Todd warmly, with a delightful smile.

Later they spoke of a promised visit which was to be made in the Indian summer to the Landing and Green Island, but I observed that Mrs. Todd presented the little parcel of dried herbs, with full directions, for a cure-all in the spring, as if there were no real chance of their meeting again first. As we looked back from the turn of the road the Queen's Twin was still standing on the doorstep watching us away, and Mrs. Todd stopped, and stood still for a moment before she waved her hand again.

"There's one thing certain, dear," she said to me with great discernment; "it ain't as if we left her all alone!"

Then we set out upon our long way home over the hill, where we lingered in the afternoon sunshine, and through the dark woods across the heron-swamp.

A DUNNET SHEPHERDESS

I

EARLY ONE MORNING AT Dunnet Landing, as if it were still night, I waked, suddenly startled by a spirited conversation beneath my window. It was not one of Mrs. Todd's morning soliloquies; she was not addressing her plants and flowers in words of either praise or blame. Her voice was declamatory though perfectly good-humored, while the second voice, a man's, was of lower pitch and somewhat deprecating.

The sun was just above the sea, and struck straight across my room through a crack in the blind. It was a strange hour for the arrival of a guest, and still too soon for the general run of business, even in that tiny eastern haven where daybreak fisheries and early tides must often rule the day.

The man's voice suddenly declared itself to my sleepy ears. It was Mr. William Blackett's.

"Why, sister Almiry," he protested gently, "I don't need one o' your nostrums!"*

"Pick me a small han'ful," she commanded. "No, no, a *small* han'ful I said—o' them large pennyr'yal† sprigs! I go to all the trouble an' cossetin' of 'em just so as to have you ready to meet such occasions, an' last year, you may remember, you never stopped here at all the day you went up country. An' the frost come at last an' blacked it. I never saw any herb that so objected to gardin ground; might as well try to flourish mayflowers in a common front yard. There, you can come in now, an' set and eat what breakfast you've got patience for. I've found everything I want, an' I'll mash 'em up an' be all ready to put 'em on."

*A *nostrum* is a medicine whose ingredients are kept secret by the inventor or proprietor to protect the profitability of the medicine; the term can also refer to a quack medicine.

†Medicinal herb.

I heard such a pleading note of appeal as the speakers went round the corner of the house, and my curiosity was so demanding, that I dressed in haste, and joined my friends a little later, with two unnoticed excuses of the beauty of the morning, and the early mail boat. William's breakfast had been slighted; he had taken his cup of tea and merely pushed back the rest on the kitchen table. He was now sitting in a helpless condition by the side window, with one of his sister's purple calico aprons pinned close about his neck. Poor William was meekly submitting to being smeared, as to his countenance, with a most pungent and unattractive lotion of pennyroyal and other green herbs which had been hastily pounded and mixed with cream in the little white stone mortar.

I had to cast two or three straightforward looks at William to reassure myself that he really looked happy and expectant in spite of his melancholy circumstances, and was not being overtaken by retribution. The brother and sister seemed to be on delightful terms with each other for once, and there was something of cheerful anticipation in their morning talk. I was reminded of Medea's anointing Jason before the great episode of the iron bulls,[5] but to-day William really could not be going up country to see a railroad for the first time. I knew this to be one of his great schemes, but he was not fitted to appear in public, or to front an observing world of strangers. As I appeared he essayed to rise, but Mrs. Todd pushed him back into the chair.

"Set where you be till it dries on," she insisted. "Land sakes, you'd think he'd get over bein' a boy some time or 'nother, gettin' along in years as he is. An' you'd think he'd seen full enough o' fish, but once a year he has to break loose like this, an' travel off way up back o' the Bowden place—far out o' my beat, 't is—an' go a trout fishin'!"

Her tone of amused scorn was so full of challenge that William changed color even under the green streaks.

"I want some change," he said, looking at me and not at her. " 'T is the prettiest little shady brook you ever saw."

"If he ever fetched home more 'n a couple o' minnies, 't would seem worth while," Mrs. Todd concluded, putting a last dab of the mysterious compound so perilously near her brother's mouth that William flushed again and was silent.

A little later I witnessed his escape, when Mrs. Todd had taken the foolish risk of going down cellar. There was a horse and wagon outside the garden fence, and presently we stood where we could see him driving up the hill with thoughtless speed. Mrs. Todd said nothing, but watched him affectionately out of sight.

"It serves to keep the mosquitoes off," she said, and a moment later it occurred to my slow mind that she spoke of the pennyroyal lotion. "I don't know sometimes but William's kind of poetical," she continued, in her gentlest voice. "You'd think if anything could cure him of it, 't would be the fish business."

It was only twenty minutes past six on a summer morning, but we both sat down to rest as if the activities of the day were over. Mrs. Todd rocked gently for a time, and seemed to be lost, though not poorly, like Macbeth,* in her thoughts. At last she resumed relations with her actual surroundings. "I shall now put my lobsters on. They'll make us a good supper," she announced. "Then I can let the fire out for all day; give it a holiday, same's William. You can have a little one now, nice an' hot, if you ain't got all the breakfast you want. Yes, I'll put the lobsters on. William was very thoughtful to bring 'em over; William *is* thoughtful; if he only had a spark o' ambition, there be few could match him."

This unusual concession was afforded a sympathetic listener from the depths of the kitchen closet. Mrs. Todd was getting out her old lobster pot, and began to speak of prosaic affairs. I hoped that I should hear something more about her brother and their island life, and sat idly by the kitchen window looking at the morning glories that shaded it, believing that some flaw of wind might set Mrs. Todd's mind on its former course. Then it occurred to me that she had spoken about our supper rather than our dinner, and I guessed that she might have some great scheme before her for the day.

When I had loitered for some time and there was no further word about William, and at last I was conscious of receiving no attention whatever, I went away. It was something of a disappointment to find that she put no hindrance in the way of my usual morning affairs, of going up to the empty little white schoolhouse

---

*Reference to Shakespeare's play *Macbeth*.

on the hill where I did my task of writing. I had been almost sure of a holiday when I discovered that Mrs. Todd was likely to take one herself; we had not been far afield to gather herbs and pleasures for many days now, but a little later she had silently vanished. I found my luncheon ready on the table in the little entry, wrapped in its shining old homespun napkin, and as if by way of special consolation, there was a stone bottle of Mrs. Todd's best spruce beer, with a long piece of cod line would round it by which it could be lowered for coolness into the deep schoolhouse well.

I walked away with a dull supply of writing-paper and these provisions, feeling like a reluctant child who hopes to be called back at every step. There was no relenting voice to be heard, and when I reached the schoolhouse, I found that I had left an open window and a swinging shutter the day before, and the sea wind that blew at evening had fluttered my poor sheaf of papers all about the room.

So the day did not begin very well, and I began to recognize that it was one of the days when nothing could be done without company. The truth was that my heart had gone trouting with William, but it would have been too selfish to say a word even to one's self about spoiling his day. If there is one way above another of getting so close to nature that one simply is a piece of nature, following a primeval instinct with perfect self-forgetfulness and forgetting everything except the dreamy consciousness of pleasant freedom, it is to take the course of a shady trout brook. The dark pools and the sunny shallows beckon one on; the wedge of sky between the trees on either bank, the speaking, companioning noise of the water, the amazing importance of what one is doing, and the constant sense of life and beauty make a strange transformation of the quick hours. I had a sudden memory of all this, and another, and another. I could not get myself free from "fishing and wishing."

At that moment I heard the unusual sound of wheels, and I looked past the high-growing thicket of wild-roses and straggling sumac to see the white nose and meagre shape of the Caplin horse; then I saw William sitting in the open wagon, with a small expectant smile upon his face.

"I've got two lines," he said. "I was quite a piece up the road. I thought perhaps 't was so you'd feel like going."

There was enough excitement for most occasions in hearing William speak three sentences at once. Words seemed but vain to me at that bright moment. I stepped back from the schoolhouse window with a beating heart. The spruce-beer bottle was not yet in the well, and with that and my luncheon, and Pleasure at the helm, I went out into the happy world. The land breeze was blowing, and, as we turned away, I saw a flutter of white go past the window as I left the schoolhouse and my morning's work to their neglected fate.

II

One seldom gave way to a cruel impulse to look at an ancient seafaring William, but one felt as if he were a growing boy; I only hope that he felt much the same about me. He did not wear the fishing clothes that belonged to his sea-going life, but a strangely shaped old suit of tea-colored linen garments that might have been brought home years ago from Canton or Bombay. William had a peculiar way of giving silent assent when one spoke, but of answering your unspoken thoughts as if they reached him better than words. "I find them very easy," he said, frankly referring to the clothes. "Father had them in his old sea-chest."

The antique fashion, a quaint touch of foreign grace and even imagination about the cut were very pleasing; if ever Mr. William Blackett had faintly resembled an old beau, it was upon that day. He now appeared to feel as if everything had been explained between us, as if everything were quite understood; and we drove for some distance without finding it necessary to speak again about anything. At last, when it must have been a little past nine o'clock, he stopped the horse beside a small farmhouse, and nodded when I asked if I should get down from the wagon. "You can steer about northeast right across the pasture," he said, looking from under the eaves of his hat with an expectant smile. "I always leave the team here."

I helped to unfasten the harness, and William led the horse away to the barn. It was a poor-looking little place, and a forlorn woman looked at us through the window before she appeared at the door. I told her that Mr. Blackett and I came up from the Landing to go fishing. "He keeps a-comin', don't he?" she answered, with a funny little laugh, to which I was at a loss to find answer. When he joined us, I could not see that he took notice of her presence in any way, except to take an armful of dried salt fish from a corded stack in the back of the wagon which had been carefully covered with a piece of old sail. We had left a wake of their pungent flavor behind us all the way. I wondered what was going to become of the rest of them and some fresh lobsters which were also disclosed to view, but he laid the present gift on the doorstep without a word, and a few minutes later, when I looked back as we crossed the pasture, the fish were being carried into the house.

I could not see any signs of a trout brook until I came close upon it in the bushy pasture, and presently we struck into the low woods of straggling spruce and fir mixed into a tangle of swamp maples and alders which stretched away on either hand up and down stream. We found an open place in the pasture where some taller trees seemed to have been overlooked rather than spared. The sun was bright and hot by this time, and I sat down in the shade while William produced his lines and cut and trimmed us each a slender rod. I wondered where Mrs. Todd was spending the morning, and if later she would think that pirates had landed and captured me from the schoolhouse.

III

THE BROOK WAS GIVING that live, persistent call to a listener that trout brooks always make; it ran with a free, swift current even here, where it crossed an apparently level piece of land. I saw two unpromising, quick barbel* chase each other upstream from bank to bank as we solemnly arranged our hooks and sinkers. I felt that William's glances changed from anxiety to relief when he found that I was used to such gear; perhaps he felt that we must stay together if I could not bait my own hook, but we parted happily, full of a pleasing sense of companionship.

*Type of fish featuring barbels (projections from the upper jaw that look like whiskers), possibly a catfish.

William had pointed me up the brook, but I chose to go down, which was only fair because it was his day, though one likes as well to follow and see where a brook goes as to find one's way to the places it comes from, and its tiny springs and headwaters, and in this case trout were not to be considered. William's only real anxiety was lest I might suffer from mosquitoes. His own complexion was still strangely impaired by its defenses, but I kept forgetting it, and looking to see if we were treading fresh pennyroyal underfoot, so efficient was Mrs. Todd's remedy. I was conscious, after we parted, and I turned to see if he were already fishing, and saw him wave his hand gallantly as he went away, that our friendship had made a great gain.

The moment that I began to fish the brook, I had a sense of its emptiness; when my bait first touched the water and went lightly down the quick stream, I knew that there was nothing to lie in wait for it. It is the same certainty that comes when one knocks at the door of an empty house, a lack of answering consciousness and of possible response; it is quite different if there is any life within. But it was a lovely brook, and I went a long way through the woods and breezy open pastures, and found a forsaken house and overgrown farm, and laid up many pleasures for future joy and remembrance. At the end of the morning I came back to our meeting-place hungry and without any fish. William was already waiting, and we did not mention the matter of trout. We ate our luncheons with good appetites, and William brought our two stone bottles of spruce beer from the deep place in the brook where he had left them to cool. Then we sat awhile longer in peace and quietness on the green banks.

As for William, he looked more boyish than ever, and kept a more remote and juvenile sort of silence. Once I wondered how he had come to be so curiously wrinkled, forgetting, absent-mindedly, to recognize the effects of time. He did not expect any one else to keep up a vain show of conversation, and so I was silent as well as he. I glanced at him now and then, but I watched the leaves tossing against the sky and the red cattle moving in the pasture. "I don't know's we need head for home. It's early yet," he said at last, and I was as startled as if one of the gray firs had spoken.

"I guess I'll go up-along and ask after Thankful Hight's folks," he continued. "Mother 'd like to get word;" and I nodded a pleased assent.

IV

William led the way across the pasture, and I followed with a deep sense of pleased anticipation. I do not believe that my companion had expected me to make any objection, but I knew that he was gratified by the easy way that his plans for the day were being seconded. He gave a look at the sky to see if there were any portents, but the sky was frankly blue; even the doubtful morning haze had disappeared.

We went northward along a rough, clayey road, across a barelooking, sunburnt country full of tiresome long slopes where the sun was hot and bright, and I could not help observing the forlorn look of the farms. There was a great deal of pasture, but it looked deserted, and I wondered afresh why the people did not raise more sheep when that seemed the only possible use to make of their land. I said so to Mr. Blackett, who gave me a look of pleased surprise.

"That's what She always maintains," he said eagerly. "She's right about it, too; well, you'll see!" I was glad to find myself approved, but I had not the least idea whom he meant, and waited until he felt like speaking again.

A few minutes later we drove down a steep hill and entered a large tract of dark spruce woods. It was delightful to be sheltered from the afternoon sun, and when we had gone some distance in the shade, to my great pleasure William turned the horse's head toward some bars, which he let down, and I drove through into one of those narrow, still, sweet-scented by-ways which seem to be paths rather than roads. Often we had to put aside the heavy drooping branches which barred the way, and once, when a sharp twig struck William in the face, he announced with such spirit that somebody ought to go through there with an axe, that I felt unexpectedly guilty. So far as I now remember, this was William's only remark all the way through the woods to Thankful Hight's folks, but from time to time he pointed or nodded at something which I might have missed: a sleepy little owl snuggled into the bend of a branch, or a tall stalk of cardinal flowers where the sunlight came down at the edge of a small, bright piece of marsh. Many times, being used to the company of Mrs. Todd and other friends who were in the habit of talking, I came near making an idle remark to William, but I was for the most part happily preserved; to be with him only for a short time was to live on a different level, where thoughts served best because they were thoughts in common; the primary effect upon our minds of the simple things and beauties that we saw. Once when I caught sight of a lovely gay pigeon-woodpecker* eyeing us curiously from a dead branch, and instinctively turned toward William, he gave an indulgent, comprehending nod which silenced me all the rest of the way. The wood-road was not a place for common noisy conversation; one would interrupt the birds and all the still little beasts that belonged there. But it was mortifying to find how strong the habit of idle speech may become in one's self. One need not always be saying something in this noisy world. I grew conscious of the difference between William's usual fashion of life and mine; for him there were long days of silence in a sea-going boat, and I could believe that he and his mother usually spoke very little because they so perfectly understood each other. There was something peculiarly unresponding about their quiet island in the sea, solidly fixed into the still foundations of the world, against whose rocky shores the sea beats and calls and is unanswered.

We were quite half an hour going through the woods; the horse's feet made no sound on the brown, soft track under the dark evergreens. I thought that we should come out at last into more pastures, but there was no half-wooded strip of land at the end; the high woods grew squarely against an old stone wall and a sunshiny open field, and we came out suddenly into broad daylight that startled us and even startled the horse, who might have been napping as he walked, like an old soldier. The field sloped up to a low unpainted house that faced the east. Behind it were long, frost-whitened ledges that made the hill, with strips of green turf

*Folk term for the bird generally known as the flicker.

and bushes between. It was the wildest, most Titanic sort of pasture country up there;* there was a sort of daring in putting a frail wooden house before it, though it might have the homely field and honest woods to front against. You thought of the elements and even of possible volcanoes as you looked up the stony heights. Suddenly I saw that a region of what I had thought gray stones was slowly moving, as if the sun was making my eyesight unsteady.

"There's the sheep!" exclaimed William, pointing eagerly. "You see the sheep?" and sure enough, it was a great company of woolly backs, which seemed to have taken a mysterious protective resemblance to the ledges themselves. I could discover but little chance for pasturage on that high sunburnt ridge, but the sheep were moving steadily in a satisfied way as they fed along the slopes and hollows.

"I never have seen half so many sheep as these, all summer long!" I cried with admiration.

"There ain't so many," answered William soberly. "It's a great sight. They do so well because they're shepherded, but you can't beat sense into some folks."

"You mean that somebody stays and watches them?" I asked.

"She observed years ago in her readin' that they don't turn out their flocks without protection anywhere but in the State o' Maine," returned William. "First thing that put it into her mind was a little old book mother's got; she read it one time when she come out to the Island. They call it the 'Shepherd o' Salisbury Plain.'† 'T wasn't the purpose o' the book to most, but when she read it, 'There, Mis' Blackett!' she said, 'that's where we've all lacked sense; our Bibles ought to have taught us that what sheep need is a shepherd.'‡ You see most folks about here gave up sheep-raisin' years ago 'count o' the dogs. So she gave up school-teachin'

---

*Greek mythology alleged that the Titans were giants; hence, the pasture country is metaphorically suitable for giants.

†This "little old book," widely circulated in nineteenth-century New England, was written in 1795 by Hannah More (1745–1833); it concerned a Christian protagonist who was both devout and wise.

‡Reference to the Bible, John 10:11–14.

and went out to tend her flock, and has shepherded ever since, an' done well."

For William, this approached an oration. He spoke with enthusiasm, and I shared the triumph of the moment. "There she is now!" he exclaimed, in a different tone, as the tall figure of a woman came following the flock and stood still on the ridge, looking toward us as if her eyes had been quick to see a strange object in the familiar emptiness of the field. William stood up in the wagon, and I thought he was going to call or wave his hand to her, but he sat down again more clumsily than if the wagon had made the familiar motion of a boat, and we drove on toward the house.

It was a most solitary place to live—a place where one might think that a life could hide itself. The thick woods were between the farm and the main road, and as one looked up and down the country, there was no other house in sight.

"Potatoes look well," announced William. "The old folks used to say that there wa'n't no better land outdoors than the Hight field."

I found myself possessed of a surprising interest in the shepherdess, who stood far away in the hill pasture with her great flock, like a figure of Millet's,* high against the sky.

V

EVERYTHING ABOUT THE OLD farmhouse was clean and orderly, as if the green door-yard were not only swept, but dusted. I saw a flock of turkeys stepping off carefully at a distance, but there was not the usual untidy flock of hens about the place to make everything look in disarray. William helped me out of the wagon as carefully as if I had been his mother, and nodded toward the open door with a reassuring look at me; but I waited until he had tied the horse and could lead the way, himself. He took off his hat just as we were going in, and stopped for a moment to smooth his thin gray hair with his hand, by which I saw that we had an affair of some ceremony.

---

*Jewett is referring to paintings by French painter Jean-Francois Millet (1814–1875).

We entered an old-fashioned country kitchen, the floor scrubbed into unevenness, and the doors well polished by the touch of hands. In a large chair facing the window there sat a masterful-looking old woman with the features of a warlike Roman emperor, emphasized by a bonnet-like black cap with a band of green ribbon. Her scepter was a palm-leaf fan.

William crossed the room toward her, and bent his head close to her ear.

"Feelin' pretty well to-day, Mis' Hight?" he asked, with all the voice his narrow chest could muster.

"No, I ain't, William. Here I have to set," she answered coldly, but she gave an inquiring glance over his shoulder at me.

"This is the young lady who is stopping with Almiry this summer," he explained, and I approached as if to give the countersign. She offered her left hand with considerable dignity, but her expression never seemed to change for the better. A moment later she said that she was pleased to meet me, and I felt as if the worst were over. William must have felt some apprehension, while I was only ignorant, as we had come across the field. Our hostess was more than disapproving, she was forbidding; but I was not long in suspecting that she felt the natural resentment of a strong energy that has been defeated by illness and made the spoil of captivity.

"Mother well as usual since you was up last year?" and William replied by a series of cheerful nods. The mention of dear Mrs. Blackett was a help to any conversation.

"Been fishin', ashore," he explained, in a somewhat conciliatory voice. "Thought you'd like a few for winter," which explained at once the generous freight we had brought in the back of the wagon. I could see that the offering was no surprise, and that Mrs. Hight was interested.

"Well, I expect they're good as the last," she said, but did not even approach a smile. She kept a straight, discerning eye upon me.

"Give the lady a cheer," she admonished William, who hastened to place close by her side one of the straight-backed chairs that stood against the kitchen wall. Then he lingered for a moment like a timid boy. I could see that he wore a look of resolve, but he did not ask the permission for which he evidently waited.

"You can go search for Esther," she said, at the end of a long pause that became anxious for both her guests. "Esther'd like to see her;" and William in his pale nankeens disappeared with one light step and was off.

VI

"Don't speak too loud, it jars a person's head," directed Mrs. Hight plainly. "Clear an' distinct is what reaches me best. Any news to the Landin'?"

I was happily furnished with the particulars of a sudden death, and an engagement of marriage between a Caplin, a seafaring widower home from his voyage, and one of the younger Harrises; and now Mrs. Hight really smiled and settled herself in her chair. We exhausted one subject completely before we turned to the other. One of the returning turkeys took an unwarrantable liberty, and, mounting the doorstep, came in and walked about the kitchen without being observed by its strict owner; and the tin dipper slipped off its nail behind us and made an astonishing noise, and jar enough to reach Mrs. Hight's inner ear and make her turn her head to look at it; but we talked straight on. We came at last to understand each other upon such terms of friendship that she unbent her majestic port and complained to me as any poor old woman might of the hardships of her illness. She had already fixed various dates upon the sad certainty of the year when she had the shock, which had left her perfectly helpless except for a clumsy left hand which fanned and gestured, and settled and resettled the folds of her dress, but could do no comfortable time-shortening work.

"Yes'm, you can feel sure I use it what I can," she said severely. "'T was a long spell before I could let Esther go forth in the mornin' till she'd got me up an' dressed me, but now she leaves things ready overnight and I get 'em as I want 'em with my light pair o' tongs, and I feel very able about helpin' myself to what I once did. Then when Esther returns, all she has to do is to push out here into the kitchen. Some parts o' the year Esther stays out all night, them moonlight nights when the dogs are apt to be after the sheep, but she don't use herself as hard as she once had to. She's well able to

hire somebody, Esther is, but there, you can't find no hired man that wants to git up before five o'clock nowadays; 't ain't as 't was in my time. They're liable to fall asleep, too, and them moonlight nights she's so anxious she can't sleep, and out she goes. There's a kind of a fold, she calls it, up there in a sheltered spot, and she sleeps up in a little shed she's got—built it herself for lambin' time and when the poor foolish creatur's gets hurt or anything. I've never seen it, but she says it's in a lovely spot and always pleasant in any weather. You see off, other side of the ridge, to the south'ard, where there's houses. I used to think some time I'd get up to see it again, and all them spots she lives in, but I sha'nt now. I'm beginnin' to go back; an' 't ain't surprisin'. I've kind of got used to disappointments," and the poor soul drew a deep sigh.

VII

It was long before we noticed the lapse of time; I not only told every circumstance known to me of recent events among the households of Mrs. Todd's neighborhood at the shore, but Mrs. Hight became more and more communicative on her part, and went carefully into the genealogical descent and personal experience of many acquaintances, until between us we had pretty nearly circumnavigated the globe and reached Dunnet Landing from an opposite direction to that in which we had started. It was long before my own interest began to flag; there was a flavor of the best sort in her definite and descriptive fashion of speech. It may be only a fancy of my own that in the sound and value of many words, with their lengthened vowels and doubled cadences, there is some faint survival on the Maine coast of the sound of English speech of Chaucer's time.*

At last Mrs. Thankful Hight gave a suspicious look through the window.

"Where do you suppose they be?" she asked me. "Esther must ha' been off to the far edge o' everything. I doubt William ain't been able to find her; can't he hear their bells? His hearin' all right?"

---

*English poet Geoffrey Chaucer lived from around 1342 to 1400.

William had heard some herons that morning which were beyond the reach of my own ears, and almost beyond eyesight in the upper skies, and I told her so. I was luckily preserved by some unconscious instinct from saying that we had seen the shepherdess so near as we crossed the field. Unless she had fled faster than Atalanta,* William must have been but a few minutes in reaching her immediate neighborhood. I now discovered with a quick leap of amusement and delight in my heart that I had fallen upon a serious chapter of romance. The old woman looked suspiciously at me, and I made a dash to cover with a new piece of information; but she listened with lofty indifference, and soon interrupted my eager statements.

"Ain't William been gone some considerable time?" she demanded, and then in a milder tone: "The time has re'lly flown; I do enjoy havin' company. I set here alone a sight o' long days. Sheep is dreadful fools; I expect they heard a strange step, and set right off through bush an' brier, spite of all she could do. But William might have the sense to return, 'stead o' searchin' about. I want to inquire of him about his mother. What was you goin' to say? I guess you'll have time to relate it."

My powers of entertainment were on the ebb, but I doubled my diligence and we went on for another half-hour at least with banners flying, but still William did not reappear. Mrs. Hight frankly began to show fatigue.

"Somethin' 's happened, an' he's stopped to help her," groaned the old lady, in the middle of what I had found to tell her about a rumor of disaffection with the minister of a town I merely knew by name in the weekly newspaper to which Mrs. Todd subscribed. "You step to the door, dear, an' look if you can't see 'em." I promptly stepped, and once outside the house I looked anxiously in the direction which William had taken.

To my astonishment I saw all the sheep so near that I wonder we had not been aware in the house of every bleat and tinkle. And there, within a stone's-throw, on the first long gray ledge that showed above the juniper, were William and the shepherdess engaged in

*In Roman mythology, the heroine Atalanta, rejected by her father, was raised by hunters to be fast and strong; as an adult, she vowed to marry only that man who could out-race her.

pleasant conversation. At first I was provoked and then amused, and a thrill of sympathy warmed my whole heart. They had seen me and risen as if by magic; I had a sense of being the messenger of Fate. One could almost hear their sighs of regret as I appeared; they must have passed a lovely afternoon. I hurried into the house with the reassuring news that they were not only in sight but perfectly safe, with all the sheep.

VIII

Mrs. Hight, like myself, was spent with conversation, and had ceased even the one activity of fanning herself. I brought a desired drink of water, and happily remembered some fruit that was left from my luncheon. She revived with splendid vigor, and told me the simple history of her later years since she had been smitten in the prime of her life by the stroke of paralysis, and her husband had died and left her alone with Esther and a mortgage on their farm. There was only one field of good land, but they owned a great region of sheep pasture and a little woodland. Esther had always been laughed at for her belief in sheep-raising when one by one their neighbors were giving up their flocks, and when everything had come to the point of despair she had raised all the money and bought all the sheep she could, insisting that Maine lambs were as good as any, and that there was a straight path by sea to Boston market. And by tending her flock herself she had managed to succeed; she had made money enough to pay off the mortgage five years ago, and now what they did not spend was safe in the bank. "It has been stubborn work, day and night, summer and winter, an' now she's beginnin' to get along in years," said the old mother sadly. "She's tended me 'long o' the sheep, an' she's been a good girl right along, but she ought to have been a teacher;" and Mrs. Hight sighed heavily and plied the fan again.

We heard voices, and William and Esther entered; they did not know that it was so late in the afternoon. William looked almost bold, and oddly like a happy young man rather than an ancient boy. As for Esther, she might have been Jeanne d'Arc* returned to her sheep,

*That is, Joan of Arc (c.1412–1431).

touched with age and gray with the ashes of a great remembrance. She wore the simple look of sainthood and unfeigned devotion. My heart was moved by the sight of her plain sweet face, weather-worn and gentle in its looks, her thin figure in its close dress, and the strong hand that clasped a shepherd's staff, and I could only hold William in new reverence; this silent farmer-fisherman who knew, and he alone, the noble and patient heart that beat within her breast. I am not sure that they acknowledged even to themselves that they had always been lovers; they could not consent to anything so definite or pronounced; but they were happy in being together in the world. Esther was untouched by the fret and fury of life; she had lived in sunshine and rain among her silly sheep, and been refined instead of coarsened, while her touching patience with a ramping* old mother, stung by the sense of defeat and mourning her lost activities, had given back a lovely self-possession, and habit of sweet temper. I had seen enough of old Mrs. Hight to know that nothing a sheep might do could vex a person who was used to the uncertainties and severities of her companionship.

IX

Mrs. Hight told her daughter at once that she had enjoyed a beautiful call, and got a great many new things to think of. This was said so frankly in my hearing that it gave a consciousness of high reward, and I was indeed recompensed by the grateful look in Esther's eyes. We did not speak much together, but we understood each other. For the poor old woman did not read, and could not sew or knit with her helpless hand, and they were far from any neighbors, while her spirit was as eager in age as in youth, and expected even more from a disappointing world. She had lived to see the mortgage paid and money in the bank, and Esther's success acknowledged on every hand, and there were still a few pleasures left in life. William had his mother, and Esther had hers, and they had not seen each other for a year, though Mrs. Hight had spoken of a year's making

---

*Colloquialism; possibly a variation of the word *rampaging*.

no change in William even at his age. She must have been in the far eighties herself, but of a noble courage and persistence in the world she ruled from her stiff-backed rocking-chair.

William unloaded his gift of dried fish, each one chosen with perfect care, and Esther stood by, watching him, and then she walked across the field with us beside the wagon. I believed that I was the only one who knew their happy secret, and she blushed a little as we said good-by.

"I hope you ain't goin' to feel too tired, mother's so deaf; no, I hope you won't be tired," she said kindly, speaking as if she well knew what tiredness was. We could hear the neglected sheep bleating on the hill in the next moment's silence. Then she smiled at me, a smile of noble patience, of uncomprehended sacrifice, which I can never forget. There was all the remembrance of disappointed hopes, the hardships of winter, the loneliness of single-handedness in her look, but I understood, and I love to remember her worn face and her young blue eyes.

"Good-by, William," she said gently, and William said good-by, and gave her a quick glance, but he did not turn to look back, though I did, and waved my hand as she was putting up the bars behind us. Nor did he speak again until we had passed through the dark woods and were on our way homeward by the main road. The grave yearly visit had been changed from a hope into a happy memory.

"You can see the sea from the top of her pasture hill," said William at last.

"Can you?" I asked, with surprise.

"Yes, it's very high land; the ledges up there show very plain in clear weather from the top of our island, and there's a high upstandin' tree that makes a landmark for the fishin' grounds." And William gave a happy sigh.

When we had nearly reached the Landing, my companion looked over into the back of the wagon and saw that the piece of sailcloth was safe, with which he had covered the dried fish. "I wish we had got some trout," he said wistfully. "They always appease Almiry, and make her feel 't was worth while to go."

I stole a glance at William Blackett. We had not seen a solitary mosquito, but there was a dark stripe across his mild face, which might have been an old scar won long ago in battle.

THE FOREIGNER

I

One evening, at the end of August, in Dunnet Landing, I heard Mrs. Todd's firm footstep crossing the small front entry outside my door, and her conventional cough which served as a herald's trumpet, or a plain New England knock, in the harmony of our fellowship.

"Oh, please come in!" I cried, for it had been so still in the house that I supposed my friend and hostess had gone to see one of her neighbors. The first cold northeasterly storm of the season was blowing hard outside. Now and then there was a dash of great raindrops and a flick of wet lilac leaves against the window, but I could hear that the sea was already stirred to its dark depths, and the great rollers were coming in heavily against the shore. One might well believe that Summer was coming to a sad end that night, in the darkness and rain and sudden access of autumnal cold. It seemed as if there must be danger offshore among the outer islands.

"Oh, there!" exclaimed Mrs. Todd, as she entered. "I know nothing ain't ever happened out to Green Island since the world began, but I always do worry about mother in these great gales. You know those tidal waves occur sometimes down to the West Indies, and I get dwellin' on 'em so I can't set still in my chair, nor knit a common row to a stocking. William might get mooning, out in his small bo't, and not observe how the sea was making, an' meet with some accident. Yes, I thought I'd come in and set with you if you wa'n't busy. No, I never feel any concern about 'em in winter 'cause then they're prepared, and all ashore and everything snug. William ought to keep help, as I tell him; yes, he ought to keep help."

I hastened to reassure my anxious guest by saying that Elijah Tilley had told me in the afternoon, when I came along the shore past the fishhouses, that Johnny Bowden and the Captain were out at Green Island; he had seen them beating up the bay, and thought they must have put into Burnt Island cove, but one of the lobstermen brought word later that he saw them hauling out at Green Island as he came by, and Captain Bowden pointed ashore and shook his head to say that he did not mean to try to get in. "The old Miranda just managed it, but she will have to stay at home a day or two and put new patches in her sail," I ended, not without pride in so much circumstantial evidence.

Mrs. Todd was alert in a moment. "Then they'll all have a very pleasant evening," she assured me, apparently dismissing all fears of tidal waves and other seagoing disasters. "I was urging Alick Bowden to go ashore some day and see mother before cold weather. He's her own nephew; she sets a great deal by him. And Johnny's a great chum o' William's; don't you know the first day we had Johnny out 'long of us, he took an' give William his money to keep for him that he'd been a-savin', and William showed it to me an' was so affected I thought he was goin' to shed tears? 'T was a dollar an' eighty cents; yes, they'll have a beautiful evenin' all together, and like's not the sea'll be flat as a doorstep come morning."

I had drawn a large wooden rocking-chair before the fire, and Mrs. Todd was sitting there jogging herself a little, knitting fast, and wonderfully placid of countenance. There came a fresh gust of wind and rain, and we could feel the small wooden house rock and hear it creak as if it were a ship at sea.

"Lord, hear the great breakers!" exclaimed Mrs. Todd. "How they pound!—there, there! I always run of an idea that the sea knows anger these nights and gets full o' fight. I can hear the rote* o' them old black ledges way down the thoroughfare. Calls up all those stormy verses in the Book o' Psalms;† David he knew how old seagoin' folks have to quake at the heart."

I thought as I had never thought before of such anxieties. The families of sailors and coastwise adventurers by sea must always be worrying about somebody, this side of the world or the other. There was hardly one of Mrs. Todd's elder acquaintances, men or women, who had not at some time or other made a sea voyage, and there was often no news until the voyagers themselves came back to bring it.

"There's a roaring high overhead, and a roaring in the deep sea," said Mrs. Todd solemnly, "and they battle together nights like this.

---

*Sound of the surf pounding against the shore.

†Reference to the Bible, Psalms 55.

No, I couldn't sleep; some women folks always goes right to bed an' to sleep, so's to forget, but 't ain't my way. Well, it's a blessin' we don't feel alike; there's hardly any of our folks at sea to worry about, nowadays, but I can't help my feelin's, an' I got thinking of mother all alone, if William had happened to be out lobsterin' and couldn't make the cove gettin' back."

"They will have a pleasant evening," I repeated. "Captain Bowden is the best of good company."

"Mother'll make him some pancakes for his supper, like's not," said Mrs. Todd, clicking her knitting needles and giving a pull at her yarn. Just then the old cat pushed open the unlatched door and came straight toward her mistress's lap. She was regarded severely as she stepped about and turned on the broad expanse, and then made herself into a round cushion of fur, but was not openly admonished. There was another great blast of wind overhead, and a puff of smoke came down the chimney.

"This makes me think o' the night Mis' Cap'n Tolland died," said Mrs. Todd, half to herself. "Folks used to say these gales only blew when somebody's a-dyin', or the devil was a-comin' for his own, but the worst man I ever knew died a real pretty mornin' in June."

"You have never told me any ghost stories," said I; and such was the gloomy weather and the influence of the night that I was instantly filled with reluctance to have this suggestion followed. I had not chosen the best of moments; just before I spoke we had begun to feel as cheerful as possible. Mrs. Todd glanced doubtfully at the cat and then at me, with a strange absent look, and I was really afraid that she was going to tell me something that would haunt my thoughts on every dark stormy night as long as I lived.

"Never mind now; tell me to-morrow by daylight, Mrs. Todd," I hastened to say, but she still looked at me full of doubt and deliberation.

"Ghost stories!" she answered. "Yes, I don't know but I've heard a plenty of 'em first an' last. I was just sayin' to myself that this is like the night Mis' Cap'n Tolland died. 'T was the great line storm*

---

*A tropical storm often occurring on or around the autumnal equinox.

in September all of thirty, or maybe forty, year ago. I ain't one that keeps much account o' time."

"Tolland? That's a name I have never heard in Dunnet," I said.

"Then you haven't looked well about the old part o' the buryin' ground, no'theast corner," replied Mrs. Todd. "All their women folks lies there; the sea's got most o' the men. They were a known family o' shipmasters in early times. Mother had a mate, Ellen Tolland, that she mourns to this day; died right in her bloom with quick consumption, but the rest o' that family was all boys but one, and older than she, an' they lived hard seafarin' lives an' all died hard. They were called very smart seamen. I've heard that when the youngest went into one o' the old shippin' houses in Boston, the head o' the firm called out to him: 'Did you say Tolland from Dunnet? That's recommendation enough for any vessel!' There was some o' them old shipmasters as tough as iron, an' they had the name o' usin' their crews very severe, but there wa'n't a man that wouldn't rather sign with 'em an' take his chances, than with the slack ones that didn't know how to meet accidents."

II

THERE WAS SO LONG a pause, and Mrs. Todd still looked so absent-minded, that I was afraid she and the cat were growing drowsy together before the fire, and I should have no reminiscences at all. The wind struck the house again, so that we both started in our chairs and Mrs. Todd gave a curious, startled look at me. The cat lifted her head and listened too, in the silence that followed, while after the wind sank we were more conscious than ever of the awful roar of the sea. The house jarred now and then, in a strange, disturbing way.

"Yes, they'll have a beautiful evening out to the island," said Mrs. Todd again; but she did not say it gayly. I had not seen her before in her weaker moments.

"Who was Mrs. Captain Tolland?" I asked eagerly, to change the current of our thoughts.

"I never knew her maiden name; if I ever heard it, I've gone an' forgot; 't would mean nothing to me," answered Mrs. Todd.

"She was a foreigner, an' he met with her out in the Island o' Jamaica. They said she'd been left a widow with property. Land knows what become of it; she was French born, an' her first husband was a Portugee, or somethin'."

I kept silence now, a poor and insufficient question being worse than none.

"Cap'n John Tolland was the least smartest of any of 'em, but he was full smart enough, an' commanded a good brig at the time, in the sugar trade; he'd taken out a cargo o' pine lumber to the islands from somewheres up the river, an' had been loadin' for home in the port o' Kingston, an' had gone ashore that afternoon for his papers, an' remained afterwards 'long of three friends o' his, all shipmasters. They was havin' their suppers together in a tavern; 't was late in the evenin' an' they was more lively than usual, an' felt boyish; and over opposite was another house full o' company, real bright and pleasant lookin', with a lot o' lights, an' they heard somebody singin' very pretty to a guitar. They wa'n't in no go-to-meetin' condition, an' one of 'em, he slapped the table an' said, 'Le' 's go over an' hear that lady sing!' an' over they all went, good honest sailors, but three sheets in the wind, and stepped in as if they was invited, an' made their bows inside the door, an' asked if they could hear the music; they were all respectable well-dressed men. They saw the woman that had the guitar, an' there was a company a-listenin', regular highbinders* all of 'em; an' there was a long table all spread out with big candlesticks like little trees o' light, and a sight o' glass an' silver ware; an' part o' the men was young officers in uniform, an' the colored folks was steppin' round servin' 'em, an' they had the lady singin'. 'T was a wasteful scene, an' a loud talkin' company, an' though they was three sheets in the wind themselves there wa'n't one o' them cap'ns but had sense to perceive it. The others had pushed back their chairs, an' their decanters an' glasses was standin' thick about, an' they was teasin' the one that was singin' as if they'd just got her in to amuse 'em. But they quieted down; one o' the young officers had beautiful manners, an' invited the four cap'ns to join 'em, very polite; 't was a kind of public house, and after they'd all heard another song, he

*Group of people who behave badly.

come to consult with 'em whether they wouldn't git up and dance a hornpipe or somethin' to the lady's music.

"They was all elderly men an' shipmasters, and owned property; two of 'em was church members in good standin'," continued Mrs. Todd loftily, "an' they wouldn't lend theirselves to no such kick-shows* as that, an' spite o' bein' three sheets in the wind, as I have once observed; they waved aside the tumblers of wine the young officer was pourin' out for 'em so freehanded, and said they should rather be excused. An' when they all rose, still very dignified, as I've been well informed, and made their partin' bows and was goin' out, them young sports got round 'em an' tried to prevent 'em, and they had to push an' strive considerable, but out they come. There was this Cap'n Tolland and two Cap'n Bowdens, and the fourth was my own father." (Mrs. Todd spoke slowly, as if to impress the value of her authority.) "Two of them was very religious, upright men, but they would have their night off sometimes, all o' them old-fashioned cap'ns, when they was free of business and ready to leave port.

"An' they went back to their tavern an' got their bills paid, an' set down kind o' mad with everybody by the front windows, mistrusting some o' their tavern charges, like's not, by that time, an' when they got tempered down, they watched the house over across, where the party was.

"There was a kind of a grove o' trees between the house an' the road, an' they heard the guitar a-goin' an' a-stoppin' short by turns, and pretty soon somebody began to screech, an' they saw a white dress come runnin' out through the bushes, an' tumbled over each other in their haste to offer help; an' out she come, with the guitar, cryin' into the street, and they just walked off four square with her amongst 'em, down toward the wharves where they felt more to home. They couldn't make out at first what 't was she spoke—Cap'n Lorenzo Bowden was well acquainted in Havre† an' Bordeaux, an' spoke a poor quality o' French, an' she knew a little mite o' English, but not much; and they come somehow or other

---

*Kickshaws: trifles, tidbits.

†Le Havre, a seaport in northern France.

to discern that she was in real distress. Her husband and her children had died o' yellow fever; they'd all come up to Kingston from one o' the far Wind'ard Islands* to get passage on a steamer to France, an' a negro had stole their money off her husband while he lay sick o' the fever, an' she had been befriended some, but the folks that knew about her had died too; it had been a dreadful run o' the fever that season, an' she fell at last to playin' an' singin' for hire, and for what money they'd throw to her round them harbor houses.

"'T was a real hard case, an' when them cap'ns made out about it, there wa'n't one that meant to take leave without helpin' of her. They was pretty mellow, an' whatever they might lack o' prudence they more'n made up with charity: they didn't want to see nobody abused, an' she was sort of a pretty woman, an' they stopped in the street then an' there an' drew lots who should take her aboard, bein' all bound home. An' the lot fell to Cap'n Jonathan Bowden who did act discouraged; his vessel had but small accommodations, though he could stow a big freight, an' she was a dreadful slow sailer through bein' square as a box, an' his first wife, that was livin' then, was a dreadful jealous woman. He threw himself right onto the mercy o' Cap'n Tolland."

Mrs. Todd indulged herself for a short time in a season of calm reflection.

"I always thought they'd have done better, and more reasonable, to give her some money to pay her passage home to France, or wherever she may have wanted to go," she continued.

I nodded and looked for the rest of the story.

"Father told mother," said Mrs. Todd confidentially, "that Cap'n Jonathan Bowden an' Cap'n John Tolland had both taken a little more than usual; I wouldn't have you think, either, that they both wasn't the best o' men, an' they was solemn as owls, and argued the matter between 'em, an' waved aside the other two when they tried to put their oars in. An' spite o' Cap'n Tolland's bein' a settled old bachelor they fixed it that he was to take the prize on his brig; she

---

*The Windward Islands are located in the southern part of the Lesser Antilles in the West Indies.

was a fast sailer, and there was a good spare cabin or two where he'd sometimes carried passengers, but he'd filled 'em with bags o' sugar on his own account an' was loaded very heavy beside. He said he'd shift the sugar an' get along somehow, an' the last the other three cap'ns saw of the party was Cap'n John handing the lady into his bo't, guitar and all, an' off they all set tow'ds their ships with their men rowin' 'em in the bright moonlight down to Port Royal where the anchorage was, an' where they all lay, goin' out with the tide an mornin' wind at break o' day. An' the others thought they heard music of the guitar, two o' the bo'ts kept well together, but it may have come from another source."

"Well; and then?" I asked eagerly after a pause. Mrs. Todd was almost laughing aloud over her knitting and nodding emphatically. We had forgotten all about the noise of the wind and sea.

"Lord bless you! he come sailing into Portland with his sugar, all in good time, an' they stepped right afore a justice o' the peace, and Cap'n John Tolland come paradin' home to Dunnet Landin' a married man. He owned one o' them thin, narrow-lookin' houses with one room each side o' the front door, and two slim black spruce spindlin' up against the front windows to make it gloomy inside. There was no horse nor cattle of course, though he owned pasture land, an' you could see rifts o' light right through the barn as you drove by. And there was a good excellent kitchen, but his sister reigned over that; she had a right to two rooms, and took the kitchen an' a bedroom that led out of it; an' bein' given no rights in the kitchen had angered the cap'n so they weren't on no kind o' speakin' terms. He preferred his old brig for comfort, but now and then, between voyages, he'd come home for a few days, just to show he was master over his part o' the house, and show Eliza she couldn't commit no trespass.

"They stayed a little while; 't was pretty spring weather, an' I used to see Cap'n John rollin' by with his arms full o' bundles from the store, lookin' as pleased and important as a boy; an' then they went right off to sea again, an' was gone a good many months. Next time he left her to live there alone, after they'd stopped at home together some weeks, an' they said she suffered from bein' at sea, but some said that the owners wouldn't have a woman aboard. 'T was before father was lost on that last voyage of his, an' he and mother went up once or twice to see them. Father said there wa'n't a mite o' harm in her, but somehow or other a sight o' prejudice arose; it may have been caused by remarks of Eliza an' her feelin's tow'ds her brother. Even my mother had no regard for Eliza Tolland. But mother asked the cap'n's wife to come with her one evenin' to a social circle that was down to the meetin'house vestry, so she'd get acquainted a little, an' she appeared very pretty until they started to have some singin' to the melodeon. Mari' Harris an' one o' the younger Caplin girls undertook to sing a duet, an' they sort o' flatted, an' she put her hands right up to her ears, and give a little squeal, an' went quick as could be an' give 'em the right notes, for she could read the music like plain print, an' made 'em try it over again. She was real willin' an' pleasant, but that didn't suit, an' she made faces when they got it wrong. An' then there fell a dead calm, an' we was all settin' round prim as dishes, an' my mother, that never expects ill feelin', asked her if she wouldn't sing somethin', an' up she got—poor creatur', it all seems so different to me now—an' sung a lovely little song standin' in the floor; it seemed to have something gay about it that kept a-repeatin', an' nobody could help keepin' time, an' all of a sudden she looked round at the tables and caught up a tin plate that somebody's fetched a Washin'ton pie* in, an' she begun to drum on it with her fingers like one o' them tambourines, an' went right on singin' faster an' faster, and next minute she began to dance a little pretty dance between the verses, just as light and pleasant as a child. You couldn't help seein' how pretty 't was; we all got to trottin' a foot, an' some o' the men clapped their hands quite loud, a-keepin' time, 't was so catchin', an' seemed so natural to her. There wa'n't one of 'em but enjoyed it; she just tried to do her part, an' some urged her on, till she stopped with a little twirl of her skirts an' went to her place again by mother. And I can see mother now, reachin' over an' smilin' an' pattin' her hand.

"But next day there was an awful scandal goin' in the parish, an' Mari' Harris reproached my mother to her face, an' I never wanted to see her since, but I've had to a good many times. I said Mis'

---

*Washington pie is made by alternating cake layers with fruit filling.

Tolland didn't intend no impropriety—I reminded her of David's dancin' before the Lord;* but she said such a man as David never would have thought o' dancin' right there in the Orthodox† vestry, and she felt I spoke with irreverence.

"And next Sunday Mis' Tolland came walkin' into our meeting, but I must say she acted like a cat in a strange garret, and went right down the aisle with her head in the air, from the pew Deacon Caplin had showed her into. 'T was just in the beginning of the long prayer. I wished she'd stayed through, whatever her reasons were. Whether she'd expected somethin' different, or misunderstood some o' the pastor's remarks, or what 't was, I don't really feel able to explain, but she kind o' declared war, at least folks thought so, an' war 't was from that time. I see she was cryin', or had been, as she passed by me; perhaps bein' in meetin' was what had power to make her feel homesick and strange.

"Cap'n John Tolland was away fittin' out; that next week he come home to see her and say farewell. He was lost with his ship in the Straits of Malacca,‡ and she lived there alone in the old house a few months longer till she died. He left her well off; 't was said he hid his money about the house and she knew where 't was. Oh, I expect you've heard that story told over an' over twenty times, since you've been here at the Landin'?"

"Never one word," I insisted.

"It was a good while ago," explained Mrs. Todd, with reassurance. "Yes, it all happened a great while ago."

III

At this moment, with a sudden flaw of the wind, some wet twigs outside blew against the window panes and made a noise like a distressed creature trying to get in. I started with sudden fear, and so

---

*Based on the Bible, 2 Samuel 6:14 (King James Version, henceforth KJV): "And David danced before the Lord with all his might."

†Probably a reference to the Congregationalist denomination.

‡Situated between Sumatra and the Malay Peninsula, joining the South China Sea and the Indian Ocean.

did the cat, but Mrs. Todd knitted away and did not even look over her shoulder.

"She was a good-looking woman; yes, I always thought Mis' Tolland was good-looking, though she had, as was reasonable, a sort of foreign cast, and she spoke very broken English, no better than a child. She was always at work about her house, or settin' at a front window with her sewing; she was a beautiful hand to embroider. Sometimes, summer evenings, when the windows was open, she'd set an' drum on her guitar, but I don't know as I ever heard her sing but once after the cap'n went away. She appeared very happy about havin' him, and took on dreadful at partin' when he was down here on the wharf, going back to Portland by boat to take ship for that last v'y'ge. He acted kind of ashamed, Cap'n John did; folks about here ain't so much accustomed to show their feelings. The whistle had blown an' they was waitin' for him to get aboard, an' he was put to it to know what to do and treated her very affectionate in spite of all impatience; but mother happened to be there and she went an' spoke, and I remember what a comfort she seemed to be. Mis' Tolland clung to her then, and she wouldn't give a glance after the boat when it started, though the captain was very eager a-wavin' to her. She wanted mother to come home with her an' wouldn't let go her hand, and mother had just come in to stop all night with me an' had plenty o' time ashore, which didn't always happen, so they walked off together, an' 't was some considerable time before she got back.

"'I want you to neighbor with that poor lonesome creatur',' says mother to me, lookin' reproachful. 'She's a stranger in a strange land,'* says mother. 'I want you to make her have a sense that somebody feels kind to her.'

"'Why, since that time she flaunted out o' meetin', folks have felt she liked other ways better'n our'n,' says I. I was provoked, because I'd had a nice supper ready, an' mother'd let it wait so long 't was spoiled. 'I hope you'll like your supper!' I told her. I was dreadful ashamed afterward of speakin' so to mother.

*From the Bible, Exodus 2:22 (KJV).

"'What consequence is my supper?' says she to me; mother can be very stern—'or your comfort or mine, beside letting a foreign person an' a stranger feel so desolate; she's done the best a woman could do in her lonesome place, and she asks nothing of anybody except a little common kindness. Think if 't was you in a foreign land!'

"And mother set down to drink her tea, an' I set down humbled enough over by the wall to wait till she finished. An' I did think it all over, an' next day I never said nothin', but I put on my bonnet, and went to see Mis' Cap'n Tolland, if 't was only for mother's sake. 'T was about three quarters of a mile up the road here, beyond the schoolhouse. I forgot to tell you that the cap'n had bought out his sister's right at three or four times what 't was worth, to save trouble, so they'd got clear o' her, an' I went round into the side yard sort o' friendly an' sociable, rather than stop an' deal with the knocker an' the front door. It looked so pleasant an' pretty I was glad I come; she had set a little table for supper, though 't was still early, with a white cloth on it, right out under an old apple tree close by the house. I noticed 't was same as with me at home, there was only one plate. She was just coming out with a dish; you couldn't see the door nor the table from the road.

"In the few weeks she'd been there she'd got some bloomin' pinks an' other flowers next the doorstep. Somehow it looked as if she'd known how to make it homelike for the cap'n. She asked me to set down; she was very polite, but she looked very mournful, and I spoke of mother, an' she put down her dish and caught holt o' me with both hands an' said my mother was an angel. When I see the tears in her eyes 't was all right between us, and we were always friendly after that, and mother had us come out and make a little visit that summer; but she come a foreigner and she went a foreigner, and never was anything but a stranger among our folks. She taught me a sight o' things about herbs I never knew before nor since; she was well acquainted with the virtues o' plants. She'd act awful secret about some things too, an' used to work charms for herself sometimes, an' some o' the neighbors told to an' fro after she died that they knew enough not to provoke her, but 't was all nonsense; 't is the believin' in such things that causes 'em to be any harm, an' so I told 'em," confided Mrs. Todd contemptuously. "That first night I stopped to tea with her she'd cooked some eggs with some herb or other sprinkled all through, and 't was she that first led me to discern mushrooms; an' she went right down on her knees in my garden here when she saw I had my different officious* herbs. Yes, 't was she that learned me the proper use o' parsley too; she was a beautiful cook."

Mrs. Todd stopped talking, and rose, putting the cat gently in the chair, while she went away to get another stick of apple-tree wood. It was not an evening when one wished to let the fire go down, and we had a splendid bank of bright coals. I had always wondered where Mrs. Todd had got such an unusual knowledge of cookery, of the varieties of mushrooms, and the use of sorrel as a vegetable, and other blessings of that sort. I had long ago learned that she could vary her omelettes like a child of France, which was indeed a surprise in Dunnet Landing.

IV

All these revelations were of the deepest interest, and I was ready with a question as soon as Mrs. Todd came in and had well settled the fire and herself and the cat again.

"I wonder why she never went back to France, after she was left alone?"

"She come here from the French islands," explained Mrs. Todd. "I asked her once about her folks, an' she said they were all dead; 't was the fever took 'em. She made this her home, lonesome as 't was; she told me she hadn't been in France since she was 'so small,' and measured me off a child o' six. She'd lived right out in the country before, so that part wa'n't unusual to her. Oh yes, there was something very strange about her, and she hadn't been brought up in high circles nor nothing o' that kind. I think she'd been really pleased to have the cap'n marry her an' give her a good home, after all she'd passed through, and leave her free with his money an' all that. An' she got over bein' so strange-looking to me after a while,

*That is, helpful.

but 't was a very singular expression: she wore a fixed smile that wa'n't a smile; there wa'n't no light behind it, same's a lamp can't shine if it ain't lit. I don't know just how to express it, 't was a sort of made countenance."

One could not help thinking of Sir Philip Sidney's phrase.* "A made countenance, between simpering and smiling."

"She took it hard, havin' the captain go off on that last voyage," Mrs. Todd went on. "She said somethin' told her when they was partin' that he would never come back. He was lucky to speak a home-bound ship this side o' the Cape o' Good Hope, an' got a chance to send her a letter, an' that cheered her up. You often felt as if you was dealin' with a child's mind, for all she had so much information that other folks hadn't. I was a sight younger than I be now, and she made me imagine new things, and I got interested watchin' her an' findin' out what she had to say, but you couldn't get to no affectionateness with her. I used to blame me sometimes; we used to be real good comrades goin' off for an afternoon, but I never gave her a kiss till the day she laid in her coffin and it come to my heart there wa'n't no one else to do it."

"And Captain Tolland died," I suggested after a while.

"Yes, the cap'n was lost," said Mrs. Todd, "and of course word didn't come for a good while after it happened. The letter come from the owners to my uncle, Cap'n Lorenzo Bowden, who was in charge of Cap'n Tolland's affairs at home, and he come right up for me an' said I must go with him to the house. I had known what it was to be a widow, myself, for near a year, an' there was plenty o' widow women along this coast that the sea had made desolate, but I never saw a heart break as I did then.

" 'T was this way: we walked together along the road, me an' uncle Lorenzo. You know how it leads straight from just above the schoolhouse to the brook bridge, and their house was just this side o' the brook bridge on the left hand; the cellar's there now, and a couple or three good-sized gray birches growin' in it. And when we come near enough I saw that the best room, this way, where she most never set, was all lighted up, and the curtains up so that the

---

*From book 1 of Sidney's *New Arcadia* (c.1583–1584).

light shone bright down the road, and as we walked, those lights would dazzle and dazzle in my eyes, and I could hear the guitar a-goin', an' she was singin'. She heard our steps with her quick ears and come running to the door with her eyes a-shinin', an' all that set look gone out of her face, an' begun to talk French, gay as a bird, an' shook hands and behaved very pretty an' girlish, sayin' 't was her fête day.* I didn't know what she meant then. And she had gone an' put a wreath o' flowers on her hair an' wore a handsome gold chain that the cap'n had given her; an' there she was, poor creatur', makin' believe have a party all alone in her best room; 't was prim enough to discourage a person, with too many chairs set close to the walls, just as the cap'n's mother had left it, but she had put sort o' long garlands on the walls, droopin' very graceful, and a sight of green boughs in the corners, till it looked lovely, and all lit up with a lot o' candles."

"Oh dear!" I sighed. "Oh, Mrs. Todd, what did you do?"

"She beheld our countenances," answered Mrs. Todd solemnly. "I expect they was telling everything plain enough, but Cap'n Lorenzo spoke the sad words to her as if he had been her father; and she wavered a minute and then over she went on the floor before we could catch hold of her, and then we tried to bring her to herself and failed, and at last we carried her upstairs, an' I told uncle to run down and put out the lights, and then go fast as he could for Mrs. Begg, being very experienced in sickness, an' he so did. I got off her clothes and her poor wreath, and cried as I done it. We both stayed there that night and the doctor said 't was a shock† when he come in the morning; he'd been over to Black Island an' had to stay all night with a very sick child."

"You said that she lived alone some time after the news came," I reminded Mrs. Todd then.

"Oh yes, dear," answered my friend sadly, "but it wa'n't what you'd call livin'; no, it was only dyin', though at a snail's pace. She never went out again those few months, but for a while she could

---

*In a Catholic tradition, a feast (*fête* in French) day commemorates the day a saint died; on that day, an individual named after that saint celebrates his "name day"—often considered a more important day than the natural birthday.

†Stroke.

manage to get about the house a little, and do what she needed, an' I never let two days go by without seein' her or hearin' from her. She never took much notice as I came an' went except to answer if I asked her anything. Mother was the one who gave her the only comfort."

"What was that?" I asked softly.

"She said that anybody in such trouble ought to see their minister, mother did, and one day she spoke to Mis' Tolland, and found that the poor soul had been believin' all the time that there weren't any priests here. We'd come to know she was a Catholic by her beads* and all, and that had set some narrow minds against her. And mother explained it just as she would to a child; and uncle Lorenzo sent word right off somewheres up river by a packet that was bound up the bay, and the first o' the week a priest come by the boat, an' uncle Lorenzo was on the wharf 'tendin' to some business; so they just come up for me, and I walked with him to show him the house. He was a kind-hearted old man; he looked so benevolent an' fatherly I could ha' stopped an' told him my own troubles; yes, I was satisfied when I first saw his face, an' when poor Mis' Tolland beheld him enter the room, she went right down on her knees and clasped her hands together to him as if he'd come to save her life, and he lifted her up and blessed her, an' I left 'em together, and slipped out into the open field and walked there in sight so if they needed to call me, and I had my own thoughts. At last I saw him at the door; he had to catch the return boat. I meant to walk back with him and offer him some supper, but he said no, and said he was comin' again if needed, and signed me to go into the house to her, and shook his head in a way that meant he understood everything. I can see him now; he walked with a cane, rather tired and feeble; I wished somebody would come along, so's to carry him down to the shore.

"Mis' Tolland looked up at me with a new look when I went in, an' she even took hold o' my hand and kept it. He had put some oil on her forehead,† but nothing anybody could do would keep her

---

*That is, she had a rosary.

†Anointing a sick person with holy oil is a Roman Catholic rite of healing.

alive very long; 't was his medicine for the soul rather 'n the body. I helped her to bed, and next morning she couldn't get up to dress her, and that was Monday, and she began to fail, and 't was Friday night she died." (Mrs. Todd spoke with unusual haste and lack of detail.) "Mrs. Begg and I watched with her, and made everything nice and proper, and after all the ill will there was a good number gathered to the funeral. 'T was in Reverend Mr. Bascom's day, and he done very well in his prayer, considering he couldn't fill in with mentioning all the near connections by name as was his habit. He spoke very feeling about her being a stranger and twice widowed, and all he said about her being reared among the heathen was to observe that there might be roads leadin' up to the New Jerusalem* from various points. I says to myself that I guessed quite a number must ha' reached there that wa'n't able to set out from Dunnet Landin'!"

Mrs. Todd gave an odd little laugh as she bent toward the firelight to pick up a dropped stitch in her knitting, and then I heard a heartfelt sigh.

"'T was most forty years ago," she said; "most everybody's gone a'ready that was there that day."

V

Suddenly Mrs. Todd gave an energetic shrug of her shoulders, and a quick look at me, and I saw that the sails of her narrative were filled with a fresh breeze.

"Uncle Lorenzo, Cap'n Bowden that I have referred to"—

"Certainly!" I agreed with eager expectation.

"He was the one that had been left in charge of Cap'n John Tolland's affairs, and had now come to be of unforeseen importance.

"Mrs. Begg an' I had stayed in the house both before an' after Mis' Tolland's decease, and she was now in haste to be done, having affairs to call her home; but uncle come to me as the exercises was beginning, and said he thought I'd better remain at the house while they went to the buryin' ground. I couldn't understand his

---

*From the Bible, Revelation 21:2 (KJV).

reasons, an' I felt disappointed, bein' as near to her as most anybody; 't was rough weather, so mother couldn't get in, and didn't even hear Mis' Tolland was gone till next day. I just nodded to satisfy him, 't wa'n't no time to discuss anything. Uncle seemed flustered; he'd gone out deep-sea fishin' the day she died, and the storm I told you of rose very sudden, so they got blown off way down the coast beyond Monhegan, and he'd just got back in time to dress himself and come.

"I set there in the house after I'd watched her away down the straight road far's I could see from the door; 't was a little short walkin' funeral an' a cloudy sky, so everything looked dull an' gray, an' it crawled along all in one piece, same's walking funerals do, an' I wondered how it ever come to the Lord's mind to let her begin down among them gay islands all heat and sun, and end up here among the rocks with a north wind blowin'. 'T was a gale that begun the afternoon before she died, and had kept blowin' off an' on ever since. I'd thought more than once how glad I should be to get home an' out o' sound o' them black spruces a-beatin' an' scratchin' at the front windows.

"I set to work pretty soon to put the chairs back, an' set outdoors some that was borrowed, an' I went out in the kitchen, an' I made up a good fire in case somebody come an' wanted a cup o' tea; but I didn't expect anyone to travel way back to the house unless 't was uncle Lorenzo. 'T was grown' so chilly that I fetched some kindlin' wood and made fires in both the fore rooms. Then I set down an' begun to feel as usual, and I got my knittin' out of a drawer. You can't be sorry for a poor creatur' that's come to the end o' all her troubles; my only discomfort was I thought I'd ought to feel worst at losin' her than I did; I was younger then than I be now. And as I set there, I begun to hear some long notes o' dronin' music from upstairs that chilled me to the bone."

Mrs. Todd gave a hasty glance at me.

"Quick's I could gather me, I went right upstairs to see what 't was," she added eagerly, "an' 't was just what I might ha' known. She'd always kept her guitar hangin' right against the wall in her room; 't was tied by a blue ribbon, and there was a window left wide open the wind was veerin' a good deal, an' it slanted in and searched the room. The strings was jarrin' yet.

" 'T was growin' pretty late in the afternoon, an' I begun to feel lonesome as I shouldn't now, and I was disappointed at having to stay there, the more I thought it over, but after a while I saw Cap'n Lorenzo poulin' back up the road all alone, and when he come nearer I could see he had a bundle under his arm and had shifted his best black clothes for his everyday ones. I ran out and put some tea into the teapot and set it back on the stove to draw, an' when he come in I reached down a little jug o' spirits—Cap'n Tolland had left his house well provisioned as if his wife was goin' to put to sea same's himself, an' there she'd gone an' left it. There was some cake that Mis' Begg an' I had made the day before. I thought that uncle an' me had a good right to the funeral supper, even if there wa'n't anyone to join us. I was lookin' forward to my cup o' tea; 't was beautiful tea out of a green lacquered chest that I've got now."

"You must have felt very tired," said I, eagerly listening.

"I was 'most beat out, with watchin' an' tendin' and all," answered Mrs. Todd, with as much sympathy in her voice as if she were speaking of another person. "But I called out to uncle as he came in, 'Well, I expect it's all over now, an' we've all done what we could. I thought we'd better have some tea or somethin' before we go home. Come right out in the kitchen, sir,' says I, never thinking but we only had to let the fires out and lock up everything safe an' eat our refreshment, an' go home.'

" 'I want both of us to stop here tonight,' says uncle, looking at me very important.

" 'Oh, what for?' says I, kind o' fretful.

" 'I've got my proper reasons,' says uncle. 'I'll see you well satisfied, Almira. Your tongue ain't so easy-goin' as some o' the women folks, an' there's property here to take charge of that you don't know nothin' at all about.'

" 'What do you mean?' says I.

" 'Cap'n Tolland acquainted me with his affairs; he hadn't no sort o' confidence in nobody but me an' his wife, after he was tricked into signin' that Portland note, an' lost money. An' she didn't know nothin' about business; but what he didn't take to sea to be sunk with him he's hid somewhere in this house. I expect Mis' Tolland may have told you where she kept things?' said uncle.

"I see he was dependin' a good deal on my answer," said Mrs. Todd, "but I had to disappoint him; no, she had never said nothin' to me.

"'Well, then, we've got to make a search,' says he, with considerable relish; but he was all tired and worked up, and we set down to the table, an' he had somethin', an' I took my desired cup o' tea, and then I begun to feel more interested.

"'Where you goin' to look first?' says I, but he give me a short look an' made no answer, an' begun to mix me a very small portion out of the jug, in another glass. I took it to please him; he said I looked tired, speakin' real fatherly, and I did feel better for it, and we set talkin' a few minutes, an' then he started for the cellar, carrying an old ship's lantern he fetched out o' the stairway an' lit.

"'What are you lookin' for, some kind of a chist?' I inquired, and he said yes. All of a sudden it come to me to ask who was the heirs; Eliza Tolland, Cap'n John's own sister, had never demeaned herself to come near the funeral, and uncle Lorenzo faced right about and begun to laugh, sort o' pleased. I thought queer of it; 't wa'n't what he'd taken, which would be nothin' to an old weathered sailor like him.

"'Who's the heir?' says I the second time.

"'Why, it's *you*, Almiry,' says he; and I was so took aback I set right down on the turn o' the cellar stairs.

"'Yes 't is,' said Uncle Lorenzo. 'I'm glad of it too. Some thought she didn't have no sense but foreign sense, an' a poor stock o' that, but she said you was friendly to her, an' one day after she got news of Tolland's death, an' I had fetched up his will that left everything to her, she said she was goin' to make a writin', so's you could have things after she was gone, an' she give five hundred to me for bein' executor. Square Pease* fixed up the paper, an' she signed it; it's all accordin' to law.' There, I begun to cry," said Mrs. Todd; "I couldn't help it. I wished I had her back again to do somethin' for, an' to make her know I felt sisterly to her more'n I'd ever showed, an' it come over me 't was all too late, an' I cried the more, till uncle

*Squire Pease.

showed impatience, an' I got up an' stumbled along down cellar with my apern to my eyes the greater part of the time.

"'I'm goin' to have a clean search,' says he; 'you hold the light.' An' I held it and he rummaged in the arches an' under the stairs, an' over in some old closet where he reached out bottles an' stone jugs an' canted some kags an' one or two casks, an' chuckled well when he heard there was somethin' inside—but there wa'n't nothin' to find but things usual in a cellar, an' then the old lantern was givin' out an' we come away.

"'He spoke to me of a chist, Cap'n Tolland did,' says uncle in a whisper. 'He said a good sound chist was as safe a bank as there was, an' I beat him out of such nonsense, 'count o' fire an' other risks.' 'There's no chist in the rooms above,' says I; 'no, uncle, there ain't no sea-chist, for I've been here long enough to see what there was to be seen.' Yet he wouldn't feel contented till he'd mounted up into the top-loft; 't was one o' them single, hip-roofed houses that don't give proper accommodation for a real garret, like Cap'n Littlepage's down here at the Landin'. There was broken furniture and rubbish, an' he let down a terrible sight o' dust into the front entry, but sure enough there wasn't no chist. I had it all to sweep up next day.

"'He must have took it away to sea,' says I to the cap'n, an' even then he didn't want to agree, but we was both beat out. I told him where I'd always seen Mis' Tolland get her money from, and we found much as a hundred dollars there in an old red morocco wallet. Cap'n John had been gone a good while a'ready, and she had spent what she needed. 'T was in an old desk o' his in the settin' room that we found the wallet."

"At the last minute he may have taken his money to sea," I suggested.

"Oh yes," agreed Mrs. Todd. "He did take considerable to make his venture to bring home, as was customary, an' that was drowned with him as uncle agreed; but he had other property in shipping, and a thousand dollars invested in Portland in a cordage shop, but 't was about the time shipping begun to dacay,* and the cordage shop

*That is, the Embargo Act of 1807, which prohibited shipping trade between the United States and other countries.

failed, and in the end I wa'n't so rich as I thought I was goin' to be for those few minutes on the cellar stairs. There was an auction that accumulated something. Old Mis' Tolland, the cap'n's mother, had heired some good furniture from a sister: there was above thirty chairs in all, and they're apt to sell well. I got over a thousand dollars when we come to settle up, and I made uncle take his five hundred; he was getting along in years and had met with losses in navigation, and he left it back to me when he died, so I had a real good lift. It all lays in the bank over to Rockland, and I draw my interest fall an' spring, with the little Mr. Todd was able to leave me; but that's kind o' sacred money; 't was earnt and saved with the hope o' youth, an' I'm very particular what I spend it for. Oh yes, what with ownin' my house, I've been enabled to get along very well, with prudence!" said Mrs. Todd contentedly.

"But there was the house and land," I asked—"What became of that part of the property?"

Mrs. Todd looked into the fire, and a shadow of disapproval flitted over her face.

"Poor old uncle!" she said, "he got childish about the matter. I was hoping to sell at first, and I had an offer, but he always run of an idea that there was more money hid away, and kept wanting me to delay; an' he used to go up there all alone and search, and dig in the cellar, empty an' bleak as 't was in winter weather or any time. An' he'd come and tell me he'd dreamed he found gold behind a stone in the cellar wall, or somethin'. And one night we all see the light o' fire up that way, an' the whole Landin' took the road, and run to look, and the Tolland property was all in a light blaze. I expect the old gentleman had dropped fire about; he said he'd been up there to see if everything was safe in the afternoon. As for the land, 't was so poor that everybody used to have a joke that the Tolland boys preferred to farm the sea instead. It's 'most all grown up to bushes now where it ain't poor water grass in the low places. There's some upland that has a pretty view, after you cross the brook bridge. Years an' years after she died, there was some o' her flowers used to come up an' bloom in the door garden. I brought two or three that was unusual down here; they always come up and remind me of her, constant as the spring. But I never did want to fetch home that guitar, some way or 'nother; I wouldn't let it go at the auction, either. It was hangin' right there in the house when the fire took place. I've got some o' her other little things scattered about the house: that picture on the mantelpiece belonged to her."

I had often wondered where such a picture had come from, and why Mrs. Todd had chosen it; it was a French print of the statue of the Empress Josephine in the Savane at old Fort Royal, in Martinique.*

VI

MRS. TODD DREW HER chair closer to mine; she held the cat and her knitting with one hand as she moved, but the cat was so warm and so sound asleep that she only stretched a lazy paw in spite of what must have felt like a slight earthquake. Mrs. Todd began to speak almost in a whisper.

"I ain't told you all," she continued; "no, I haven't spoken of all to but very few. The way it came was this," she said solemnly, and then stopped to listen to the wind, and sat for a moment in deferential silence, as if she waited for the wind to speak first. The cat suddenly lifted her head with quick excitement and gleaming eyes, and her mistress was leaning forward toward the fire with an arm laid on either knee, as if they were consulting the glowing coals for some augury. Mrs. Todd looked like an old prophetess as she sat there with the firelight shining on her strong face; she was posed for some great painter. The woman with the cat was as unconscious and as mysterious as any sibyl of the Sistine Chapel.†

"There, that's the last struggle o' the gale," said Mrs. Todd, nodding her head with impressive certainty and still looking into the bright embers of the fire. "You'll see!" She gave me another quick glance, and spoke in a low tone as if we might be overheard.

"'T was such a gale as this the night Mis' Tolland died. She appeared more comfortable the first o' the evenin'; and Mrs. Begg was

---

*Empress Josephine was Napoléon Bonaparte's wife; Martinique, a French colony, is an island in the Lesser Antilles (West Indies).

†Michelangelo (1474–1564) included images of sibyls (female prophets) in the frescoes he painted on the ceiling of the Sistine Chapel.

more spent than I, bein' older, and a beautiful nurse that was the first to see and think of everything, but perfectly quiet an' never asked a useless question. You remember her funeral when you first come to the Landing? And she consented to goin' an' havin' a good sleep while she could, and left me one o' those good little pewter lamps that burnt whale oil an' made plenty o' light in the room, but not too bright to be disturbin'.

"Poor Mis' Tolland had been distressed the night before, an' all that day, but as night come on she grew more and more easy, an' was layin' there asleep; 't was like settin' by any sleepin' person, and I had none but usual thoughts. When the wind lulled and the rain, I could hear the seas, though more distant than this, and I don' know's I observed any other sound than what the weather made; 't was a very solemn feelin' night. I set close by the bed; there was times she looked to find somebody when she was awake. The light was on her face, so I could see her plain; there was always times when she wore a look that made her seem a stranger you'd never set eyes on before. I did think what a world it was that her an' me should have come together so, and she have nobody but Dunnet Landin' folks about her in her extremity. 'You're one o' the stray ones, poor creatur',' I said. I remember those very words passin' through my mind, but I saw reason to be glad she had some comforts, and didn't lack friends at the last, though she'd seen misery an' pain. I was glad she was quiet; all day she'd been restless, and we couldn't understand what she wanted from her French speech. We had the window open to give her air, an' now an' then a gust would strike that guitar that was on the wall and set it swinging by the blue ribbon, and soundin' as if somebody begun to play it. I come near takin' it down, but you never know what'll fret a sick person an' put 'em on the rack, an' that guitar was one o' the few things she'd brought with her."

I nodded assent, and Mrs. Todd spoke still lower.

"I set there close by the bed; I'd been through a good deal for some days back, and I thought I might's well be droppin' asleep too, bein' a quick person to wake. She looked to me as if she might last a day longer, certain, now she'd got more comfortable, but I was real tired, an' sort o' cramped as watchers will get, an' a fretful feeling begun to creep over me such as they often do have. If you give way, there ain't no support for the sick person; they can't count on no composure o' their own. Mis' Tolland moved then, a little restless, an' I forgot me quick enough, an' begun to hum out a little part of a hymn tune just to make her feel everything was as usual an' not wake up into a poor uncertainty. All of a sudden she set right up in bed with her eyes wide open, an' I stood an' put my arm behind her; she hadn't moved like that for days. And she reached out both her arms toward the door, an' I looked the way she was lookin', an' I see someone was standin' there against the dark. No, 't wa'n't Mis' Begg; 't was somebody a good deal shorter than Mis' Begg. The lamplight struck across the room between us. I couldn't tell the shape, but 't was a woman's dark face lookin' right at us; 't wa'n't but an instant I could see. I felt dreadful cold, and my head begun to swim; I thought the light went out; 't wa'n't but an instant, as I say, an' when my sight come back I couldn't see nothing there. I was one that didn't know what it was to faint away, no matter what happened; time was I felt above it in others, but 't was somethin' that made poor human natur' quail. I saw very plain while I could see; 't was a pleasant enough face, shaped somethin' like Mis' Tolland's, and a kind of expectin' look.

"No, I don't expect I was asleep," Mrs. Todd assured me quietly, after a moment's pause, though I had not spoken. She gave a heavy sigh before she went on. I could see that the recollection moved her in the deepest way.

"I suppose if I hadn't been so spent an' quavery with long watchin', I might have kept my head an' observed much better," she added humbly; "but I see all I could bear. I did try to act calm, an' I laid Mis' Tolland down on her pillow, an' I was a-shakin' as I done it. All she did was to look up to me so satisfied and sort o' questioning, an' I looked back to her.

"'You saw her, didn't you?' she says to me, speakin' perfectly reasonable. ''T is my mother,' she says again, very feeble, but lookin' straight up at me, kind of surprised with the pleasure, and smiling as if she saw I was overcome, an' would have said more if she could, but we had hold of hands. I see then her change was comin', but I didn't call Mis' Begg, nor make no uproar. I felt calm then, an' lifted to somethin' different as I never was since. She opened her eyes just as she was goin'—

"'You saw her, didn't you?' she said the second time, an' I says, '*Yes, dear, I did; you ain't never goin' to feel strange an' lonesome no more.*' An' then in a few quiet minutes 't was all over. I felt they'd gone away together. No, I wa'n't alarmed afterward; 't was just that one moment I couldn't live under, but I never called it beyond reason I should see the other watcher. I saw plain enough there was somebody there with me in the room.

VII

"'T WAS JUST SUCH a night as this Mis' Tolland died," repeated Mrs. Todd, returning to her usual tone and leaning back comfortably in her chair as she took up her knitting. "'T was just such a night as this. I've told the circumstances to but very few; but I don't call it beyond reason. When folks is goin' 't is all natural, and only common things can jar upon the mind. You know plain enough there's somethin' beyond this world; the doors stand wide open. There's somethin' of us that must still live on; we've got to join both worlds together an' live in one but for the other. The doctor said that to me one day, an' I never could forget it; he said 't was in one o' his old doctor's books."

We sat together in silence in the warm little room; the rain dropped heavily from the eaves, and the sea still roared, but the high wind had done blowing. We heard the far complaining fog horn of a steamer up the Bay.

"There goes the Boston boat out, pretty near on time," said Mrs. Todd with satisfaction. "Sometimes these late August storms'll sound a good deal worse than they really be. I do hate to hear the poor steamers callin' when they're bewildered in thick nights in winter, comin' on the coast. Yes, there goes the boat; they'll find it rough at sea, but the storm's all over."

WILLIAM'S WEDDING

I

THE HURRY OF LIFE in a large town, the constant putting aside of preference to yield to a most unsatisfactory activity, began to vex me, and one day I took the train, and only left it for the eastward-bound boat. Carlyle* says somewhere that the only happiness a man ought to ask for is happiness enough to get his work done; and against this the complexity and futile ingenuity of social life seems a conspiracy. But the first salt wind from the east, the first sight of a lighthouse set boldly on its outer rock, the flash of a gull, the waiting procession of seaward-bound firs on an island, made me feel solid and definite again, instead of a poor, incoherent being. Life was resumed, and anxious living blew away as if it had not been. I could not breathe deep enough or long. It was a return to happiness.

The coast had still a wintry look; it was far on in May, but all the shore looked cold and sterile. One was conscious of going north as well as east and as the day went on the sea grew colder, and all the warmer air and bracing strength and stimulus of the autumn weather, and storage of the heat of summer, were quite gone. I was very cold and very tired when I came at evening up the lower bay, and saw the white houses of Dunnet Landing climbing the hill. They had a friendly look; these little houses, not as if they were climbing up the shore, but as if they were rather all coming down to meet a fond and weary traveler, and I could hardly wait with patience to step off the boat. It was not the usual eager company on the wharf. The coming-in of the mail-boat was the one large public event of a summer day, and I was disappointed at seeing none of my intimate friends but Johnny Bowden, who had evidently done nothing all winter but grow, so that his short sea-smitten clothes gave him a look of poverty.

---

*Reference to the 1843 book *Past and Present* (book 3, chapter 4), by English author Thomas Carlyle (1795–1881).

Johnny's expression did not change as we greeted each other, but I suddenly felt that I had shown indifference and inconvenient delay by not coming sooner; before I could make an apology he took my small portmanteau,* and walking before me in his old fashion he made straight up the hilly road toward Mrs. Todd's. Yes, he was much grown—it had never occurred to me the summer before that Johnny was likely, with the help of time and other forces, to grow into a young man; he was such a well-framed and well-settled chunk of a boy that nature seemed to have set him aside as something finished, quite satisfactory, and entirely completed.

The wonderful little green garden had been enchanted away by winter. There were a few frost-bitten twigs and some thin shrubbery against the fence, but it was a most unpromising small piece of ground. My heart was beating like a lover's as I passed it on the way to the door of Mrs. Todd's house, which seemed to have become much smaller under the influence of winter weather.

"She hasn't gone away?" I asked Johnny Bowden with a sudden anxiety just as we reached the doorstep.

"Gone away!" he faced me with blank astonishment—"I see her settin' by Mis' Caplin's window, the one nighest the road, about four o'clock!" And eager with suppressed news of my coming he made his entrance as if the house were a burrow.

Then on my homesick heart fell the voice of Mrs. Todd. She stopped, through what I knew to be excess of feeling, to rebuke Johnny for bringing in so much mud, and I dallied without for one moment during the ceremony; then we met again face to face.

II

"I DARE SAY YOU can advise me what shapes they are goin' to wear. My meetin'-bunnit ain't goin' to do me again this year; no! I can't expect 't would do me forever," said Mrs. Todd, as soon as she could say anything. "There! do set down and tell me how you have been! We've got a weddin' in the family, I s'pose you know?"

---

*Carrying case made of leather.

"A wedding!" said I, still full of excitement.

"Yes; I expect if the tide serves and the line storm* don't overtake him they'll come in and appear out on Sunday, I shouldn't have concerned me about the bunnit for a month yet, nobody would notice, but havin' an occasion like this I shall show consider'ble. 'Twill be an ordeal for William!"

"For *William*!" I exclaimed. "What do you mean, Mrs. Todd?"

She gave a comfortable little laugh. "Well, the Lord's seen reason at last an' removed Mis' Cap'n Hight up to the farm, an' I don't know but the weddin's goin' to be this week. Esther's had a great deal of business disposin' of her flock, but she's done extra well—the folks that owns the next place goin' up country are well off. 'Tis elegant land north side o' that bleak ridge, an' one o' the boys has been Esther's right-hand man of late. She instructed him in all matters, and after she markets the early lambs he's goin' to take the farm on halves, an' she's give the refusal to him to buy her out within two years. She's reserved the buryin' lot, an' the right o' way in, an'—"

I couldn't stop for details. I demanded reassurance of the central fact.

"William going to be married?" I repeated; whereat Mrs. Todd gave me a searching look that was not without scorn.

"Old Mis' Hight's funeral was a week ago Wednesday, and 't was very well attended," she assured me after a moment's pause.

"Poor thing!" said I, with a sudden vision of her helplessness and angry battle against the fate of illness; "it was very hard for her."

"I thought it was hard for Esther!" said Mrs. Todd without sentiment.

III

I HAD AN ODD feeling of strangeness: I missed the garden, and the little rooms, to which I had added a few things of my own the summer before, seemed oddly unfamiliar. It was like the hermit crab in

*A tropical storm often occurring on or around the autumnal equinox.

a cold new shell—and with the windows shut against the raw May air, and a strange silence and grayness of the sea all that first night and day of my visit, I felt as if I had after all lost my hold of that quiet life.

Mrs. Todd made the apt suggestion that city persons were prone to run themselves to death, and advised me to stay and get properly rested now that I had taken the trouble to come. She did not know how long I had been homesick for the conditions of life at the Landing the autumn before—it was natural enough to feel a little unsupported by compelling incidents on my return.

Some one has said that one never leaves a place, or arrives at one, until the next day! But on the second morning I woke with the familiar feeling of interest and ease, and the bright May sun was streaming in, while I could hear Mrs. Todd's heavy footsteps pounding about in the other part of the house as if something were going to happen. There was the first golden robin* singing somewhere close to the house, and a lovely aspect of spring now, and I looked at the garden to see that in the warm night some of its treasures had grown a hand's breadth; the determined spikes of yellow daffies† stood tall against the doorsteps, and the blood-root was unfolding leaf and flower. The belated spring which I had left behind farther south had overtaken me on this northern coast. I even saw a presumptuous dandelion in the garden border.

It is difficult to report the great events of New England; expression is so slight, and those few words which escape us in moments of deep feeling look but meager on the printed page. One has to assume too much of the dramatic fervor as one reads; but as I came out of my room at breakfast-time I met Mrs. Todd face to face, and when she said to me, "This weather'll bring William in after her; 'tis their happy day!" I felt something take possession of me which ought to communicate itself to the least sympathetic reader of this cold page. It is written for those who have a Dunnet Landing of their own: who either kindly share this with the writer, or possess another.

---

*Baltimore oriole (in recent years known as the northern oriole).
†Daffodils.

"I ain't seen his comin' sail yet; he'll be likely to dodge round among the islands so he'll be the less observed," continued Mrs. Todd. "You can get a dory up the bay, even a clean new painted one, if you know as how, keepin' it against the high land." She stepped to the door and looked off to sea as she spoke. I could see her eye follow the gray shores to and fro, and then a bright light spread over her calm face. "There he comes, and he's strikin' right in across the open bay like a man!" she said with splendid approval. "See, there he comes! Yes, there's William, and he's bent his new sail."

I looked too, and saw the fleck of white no larger than a gull's wing yet, but present to her eager vision.

I was going to France for the whole long summer that year, and the more I thought of such an absence from these simple scenes the more dear and delightful they became. Santa Teresa says* that the true proficiency of the soul is not in much thinking, but in much loving, and sometimes I believed that I had never found love in its simplicity as I had found it at Dunnet Landing in the various hearts of Mrs. Blackett and Mrs. Todd and William. It is only because one came to know them, these three, loving and wise and true, in their own habitations. Their counterparts are in every village in the world, thank heaven, and the gift to one's life is only in its discernment. I had only lived in Dunnet until the usual distractions and artifices of the world were no longer in control, and I saw these simple natures clear. "The happiness of life is in its recognitions. It seems that we are not ignorant of these truths, and even that we believe them; but we are so little accustomed to think of them, they are so strange to us—"

"Well now, deary me!" said Mrs. Todd, breaking into exclamation: "I've got to fly round—I thought he'd have to beat; he can't sail far on that tack, and he won't be in for a good hour yet—I expect he's made every arrangement, but he said he shouldn't go up after Esther unless the weather was good, and I declare it did look doubtful this morning."

---

*Paraphrase from Saint Teresa of Avila's *Interior Castle* (1577), chapter 1: "Fourth Mansions."

I remembered Esther's weather-worn face. She was like a Frenchwoman who had spent her life in the fields. I remembered her pleasant look, her childlike eyes, and thought of the astonishment of joy she would feel now in being taken care of and tenderly sheltered from wind and weather after all these years. They were going to be young again now, she and William, to forget work and care in the spring weather. I could hardly wait for the boat to come to land, I was so eager to see his happy face.

"Cake an' wine I'm goin' to set 'em out!" said Mrs. Todd. "They won't stop to set down for an ordered meal, they'll want to get right out home quick's they can. Yes, I'll give 'em some cake an' wine—I've got a rare plum-cake from my best receipt, and a bottle o' wine that the old Cap'n Denton of all give me, one of two, the day I was married, one we had and one we saved, and I've never touched it till now. He said there wa'n't none like it in the State o' Maine."

It was a day of waiting, that day of spring; the May weather was as expectant as our fond hearts, and one could see the grass grow green hour by hour. The warm air was full of birds, there was a glow of light on the sea instead of the cold shining of chilly weather which had lingered late. There was a look on Mrs. Todd's face which I saw once and could not meet again. She was in her highest mood. Then I went out early for a walk, and when I came back we sat in different rooms for the most part. There was such a thrill in the air that our only conversation was in her most abrupt and incisive manner. She was knitting, I believe, and as for me I dallied with a book. I heard her walking to and fro, and the door being wide open now, she went out and paced the front walk to the gate as if she walked a quarter-deck.

It is very solemn to sit waiting for the great events of life—most of us have done it again and again—to be expectant of life or expectant of death gives one the same feeling.

But at the last Mrs. Todd came quickly back from the gate, and standing in the sunshine of the door, she beckoned me as if she were a sibyl.

"I thought you comprehended everything the day you was up there," she added with a little more patience in her tone, but I felt that she thought I had lost instead of gained since we parted the autumn before.

"William's made this pretext o' goin' fishin' for the last time. 'T wouldn't done to take notice, 't would 'a scared him to death! but there never was nobody took less comfort out o' forty years courtin'. No, he won't have to make no further pretexts," said Mrs. Todd, with an air of triumph.

"Did you know where he was going that day?" I asked, with a sudden burst of admiration at such discernment.

"I did!" replied Mrs. Todd grandly.

"Oh! but that pennyroyal lotion," I indignantly protested, remembering that under pretext of mosquitoes she had besmeared the poor lover in an awful way—why, it was outrageous! Medea could not have been more conscious of high ultimate purposes.[6]

"Darlin'," said Mrs. Todd, in the excitement of my arrival and the great concerns of marriage, "he's got a beautiful shaped face and they pison him very unusual—you wouldn't have had him present himself to his lady all lop-sided with a mosquito-bite? Once when he was young I rode up with him, and they set upon him in concert the minute we entered the woods." She stood before me reproachfully, and I was conscious of deserved rebuke. "Yes, you've come just in the nick of time to advise me about a bunnit. They say large bows on top is liable to be worn."

IV

THE PERIOD OF WAITING was one of direct contrast to these high moments of recognition. The very slowness of the morning hours wasted that sense of excitement with which we had begun the day. Mrs. Todd came down from the mount where her face had shone so bright,* to the cares of common life, and some acquaintances from Black Island for whom she had little natural preference or liking came, bringing a poor, sickly child to get medical advice. They were noisy women, with harsh, clamorous voices, and they stayed a long time. I heard the clink of teacups, however, and could detect no impatience in the tones of Mrs. Todd's voice; but when they were at

*Reference to the Bible, Matthew 17:2.

last going away, she did not linger unduly over her leave-taking, and returned to me to explain that they were people she had never liked, and they had made an excuse of a friendly visit to save their doctor's bill; but she pitied the poor little child, and knew beside that the doctor was away.

"I had to give 'em the remedies right out," she told me; "they wouldn't have bought a cent's worth o' drugs down to the store for that dwindlin' thing. She needed feedin' up, and I don't expect she gets milk enough; they're great butter-makers down to Black Island, 't is excellent pasturage, but they use no milk themselves, and their butter is heavy laden with salt to make weight, so that you'd think all their ideas come down from Sodom."*

She was very indignant and very wistful about the pale little girl. "I wish they'd let me kept her," she said. "I kind of advised it, and her eyes was so wishful in that pinched face when she heard me, so that I could see what was the matter with her, but they said she wa'n't prepared. Prepared!" And Mrs. Todd snuffed like an offended war-horse and departed; but I could hear her still grumbling and talking to herself in high dudgeon an hour afterward.

At the end of that time her arch enemy, Mari' Harris, appeared at the side-door with gingham handkerchief over her head. She was always on hand for the news, and made some formal excuse for her presence—she wished to borrow the weekly paper. Captain Littlepage, whose housekeeper she was, had taken it from the post-office in the morning, but had forgotten, being of failing memory, what he had done with it.

"How is the poor old gentleman?" asked Mrs. Todd with solicitude, ignoring the present errand of Maria and all her concerns.

I had spoken the evening before of intended visits to Captain Littlepage and Elijah Tilley, and I now heard Mrs. Todd repeating my inquiries and intentions, and fending off with unusual volubility of her own the curious questions that were sure to come. But at last Maria Harris secured an opportunity and boldly inquired if she had not seen William ashore early that morning.

---

*Reference to the Bible, Genesis 18 and 19.

"I don't say he wasn't," replied Mrs. Todd; "Thu'sday's a very usual day with him to come ashore."

"He was all dressed up," insisted Maria—she really had no sense of propriety. "I didn't know but they was going to be married?"

Mrs. Todd did not reply. I recognized from the sounds that reached me that she had retired to the fastnesses of the kitchen-closet and was clattering the tins.

"I expect they'll marry soon anyway," continued the visitor.

"I expect they will if they want to," answered Mrs. Todd. "I don't know nothin' 't all about it; that's what folks say." And presently the gingham handkerchief retreated past my window.

"I routed her, horse and foot,"* said Mrs. Todd proudly, coming at once to stand at my door. "Who's comin' now?" as two figures passed inward bound to the kitchen.

They were Mrs. Begg and Johnny Bowden's mother, who were favorites, and were received with Mrs. Todd's usual civilities. Then one of the Mrs. Caplins came with a cup in hand to borrow yeast. On one pretext or another nearly all our acquaintances came to satisfy themselves of the facts, and see what Mrs. Todd would impart about the wedding. But she firmly avoided the subject through the length of every call and errand, and answered the final leading question of each curious guest with her noncommittal phrase, "I don't know nothin' 't all about it; that's what folks say!"

She had just repeated this for the fourth or fifth time and shut the door upon the last comers, when we met in the little front entry. Mrs. Todd was not in a bad temper, but highly amused. "I've been havin' all sorts o' social privileges, you may have observed. They didn't seem to consider that if they could only hold out till afternoon they'd know as much as I did. There wa'n't but one o' the whole sixteen that showed real interest, the rest demeaned themselves to ask out o' cheap curiosity; no, there wa'n't but one showed any real feelin'."

"Miss Maria Harris, you mean?" and Mrs. Todd laughed.

"Certain, dear," she agreed, "how you do understand poor human natur'!"

---

*That is, it was a total victory; refers to a military expression about the vanquishing of one army by another, in terms of both its cavalry and its foot soldiers.

A short distance down the hilly street stood a narrow house that was newly painted white. It blinded one's eyes to catch the reflection of the sun. It was the house of the minister, and a wagon had just stopped before it; a man was helping a woman to alight, and they stood side by side for a moment, while Johnny Bowden appeared as if by magic, and climbed to the wagon-seat. Then they went into the house and shut the door. Mrs. Todd and I stood close together and watched; the tears were running down her cheeks. I watched Johnny Bowden, who made light of so great a moment by so handling the whip that the old white Caplin horse started up from time to time and was inexorably stopped as if he had some idea of running away. There was something in the back of the wagon which now and then claimed the boy's attention; he leaned over as if there were something very precious left in his charge; perhaps it was only Esther's little trunk going to its new home.

At last the door of the parsonage opened, and two figures came out. The minister followed them and stood in the doorway, delaying them with parting words; he could not have thought it was a time for admonition.

"He's all alone; his wife's up to Portland to her sister's," said Mrs. Todd aloud, in a matter-of-fact voice. "She's a nice woman, but she might ha' talked too much. There! see, they're comin' here. I didn't know how 't would be. Yes, they're comin' up to see us before they go home. I declare, if William ain't lookin' just like a king!"

Mrs. Todd took one step forward, and we stood and waited. The happy pair came walking up the street, Johnny Bowden driving ahead. I heard a plaintive little cry from time to time to which in the excitement of the moment I had not stopped to listen; but when William and Esther had come and shaken hands with Mrs. Todd and then with me, all in silence, Esther stepped quickly to the back of the wagon, and unfastening some cords returned to us carrying a little white lamb. She gave a shy glance at William as she fondled it and held it to her heart, and then, still silent, we went into the house together. The lamb had stopped bleating. It was lovely to see Esther carry it in her arms.

When we got into the house, all the repression of Mrs. Todd's usual manner was swept away by her flood of feeling. She took Esther's thin figure, lamb and all, to her heart and held her there, kissing her as she might have kissed a child, and then held out her hand to William and they gave each other the kiss of peace.* This was so moving, so tender, so free from their usual fetters of self-consciousness, that Esther and I could not help giving each other a happy glance of comprehension. I never saw a young bride half so touching in her happiness as Esther was that day of her wedding. We took the cake and wine of the marriage feast together, always in silence, like a true sacrament, and then to my astonishment I found that sympathy and public interest in so great an occasion were going to have their way. I shrank from the thought of William's possible sufferings, but he welcomed both the first group of neighbors and the last with heartiness; and when at last they had gone, for there were thoughtless loiterers in Dunnet Landing, I made ready with eager zeal and walked with William and Esther to the water-side. It was only a little way, and kind faces nodded reassuringly from the windows, while kind voices spoke from the doors. Esther carried the lamb on one arm; she had found time to tell me that its mother had died that morning and she could not bring herself to the thought of leaving it behind. She kept the other hand on William's arm until we reached the landing. Then he shook hands with me, and looked me full in the face to be sure I understood how happy he was, and stepping into the boat held out his arms to Esther—at last she was his own.

I watched him make a nest for the lamb out of an old sea-cloak at Esther's feet, and then he wrapped her own shawl round her shoulders, and finding a pin in the lapel of his Sunday coat he pinned it for her. She looked at him fondly while he did this, and then glanced up at us, a pretty, girlish color brightening her cheeks.

We stood there together and watched them go far out into the bay. The sunshine of the May day was low now, but there was a steady breeze, and the boat moved well.

"Mother'll be watching for them," said Mrs. Todd. "Yes, mother'll be watching all day, and waiting. She'll be so happy to have Esther come."

We went home together up the hill, and Mrs. Todd said nothing more; but we held each other's hands all the way.

---

*A Christian ceremonial gesture; reference to the Bible, Romans 16:16.

SELECTED OTHER STORIES

CONTENTS

A WHITE HERON

I

THE WOODS WERE ALREADY filled with shadows one June evening, just before eight o'clock, though a bright sunset still glimmered faintly among the trunks of the trees. A little girl was driving home her cow, a plodding, dilatory, provoking creature in her behavior, but a valued companion for all that. They were going away from the western light, and striking deep into the dark woods, but their feet were familiar with the path, and it was no matter whether their eyes could see it or not.

There was hardly a night the summer through when the old cow could be found waiting at the pasture bars; on the contrary, it was her greatest pleasure to hide herself away among the high huckleberry bushes, and though she wore a loud bell she had made the discovery that if one stood perfectly still it would not ring. So Sylvia had to hunt for her until she found her, and call Co'! Co'! with never an answering Moo, until her childish patience was quite spent. If the creature had not given good milk and plenty of it, the case would have seemed very different to her owners. Besides, Sylvia had all the time there was, and very little use to make of it. Sometimes in pleasant weather it was a consolation to look upon the cow's pranks as an intelligent attempt to play hide and seek, and as the child had no playmates she lent herself to this amusement with a good deal of zest. Though this chase had been so long that the wary animal herself had given an unusual signal of her whereabouts, Sylvia had only laughed when she came upon Mistress Moolly at the swamp-side, and urged her affectionately homeward with a twig of birch leaves. The old cow was not inclined to wander farther, she even turned in the right direction for once as they left the pasture, and stepped along the road at a good pace. She was quite ready to be milked now, and seldom stopped to browse. Sylvia wondered what her grandmother would say because they were so late. It was a great while since she had left home at half past five o'clock, but everybody knew the difficulty of making this errand a short one. Mrs. Tilley had chased the horned torment too many summer evenings herself to blame any one else for lingering, and was only thankful as she waited that she had Sylvia, nowadays, to give such valuable assistance. The good woman suspected that Sylvia loitered occasionally on her own account; there never was such a child for straying about out-of-doors since the world was made! Everybody said that it was a good change for a little maid who had tried to grow for eight years in a crowded manufacturing town, but, as for Sylvia herself, it seemed as if she never had been alive at all before she came to live at the farm. She thought often with wistful compassion of a wretched dry geranium that belonged to a town neighbor.

"'Afraid of folks,'" old Mrs. Tilley said to herself, with a smile, after she had made the unlikely choice of Sylvia from her daughter's houseful of children, and was returning to the farm. "'Afraid of folks,' they said! I guess she won't be troubled no great with 'em up to the old place!" When they reached the door of the lonely house and stopped to unlock it, and the cat came to purr loudly, and rub against them, a deserted pussy, indeed, but fat with young robins, Sylvia whispered that this was a beautiful place to live in, and she never should wish to go home.

The companions followed the shady wood-road, the cow taking slow steps, and the child very fast ones. The cow stopped long at the brook to drink, as if the pasture were not half a swamp, and Sylvia stood still and waited, letting her bare feet cool themselves in the shoal water, while the great twilight moths struck softly against her. She waded on through the brook as the cow moved away, and listened to the thrushes with a heart that beat fast with pleasure. There was a stirring in the great boughs overhead. They were full of little birds and beasts that seemed to be wide-awake, and going about their world, or else saying good-night to each other in sleepy twitters. Sylvia herself felt sleepy as she walked along. However, it was not much farther to the house, and the air was soft and sweet. She was not often in the woods so late as this, and it made her feel as if she were a part of the gray shadows and the moving leaves. She was just thinking how long it seemed since she first came to the farm a year ago, and wondering if everything went on in the noisy town just the same as when she was there; the thought of the great red-faced boy who used to chase and frighten her made her hurry along the path to escape from the shadow of the trees.

Suddenly this little woods-girl is horror-stricken to hear a clear whistle not very far away. Not a bird's whistle, which would have a sort of friendliness, but a boy's whistle, determined, and somewhat aggressive. Sylvia left the cow to whatever sad fate might await her, and stepped discreetly aside into the bushes, but she was just too late. The enemy had discovered her, and called out in a very cheerful and persuasive tone, "Halloa, little girl, how far is it to the road?" and trembling Sylvia answered almost inaudibly, "A good ways."

She did not dare to look boldly at the tall young man, who carried a gun over his shoulder, but she came out of her bush and again followed the cow, while he walked alongside.

"I have been hunting for some birds," the stranger said kindly, "and I have lost my way, and need a friend very much. Don't be afraid," he added gallantly. "Speak up and tell me what your name is, and whether you think I can spend the night at your house, and go out gunning early in the morning."

Sylvia was more alarmed than before. Would not her grandmother consider her much to blame? But who could have foreseen such an accident as this? It did not appear to be her fault, and she hung her head as if the stem of it were broken, but managed to answer "Sylvy," with much effort when her companion again asked her name.

Mrs. Tilley was standing in the doorway when the trio came into view. The cow gave a loud moo by way of explanation.

"Yes, you'd better speak up for yourself, you old trial! Where'd she tucked herself away this time, Sylvy?" Sylvia kept an awed silence; she knew by instinct that her grandmother did not comprehend the gravity of the situation. She must be mistaking the stranger for one of the farmer-lads of the region.

The young man stood his gun beside the door, and dropped a heavy game-bag beside it; then he bade Mrs. Tilley good-evening, and repeated his wayfarer's story, and asked if he could have a night's lodging.

"Put me anywhere you like," he said. "I must be off early in the morning, before day; but I am very hungry, indeed. You can give me some milk at any rate, that's plain."

"Dear sakes, yes," responded the hostess, whose long slumbering hospitality seemed to be easily awakened. "You might fare better if you went out on the main road a mile or so, but you're welcome to what we've got. I'll milk right off, and you make yourself at home. You can sleep on husks or feathers," she proffered graciously. "I raised them all myself. There's good pasturing for geese just below here towards the ma'sh. Now step round and set a plate for the gentleman, Sylvy!" And Sylvia promptly stepped. She was glad to have something to do, and she was hungry herself.

It was a surprise to find so clean and comfortable a little dwelling in this New England wilderness. The young man had known the horrors of its most primitive housekeeping, and the dreary squalor of that level of society which does not rebel at the companionship of hens. This was the best thrift of an old-fashioned farmstead, though on such a small scale that it seemed like a hermitage. He listened eagerly to the old woman's quaint talk, he watched Sylvia's pale face and shining gray eyes with ever growing enthusiasm, and insisted that this was the best supper he had eaten for a month; then, afterward, the new-made friends sat down in the doorway together while the moon came up.

Soon it would be berry-time, and Sylvia was a great help at picking. The cow was a good milker, though a plaguy thing to keep track of, the hostess gossiped frankly, adding presently that she had buried four children, so that Sylvia's mother, and a son (who might be dead) in California were all the children she had left. "Dan, my boy, was a great hand to go gunning," she explained sadly. "I never wanted for pa'tridges or gray squer'ls while he was to home. He's been a great wand'rer, I expect, and he's no hand to write letters. There, I don't blame him, I'd ha' seen the world myself if it had been so I could.

"Sylvia takes after him," the grandmother continued affectionately, after a minute's pause. "There ain't a foot o' ground she don't know her way over, and the wild creatur's counts her one o' themselves. Squer'ls she'll tame to come an' feed right out o' her hands, and all sorts o' birds. Last winter she got the jay-birds to bangeing*

*In the rural speech of nineteenth-century New England, being idle or lazy.

here, and I believe she'd 'a' scanted herself of her own meals to have plenty to throw out amongst 'em, if I hadn't kep' watch. Anything but crows, I tell her, I'm willin' to help support,—though Dan he went an' tamed one o' them that did seem to have reason same as folks. It was round here a good spell after he went away. Dan an' his father they didn't hitch,—but he never held up his head ag'in after Dan had dared him an' gone off."

The guest did not notice this hint of family sorrows in his eager interest in something else.

"So Sylvy knows all about birds, does she?" he exclaimed, as he looked round at the little girl who sat, very demure but increasingly sleepy, in the moonlight. "I am making a collection of birds myself. I have been at it ever since I was a boy." (Mrs. Tilley smiled.) "There are two or three very rare ones I have been hunting for these five years. I mean to get them on my own ground if they can be found."

"Do you cage 'em up?" asked Mrs. Tilley doubtfully, in response to this enthusiastic announcement.

"Oh, no, they're stuffed and preserved, dozens and dozens of them," said the ornithologist, "and I have shot or snared every one myself. I caught a glimpse of a white heron three miles from here on Saturday, and I have followed it in this direction. They have never been found in this district at all. The little white heron, it is,"[7] and he turned again to look at Sylvia with the hope of discovering that the rare bird was one of her acquaintances.

But Sylvia was watching a hop-toad in the narrow footpath.

"You would know the heron if you saw it," the stranger continued eagerly. "A queer tall white bird with soft feathers and long thin legs. And it would have a nest perhaps in the top of a high tree, made of sticks, something like a hawk's nest."

Sylvia's heart gave a wild beat; she knew that strange white bird, and had once stolen softly near where it stood in some bright green swamp grass, away over at the other side of the woods. There was an open place where the sunshine always seemed strangely yellow and hot, where tall, nodding rushes grew, and her grandmother had warned her that she might sink in the soft black mud underneath and never be heard of more. Not far beyond were the salt marshes and beyond those was the sea, the sea which Sylvia wondered and dreamed about, but never had looked upon, though its great voice could often be heard above the noise of the woods on stormy nights.

"I can't think of anything I should like so much as to find that heron's nest," the handsome stranger was saying. "I would give ten dollars to anybody who could show it to me," he added desperately, "and I mean to spend my whole vacation hunting for it if need be. Perhaps it was only migrating, or had been chased out of its own region by some bird of prey."

Mrs. Tilley gave amazed attention to all this, but Sylvia still watched the toad, not divining, as she might have done at some calmer time, that the creature wished to get to its hole under the doorstep, and was much hindered by the unusual spectators at that hour of the evening. No amount of thought, that night, could decide how many wished-for treasures the ten dollars, so lightly spoken of, would buy.

The next day the young sportsman hovered about the woods, and Sylvia kept him company, having lost her first fear of the friendly lad, who proved to be most kind and sympathetic. He told her many things about the birds and what they knew and where they lived and what they did with themselves. And he gave her a jack-knife, which she thought as great a treasure as if she were a desert-islander. All day long he did not once make her troubled or afraid except when he brought down some unsuspecting singing creature from its bough. Sylvia would have liked him vastly better without his gun; she could not understand why he killed the very birds he seemed to like so much. But as the day waned, Sylvia still watched the young man with loving admiration. She had never seen anybody so charming and delightful; the woman's heart, asleep in the child, was vaguely thrilled by a dream of love. Some premonition of that great power stirred and swayed these young foresters who traversed the solemn woodlands with soft-footed silent care. They stopped to listen to a bird's song; they pressed forward again eagerly, parting the branches,—speaking to each other rarely and in whispers; the young man going first and Sylvia following, fascinated, a few steps behind, with her gray eyes dark with excitement.

She grieved because the longed-for white heron was elusive, but she did not lead the guest, she only followed, and there was no such thing as speaking first. The sound of her own unquestioned voice would have terrified her,—it was hard enough to answer yes or no when there was need of that. At last evening began to fall, and they drove the cow home together, and Sylvia smiled with pleasure when they came to the place where she heard the whistle and was afraid only the night before.

II

Half a mile from home, at the farther edge of the woods, where the land was highest, a great pine-tree stood, the last of its generation. Whether it was left for a boundary mark, or for what reason, no one could say; the woodchoppers who had felled its mates were dead and gone long ago, and a whole forest of sturdy trees, pines and oaks and maples, had grown again. But the stately head of this old pine towered above them all and made a landmark for sea and shore miles and miles away. Sylvia knew it well. She had always believed that whoever climbed to the top of it could see the ocean; and the little girl had often laid her hand on the great rough trunk and looked up wistfully at those dark boughs that the wind always stirred, no matter how hot and still the air might be below. Now she thought of the tree with a new excitement, for why, if one climbed it at break of day, could not one see all the world, and easily discover whence the white heron flew, and mark the place, and find the hidden nest?

What a spirit of adventure, what wild ambition! What fancied triumph and delight and glory for the later morning when she could make known the secret! It was almost too real and too great for the childish heart to bear.

All night the door of the little house stood open, and the whippoorwills came and sang upon the very step. The young sportsman and his old hostess were sound asleep, but Sylvia's great design kept her broad awake and watching. She forgot to think of sleep. The short summer night seemed as long as the winter darkness, and at last when the whippoorwills ceased, and she was afraid the morning would after all come too soon, she stole out of the house and followed the pasture path through the woods, hastening toward the open ground beyond, listening with a sense of comfort and companionship to the drowsy twitter of a half-awakened bird, whose perch she had jarred in passing. Alas, if the great wave of human interest which flooded for the first time this dull little life should sweep away the satisfactions of an existence heart to heart with nature and the dumb life of the forest!

There was the huge tree asleep yet in the paling moonlight, and small and hopeful Sylvia began with utmost bravery to mount to the top of it, with tingling, eager blood coursing the channels of her whole frame, with her bare feet and fingers, that pinched and held like bird's claws to the monstrous ladder reaching up, up, almost to the sky itself. First she must mount the white oak tree that grew alongside, where she was almost lost among the dark branches and the green leaves heavy and wet with dew; a bird fluttered off its nest, and a red squirrel ran to and fro and scolded pettishly at the harmless housebreaker. Sylvia felt her way easily. She had often climbed there, and knew that higher still one of the oak's upper branches chafed against the pine trunk, just where its lower boughs were set close together. There, when she made the dangerous pass from one tree to the other, the great enterprise would really begin.

She crept out along the swaying oak limb at last, and took the daring step across into the old pine-tree. The way was harder than she thought; she must reach far and hold fast, the sharp dry twigs caught and held her and scratched her like angry talons, the pitch made her thin little fingers clumsy and stiff as she went round and round the tree's great stem, higher and higher upward. The sparrows and robins in the woods below were beginning to wake and twitter to the dawn, yet it seemed much lighter there aloft in the pine-tree, and the child knew that she must hurry if her project were to be of any use.

The tree seemed to lengthen itself out as she went up, and to reach farther and farther upward. It was like a great main-mast to the voyaging earth; it must truly have been amazed that morning through all its ponderous frame as it felt this determined spark of human spirit creeping and climbing from higher branch to branch. Who knows how steadily the least twigs held themselves to advantage this light, weak creature on her way! The old pine must have loved his new dependent. More than all the hawks, and bats, and moths, and even the sweet-voiced thrushes, was the brave, beating heart of the solitary gray-eyed child. And the tree stood still and held away the winds that June morning while the dawn grew bright in the east.

Sylvia's face was like a pale star, if one had seen it from the ground, when the last thorny bough was past, and she stood trembling and tired but wholly triumphant, high in the tree-top. Yes, there was the sea with the dawning sun making a golden dazzle over it, and toward that glorious east flew two hawks with slow-moving pinions. How low they looked in the air from that height when before one had only seen them far up, and dark against the blue sky. Their gray feathers were as soft as moths; they seemed only a little way from the tree, and Sylvia felt as if she too could go flying away among the clouds. Westward, the woodlands and farms reached miles and miles into the distance; here and there were church steeples, and white villages; truly it was a vast and awesome world.

The birds sang louder and louder. At last the sun came up bewilderingly bright. Sylvia could see the white sails of ships out at sea, and the clouds that were purple and rose-colored and yellow at first began to fade away. Where was the white heron's nest in the sea of green branches, and was this wonderful sight and pageant of the world the only reward for having climbed to such a giddy height? Now look down again, Sylvia, where the green marsh is set among the shining birches and dark hemlocks; there where you saw the white heron once you will see him again; look, look! a white spot of him like a single floating feather comes up from the dead hemlock and grows larger, and rises, and comes close at last, and goes by the landmark pine with steady sweep of wing and outstretched slender neck and crested head. And wait! wait! do not move a foot or a finger, little girl, do not send an arrow of light and consciousness from your two eager eyes, for the heron has perched on a pine bough not far beyond yours, and cries back to his mate on the nest, and plumes his feathers for the new day!

The child gives a long sigh a minute later when a company of shouting cat-birds comes also to the tree, and vexed by their fluttering and lawlessness the solemn heron goes away. She knows his secret now, the wild, light, slender bird that floats and wavers, and goes back like an arrow presently to his home in the green world beneath. Then Sylvia, well satisfied, makes her perilous way down again, not daring to look far below the branch she stands on, ready to cry sometimes because her fingers ache and her lamed feet slip. Wondering over and over again what the stranger would say to her, and what he would think when she told him how to find his way straight to the heron's nest.

"Sylvy, Sylvy!" called the busy old grandmother again and again, but nobody answered, and the small husk bed was empty, and Sylvia had disappeared.

The guest waked from a dream, and remembering his day's pleasure hurried to dress himself that it might sooner begin. He was sure from the way the shy little girl looked once or twice yesterday that she had at least seen the white heron, and now she must really be persuaded to tell. Here she comes now, paler than ever, and her worn old frock is torn and tattered, and smeared with pine pitch. The grandmother and the sportsman stand in the door together and question her, and the splendid moment has come to speak of the dead hemlock-tree by the green marsh.

But Sylvia does not speak after all, though the old grandmother fretfully rebukes her, and the young man's kind appealing eyes are looking straight in her own. He can make them rich with money; he has promised it, and they are poor now. He is so well worth making happy, and he waits to hear the story she can tell.

No, she must keep silence! What is it that suddenly forbids her and makes her dumb? Has she been nine years growing, and now, when the great world for the first time puts out a hand to her, must she thrust it aside for a bird's sake? The murmur of the pine's green branches is in her ears, she remembers how the white heron came flying through the golden air and how they watched the sea and the morning together, and Sylvia cannot speak; she cannot tell the heron's secret and give its life away.

Dear loyalty, that suffered a sharp pang as the guest went away disappointed later in the day, that could have served and followed him and loved him as a dog loves! Many a night Sylvia heard the echo of his whistle haunting the pasture path as she came home with the loitering cow. She forgot even her sorrow at the sharp report of his gun and the piteous sight of thrushes and sparrows dropping silent to the ground, their songs hushed and their pretty feathers stained and wet with blood. Were the birds better friends than their hunter might have been,—who can tell? Whatever treasures were lost to her, woodlands and summer-time, remember! Bring your gifts and graces and tell your secrets to this lonely country child!

THE DULHAM LADIES

To be leaders of society in the town of Dulham was as satisfactory to Miss Dobin and Miss Lucinda Dobin[8] as if Dulham were London itself. Of late years, though they would not allow themselves to suspect such treason, the most ill-bred of the younger people in the village made fun of them behind their backs, and laughed at their treasured summer mantillas,* their mincing steps, and the shape of their parasols.

They were always conscious of the fact that they were the daughters of a once eminent Dulham minister; but beside this unanswerable claim to the respect of the First Parish,† they were aware that their mother's social position was one of superior altitude. Madam Dobin's grandmother was a Greenaple, of Boston. In her younger days she had often visited her relatives, the Greenaples and Hightrees, and in seasons of festivity she could relate to a select and properly excited audience her delightful experiences of town life. Nothing could be finer than her account of having taken tea at Governor Clovenfoot's on Beacon Street‡ in company with an English lord, who was indulging himself in a brief vacation from his arduous duties at the Court of St. James.§

"He exclaimed that he had seldom seen in England so beautiful and intelligent a company of ladies," Madam Dobin would always say in conclusion. "He was decorated with the blue ribbon of the Knights of the Garter."‖ Miss Dobin and Miss Lucinda thought for

*Lace scarves worn over the head and the shoulders by women, initially in Spain and Latin America and later in other Western countries.

†The first church of a denomination to be established within a given New England community. In "The Dulham Ladies," the First Parish Church is likely either Episcopal or Congregational.

‡Central, historically important street in Boston.

§Great Britain's royal court.

‖ Reference to the order of British knighthood that is at the peak of the British honors system.

many years that this famous blue ribbon was tied about the noble gentleman's leg. One day they even discussed the question openly; Miss Dobin placing the decoration at his knee, and Miss Lucinda locating it much lower down, according to the length of the short gray socks with which she was familiar.

"You have no imagination, Lucinda," the elder sister replied impatiently. "Of course, those were the days of small-clothes and long silk stockings!"[9]—whereat Miss Lucinda was rebuked, but not persuaded.

"I wish that my dear girls could have the outlook upon society which fell to my portion," Madam Dobin sighed, after she had set these ignorant minds to rights, and enriched them by communicating the final truth about the blue ribbon. "I must not chide you for the absence of opportunities, but if our cousin Harriet Greenaple were only living you would not lack enjoyment or social education."

Madam Dobin had now been dead a great many years. She seemed an elderly woman to her daughters some time before she left them; later they thought that she had really died comparatively young, since their own years had come to equal the record of hers. When they visited her tall white tombstone in the orderly Dulham burying-ground, it was a strange thought to both the daughters that they were older women than their mother had been when she died. To be sure, it was the fashion to appear older in her day,—they could remember the sober effect of really youthful married persons in cap and frisette; but, whether they owed it to the changed times or to their own qualities, they felt no older themselves than ever they had. Beside upholding the ministerial dignity of their father, they were obliged to give a lenient sanction to the ways of the world for their mother's sake; and they combined the two duties with reverence and impartiality.

Madam Dobin was, in her prime, a walking example of refinements and courtesies. If she erred in any way, it was by keeping too strict watch and rule over her small kingdom. She acted with great dignity in all matters of social administration and etiquette, but, while it must be owned that the parishioners felt a sense of freedom for a time after her death, in their later years they praised and valued her more and more, and often lamented her generously and sincerely.

Several of her distinguished relatives attended Madam Dobin's funeral, which was long considered the most dignified and elegant pageant of that sort which had ever taken place in Dulham. It seemed to mark the close of a famous epoch in Dulham history, and it was increasingly difficult forever afterward to keep the tone of society up to the old standard. Somehow, the distinguished relatives had one by one disappeared, though they all had excellent reasons for the discontinuance of their visits. A few had left this world altogether, and the family circle of the Greenaples and Hightrees was greatly reduced in circumference. Sometimes, in summer, a stray connection drifted Dulham-ward, and was displayed to the townspeople (not to say paraded) by the gratified hostesses. It was a disappointment if the guest could not be persuaded to remain over Sunday and appear at church. When household antiquities became fashionable, the ladies remarked a surprising interest in their corner cupboard and best chairs, and some distant relatives revived their almost forgotten custom of paying a summer visit to Dulham. They were not long in finding out with what desperate affection Miss Dobin and Miss Lucinda clung to their mother's wedding china and other inheritances, and were allowed to depart without a single teacup. One graceless descendant of the Hightrees prowled from garret to cellar, and admired the household belongings diligently, but she was not asked to accept even the dislocated cherry-wood footstool that she had discovered in the far corner of the parsonage pew.

Some of the Dulham friends had long suspected that Madam Dobin made a social misstep when she chose the Reverend Edward Dobin for her husband. She was no longer young when she married, and though she had gone through the wood and picked up a crooked stick at last, it made a great difference that her stick possessed an ecclesiastical bark. The Reverend Edward was, moreover, a respectable graduate of Harvard College, and to a woman of her standards a clergyman was by no means insignificant. It was impossible not to respect his office, at any rate, and she must have treated him with proper veneration for the sake of that, if for no other reason, though his early advantages had been insufficient, and he was quite insensible to the claims of the Greenaple pedigree, and preferred an Indian pudding* to pie crust that was, without exaggeration,

*Baked pudding of cornmeal, milk, and molasses.

half a quarter high.* The delicacy of Madam Dobin's touch and preference in everything, from hymns to cookery, was quite lost upon this respected preacher, yet he was not without pride or complete confidence in his own decisions.

The Reverend Mr. Dobin was never very enlightening in his discourses, and was providentially stopped short by a stroke of paralysis in the middle of his clerical career. He lived on and on through many dreary years, but his children never accepted the fact that he was a tyrant, and served him humbly and patiently. He fell at last into a condition of great incapacity and chronic trembling, but was able for nearly a quarter of a century to be carried to the meeting-house from time to time to pronounce farewell discourses. On high days of the church he was always placed in the pulpit, and held up his shaking hands when the benediction was pronounced, as if the divine gift were exclusively his own, and the other minister did but say empty words. Afterward, he was usually tired and displeased and hard to cope with, but there was always a proper notice taken of these too often recurring events. For old times' and for pity's sake and from natural goodness of heart, the elder parishioners rallied manfully about the Reverend Mr. Dobin; and whoever his successor or colleague might be, the Dobins were always called the minister's folks, while the active laborer in that vineyard† was only Mr. Smith or Mr. Jones, as the case might be. At last the poor old man died, to everybody's relief and astonishment; and after he was properly preached about and lamented, his daughters, Miss Dobin and Miss Lucinda, took a good look at life from a new standpoint, and decided that now they were no longer constrained by home duties they must make themselves a great deal more used to the town.

Sometimes there is such a household as this (which has been perhaps too minutely described), where the parents linger until their children are far past middle age, and always keep them in a too childish and unworthy state of subjection. The Misses Dobin's

---

*Reference to an English measurement, likely half a quarter of a yard—that is, 4.5 inches.

†Reference to the Bible, Matthew 20.

characters were much influenced by such an unnatural prolongation of the filial relationship, and they were amazingly slow to suspect that they were not so young as they used to be. There was nothing to measure themselves by but Dulham people and things. The elm-trees were growing yet, and many of the ladies of the First Parish were older than they, and called them, with pleasant familiarity, the Dobin girls. These elderly persons seemed really to be growing old, and Miss Lucinda frequently lamented the change in society; she thought it a freak of nature and too sudden blighting of earthly hopes that several charming old friends of her mother's were no longer living. They were advanced in age when Miss Lucinda was a young girl, though time and space are but relative, after all.

Their influence upon society would have made a great difference in many ways. Certainly, the new parishioners, who had often enough been instructed to pronounce their pastor's name as if it were spelled with one "b," would not have boldly returned again and again to their obnoxious habit of saying Dobbin. Miss Lucinda might carefully speak to the neighbor and new-comers of "my sister, Miss Do-bin;" only the select company of intimates followed her lead, and at last there was something humiliating about it, even though many persons spoke of them only as "the ladies."

"The name was originally *D' Aubigne*, we think," Miss Lucinda would say coldly and patiently, as if she had already explained this foolish mistake a thousand times too often. It was like the sorrows in many a provincial château in the Reign of Terror.* The ladies looked on with increasing dismay at the retrogression in society. They felt as if they were a feeble garrison, to whose lot it had fallen to repulse a noisy, irreverent mob, an increasing band of marauders who would overthrow all land-marks of the past, all etiquette and social rank. The new minister himself was a round-faced, unspiritual-looking young man, whom they would have instinctively ignored if he had not been a minister. The new people who came to Dulham were not

*Reference to the period between September 5, 1793, and July 27, 1794, when the French government began to persecute and often execute opponents of the Revolution.

like the older residents, and they had no desire to be taught better. Little they cared about the Greenaples or the Hightrees; and once, when Miss Dobin essayed to speak of some detail of her mother's brilliant opportunities in Boston high life, she was interrupted, and the new-comer who sat next her at the parish sewing society began to talk about something else. We cannot believe that it could have been the tea-party at Governor Clovenfoot's which the rude creature so disrespectfully ignored, but some persons are capable of showing any lack of good taste.

The ladies had an unusual and most painful sense of failure, as they went home together that evening. "I have always made it my object to improve and interest the people at such times; it would seem so possible to elevate their thoughts and direct them into higher channels," said Miss Dobin sadly. "But as for that Woolden woman, there is no use in casting pearls before swine!"*

Miss Lucinda murmured an indignant assent. She had a secret suspicion that the Woolden woman had heard the story in question oftener than had pleased her. She was but an ignorant creature; though she had lived in Dulham twelve or thirteen years, she was no better than when she came. The mistake was in treating sister Harriet as if she were on a level with the rest of the company. Miss Lucinda had observed more than once, lately, that her sister sometimes repeated herself, unconsciously, a little oftener than was agreeable. Perhaps they were getting a trifle dull; toward spring it might be well to pass a few days with some of their friends, and have a change.

"If I have tried to do anything," said Miss Dobin in an icy tone, "it has been to stand firm in my lot and place, and to hold the standard of cultivated mind and elegant manners as high as possible. You would think it had been a hundred years since our mother's death, so completely has the effect of her good breeding and exquisite hospitality been lost sight of, here in Dulham. I could wish that our father had chosen to settle in a larger and more appreciative place. They would like to put us on the shelf, too. I can see that plainly."

---

*Based on the Bible, Matthew 7:6 (KJV): "Neither cast ye your pearls before swine, lest they trample them under their feet."

"I am sure we have our friends," said Miss Lucinda anxiously, but with a choking voice. "We must not let them think we do not mean to keep up with the times, as we always have. I do feel as if perhaps—our hair"—

And the sad secret was out at last. Each of the sisters drew a long breath of relief at this beginning of a confession.

It was certain that they must take some steps to retrieve their lost ascendency. Public attention had that evening been called to their fast-disappearing locks, poor ladies; and Miss Lucinda felt the discomfort most, for she had been the inheritor of the Hightree hair, long and curly, and chestnut in color. There used to be a waviness about it, and sometimes pretty escaping curls, but these were gone long ago. Miss Dobin resembled her father, and her hair had not been luxuriant, so that she was less changed by its absence than one might suppose. The straightness and thinness had increased so gradually that neither sister had quite accepted the thought that other persons would particularly notice their altered appearance.

They had shrunk, with the reticence born of close family association, from speaking of the cause even to each other, when they made themselves pretty little lace and dotted muslin caps. Breakfast caps, they called them, and explained that these were universally worn in town; the young Princess of Wales* originated them, or at any rate adopted them. The ladies offered no apology for keeping the breakfast caps on until bedtime, and in spite of them a forward child had just spoken, loud and shrill, an untimely question in the ears of the for once silent sewing society. "Do Miss Dobbinses wear them great caps because their bare heads is cold?" the little beast had said; and everybody was startled and dismayed.

Miss Dobin had never shown better her good breeding and valor, the younger sister thought.

"No, little girl," replied the stately Harriet, with a chilly smile. "I believe that our headdresses are quite in the fashion for ladies of all ages. And you must remember that it is never polite to make such

---

*Likely a reference to Alexandra, wife of Queen Victoria's son Albert Edward, prince of Wales, who in 1901 became King Edward VII; Alexandra and Albert were married on March 10, 1863.

personal remarks." It was after this that Miss Dobin had been reminded of Madam Somebody's unusual headgear at the evening entertainment in Boston. Nobody but the Woolden woman could have interrupted her under such trying circumstances.

Miss Lucinda, however, was certain that the time had come for making some effort to replace her lost adornment. The child had told an unwelcome truth, but had paved the way for further action, and now was the time to suggest something that had slowly been taking shape in Miss Lucinda's mind. A young grand-nephew of their mother and his bride had passed a few days with them, two or three summers before, and the sisters had been quite shocked to find that the pretty young woman wore a row of frizzes, not originally her own, over her smooth forehead. At the time, Miss Dobin and Miss Lucinda had spoken severely with each other of such bad taste, but now it made a great difference that the wearer of the frizzes was not only a relative by marriage and used to good society, but also that she came from town, and might be supposed to know what was proper in the way of toilet.

"I really think, sister, that we had better see about having some—arrangements, next time we go anywhere," Miss Dobin said unexpectedly, with a slight tremble in her voice, just as they reached their own door. "There seems to be quite a fashion for them nowadays. For the parish's sake we ought to recognize"—and Miss Lucinda responded with instant satisfaction. She did not like to complain, but she had been troubled with neuralgic pains in her forehead on suddenly meeting the cold air. The sisters felt a new bond of sympathy in keeping this secret with and for each other; they took pains to say to several acquaintances that they were thinking of going to the next large town to do a few errands for Christmas.

A bright, sunny morning seemed to wish the ladies good-fortune. Old Hetty Downs, their faithful maid-servant and protector, looked after them in affectionate foreboding. "Dear sakes, what devil's wiles may be played on them blessed innocents afore they're safe home again!" she murmured, as they vanished round the corner of the street that led to the railway station.

Miss Dobin and Miss Lucinda paced discreetly side by side down the main street of Westbury. It was nothing like Boston, of course, but the noise was slightly confusing, and the passers-by sometimes roughly pushed against them. Westbury was a consequential manufacturing town, but a great convenience at times like this. The trifling Christmas gifts for their old neighbors and Sunday-school scholars were purchased and stowed away in their neat Fayal* basket before the serious commission of the day was attended to. Here and there, in the shops, disreputable frizzes were displayed in unblushing effrontery, but no such vulgar shopkeeper merited the patronage of the Misses Dobin. They pretended not to observe the unattractive goods, and went their way to a low, one-storied building on a side street, where an old tradesman lived. He had been useful to the minister while he still remained upon the earth and had need of a wig, sandy in hue and increasingly sprinkled with gray, as if it kept pace with other changes of existence. But old Paley's shutters were up, and a bar of rough wood was nailed firmly across the one that had lost its fastening and would rack its feeble hinges in the wind. Old Paley had always been polite and bland; they really had looked forward to a little chat with him; they had heard a year or two before of his wife's death, and meant to offer sympathy. His business of hair-dressing had been carried on with that of parasol and umbrella mending, and the condemned umbrella which was his sign cracked and swung in the rising wind, a tattered skeleton before the closed door. The ladies sighed and turned away; they were beginning to feel tired; the day was long, and they had not met with any pleasures yet. "We might walk up the street a little farther," suggested Miss Lucinda; "that is, if you are not tired," as they stood hesitating on the corner after they had finished a short discussion of Mr. Paley's disappearance. Happily it was only a few minutes before they came to a stop together in front of a new, shining shop, where smirking waxen heads all in a row were decked with the latest fashions of wigs and frizzes. One smiling fragment of a gentleman stared so straight at Miss Lucinda with his black eyes that she felt quite coy and embarrassed, and was obliged to feign not to be conscious of his admiration. But Miss Dobin, after a brief delay,

*Older spelling of "Faial," as in Faial Island in the Portuguese Azores, where many women made fine baskets.

boldly opened the door and entered; it was better to be sheltered in the shop than exposed to public remark as they gazed in at the windows. Miss Lucinda felt her heart beat and her courage give out; she, coward like, left the transaction of their business to her sister, and turned to contemplate the back of the handsome model. It was a slight shock to find that he was not so attractive from this point of view. The wig he wore was well made all round, but his shoulders were roughly finished in a substance that looked like plain plaster of Paris.

"What can I have ze pleasure of showing you, young ladees?" asked a person who advanced; and Miss Lucinda faced about to discover a smiling, middle-aged Frenchman, who rubbed his hands together and looked at his customers, first one and then the other, with delightful deference. He seemed a very civil, nice person, the young ladies thought.

"My sister and I were thinking of buying some little arrangements to wear above the forehead." Miss Dobin explained, with pathetic dignity; but the Frenchman spared her any further words. He looked with eager interest at the bonnets, as if no lack had attracted his notice before. "Ah, yes. *Je comprends*; ze high foreheads are not now ze mode. Je prefer them, moi, yes, yes, but ze ladies must accept ze fashion; zay must now cover ze forehead with ze frizzes, ze bangs, you say. As you wis', as you wis'!" and the tactful little man, with many shrugs and merry gestures at such girlish fancies, pulled down one box after another.

It was a great relief to find that this was no worse, to say the least, than any other shopping, though the solemnity and secrecy of the occasion were infringed upon by the great supply of "arrangements" and the loud discussion of the color of some crimps a noisy girl was buying from a young saleswoman the other side of the shop.

Miss Dobin waved aside the wares which were being displayed for her approval. "Something—more simple, if you please,"—she did not like to say "older."

"But these are *très simple*,"* protested the Frenchman. "We have nothing younger;" and Miss Dobin and Miss Lucinda blushed, and

*Very simple (French).

said no more. The Frenchman had his own way; he persuaded them that nothing was so suitable as some conspicuous forelocks that matched their hair as it used to be. They would have given anything rather than leave their breakfast caps at home, if they had known that their proper winter bonnets must come off. They hardly listened to the wig merchant's glib voice as Miss Dobin stood revealed before the merciless mirror at the back of the shop.

He made everything as easy as possible, the friendly creature, and the ladies were grateful to him. Beside, now that the bonnet was on again there was a great improvement in Miss Dobin's appearance. She turned to Miss Lucinda, and saw a gleam of delight in her eager countenance. "It really is very becoming. I like the way it parts over your forehead," said the younger sister, "but if it were long enough to go behind the ears"—"*Non, non,*" entreated the Frenchman. "To make her the old woman at once would be cruelty!" And Lucinda who was wondering how well she would look in her turn, succumbed promptly to such protestations. Yes, there was no use in being old before their time. Dulham was not quite keeping pace with the rest of the world in these days, but they need not drag behind everybody else, just because they lived there.

The price of the little arrangements was much less than the sisters expected, and the uncomfortable expense of their reverend father's wigs had been, it was proved, a thing of the past. Miss Dobin treated her polite Frenchman with great courtesy; indeed, Miss Lucinda had more than once whispered to her to talk French, and as they were bowed out of the shop the gracious *Bong-sure** of the elder lady seemed to act like the string of a showerbath† and bring down an awesome torrent of foreign words upon the two guileless heads. It was impossible to reply; the ladies bowed again, however, and Miss Lucinda caught a last smile from the handsome wax countenance in the window. He appeared to regard her with fresh approval, and she departed down the street with mincing steps.

---

*Corruption of the French phrase *bon jour* ("good day").

†In the nineteenth century, one took a shower by pulling on a string that released water from an overhead tank.

"I feel as if anybody might look at me now, sister," said gentle Miss Lucinda. "I confess, I have really suffered sometimes, since I knew I looked so distressed."

"Yours is lighter than I thought it was in the shop," remarked Miss Dobin, doubtfully, but she quickly added that perhaps it would change a little. She was so perfectly satisfied with her own appearance that she could not bear to dim the pleasure of any one else. The truth remained that she never would have let Lucinda choose that particular arrangement if she had seen it first in a good light. And Lucinda was thinking exactly the same of her companion.

"I am sure we shall have no more neuralgia," said Miss Dobin. "I am sorry we waited so long, dear," and they tripped down the main street of Westbury, confident that nobody would suspect them of being over thirty. Indeed, they felt quite girlish, and unconsciously looked sideways as they went along, to see their satisfying reflections in the windows. The great panes made excellent mirrors, with not too clear or lasting pictures of these comforted passers-by.

The Frenchman in the shop was making merry with his assistants. The two great frisettes had long been out of fashion; he had been lying in wait with them for two unsuspecting country ladies, who could be cajoled into such a purchase.

"Sister," Miss Lucinda was saying, "you know there is still an hour to wait before our train goes. Suppose we take a little longer walk down the other side of the way;" and they strolled slowly back again. In fact, they nearly missed the train, naughty girls! Hetty would have been so worried, they assured each other, but they reached the station just in time.

"Lutie," said Miss Dobin, "put up your hand and part it from your forehead; it seems to be getting out of place a little;" and Miss Lucinda, who had just got breath enough to speak, returned the information that Miss Dobin's was almost covering her eyebrows. They might have to trim them a little shorter; of course it could be done. The darkness was falling; they had taken an early dinner before they started, and now they were tired and hungry after the exertion of the afternoon, but the spirit of youth flamed afresh in their hearts, and they were very happy. If one's heart remains young, it is a sore trial to have the outward appearance entirely at variance. It was the ladies' nature to be girlish, and they found it impossible not to be grateful to the flimsy, ineffectual disguise which seemed to set them right with the world. The old conductor, who had known them for many years, looked hard at them as he took their tickets, and, being a man of humor and compassion, affected not to notice anything remarkable in their appearance. "You ladies never mean to grow old, like the rest of us," he said gallantly, and the sisters fairly quaked with joy.

"Bless us!" the obnoxious Mrs. Woolden was saying, at the other end of the car. "There's the old maid Dobbinses, and they've bought 'em some bangs. I expect they wanted to get thatched in a little before real cold weather; but don't they look just like a pair o' poodle dogs."

The little ladies descended wearily from the train. Somehow they did not enjoy a day's shopping as much as they used. They were certainly much obliged to Hetty for sending her niece's boy to meet them, with a lantern; also for having a good warm supper ready when they came in. Hetty took a quick look at her mistresses, and returned to the kitchen. "I knew somebody would be foolin' of 'em," she assured herself angrily, but she had to laugh. Their dear, kind faces were wrinkled and pale, and the great frizzes had lost their pretty curliness, and were hanging down, almost straight and very ugly, into the ladies' eyes. They could not tuck them up under their caps, as they were sure might be done.

Then came a succession of rainy days, and nobody visited the rejuvenated household. The frisettes looked very bright chestnut by the light of day, and it must be confessed that Miss Dobin took the scissors and shortened Miss Lucinda's half an inch, and Miss Lucinda returned the compliment quite secretly, because each thought her sister's forehead lower than her own. Their dear gray eyebrows were honestly displayed, as if it were the fashion not to have them match with wigs. Hetty at last spoke out, and begged her mistresses, as they sat at breakfast, to let her take the frizzes back and change them. Her sister's daughter worked in that very shop, and, though in the work-room, would be able to oblige them, Hetty was sure.

But the ladies looked at each other in pleased assurance, and then turned together to look at Hetty, who stood already a little apprehensive near the table, where she had just put down a plateful of smoking drop-cakes.* The good creature really began to look old.

"They are worn very much in town," said Miss Dobin. "We think it was quite fortunate that the fashion came in just as our hair was growing a trifle thin. I dare say we may choose those that are a shade duller in color when these are a little past. Oh, we shall not want tea this evening, you remember, Hetty. I am glad there is likely to be such a good night for the sewing circle." And Miss Dobin and Miss Lucinda nodded and smiled.

"Oh, my sakes alive!" the troubled handmaiden groaned. "Going to the circle, be they, to be snickered at! Well, the Dobbin girls they was born, and the Dobbin girls they will remain till they die; but if they ain't innocent Christian babes to those that knows 'em well, mark me down for an idjit myself! They believe them front-pieces has set the clock back forty year or more, but if they're pleased to think so, let 'em!"

Away paced the Dulham ladies, late in the afternoon, to grace the parish occasion, and face the amused scrutiny of their neighbors. "I think we owe it to society to observe the fashions of the day," said Miss Lucinda. "A lady cannot afford to be unattractive. I feel now as if we were prepared for anything!"

---

*Small cakes cooked by dropping batter in hot fat and then baking it in an oven.

THE COURTING OF SISTER WISBY

ALL THE MORNING THERE had been an increasing temptation to take an out-door holiday, and early in the afternoon the temptation outgrew my power of resistance. A far-away pasture on the long southwestern slope of a high hill was persistently present to my mind, yet there seemed to be no particular reason why I should think of it. I was not sure that I wanted anything from the pasture, and there was no sign, except the temptation, that the pasture wanted anything of me. But I was on the farther side of as many as three fences before I stopped to think again where I was going, and why.

There is no use in trying to tell another person about that afternoon unless he distinctly remembers weather exactly like it. No number of details concerning an Arctic ice-blockade will give a single shiver to a child of the tropics. This was one of those perfect New England days in late summer, when the spirit of autumn takes a first stealthy flight, like a spy, through the ripening country-side, and, with feigned sympathy for those who droop with August heat, puts her cool cloak of bracing air about leaf and flower and human shoulders. Every living thing grows suddenly cheerful and strong; it is only when you catch sight of a horror-stricken little maple in swampy soil,—a little maple that has second sight and foreknowledge of coming disaster to her race,—only then does a distrust of autumn's friendliness dim your joyful satisfaction.

In midwinter there is always a day when one has the first foretaste of spring; in late August there is a morning when the air is for the first time autumn like. Perhaps it is a hint to the squirrels to get in their first supplies for the winter hoards, or a reminder that summer will soon end, and everybody had better make the most of it. We are always looking forward to the passing and ending of winter, but when summer is here it seems as if summer must always last. As I went across the fields that day, I found myself half lamenting that the world must fade again, even that the best of her budding and bloom was only a preparation for another spring-time, for an awakening beyond the coming winter's sleep.

The sun was slightly veiled; there was a chattering group of birds, which had gathered for a conference about their early migration. Yet, oddly enough, I heard the voice of a belated bobolink, and presently saw him rise from the grass and hover leisurely, while he sang a brief tune. He was much behind time if he were still a housekeeper; but as for the other birds, who listened, they cared only for their own notes. An old crow went sagging by, and gave a croak at his despised neighbor, just as a black reviewer croaked at Keats:[10] so hard it is to be just to one's contemporaries. The bobolink was indeed singing out of season, and it was impossible to say whether he really belonged most to this summer or to the next. He might have been delayed on his northward journey; at any rate, he had a light heart now, to judge from his song, and I wished that I could ask him a few questions,—how he liked being the last man among the bobolinks, and where he had taken singing lessons in the South.

Presently I left the lower fields, and took a path that led higher, where I could look beyond the village to the northern country mountainward. Here the sweet fern grew, thick and fragrant, and I also found myself heedlessly treading on pennyroyal. Near by, in a field corner, I long ago made a most comfortable seat by putting a stray piece of board and bit of rail across the angle of the fences. I have spent many a delightful hour there, in the shade and shelter of a young pitch-pine and a wild-cherry tree, with a lovely outlook toward the village, just far enough away beyond the green slopes and tall elms of the lower meadows. But that day I still had the feeling of being outward bound, and did not turn aside nor linger. The high pasture land grew more and more enticing.

I stopped to pick some blackberries that twinkled at me like beads among their dry vines, and two or three yellow-birds fluttered up from the leaves of a thistle, and then came back again, as if they had complacently discovered that I was only an overgrown yellow-bird,* in strange disguise but perfectly harmless. They made me feel

---

*Folk name for the American goldfinch.

as if I were an intruder, though they did not offer to peck at me, and we parted company very soon. It was good to stand at last on the great shoulder of the hill. The wind was coming in from the sea, there was a fine fragrance from the pines, and the air grew sweeter every moment. I took new pleasure in the thought that in a piece of wild pasture land like this one may get closest to Nature, and subsist upon what she gives of her own free will. There have been no drudging, heavy-shod ploughmen to overturn the soil, and vex it into yielding artificial crops. Here one has to take just what Nature is pleased to give, whether one is a yellow-bird or a human being. It is very good entertainment for a summer wayfarer, and I am asking my reader now to share the winter provision which I harvested that day. Let us hope that the small birds are also faring well after their fashion, but I give them an anxious thought while the snow goes hurrying in long waves across the buried fields, this windy winter night.

I next went farther down the hill, and got a drink of fresh cool water from the brook, and pulled a tender sheaf of sweet flag beside it. The mossy old fence just beyond was the last barrier between me and the pasture which had sent an invisible messenger earlier in the day, but I saw that somebody else had come first to the rendezvous: there was a brown gingham cape-bonnet and a sprigged shoulder-shawl bobbing up and down, a little way off among the junipers. I had taken such uncommon pleasure in being alone that I instantly felt a sense of disappointment; then a warm glow of pleasant satisfaction rebuked-my selfishness. This could be no one but dear old Mrs. Goodsoe, the friend of my childhood and fond dependence of my maturer years. I had not seen her for many weeks, but here she was, out on one of her famous campaigns for herbs, or perhaps just returning from a blueberrying expedition. I approached with care, so as not to startle the gingham bonnet; but she heard the rustle of the bushes against my dress, and looked up quickly, as she knelt, bending over the turf. In that position she was hardly taller than the luxuriant junipers themselves.

"I'm a-gittin' in my mulleins," she said briskly, "an' I've been thinking o' you these twenty times since I come out o' the house. I begun to believe you must ha' forgot me at last."

"I have been away from home," I explained. "Why don't you get in your pennyroyal too? There's a great plantation of it beyond the next fence but one."

"Pennyr'yal!" repeated the dear little old woman, with an air of compassion for inferior knowledge; "'t ain't the right time, darlin'. Pennyr'yal's too rank now. But for mulleins this day is prime. I've got a dreadful graspin' fit for 'em this year; seems if I must be goin' to need 'em extry. I feel like the squirrels must when they know a hard winter's comin'." And Mrs. Goodsoe bent over her work again, while I stood by and watched her carefully cut the best fullgrown leaves with a clumsy pair of scissors, which might have served through at least half a century of herb-gathering. They were fastened to her apron-strings by a long piece of list.*

"I'm going to take my jack-knife and help you," I suggested, with some fear of refusal. "I just passed a flourishing family of six or seven heads that must have been growing on purpose for you."

"Now be keerful, dear heart," was the anxious response; "choose 'em well. There's odds in mulleins same's there is in angels. Take a plant that's all run up to stalk, and there ain't but little goodness in the leaves. This one I'm at now must ha' been stepped on by some creatur' and blighted of its bloom, and the leaves is han'some! When I was small I used to have a notion that Adam an' Eve must a took mulleins fer their winter wear. Ain't they just like flannel, for all the world? I've had experience, and I know there's plenty of sickness might be saved to folks if they'd quit horse-radish and such fiery, exasperating things, and use mullein drarves† in proper season. Now I shall spread these an' dry 'em nice on my spare floor in the garrit, an' come to steam 'em for use along in the winter there'll be the vally of the whole summer's goodness in 'em, sartin." And she snipped away with the dull scissors, while I listened respectfully, and took great pains to have my part of the harvest present a good appearance.

"This is most too dry a head," she added presently, a little out of

---

*Strip of material cut out of a larger piece.

†Likely a reference to poultices fashioned from the leaves of the mullein plant.

‡Windrows: rows of recently mowed and raked hay.

breath. "There! I can tell you there's win'rows[‡] o' young doctors, bilin' over with book-larnin', that is truly ignorant of what to do for the sick, or how to p'int out those paths that well people foller toward sickness. Book-fools I call 'em, them young men, an' some on 'em never'll live to know much better, if they git to be Methuselahs.[*] In my time every middle-aged woman, who had brought up a family, had some proper ideas o' dealin' with complaints. I won't say but there was some fools amongst *them*, but I'd rather take my chances, unless they'd forsook herbs and gone to dealin' with patent stuff.[†] Now my mother really did sense the use of herbs and roots. I never see anybody that come up to her. She was a meek-looking woman, but very understandin', mother was."

"Then that's where you learned so much yourself, Mrs. Goodsoe," I ventured to say.

"Bless your heart, I don't hold a candle to her; 't is but little I can recall of what she used to say. No, her l'arnin' died with her," said my friend, in a self-deprecating tone. "Why, there was as many as twenty kinds of roots alone that she used to keep by her, that I forget the use of; an' I'm sure I shouldn't know where to find the most of 'em, any. There was an herb"—*airb*, she called it—"an herb called masterwort, that she used to get way from Pennsylvany; and she used to think everything of noble-liverwort,[‡] but I never could seem to get the right effects from it as she could. Though I don't know as she ever really did use masterwort where somethin' else wouldn't a served. She had a cousin married out in Pennsylvany that used to take pains to get it to her every year or two, and so she felt 't was important to have it. Some set more by such things as come from a distance, but I rec'lect mother always used to maintain that folks was meant to be doctored with the stuff that grew right about 'em; 't was sufficient, an' so ordered. That was before the whole population took to livin' on wheels, the way they do now.

---

*According to the Bible (Genesis 5:25–26), Methuselah lived for more than 900 years.

†Patent medicine contained ingredients that, for the commercial benefit of the maker, were not publicly disclosed, unlike the widely known ingredients of herbal medicines.

‡An herb.

'T was never my idee that we was meant to know what's goin' on all over the world to once. There's goin' to be some sort of a set-back one o' these days, with these telegraphs an' things, an' letters comin' every hand's turn, and folks leavin' their proper work to answer 'em.* I may not live to see it. 'T was allowed to be difficult for folks to git about in old times, or to git word across the country, and they stood in their lot an' place, and weren't all just alike, either, same as pine-spills."†

We were kneeling side by side now, as if in penitence for the march of progress, but we laughed as we turned to look at each other.

"Do you think it did much good when everybody brewed a cracked quart mug of herb-tea?" I asked, walking away on my knees to a new mullein.

"I've always lifted my voice against the practice, far's I could," declared Mrs. Goodsoe; "an' I won't deal out none o' the herbs I save for no such nonsense. There was three houses along our road,—I call no names,—where you couldn't go into the livin' room without findin' a mess o' herb-tea drorin'‡ on the stove or side o' the fireplace, winter or summer, sick or well. One was thoroughwut,§ one would be camomile, and the other, like as not, yellow dock; but they all used to put in a little new rum to git out the goodness, or keep it from spilin'." (Mrs. Goodsoe favored me with a knowing smile.) "Land, how mother used to laugh! But, poor creaturs, they had to work hard, and I guess it never done 'em a mite o' harm; they was all good herbs. I wish you could hear the quawkin'‖ there used to be when they was indulged with a real case o' sickness. Everybody would collect from far an' near; you'd see 'em coming along the road and across the pastures then; everybody clamorin' that nothin' wouldn't do no kind o' good but her choice o' teas or drarves to the feet. I wonder there was a babe lived to grow up in the whole lower part o' the town; an' if nothin' else 'peared to ail 'em, word was

---

*Echo of a passage in the second chapter of Henry David Thoreau's Walden (1854).

†Colloquial expression for pine splinters.

‡Drawing, used in the sense of brewing.

§The plant known as thoroughwort, an herb.

‖Likely means either "squawking" or "cawing."

passed about that 't was likely Mis' So-and-So's last young one was goin' to be foolish. Land, how they'd gather! I know one day the doctor come to Widder Peck's and the house was crammed so 't he could scercely git inside the door; and he says, just as polite, 'Do send for some of the neighbors!' as if there wa'n't a soul to turn to, right or left. You'd ought to seen 'em begin to scatter."

"But don't you think the cars and telegraphs have given people more to interest them, Mrs. Goodsoe? Don't you believe people's lives were narrower then, and more taken up with little things?" I asked, unwisely, being a product of modern times.

"Not one mite, dear," said my companion stoutly. "There was as big thoughts then as there is now; these times was born o' them. The difference is in folks themselves; but now, instead o' doin' their own housekeepin' and watchin' their own neighbors,—though that was carried to excess,—they git word that a niece's child is ailin' the other side o' Massachusetts, and they drop everything and git on their best clothes, and off they jiggit in the cars.* 'T is a bad sign when folks wears out their best clothes faster 'n they do their every-day ones. The other side o' Massachusetts has got to look after itself by rights. An' besides that, Sunday-keepin' 's all gone out o' fashion. Some lays it to one thing an' some another, but some o' them old ministers that folks are all a-sighin' for did preach a lot o' stuff that wa'n't nothin' but chaff; 't wa'n't the word o' God out o' either Old Testament or New. But everybody went to meetin' and heard it, and come home, and was set to fightin' with their next door neighbor over it. Now I'm a believer, and I try to live a Christian life, but I'd as soon hear a surveyor's book read out, figgers an' all, as try to get any simple truth out o' most sermons. It's them as is most to blame."

"What was the matter that day at Widow Peck's?" I hastened to ask, for I knew by experience that the good, clear-minded soul beside me was apt to grow unduly vexed and distressed when she contemplated the state of religious teaching.

"Why, there wa'n't nothin' the matter, only a gal o' Miss Peck's had met with a dis'pintment and had gone into screechin' fits.

---

*Probably "dancing in the railroad cars."

'T was a rovin' creatur' that had come along hayin' time, and he'd gone off an' forsook her betwixt two days; nobody ever knew what become of him. Them Pecks was 'Good Lord, anybody!' kind o' gals, and took up with whoever they could get. One of 'em married Heron, the Irishman; they lived in that little house that was burnt this summer, over on the edge o' the plains. He was a good-hearted creatur', with a laughin' eye and a clever word for everybody. He was the first Irishman that ever came this way, and we was all for gettin' a look at him, when he first used to go by. Mother's folks was what they call Scotch-Irish, though; there was an old race of 'em settled about here. They could foretell events, some on 'em, and had the second sight. I know folks used to say mother's grandmother had them gifts, but mother was never free to speak about it to us. She remembered her well, too."

"I suppose that you mean old Jim Heron, who was such a famous fiddler?" I asked with great interest, for I am always delighted to know more about that rustic hero, parochial Orpheus* that he must have been!

"Now, dear heart, I suppose you don't remember him, do you?" replied Mrs. Goodsoe, earnestly. "Fiddle! He'd about break your heart with them tunes of his, or else set your heels flying up the floor in a jig, though you was minister o' the First Parish† and all wound up for a funeral prayer. I tell ye there ain't no tunes sounds like them used to. It used to seem to me summer nights when I was comin' along the plains road, and he set by the window playin', as if there was a bewitched human creatur' in that old red fiddle o' his. He could make it sound just like a woman's voice tellin' somethin' over and over, as if folks could help her out o' her sorrows if she could only make 'em understand. I've set by the stone-wall and cried as if my heart was broke, and dear knows it wa'n't in them days. How he would twirl off them jigs and dance tunes! He used to make somethin' han'some out of 'em in fall an' winter, playin' at huskins‡

*In Greek mythology, Orpheus was a poet who, with a lyre given him by the god Apollo, could tame wild beasts and charm people with his music.

†The first church of a given denomination to be established in a given community.

‡Cornhuskings: a community gathering held each fall in rural areas to husk corn.

and dancin' parties; but he was unstiddy by spells, as he got along in years, and never knew what it was to be forehanded.* Everybody felt bad when he died; you couldn't help likin' the creatur'. He'd got the gift—that's all you could say about it.

"There was a Mis' Jerry Foss, that lived over by the brook bridge, on the plains road, that had lost her husband early, and was left with three child'n. She set the world by 'em, and was a real pleasant, ambitious little woman, and was workin' on as best she could with that little farm, when there come a rage o' scarlet fever, and her boy and two girls was swept off and laid dead within the same week. Every one o' the neighbors did what they could, but she'd had no sleep since they was taken sick, and after the funeral she set there just like a piece o' marble, and would only shake her head when you spoke to her. They all thought her reason would go; and 't would certain, if she couldn't have shed tears. An' one o' the neighbors—'t was like mother's sense, but it might have been somebody else—spoke o' Jim Heron. Mother an' one or two o' the women that knew her best was in the house with her. 'T was right in the edge o' the woods and some of us younger ones was over by the wall on the other side of the road where there was a couple of old willows,—I remember just how the brook damp felt; and we kept quiet's we could, and some other folks come along down the road, and stood waitin' on the little bridge, hopin' somebody'd come out, I suppose, and they'd git news. Everybody was wrought up, and felt a good deal for her, you know. By an' by Jim Heron come stealin' right out o' the shadows an' set down on the doorstep, an' 't was a good while before we heard a sound; then, oh, dear me! 't was what the whole neighborhood felt for that mother all spoke in the notes, an' they told me afterwards that Mis' Foss's face changed in a minute, and she come right over an' got into my mother's lap,—she was a little woman,—an' laid her head down, and there she cried herself into a blessed sleep. After awhile one o' the other women stole out an' told the folks, and we all went home. He only played that one tune.

"But there!" resumed Mrs. Goodsoe, after a silence, during which my eyes were filled with tears. "His wife always complained that the

---

*Ready for possible future economic difficulties.

fiddle made her nervous. She never 'peared to think nothin' o' poor Heron after she'd once got him."

"That's often the way," said I, with harsh cynicism, though I had no guilty person in my mind at the moment; and we went straying off, not very far apart, up through the pasture. Mrs. Goodsoe cautioned me that we must not get so far off that we could not get back the same day. The sunshine began to feel very hot on our backs, and we both turned toward the shade. We had already collected a large bundle of mullein leaves, which were carefully laid into a clean, calico apron, held together by the four corners, and proudly carried by me, though my companion regarded them with anxious eyes. We sat down together at the edge of the pine woods, and Mrs. Goodsoe proceeded to fan herself with her limp cape-bonnet.

"I declare, how hot it is! The east wind's all gone again," she said. "It felt so cool this forenoon that I overburdened myself with as thick a petticoat as any I've got. I'm despri't afeared of having a chill, now that I ain't so young as once. I hate to be housed up."

"It's only August, after all," I assured her unnecessarily, confirming my statement by taking two peaches out of my pocket, and laying them side by side on the brown pine needles between us.

"Dear sakes alive!" exclaimed the old lady, with evident pleasure. "Where did you get them, now? Doesn't anything taste twice better out-o'-doors? I ain't had such a peach for years. Do le's keep the stones, an' I'll plant 'em; it only takes four year for a peach pit to come to bearing, an' I guess I'm good for four year, 'thout I meet with some accident."

I could not help agreeing, or taking a fond look at the thin little figure, and her wrinkled brown face and kind, twinkling eyes. She looked as if she had properly dried herself, by mistake, with some of her mullein leaves, and was likely to keep her goodness, and to last the longer in consequence. There never was a truer, simple-hearted soul made out of the old-fashioned country dust than Mrs. Goodsoe. I thought, as I looked away from her across the wide country, that nobody was left in any of the farm-houses so original, so full of rural wisdom and reminiscence, so really able and dependable, as she. And nobody had made better use of her time in a world foolish enough to sometimes undervalue medicinal herbs.

When we had eaten our peaches we still sat under the pines, and I was not without pride when I had poked about in the ground with a little twig, and displayed to my crony a long fine root, bright yellow to the eye, and a wholesome bitter to the taste.

"Yis, dear, goldthread,"* she assented indulgently. "Seems to me there's more of it than anything except grass an' hardhack. Good for canker, but no better than two or three other things I can call to mind; but I always lay in a good wisp of it, for old times' sake. Now, I want to know why you should a bit it, and took away all the taste o' your nice peach? I was just thinkin' what a han'some entertainment we've had. I've got so I 'sociate certain things with certain folks, and goldthread was somethin' Lizy Wisby couldn't keep house without, no ways whatever. I believe she took so much it kind o' puckered her disposition."

"Lizy Wisby?" I repeated inquiringly.

"You knew her, if ever, by the name of Mis' Deacon Brimblecom," answered my friend, as if this were only a brief preface to further information, so I waited with respectful expectation. Mrs. Goodsoe had grown tired out in the sun, and a good story would be an excuse for sufficient rest. It was a most lovely place where we sat, halfway up the long hillside; for my part, I was perfectly contented and happy. "You've often heard of Deacon Brimblecom?" she asked, as if a great deal depended upon his being properly introduced.

"I remember him," said I. "They called him Deacon Brimfull, you know, and he used to go about with a witch-hazel branch to show people where to dig wells."

"That's the one," said Mrs. Goodsoe, laughing. "I didn't know's you could go so far back. I'm always divided between whether you can remember everything I can, or are only a babe in arms."

"I have a dim recollection of there being something strange about their marriage," I suggested, after a pause, which began to appear dangerous. I was so much afraid the subject would be changed.

---

*Root used as a treatment for ulcers and gangrene.

"I can tell you all about it," I was quickly answered. "Deacon Brimblecom was very pious accordin' to his lights in his early years. He lived way back in the country then, and there come a rovin' preacher along, and set everybody up that way all by the ears.* I've heard the old folks talk it over, but I forget most of his doctrine, except some of his followers was persuaded they could dwell among the angels while yet on airth, and this Deacon Brimfull, as you call him, felt sure he was called by the voice of a spirit bride. So he left a good, deservin' wife he had, an' four children, and built him a new house over to the other side of the land he'd had from his father. They didn't take much pains with the buildin', because they expected to be translated† before long, and then the spirit brides and them folks was goin' to appear and divide up the airth amongst 'em, and the world's folks and on-believers was goin' to serve 'em or be sent to torments. They had meetins about in the school-houses, an' all sorts o' goins on; some on 'em went crazy, but the deacon held on to what wits he had, an' by an' by the spirit bride didn't turn out to be much of a housekeeper, an' he had always been used to good livin', so he sneaked home ag'in. One o' mother's sisters married up to Ash Hill, where it all took place; that's how I come to have the particulars."

"Then how did he come to find his Eliza Wisby?" I inquired. "Do tell me the whole story; you've got mullein leaves enough."

"There's all yisterday's at home, if I haven't," replied Mrs. Goodsoe. "The way he come a-courtin' o' Sister Wisby was this: she went a-courtin' o' him.

"There was a spell he lived to home, and then his poor wife died, and he had a spirit bride in good earnest, an' the child'n was placed about with his folks and hers, for they was both out o' good families; and I don't know what come over him, but he had another pious fit that looked for all the world like the real thing. He hadn't no family cares, and he lived with his brother's folks, and turned his land in with theirs. He used to travel to every meetin' an' conference

---

*That is, the preacher generated a strong response in the people who heard him preach.

†That is, transferred directly from this life to Heaven.

that was within reach of his old sorrel hoss's feeble legs; he j'ined the Christian Baptists* that was just in their early prime, and he was a great exhorter, and got to be called deacon, though I guess he wa'n't deacon, 'less it was for a spare hand when deacon timber was scercer'n usual. An' one time there was a four days' protracted meetin' to the church in the lower part of the town. 'T was a real solemn time; something more'n usual was goin' forward, an' they collected from the whole country round. Women folks liked it, an' the men too; it give 'em a change, an' they was quartered round free, same as conference folks now. Some on 'em, for a joke, sent Silas Brimblecom up to Lizy Wisby's, though she'd give out she couldn't accommodate nobody, because of expectin' her cousin's folks. Everybody knew 't was a lie; she was amazin' close considerin' she had plenty to do with. There was a streak that wa'n't just right somewheres in Lizy's wits, I always thought. She was very kind in case o' sickness, I'll say that for her.

"You know where the house is, over there on what they call Windy Hill? There the deacon went, all unsuspectin', and 'stead o' Lizy 's resentin' of him she put in her own hoss, and they come back together to evenin' meetin'. She was prominent among the sect herself, an' he bawled and talked, and she bawled and talked, an' took up more 'n the time allotted in the exercises, just as if they was showin' off to each other what they was able to do at expoundin'. Everybody was laughin' at 'em after the meetin' broke up, and that next day an' the next, an' all through, they was constant, and seemed to be havin' a beautiful occasion. Lizy had always give out she scorned the men, but when she got a chance at a particular one 't was altogether different, and the deacon seemed to please her somehow or 'nother, and—There! you don't want to listen to this old stuff that's past an' gone?"

"Oh yes, I do," said I.

"I run on like a clock that's onset her striking hand," said Mrs. Goodsoe mildly. "Sometimes my kitchen timepiece goes on half the forenoon, and I says to myself the day before yisterday I would let it

---

*This Protestant denomination, dating back to 1639 in the American colonies, was started by Roger Williams in Providence, Rhode Island.

be a warnin', and keep it in mind for a check on my own speech. The next news that was heard was that the deacon an' Lizy—well, opinions differed which of 'em had spoke first, but them fools settled it before the protracted meetin' was over, and give away their hearts before he started for home. They considered 't would be wise, though, considerin' their short acquaintance, to take one another on trial a spell; 't was Lizy's notion, and she asked him why he wouldn't come over and stop with her till spring, and then, if they both continued to like, they could git married any time 't was convenient. Lizy, she come and talked it over with mother, and mother disliked to offend her, but she spoke pretty plain; and Lizy felt hurt, an' thought they was showin' excellent judgment, so much harm come from hasty unions and folks comin' to a realizin' sense of each other's failin's when 't was too late.

"So one day our folks saw Deacon Brimfull a-ridin' by with a gre't coopful of hens in the back o' his wagon, and bundles o' stuff tied on top and hitched to the exes* underneath; and he riz a hymn just as he passed the house, and was speedin' the old sorrel with a willer switch. 'T was most Thanksgivin' time, an' sooner 'n she expected him. New Year's was the time she set; but he thought he'd better come while the roads was fit for wheels. They was out to meetin' together Thanksgivin' Day, an' that used to be a gre't season for marryin'; so the young folks nudged each other, and some on' 'em ventured to speak to the couple as they come down the aisle. Lizy carried it off real well; she wa'n't afraid o' what nobody said or thought, and so home they went. They'd got out her yaller sleigh and her hoss; she never would ride after the deacon's poor old creatur', and I believe it died long o' the winter from stiffenin' up.

"Yes," said Mrs. Goodsoe emphatically, after we had silently considered the situation for a short space of time,—"yes, there was consider'ble talk, now I tell you! The raskil boys pestered 'em just about to death for a while. They used to collect up there an' rap on the winders, and they'd turn out all the deacon's hens 'long at nine o'clock 'o night, and chase 'em all over the dingle;† an' one night they even

*Wooden frame that supports a horse-drawn wagon or carriage.

†Narrow, wooded valley.

lugged the pig right out o' the sty, and shoved it into the back entry, an' run for their lives. They'd stuffed its mouth full o' somethin', so it couldn't squeal till it got there. There wa'n't a sign o' nobody to be seen when Lizy hasted out with the light, and she an' the deacon had to persuade the creatur' back as best they could; 't was a cold night, and they said it took 'em till towards mornin'. You see the deacon was just the kind of a man that a hog wouldn't budge for; it takes a masterful man to deal with a hog. Well, there was no end to the works nor the talk, but Lizy left 'em pretty much alone. She did 'pear kind of dignified about it, I must say!"

"And then, were they married in the spring?"

"I was tryin' to remember whether it was just before Fast Day* or just after," responded my friend, with a careful look at the sun, which was nearer the west than either of us had noticed. "I think likely 't was along in the last o' April, any way some of us looked out o' the window one Monday mornin' early, and says, 'For goodness' sake! Lizy's sent the deacon home again!' His old sorrel havin' passed away, he was ridin' in Ezry Welsh's hoss-cart, with his hen-coop and more bundles than he had when he come, and he looked as meechin'† as ever you see. Ezry was drivin', and he let a glance fly swiftly round to see if any of us was lookin' out; an' then I declare if he didn't have the malice to turn right in towards the barn, where he see my oldest brother, Joshuay, an' says he real natural, 'Joshuay, just step out with your wrench. I believe I hear my kingbolt‡ rattlin' kind o' loose.' Brother, he went out an' took in the sitooation, an' the deacon bowed kind of stiff. Joshuay was so full o' laugh, and Ezry Welsh, that they couldn't look one another in the face. There wa'n't nothing ailed the kingbolt, you know, an' when Josh riz up he says, 'Goin' up country for a spell, Mr. Brimblecom?'

---

*In response to the Anglican practice of celebrating Holy Days, early American Protestant dissenters observed one or more Fast Days, during which time they demonstrated their faith through fasting and prayer.

†Colloquial adjective meaning "humble" or "servile."

‡The pin on a horse cart latching the cart's body to the part of the cart known as the tongue, which was strapped to the harnessed horse.

"'I be,' says the deacon, lookin' dreadful mortified and cast down.

"'Ain't things turned out well with you an' Sister Wisby?' says Joshuay. 'You had ought to remember that the woman is the weaker vessel.'

"'Hang her, let her carry less sail, then!' the deacon bu'st out, and he stood right up an' shook his fist there by the hen-coop, he was so mad; an' Ezry's hoss was a young creatur', an' started up an set the deacon right over backwards into the chips.* We didn't know but he'd broke his neck; but when he see the women folks runnin' out, he jumped up quick as a cat, an' clim' into the cart, an' off they went. Ezry said he told him that he couldn't git along with Lizy, she was so fractious in thundery weather; if there was a rumble in the daytime she must go right to bed an' screech, and if 't was night she must git right up an' go an' call him out of a sound sleep. But everybody knew he'd never a gone home unless she'd sent him.

"Somehow they made it up agin right away, him an' Lizy, and she had him back. She'd been countin' all along on not havin' to hire nobody to work about the gardin an' so on, an' she said she wa'n't goin' to let him have a whole winter's board for nothin'. So the old hens was moved back, and they was married right off fair an' square, an' I don't know but they got along well as most folks. He brought his youngest girl down to live with 'em after a while, an' she was a real treasure to Lizy; everybody spoke well o' Phebe Brimblecom. The deacon got over his pious fit, and there was consider'ble work in him if you kept right after him. He was an amazin' cider-drinker, and he airnt the name you know him by in his latter days. Lizy never trusted him with nothin', but she kep' him well. She left everything she owned to Phebe, when she died, 'cept somethin' to satisfy the law. There, they're all gone now: seems to me sometimes, when I get thinkin,' as if I'd lived a thousand years!"

I laughed, but I found that Mrs. Goodsoe's thoughts had taken a serious turn.

"There, I come by some old graves down here in the lower edge of the pasture," she said as we rose to go. "I couldn't help thinking how I should like to be laid right out in the pasture ground, when

---

*Likely, animal scat.

my time comes; it looked sort o' comfortable, and I have ranged these slopes so many summers. Seems as if I could see right up through the turf and tell when the weather was pleasant, and get the goodness o' the sweet fern. Now, dear, just hand me my apernful o' mulleins out o' the shade. I hope you won't come to need none this winter, but I'll dry some special for you."

"I'm going home by the road," said I, "or else by the path across the meadows, so I will walk as far as the house with you. Aren't you pleased with my company?" for she demurred at my going the least bit out of the way.

So we strolled toward the little gray house, with our plunder of mullein leaves slung on a stick which we carried between us. Of course I went in to make a call, as if I had not seen my hostess before; she is the last maker of muster-gingerbread* and before I came away I was kindly measured for a pair of mittens.

"You'll be sure to come an' see them two peach-trees after I get 'em well growin'?" Mrs. Goodsoe called after me when I had said good-by, and was almost out of hearing down the road.

---

*Possibly a reference to a kind of cake known as mustard gingerbread.

A WINTER COURTSHIP

The passenger and mail transportation between the towns of North Kilby and Sanscrit Pond was carried on by Mr. Jefferson Briley, whose two-seated covered wagon was usually much too large for the demands of business. Both the Sanscrit Pond and North Kilby people were stayers-at-home, and Mr. Briley often made his seven-mile journey in entire solitude, except for the limp leather mail-bag, which he held firmly to the floor of the carriage with his heavily shod left foot. The mail-bag had almost a personality to him, born of long association. Mr. Briley was a meek and timid-looking body, but he held a warlike soul, and encouraged his fancies by reading awful tales of bloodshed and lawlessness in the far West. Mindful of stage robberies and train thieves, and of express messengers who died at their posts, he was prepared for anything; and although he had trusted to his own strength and bravery these many years, he carried a heavy pistol under his front-seat cushion for better defense. This awful weapon was familiar to all his regular passengers, and was usually shown to strangers by the time two of the seven miles of Mr. Briley's route had been passed. The pistol was not loaded. Nobody (at least not Mr. Briley himself) doubted that the mere sight of such a weapon would turn the boldest adventurer aside.

Protected by such a man and such a piece of armament, one gray Friday morning in the edge of winter, Mrs. Fanny Tobin was traveling from Sanscrit Pond to North Kilby. She was an elderly and feeble-looking woman, but with a shrewd twinkle in her eyes, and she felt very anxious about her numerous pieces of baggage and her own personal safety. She was enveloped in many shawls and smaller wrappings, but they were not securely fastened, and kept getting undone and flying loose, so that the bitter December cold seemed to be picking a lock now and then, and creeping in to steal away the little warmth she had. Mr. Briley was cold, too, and could only cheer himself by remembering the valor of those pony-express drivers of the pre-railroad days, who had to cross the Rocky Mountains on the great California route.* He spoke at length of their perils to the suffering passenger, who felt none the warmer, and at last gave a groan of weariness.

"How fur did you say 't was now?"

"I do' know 's I said, Mis' Tobin," answered the driver, with a frosty laugh. "You see them big pines, and the side of a barn just this way, with them yellow circus bills? That's my three-mile mark."

"Be we got four more to make? Oh, my laws!" mourned Mrs. Tobin. "Urge the beast, can't ye, Jeff'son? I ain't used to bein' out in such bleak weather. Seems if I couldn't git my breath. I'm all pinched up and wigglin' with shivers now. 'T ain't no use lettin' the hoss go step-a-ty-step, this fashion."

"Landy me!" exclaimed the affronted driver. "I don't see why folks expects me to race with the cars.† Everybody that gits in wants me to run the hoss to death on the road. I make a good everage o' time, and that's all I *can* do. Ef you was to go back an' forth every day but Sabbath fur eighteen years, *you*'d want to ease it all you could, and let those thrash the spokes out o' their wheels that wanted to. North Kilby, Mondays, Wednesdays, and Fridays; Sanscrit Pond, Tuesdays, Thu'sdays, an' Saturdays. Me an' the beast's done it eighteen years together, and the creatur' warn't, so to say, young when we begun it, nor I neither. I re'lly didn't know 's she'd hold out till this time. There, git up, will ye, old mar'!" as the beast of burden stopped short in the road.

There was a story that Jefferson gave this faithful creature a rest three times a mile, and took four hours for the journey by himself, and longer whenever he had a passenger. But in pleasant weather the road was delightful, and full of people who drove their own conveyances, and liked to stop and talk. There were not many farms, and the third growth of white pines made a pleasant shade, though Jefferson liked to say that when he began to carry the mail his way

---

*A legendary mail-delivery service operated between Missouri and California in 1860 and 1861, the pony express became unnecessary when telegraph was introduced.

†That is, railroad cars.

lay through an open country of stumps and sparse underbrush, where the white pines nowadays completely arched the road.

They had passed the barn with circus posters, and felt colder than ever when they caught sight of the weather-beaten acrobats in their tights.

"My gorry!" exclaimed Widow Tobin, "them pore creatur's looks as cheerless as little birch-trees in snow-time. I hope they dresses 'em warmer this time o' year. Now, there! look at that one jumpin' through the little hoop, will ye?"

"He couldn't git himself through there with two pair o' pants on," answered Mr. Briley. "I expect they must have to keep limber as eels. I used to think, when I was a boy, that 't was the only thing I could ever be reconciled to do for a livin'. I set out to run away an' follow a rovin' showman once, but mother needed me to home. There warn't nobody but me an' the little gals."

"You ain't the only one that's be'n disapp'inted o' their heart's desire," said Mrs. Tobin sadly. "'T warn't so that I could be spared from home to learn the dressmaker's trade."

"'T would a come handy later on, I declare," answered the sympathetic driver, "bein' 's you went an' had such a passel o' gals to clothe an' feed. There, them that 's livin' is all well off now, but it must ha' been some inconvenient for ye when they was small."

"Yes, Mr. Briley, but then I've had my mercies, too," said the widow somewhat grudgingly. "I take it master hard now, though, havin' to give up my own home and live round from place to place, if they be my own child'en. There was Ad'line and Susan Ellen fussin' an' bickerin' yesterday about who'd got to have me next; and, Lord be thanked, they both wanted me right off but I hated to hear 'em talkin' of it over. I'd rather live to home, and do for myself."

"I've got consider'ble used to boardin'," said Jefferson, "sence ma'am died, but it made me ache 'long at the fust* on 't. I tell ye. Bein' on the road's I be, I couldn't do no ways at keepin' house. I should want to keep right there and see to things."

"Course you would," replied Mrs. Tobin, with a sudden inspiration of opportunity which sent a welcome glow all over her. "Course

---

*Colloquial for "at first."

you would, Jeff 'son,"—she leaned toward the front seat; "that is to say, on-less you had jest the right one to do it for ye."

And Jefferson felt a strange glow also, and a sense of unexpected interest and enjoyment.

"See here, Sister Tobin," he exclaimed with enthusiasm. "Why can't ye take the trouble to shift seats, and come front here long o' me? We could put one buff'lo top o' the other,—they're both wearin' thin,—and set close, and I do' know but we sh'd be more protected ag'inst the weather."

"Well, I couldn't be no colder if I was froze to death," answered the widow, with an amiable simper. "Don't ye let me delay you, nor put you out, Mr. Briley. I don't know 's I'd set forth to-day if I'd known 't was so cold; but I had all my bundles done up, and I ain't one that puts my hand to the plough an' looks back, 'cordin' to Scriptur'."*

"You wouldn't wanted me to ride all them seven miles alone?" asked the gallant Briley sentimentally, as he lifted her down, and helped her up again to the front seat. She was a few years older than he, but they had been schoolmates, and Mrs. Tobin's youthful freshness was suddenly revived to his mind's eye. She had a little farm; there was nobody left at home now but herself, and so she had broken up housekeeping for the winter. Jefferson himself had savings of no mean amount.

They tucked themselves in, and felt better for the change, but there was a sudden awkwardness between them; they had not had time to prepare for an unexpected crisis.

"They say Elder Bickers, over to East Sanscrit, 's been and got married again to a gal that's four year younger than his oldest daughter," proclaimed Mrs. Tobin presently. "Seems to me 't was fool's business."

"I view it so," said the stage-driver. "There's goin' to be a mild open winter for that fam'ly."

"What a joker you be for a man that's had so much responsibility!" smiled Mrs. Tobin, after they had done laughing. "Ain't you

---

*Reference to the Bible, Luke 9:62 (KJV): "No man, having put his hand to the plough, and looking back, is fit for the kingdom of God."

never 'fraid, carryin' mail matter and such valuable stuff, that you'll be set on an' robbed, 'specially by night?"

Jefferson braced his feet against the dasher under the worn buffalo skin. "It is kind o' scary, or would be for some folks, but I'd like to see anybody get the better o' me. I go armed, and I don't care who knows it. Some o' them drover men that comes from Canady looks as if they didn't care what they did, but I look 'em right in the eye every time."

"Men folks is brave by natur'," said the widow admiringly. "You know how Tobin would let his fist right out at anybody that ondertook to sass him. Town-meetin' days, if he got disappointed about the way things went, he'd lay 'em out in win'rows;* and ef he hadn't been a church-member he'd been a real fightin' character. I was always 'fraid to have him roused, for all he was so willin' and meechin'† to home, and set round clever as anybody. My Susan Ellen used to boss him same's the kitten, when she was four year old."

"I've got a kind of a sideways cant to my nose, that Tobin give me when we was to school. I don't know's you ever noticed it," said Mr. Briley. "We was scufflin', as lads will. I never bore him no kind of a grudge. I pitied ye, when he was taken away. I re'lly did, now, Fanny. I liked Tobin first-rate, and I liked you. I used to say you was the han'somest girl to school."

"Lemme see your nose. 'T is all straight, for what I know," said the widow gently, as with a trace of coyness she gave a hasty glance. "I don't know but what 't is warped a little, but nothin' to speak of. You've got real nice features, like your marm's folks."

It was becoming a sentimental occasion, and Jefferson Briley felt that he was in for something more than he had bargained. He hurried the faltering sorrel horse, and began to talk of the weather. It certainly did look like snow, and he was tired of bumping over the frozen road.

"I shouldn't wonder if I hired a hand here another year, and went off out West myself to see the country."

"Why, how you talk!" answered the widow.

---

*Windrows: rows of recently mowed and raked hay.

†Humble or servile.

"Yes 'm," pursued Jefferson. "'T is tamer here than I like, and I was tellin' 'em yesterday I've got to know this road most too well. I'd like to go out an' ride in the mountains with some o' them great clipper coaches, where the driver don't know one minute but he'll be shot dead the next. They carry an awful sight o' gold down from the mines, I expect."

"I should be scairt to death," said Mrs. Tobin. "What creatur's men folks be to like such things! Well, I do declare."

"Yes," explained the mild little man. "There's sights of desp'radoes makes a han'some livin' out o' followin' them coaches, an' stoppin' an' robbin' 'em clean to the bone. Your money *or* your life!" and he flourished his stub of a whip over the sorrel mare.

"Landy me! you make me run all of a cold creep. Do tell somethin' heartenin', this cold day. I shall dream bad dreams all night."

"They put on black crape over their heads," said the driver mysteriously. "Nobody knows who most on 'em be, and like as not some o' them fellows come o' good families. They've got so they stop the cars, and go right through 'em bold as brass. I could make your hair stand on end, Mis' Tobin,—I could *so*!"

"I hope none on 'em 'll git round our way, I'm sure," said Fanny Tobin. "I don't want to see none on 'em in their crape bunnits comin' after me."

"I ain't goin' to let nobody touch a hair o' your head," and Mr. Briley moved a little nearer, and tucked in the buffaloes again.

"I feel considerable warm to what I did," observed the widow by way of reward.

"There, I used to have my fears," Mr. Briley resumed, with an inward feeling that he never would get to North Kilby depot a single man. "But you see I hadn't nobody but myself to think of. I've got cousins, as you know, but nothin' nearer, and what I've laid up would soon be parted out; and—well, I suppose some folks would think o' me if anything was to happen."

Mrs. Tobin was holding her cloud over her face,*—the wind was sharp on that bit of open road,—but she gave an encouraging sound, between a groan and a chirp.

---

*This expression refers to a scarf that Mrs. Tobin is wearing over her head.

"'T wouldn't be like nothin' to me not to see you drivin' by," she said, after a minute. "I shouldn't know the days o' the week. I says to Susan Ellen last week I was sure 't was Friday, and she said no, 't was Thursday; but next minute you druv by and headin' toward North Kilby, so we found I was right."

"I've got to be a featur' of the landscape," said Mr. Briley plaintively. "This kind o' weather the old mare and me, we wish we was done with it, and could settle down kind o' comfortable. I've been lookin' this good while, as I drove the road, and I've picked me out a piece o' land two or three times. But I can't abide the thought o' buildin',—'t would plague me to death; and both Sister Peak to North Kilby and Mis' Deacon Ash to the Pond, they vie with one another to do well by me, fear I'll like the other stoppin'-place best."

"*I* shouldn't covet livin' long o' neither one o' them women," responded the passenger with some spirit. "I see some o' Mis' Peak's cookin' to a farmers' supper once, when I was visitin' Susan Ellen's folks, an' I says 'Deliver me from sech pale-complected baked beans as them!' and she give a kind of a quack. She was settin' jest at my left hand, and couldn't help hearin' of me. I wouldn't have spoken if I had known, but she needn't have let on they was hers an' make everything unpleasant. 'I guess them beans taste just as well as other folks',' says she, and she wouldn't never speak to me afterward."

"Do' know 's I blame her," ventured Mr. Briley. "Women folks is dreadful pudjicky* about their cookin'. I've always heard you was one o' the best o' cooks, Mis' Tobin. I know them doughnuts an' things you've give me in times past, when I was drivin' by. Wish I had some on 'em now. I never let on, but Mis' Ash's cookin' 's the best by a long chalk. Mis' Peak's handy about some things, and looks after mendin' of me up."

"It doos seem as if a man o' your years and your quiet make ought to have a home you could call your own," suggested the passenger.

---

*According to the *Dictionary of American Regional English* (see "For Further Reading"), this word, historically used in colloquial New England speech, meant "sensitive," "sullen," or "grouchy."

"I kind of hate to think o' your bangein'* here and boardin' there, and one old woman mendin', and the other settin' ye down to meals that like's not don't agree with ye."

"Lor', now, Mis' Tobin, le's not fuss round no longer," said Mr. Briley impatiently. "You know you covet me same 's I do you."

"I don't nuther. Don't you go an' say fo'lish things you can't stand to."

"I've been tryin' to git a chance to put in a word with you ever sence—Well, I expected you'd want to get your feelin's kind o' calloused after losin' Tobin."

"There's nobody can fill his place," said the widow.

"I do' know but I can fight for ye town-meetin' days, on a pinch," urged Jefferson boldly.

"I never see the beat o' you men fur conceit," and Mrs. Tobin laughed. "I ain't goin' to bother with ye, gone half the time as you be, an' carryin' on with your Mis' Peaks and Mis' Ashes. I dare say you've promised yourself to both on 'em twenty times."

"I hope to gracious if I ever breathed a word to none on 'em!" protested the lover. "'T ain't for lack o' opportunities set afore me, nuther;" and then Mr. Briley craftily kept silence, as if he had made a fair proposal, and expected a definite reply.

The lady of his choice was, as she might have expressed it, much beat about. As she soberly thought, she was getting along in years, and must put up with Jefferson all the rest of the time. It was not likely she would ever have the chance of choosing again, though she was one who liked variety.

Jefferson wasn't much to look at, but he was pleasant and appeared boyish and young-feeling. "I do' know 's I should do better," she said unconsciously and half aloud. "Well, yes, Jefferson, seein' it's you. But we're both on us kind of old to change our situation." Fanny Tobin gave a gentle sigh.

"Hooray!" said Jefferson. "I was scairt you meant to keep me sufferin' here a half an hour. I declare, I'm more pleased than I calc'lated on. An' I expected till lately to die a single man!"

---

*In the rural speech of nineteenth-century New England, being idle or lazy.

"'T would re'lly have been a shame; 't ain't natur'," said Mrs. Tobin, with confidence. "I don't see how you held out so long with bein' solitary."

"I'll hire a hand to drive for me, and we'll have a good comfortable winter, me an' you an' the old sorrel. I've been promisin' of her a rest this good while."

"Better keep her a steppin'," urged thrifty Mrs. Fanny. "She'll stiffen up master, an' disapp'int ye, come spring."

"You'll have me, now, won't ye, sartin?" pleaded Jefferson, to make sure. "You ain't one o' them that plays with a man's feelin's. Say right out you'll have me."

"I s'pose I shall have to," said Mrs. Tobin somewhat mournfully. "I feel for Mis' Peak an' Mis' Ash, pore creatur's. I expect they'll be hardshipped. They've always been hard-worked, an' may have kind o' looked forward to a little ease. But one of 'em would be left lamentin', anyhow," and she gave a girlish laugh. An air of victory animated the frame of Mrs. Tobin. She felt but twenty-five years of age. In that moment she made plans for cutting her Briley's hair, and making him look smartened-up and ambitious. Then she wished that she knew for certain how much money he had in the bank; not that it would make any difference now. "He needn't bluster none before me," she thought gayly. "He's harmless as a fly."

"Who'd have thought we'd done such a piece of engineerin', when we started out?" inquired the dear one of Mr. Briley's heart, as he tenderly helped her to alight at Susan Ellen's door.

"Both on us, jest the least grain," answered the lover. "Gimme a good smack,* now, you clever creatur';" and so they parted. Mr. Briley had been taken on the road in spite of his pistol.

---

*A good kiss.

A NATIVE OF WINBY

I

On the teacher's desk, in the little roadside school-house, there was a bunch of Mayflowers, beside a dented and bent brass bell, a small Worcester's Dictionary* without any cover, and a worn morocco-covered Bible. These were placed in an orderly row, and behind them was a small wooden box which held some broken pieces of blackboard crayon. The teacher, whom no timid new scholar could look at boldly, wore her accustomed air of authority and importance. She might have been nineteen years old,—not more,—but for the time being she scorned the frivolities of youth.

The hot May sun was shining in at the smoky small-paned windows; sometimes an outside shutter swung to with a creak, and eclipsed the glare. The narrow door stood wide open, to the left as you faced the desk, and an old spotted dog lay asleep on the step, and looked wise and old enough to have gone to school with several generations of children. It was half past three o'clock in the afternoon, and the primer class, settled into the apathy of after-recess fatigue, presented a straggling front, as they stood listlessly on the floor. As for the big boys and girls, they also were longing to be at liberty, but the pretty teacher, Miss Marilla Hender, seemed quite as energetic as when school was begun in the morning.

The spring breeze blew in at the open door, and even fluttered the primer leaves, but the back of the room felt hot and close, as if it were midsummer. The children in the class read their lessons in those high-keyed, droning voices which older teachers learn to associate with faint powers of perception. Only one or two of them had an awakened human look in their eyes, such as Matthew Arnold† delighted himself in finding so often in the school-children

*First published in 1830 and widely used in classrooms, *Worcester's Dictionary* was credited to Joseph Emerson Worcester (1784–1865).

†Matthew Arnold (1822–1888) was a prominent English poet and literary and social critic.

of France. Most of these poor little students were as inadequate, at that weary moment, to the pursuit of letters as if they had been woolly spring lambs on a sunny hillside. The teacher corrected and admonished with great patience, glancing now and then toward points of danger and insurrection, whence came a suspicious buzz of whispering from behind a desk-lid or a pair of widespread large geographies. Now and then a toiling child would rise and come down the aisle, with his forefinger firm upon a puzzling word as if it were an unclassified insect. It was a lovely beckoning day out-of-doors. The children felt like captives; there was something that provoked rebellion in the droning voices, the buzzing of an early wild bee against the sunlit pane, and even in the stuffy familiar odor of the place,—the odor of apples and crumbs of doughnuts and gingerbread in the dinner pails on the high entry nails, and of all the little gowns and trousers that had brushed through junipers and young pines on their way to school.

The bee left his prisoning pane at last, and came over to the Mayflowers, which were in full bloom, although the season was very late, and deep in the woods there were still some graybacked snowdrifts, speckled with bits of bark and moss from the trees above.

"Come, come, Ezra!" urged the young teacher, rapping her desk sharply. "Stop watchin' that common bee! You know well enough what those letters spell. You won't learn to read at this rate until you are a grown man. Mind your book, now; you ought to remember who went to this school when he was a little boy. You've heard folks tell about the Honorable Joseph K. Laneway? He used to be in primer just as you are now, and 't wasn't long before he was out of it, either, and was called the smartest boy in school. He's got to be a general and a Senator, and one of the richest men out West. You don't seem to have the least mite of ambition to-day, any of you!"

The exhortation, entirely personal in the beginning, had swiftly passed to a general rebuke. Ezra looked relieved, and the other children brightened up as they recognized a tale familiar to their ears. Anything was better than trying to study in that dull last hour of afternoon school.

"Yes," continued Miss Hender, pleased that she had at last roused something like proper attention, "you all ought to be proud that you are schoolmates of District Number Four, and can remember that the celebrated General Laneway had the same early advantages as you, and think what he has made of himself by perseverance and ambition."

The pupils were familiar enough with the illustrious history of their noble predecessor. They were sure to be told, in lawless moments, that if Mr. Laneway were to come in and see them he would be mortified to death; and the members of the school committee always referred to him, and said that he had been a poor boy, and was now a self-made man,—as if every man were not self-made as to his character and reputation!

At this point, young Johnny Spencer showed his next neighbor, in the back of his Colburn's Arithmetic* an imaginary portrait of their district hero, which caused them both to chuckle derisively. The Honorable Mr. Laneway figured on the flyleaf as an extremely cross-eyed person, with strangely crooked legs and arms and a terrific expression. He was outlined with red and blue pencils as to coat and trousers, and held a reddened scalp in one hand and a blue tomahawk in the other; being closely associated in the artist's mind with the early settlements of the far West.

There was a noise of wheels in the road near by, and, though Miss Hender had much more to say, everybody ceased to listen to her, and turned toward the windows, leaning far forward over their desks to see who might be passing. They caught a glimpse of a shiny carriage; the old dog bounded out, barking, but nothing passed the open door. The carriage had stopped; some one was coming to the school; somebody was going to be called out! It could not be the committee, whose pompous and uninspiring spring visit had taken place only the week before.

Presently a well-dressed elderly man, with an expectant, masterful look, stood on the doorstep, glanced in with a smile, and knocked. Miss Marilla Hender blushed, smoothed her pretty hair anxiously with both hands, and stepped down from her little platform to answer the summons. There was hardly a shut mouth in the primer class.

---

*Reference to *First Lessons in Intellectual Arithmetic* (1821), by Warren Colburn.

"Would it be convenient for you to receive a visitor to the school?" the stranger asked politely, with a fine bow of deference to Miss Hender. He looked much pleased and a little excited, and the teacher said,—

"Certainly; step right in, won't you, sir?" in quite another tone from that in which she had just addressed the school.

The boys and girls were sitting straight and silent in their places, in something like a fit of apprehension and unpreparedness at such a great emergency. The guest represented a type of person previously unknown in District Number Four. Everything about him spoke of wealth and authority. The old dog returned to the doorstep, and after a careful look at the invader approached him, with a funny doggish grin and a desperate wag of the tail, to beg for recognition.

The teacher gave her chair on the platform to the guest, and stood beside him with very red cheeks, smoothing her hair again once or twice, and keeping the hard-wood ruler fast in hand, like a badge of office. "Primer class may now retire!" she said firmly, although the lesson was not more than half through; and the class promptly escaped to their seats, waddling and stumbling, until they all came up behind their desks, face foremost, and added themselves to the number of staring young countenances. After this there was a silence, which grew more and more embarrassing.

"Perhaps you would be pleased to hear our first class in geography, sir?" asked the fair Marilla, recovering her presence of mind; and the guest kindly assented.

The young teacher was by no means willing to give up a certainty for an uncertainty. Yesterday's lesson had been well learned; she turned back to the questions about the State of Kansota,* and at the first sentence the mysterious visitor's dignity melted into an unconscious smile. He listened intently for a minute, and then seemed to reoccupy himself with his own thoughts and purposes, looking eagerly about the old school-house, and sometimes gazing steadily at the children. The lesson went on finely, and when it was finished

---

*Jewett had intended to make the state Iowa, but the editors of the *Atlantic Monthly*, where the story was first published, asked her to change the name to a fictional one.

Miss Hender asked the girl at the head of the class to name the States and Territories, which she instantly did, mispronouncing nearly all the names of the latter; then others stated boundaries and capitals, and the resources of the New England States, passing on finally to the names of the Presidents. Miss Hender glowed with pride; she had worked hard over the geography class in the winter term, and it did not fail her on this great occasion. When she turned bravely to see if the gentleman would like to ask any questions, she found that he was apparently lost in a deep reverie, so she repeated her own question more distinctly.

"They have done very well,—very well indeed," he answered kindly; and then, to every one's surprise, he rose, went up the aisle, pushed Johnny Spencer gently along his bench, and sat down beside him. The space was cramped, and the stranger looked huge and uncomfortable, so that everybody laughed, except one of the big girls, who turned pale with fright, and thought he must be crazy. When this girl gave a faint squeak Miss Hender recovered herself, and rapped twice with the ruler to restore order; then became entirely tranquil. There had been talk of replacing the hacked and worn old school-desks with patent desks and chairs; this was probably an agent connected with that business. At once she was resolute and self-reliant, and said, "No whispering!" in a firm tone that showed she did not mean to be trifled with. The geography class was dismissed, but the elderly gentleman, in his handsome overcoat, still sat there wedged in at Johnny Spencer's side.

"I presume, sir, that you are canvassing for new desks," said Miss Hender, with dignity. "You will have to see the supervisor and the selectmen." There did not seem to be any need of his lingering, but she had an ardent desire to be pleasing to a person of such evident distinction. "We always tell strangers—I thought, sir, you might be gratified to know—that this is the school-house where the Honorable Joseph K. Laneway first attended school. All do not know that he was born in this town, and went West very young; it is only about a mile from here where his folks used to live."

At this moment the visitor's eyes fell. He did not look at pretty Marilla any more, but opened Johnny Spencer's arithmetic, and, seeing the imaginary portrait of the great General Laneway, laughed a little,—a very deep-down comfortable laugh it was,—while Johnny himself turned cold with alarm, he could not have told why.

It was very still in the school-room; the bee was buzzing and bumping at the pane again; the moment was one of intense expectation.

The stranger looked at the children right and left. "The fact is this, young people," said he, in a tone that was half pride and half apology, "I am Joseph K. Laneway myself."

He tried to extricate himself from the narrow quarters of the desk, but for an embarrassing moment found that he was stuck fast. Johnny Spencer instinctively gave him an assisting push, and once free the great soldier, statesman, and millionaire took a few steps forward to the open floor; then, after hesitating a moment, he mounted the little platform and stood in the teacher's place. Marilla Hender was as pale as ashes.

"I have thought many times," the great guest began, "that some day I should come back to visit this place, which is so closely interwoven with the memories of my childhood. In my counting-room, on the fields of war, in the halls of Congress, and most of all in my Western home, my thoughts have flown back to the hills and brooks of Winby and to this little old school-house. I could shut my eyes and call back the buzz of voices, and fear my teacher's frown, and feel my boyish ambitions waking and stirring in my breast. On that bench where I just sat I saw some notches that I cut with my first jackknife fifty-eight years ago this very spring. I remember the faces of the boys and girls who went to school with me, and I see their grandchildren before me. I know that one is a Goodsoe and another a Winn by the old family look. One generation goes, and another comes.

"There are many things that I might say to you. I meant, even in those early restricted days, to make my name known, and I dare say that you too have ambition. Be careful what you wish for in this world, for if you wish hard enough you are sure to get it. I once heard a very wise man say this, and the longer I live the more firmly I believe it to be true. But wishing hard means working hard for what you want, and the world's prizes wait for the men and women who are ready to take pains to win them. Be careful and set your minds on the best things. I meant to be a rich man when I was a boy here, and I stand before you a rich man, knowing the care and anxiety and responsibility of wealth. I meant to go to Congress, and I am one of the Senators from Kansota. I say this as humbly as I say it proudly. I used to read of the valor and patriotism of the old Greeks and Romans with my youthful blood leaping along my veins, and it came to pass that my own country was in danger, and that I could help to fight her battles. Perhaps some one of these little lads has before him a more eventful life than I have lived, and is looking forward to activity and honor and the pride of fame. I wish him all the joy that I have had, all the toil that I have had, and all the bitter disappointments even; for adversity leads a man to depend upon that which is above him, and the path of glory is a lonely path, beset by temptations and a bitter sense of the weakness and imperfection of man. I see my life spread out like a great picture, as I stand here in my boyhood's place. I regret my failures. I thank God for what in his kind providence has been honest and right. I am glad to come back, but I feel, as I look in your young faces, that I am an old man, while your lives are just beginning. When you remember, in years to come, that I came here to see the old school-house, remember that I said: Wish for the best things, and work hard to win them; try to be good men and women, for the honor of the school and the town, and the noble young country that gave you birth; be kind at home and generous abroad. Remember that I, an old man who had seen much of life, begged you to be brave and good."

The Honorable Mr. Laneway had rarely felt himself so moved in any of his public speeches, but he was obliged to notice that for once he could not hold his audience. The primer class especially had begun to flag in attention, but one or two faces among the elder scholars fairly shone with vital sympathy and a lovely prescience of their future. Their eyes met his as if they struck a flash of light. There was a sturdy boy who half rose in his place unconsciously, the color coming and going in his cheeks; something in Mr. Laneway's words lit the altar flame in his reverent heart.

Marilla Hender was pleased and a little dazed; she could not have repeated what her illustrious visitor had said, but she longed to tell everybody the news that he was in town, and had come to school to make an address. She had never seen a great man before, and really needed time to reflect upon him and to consider what she ought to say. She was just quivering with the attempt to make a proper reply and thank Mr. Laneway for the honor of his visit to the school, when he asked her which of the boys could be trusted to drive back his hired horse to the Four Corners. Eight boys, large and small, nearly every boy in the school, rose at once and snapped insistent fingers; but Johnny Spencer alone was desirous not to attract attention to himself. The Colburn's Intellectual Arithmetic with the portrait had been well secreted between his tight jacket and his shirt. Miss Hender selected a trustworthy freckled person in long trousers, who was half way to the door in an instant, and was heard almost immediately to shout loudly at the quiet horse.

Then the Hero of District Number Four made his acknowledgments to the teacher. "I fear that I have interrupted you too long," he said, with pleasing deference.

Marilla replied that it was of no consequence; she hoped he would call again. She may have spoken primly, but her pretty eyes said everything that her lips forgot. "My grandmother will want to see you, sir," she ventured to say. "I guess you will remember her,—Mis' Hender, she that was Abby Harran. She has often told me how you used to get your lessons out o' the same book."

"Abby Harran's granddaughter?" Mr. Laneway looked at her again with fresh interest. "Yes, I wish to see her more than any one else. Tell her that I am coming to see her before I go away, and give her my love. Thank you, my dear," as Marilla offered his missing hat. "Good-by, boys and girls." He stopped and looked at them once more from the boys' entry, and turned again to look back from the very doorstep.

"Good-by, sir,—good-by," piped two or three of the young voices; but most of the children only stared, and neither spoke nor moved.

"We will omit the class in Fourth Reader* this afternoon. The class in grammar may recite," said Miss Hender in her most contained and official manner.

**McGuffey's Fourth Reader* was one in a series of popular books intended for younger students published by educator William Holmes McGuffey (1800–1873).

d give him as hearty a welcome as the greeting he hem. So he rose and went his way westward to- The air was growing damp and cold, and it was e of shelter. This was hardly like the visit he had is birthplace. He wished with all his heart that he ack. But he walked briskly away, intent upon wider resh evening breeze quickened his steps. He did re he was going, but was for a time the busy man ted by the unconscious influence of his surround- gray birches and pitch pines of that neglected pas- efore seen a hat and coat exactly in the fashion. been abashed by the presence of a United States stern millionaire, though a piece of New England often felt the tread of his bare feet was not likely to a pair of smart shoes stepped hastily along the th.

III

IMPERATIVE knock at the side door of the Hender t after dark. The young school-mistress had come use she had stopped all the way along to give people er afternoon's experience. Marilla was not coy and longer, but sat by the kitchen stove telling her eager everything she could remember or could imagine.

t knocking at the door?" interrupted Mrs. Hender. yself; I'm nearest."

utside was cold and foot-weary. He was not used to hole day unrecognized, and, after being first amused, ying a sense of freedom at escaping his just dues of and respect, he had begun to feel as if he were old and l was hardly sure of a friend in the world.

Hender came to the door, with her eyes shining with eat haste to dismiss whoever had knocked, so that she he rest of Marilla's story. She opened the door wide to ht have come on some country errand, and looked the t-hearted Mr. Laneway full in the face.

The grammar class sighed like a single pupil, and obeyed. She was very stern with the grammar class, but every one in school had an inner sense that it was a great day in the history of District Number Four.

II

THE HONORABLE MR. LANEWAY found the outdoor air very fresh and sweet after the closeness of the school-house. It had just that same odor in his boyhood, and as he escaped he had a delightful sense of playing truant or of having an unexpected holiday. It was easier to think of himself as a boy, and to slip back into boyish thoughts, than to bear the familiar burden of his manhood. He climbed the tumble-down stone wall across the road, and went along a narrow path to the spring that bubbled up clear and cold under a great red oak. How many times he had longed for a drink of that water, and now here it was, and the thirst of that warm spring day was hard to quench! Again and again he stopped to fill the birch-bark dipper which the school-children had made, just as his own comrades made theirs years before. The oak-tree was dying at the top. The pine woods beyond had been cut and had grown again since his boyhood, and looked much as he remembered them. Beyond the spring and away from the woods the path led across overgrown pastures to another road, perhaps three quarters of a mile away, and near this road was the small farm which had been his former home. As he walked slowly along, he was met again and again by some reminder of his youthful days. He had always liked to refer to his early life in New England in his political addresses, and had spoken more than once of going to find the cows at nightfall in the autumn evenings, and being glad to warm his bare feet in the places where the sleepy beasts had lain, before he followed their slow steps homeward through bush and brier. The Honorable Mr. Laneway had a touch of true sentiment which added much to his really stirring and effective campaign speeches. He had often been called the "king of the platform" in his adopted State. He had long ago grown used to saying "Go" to one man, and

"Come" to another, like the ruler of old;* but all his natural power of leadership and habit of authority disappeared at once as he trod the pasture slopes, calling back the remembrance of his childhood. Here was the place where two lads, older than himself, had killed a terrible woodchuck at bay in the angle of a great rock; and just beyond was the sunny spot where he had picked a bunch of pink and white anemones under a prickly barberry thicket, to give to Abby Harran in morning school. She had put them into her desk, and let them wilt there, but she was pleased when she took them. Abby Harran, the little teacher's grandmother, was a year older than he, and had wakened the earliest thought of love in his youthful breast.

It was almost time to catch the first sight of his birthplace. From the knoll just ahead he had often seen the light of his mother's lamp, as he came home from school on winter afternoons; but when he reached the knoll the old house was gone, and so was the great walnut-tree that grew beside it, and a pang of disappointment shot through this devout pilgrim's heart. He never had doubted that the old farm was somebody's home still, and had counted upon the pleasure of spending a night there, and sleeping again in that room under the roof, where the rain sounded loud, and the walnut branches brushed to and fro when the wind blew, as if they were the claws of tigers. He hurried across the worn-out fields, long ago turned into sheep pastures, where the last year's tall grass and golden-rod stood gray and winter-killed; tracing the old walls and fences, and astonished to see how small the fields had been. The prosperous owner of Western farming lands could not help remembering those wide-spread luxuriant acres, and the broad outlooks of his Western home.

It was difficult at first to find exactly where the house had stood; even the foundations had disappeared. At last in the long, faded grass he discovered the doorstep, and near by was a little mound where the great walnut-tree stump had been. The cellar was a mere dent in the sloping ground; it had been filled in by the growing grass and slow processes of summer and winter weather. But just at the

*Reference to the Bible, Matthew 8:1–14.

pilgrim's right were so
den brightening of m
mother—dead since h
brier.* How often she h
home! So much had ch
the world of light,† and
alive! There was one slen
and getting ready to flov

The afternoon wore l
He might have laughed
sad thoughts, and found
plead his cause at the bar
hour. He had dreamed a
fashion, of this return to
grand affair, but so far he
at his poor occasion. Then
he had been undignified,
silly, in the old school-hou
path, in Johnny Spencer's a
longed-for day had held, b
remembrance and really lik
own old desk. There was an
the room, who reminded I
youth. There was a spark o
twice in the earlier afternoon
ple in the road if there were
hood, but everybody had said
had been expecting that every
and give him credit for what h
her own affairs to look after,
help.

Mr. Laneway acknowledged
weak and unmanly. There mu

*European variety of rose.
†Reference to the afterlife—that is, life

remember him, a
had brought for
ward the sunset.
time to make su
meant to pay to
had never come
thoughts as the
not consider wh
of affairs, stimul
ings. The slende
ture had never
They may have
Senator and W
ground that ha
quake because
school-house p

THERE WAS A
farmhouse, ju
home late, bec
the news of h
speechless an
grandmother

"Who's th
"No, I'll go n

The man
spending a w
and even enj
consideratio
forgotten, an

Old Mrs.
delight, in g
might hear
whoever mi
tired and fa

"Dear heart, come in!" she exclaimed, reaching out and taking him by the shoulder, as he stood humbly on a lower step. "Come right in, Joe. Why, I should know you anywhere! Why, Joe Laneway, *you same boy*!"

In they went to the warm, bright, country kitchen. The delight and kindness of an old friend's welcome and her instant sympathy seemed the loveliest thing in the world. They sat down in two old straight-backed kitchen chairs. They still held each other by the hand, and looked in each other's face. The plain old room was aglow with heat and cheerfulness; the tea-kettle was singing; a drowsy cat sat on the wood-box with her paws tucked in; and the house dog came forward in a friendly way, wagging his tail, and laid his head on their clasped hands.

"And to think I haven't seen you since your folks moved out West, the next spring after you were thirteen in the winter," said the good woman. "But I s'pose there ain't been anybody that has followed your career closer than I have, accordin' to their opportunities. You've done a great work for your country, Joe. I'm proud of you clean through. Sometimes folks has said, 'There, there, Mis' Hender, what be you goin' to say now?' but I've always told 'em to wait. I knew you saw your reasons. You was always an honest boy." The tears started and shone in her kind eyes. Her face showed that she had waged a bitter war with poverty and sorrow, but the look of affection that it wore, and the warm touch of her hard hand, misshapen and worn with toil, touched her old friend in his inmost heart, and for a minute neither could speak.

"They do say that women folks have got no natural head for politics, but I always could seem to sense what was goin' on in Washington, if there was any sense to it," said grandmother Hender at last.

"Nobody could puzzle you at school, I remember," answered Mr. Laneway, and they both laughed heartily. "But surely this granddaughter does not make your household? You have sons?"

"Two beside her father. He died; but they're both away, up toward Canada, buying cattle. We are getting along considerable well these last few years, since they got a mite o' capital together; but the old farm wasn't really able to maintain us, with the heavy expenses that fell on us unexpected year by year. I've seen a great sight of trouble, Joe. My boy John, Marilla's father, and his nice wife,—I lost 'em both early, when Marilla was but a child. John was the flower o' my family. He would have made a name for himself. You would have taken to John."

"I was sorry to hear of your loss," said Mr. Laneway. "He was a brave man. I know what he did at Fredericksburg.* You remember that I lost my wife and my only son?"

There was a silence between the friends, who had no need for words now; they understood each other's heart only too well. Marilla, who sat near them, rose and went out of the room.

"Yes, yes, daughter," said Mrs. Hender, calling her back, "we ought to be thinkin' about supper."

"I was going to light a little fire in the parlor," explained Marilla, with a slight tone of rebuke in her clear girlish voice.

"Oh, no, you ain't,—not now, at least," protested the elder woman decidedly. "Now, Joseph, what should you like to have for supper? I wish to my heart I had some fried turnovers, like those you used to come after when you was a boy. I can make 'em just about the same as mother did. I'll be bound you've thought of some old-fashioned dish that you'd relish for your supper."

"Rye drop-cakes, then, if they wouldn't give you too much trouble," answered the Honorable Joseph, with prompt seriousness, "and don't forget some cheese." He looked up at his old playfellow as she stood beside him, eager with affectionate hospitality.

"You've no idea what a comfort Marilla's been," she stooped to whisper. "Always took right hold and helped me when she was a baby. She's as good as made up already to me for my having no daughter. I want you to get acquainted with Marilla."

The granddaughter was still awed and anxious about the entertainment of so distinguished a guest when her grandmother appeared at last in the pantry.

"I ain't goin' to let you do no such a thing, darlin'," said Abby Hender, when Marilla spoke of making something that she called

---

*Town in central Virginia, the site of a major Civil War battle waged on December 13, 1862.

"fairy gems" for tea, after a new and essentially feminine recipe. "You just let me get supper to-night. The Gen'ral has enough kick-shaws* to eat; he wants a good, hearty, old-fashioned supper,—the same country cooking he remembers when he was a boy. He went so far himself as to speak of rye drop-cakes, an' there ain't one in a hundred, nowadays, knows how to make the kind he means. You go an' lay the table just as we always have it, except you can get out them old big sprigged cups o' my mother's. Don't put on none o' the parlor cluset things."

Marilla went off crestfallen and demurring. She had a noble desire to show Mr. Laneway that they knew how to have things as well as anybody, and was sure that he would consider it more polite to be asked into the best room, and to sit there alone until tea was ready; but the illustrious Mr. Laneway was allowed to stay in the kitchen, in apparent happiness, and to watch the proceedings from beginning to end. The two old friends talked industriously, but he saw his rye drop-cakes go into the oven and come out, and his tea made, and his piece of salt fish broiled and buttered, a broad piece of honeycomb set on to match some delightful thick slices of brown-crusted loaf bread, and all the simple feast prepared. There was a sufficient piece of Abby Hender's best cheese; it must be confessed that there were also some baked beans, and, as one thing after another appeared, the Honorable Joseph K. Laneway grew hungrier and hungrier, until he fairly looked pale with anticipation and delay, and was bidden at that very moment to draw up his chair and make himself a supper if he could. What cups of tea, what uncounted rye drop-cakes, went to the making of that successful supper! How gay the two old friends became, and of what old stories they reminded each other, and how late the dark spring evening grew, before the feast was over and the straight-backed chairs were set against the kitchen wall!

Marilla listened for a time with more or less interest, but at last she took one of her school-books, with slight ostentation, and went over to study by the lamp. Mrs. Hender had brought her knitting-work, a blue woolen stocking, out of a drawer, and sat

---

*Trifles, tidbits.

down serene and unruffled, prepared to keep awake as late as possible. She was a woman who had kept her youthful looks through the difficulties of farm life as few women can, and this added to her guest's sense of homelikeness and pleasure. There was something that he felt to be sisterly and comfortable in her strong figure; he even noticed the little plaid woolen shawl that she wore about her shoulders. Dear, uncomplaining heart of Abby Hender! The appealing friendliness of the good woman made no demands except to be allowed to help and to serve everybody who came in her way.

Now began in good earnest the talk of old times, and what had become of this and that old schoolmate; how one family had come to want and another to wealth. The changes and losses and windfalls of good fortune in that rural neighborhood were made tragedy and comedy by turns in Abby Hender's dramatic speech. She grew younger and more entertaining hour by hour, and beguiled the grave Senator into confidential talk of national affairs. He had much to say, to which she listened with rare sympathy and intelligence. She astonished him by her comprehension of difficult questions of the day, and by her simple good sense. Marilla grew hopelessly sleepy, and departed, but neither of them turned to notice her as she lingered a moment at the door to say good-night. When the immediate subjects of conversation were fully discussed, however, there was an unexpected interval of silence, and, after making sure that her knitting stitches counted exactly right, Abby Hender cast a questioning glance at the Senator to see if he had it in mind to go to bed. She was reluctant to end her evening so soon, but determined to act the part of considerate hostess. The guest was as wide awake as ever: eleven o'clock was the best part of his evening.

"Cider?" he suggested, with an expectant smile, and Abby Hender was on her feet in a moment. When she had brought a pitcher from the pantry, he took a candle from the high shelf and led the way.

"To think of your remembering our old cellar candlestick all these years!" laughed the pleased woman, as she followed him down the steep stairway, and then laughed still more at his delight in the familiar look of the place.

"Unchanged as the pyramids!" he said. "I suppose those pound sweetings that used to be in that farthest bin were eaten up months ago?"

It was plain to see that the household stores were waning low, as befitted the time of year, but there was still enough in the old cellar. Care and thrift and gratitude made the poor farmhouse a rich place. This woman of real ability had spent her strength from youth to age, and had lavished as much industry and power of organization in her narrow sphere as would have made her famous in a wider one. Joseph Laneway could not help sighing as he thought of it. How many things this good friend had missed, and yet how much she had been able to win that makes everywhere the very best of life! Poor and early widowed, there must have been a constant battle with poverty on that stony Harran farm, whose owners had been pitied even in his early boyhood, when the best of farming life was none too easy. But Abby Hender had always been one of the leaders of the town.

"Now, before we sit down again, I want you to step into my best room. Perhaps you won't have time in the morning, and I've got something to show you," she said persuasively.

It was a plain, old-fashioned best room, with a look of pleasantness in spite of the spring chill and the stiffness of the best chairs. They lingered before the picture of Mrs. Hender's soldier son, a poor work of a poorer artist in crayons, but the spirit of the young face shone out appealingly. Then they crossed the room and stood before some bookshelves, and Abby Hender's face brightened into a beaming smile of triumph.

"You didn't expect we should have all those books, now, did you, Joe Laneway?" she asked.

He shook his head soberly, and leaned forward to read the titles. There were no very new ones, as if times had been hard of late; almost every volume was either history, or biography, or travel. Their owner had reached out of her own narrow boundaries into other lives and into far countries. He recognized with gratitude two or three congressional books that he had sent her when he first went to Washington, and there was a life of himself, written from a partisan point of view, and issued in one of his most exciting campaigns; the sight of it touched him to the heart, and then she opened it, and showed him the three or four letters that he had written her,—one, in boyish handwriting, describing his adventures on his first Western journey.

"There are a hundred and six volumes now," announced the proud owner of such a library. "I lend 'em all I can, or most of them would look better. I have had to wait a good while for some, and some weren't what I expected 'em to be, but most of 'em 's as good books as there is in the world. I've never been so situated that it seemed best for me to indulge in a daily paper, and I don't know but it's just as well; but stories were never any great of a temptation. I know pretty well what's goin' on about me, and I can make that do. Real life's interestin' enough for me."

Mr. Laneway was still looking over the books. His heart smote him for not being thoughtful; he knew well enough that the overflow of his own library would have been delightful to this self-denying, eager-minded soul. "I've been a very busy man all my life, Abby," he said impulsively, as if she waited for some apology for his forgetfulness, "but I'll see to it now that you have what you want to read. I don't mean to lose hold of your advice on state matters." They both laughed, and he added, "I've always thought of you, if I haven't shown it."

"There's more time to read than there used to be; I've had what was best for me," answered the woman gently, with a grateful look on her face, as she turned to glance at her old friend. "Marilla takes hold wonderfully and helps me with the work. In the long winter evenings you can't think what a treat a new book is. I wouldn't change places with the queen."

They had come back to the kitchen, and she stood before the cupboard, reaching high for two old gayly striped crockery mugs. There were some doughnuts and cheese at hand; their early supper seemed quite forgotten. The kitchen was warm, and they had talked themselves thirsty and hungry; but with what an unexpected tang the cider freshened their throats! Mrs. Hender had picked the apples herself that went to the press; they were all chosen from the old russet tree* and the gnarly, red-cheeked, ungrafted fruit that

---

*Variety of apple tree.

grew along the lane. The flavor made one think of frosty autumn mornings on high hillsides, of north winds and sunny skies. "It 'livens one to the heart," as Mrs. Hender remarked proudly, when the Senator tried to praise it as much as it deserved, and finally gave a cheerful laugh, such as he had not laughed for many a day.

"Why, it seems like drinking the month of October," he told her; and at this the hostess reached over, protesting that the striped mug was too narrow to hold what it ought, and filled it up again.

"Oh, Joe Laneway, to think that I see you at last, after all these years!" she said. "How rich I shall feel with this evening to live over! I've always wanted to see somebody that I'd read about, and now I've got that to remember; but I've always known I should see you again, and I believe 't was the Lord's will."

Early the next morning they said good-by. The early breakfast had to be hurried, and Marilla was to drive Mr. Laneway to the station, three miles away. It was Saturday morning, and she was free from school.

Mr. Laneway strolled down the lane before breakfast was ready, and came back with a little bunch of pink anemones in his hand. Marilla thought that he meant to give them to her, but he laid them beside her grandmother's plate. "You mustn't put those in your desk," he said with a smile, and Abby Hender blushed like a girl.

"I've got those others now, dried and put away somewhere in one of my books," she said quietly, and Marilla wondered what they meant.

The two old friends shook hands warmly at parting. "I wish you could have stayed another day, so I could have had the minister come and see you," urged Mrs. Hender regretfully.

"You couldn't have done any more for me. I have had the best visit in the world," he answered, a little shaken, and holding her hand a moment longer, while Marilla sat, young and impatient, in the high wagon. "You're a dear good woman, Abby. Sometimes when things have gone wrong I've been sorry that I ever had to leave Winby."

The woman's clear eyes looked straight into his; then fell. "You wouldn't have done everything you have for the country," she said.

"Give me a kiss; we're getting to be old folks now," said the General; and they kissed each other gravely.

A moment later Abby Hender stood alone in her dooryard, watching and waving her hand again and again, while the wagon rattled away down the lane and turned into the highroad.

Two hours after Marilla returned from the station, and rushed into the kitchen.

"Grandma!" she exclaimed, "you never did see such a crowd in Winby as there was at the depot! Everybody in town had got word about General Laneway, and they were pushing up to shake hands, and cheering same as at election, and the cars waited much as ten minutes, and all the folks was lookin' out of the windows, and came out on the platforms when they heard who it was. Folks say that he'd been to see the selectmen yesterday before he came to school, and he's goin' to build an elegant town hall, and have the names put up in it of all the Winby men that went to the war." Marilla sank into a chair, flushed with excitement. "Everybody was asking me about his being here last night and what he said to the school. I wished that you'd gone down to the depot instead of me."

"I had the best part of anybody," said Mrs. Hender, smiling and going on with her Saturday morning work. "I'm real glad they showed him proper respect," she added a moment afterward, but her voice faltered.

"Why, you ain't been cryin', grandma?" asked the girl. "I guess you're tired. You had a real good time, now, didn't you?"

"Yes, dear heart!" said Abby Hender. "'T ain't pleasant to be growin' old, that's all. I couldn't help noticin' his age as he rode away. I've always been lookin' forward to seein' him again, an' now it's all over."

DECORATION DAY

I

A WEEK BEFORE THE thirtieth of May,[11] three friends—John Stover and Henry Merrill and Asa Brown—happened to meet on Saturday evening at Barton's store at the Plains. They were ready to enjoy this idle hour after a busy week. After long easterly rains, the sun had at last come out bright and clear, and all the Barlow farmers had been planting. There was even a good deal of ploughing left to be done, the season was so backward.

The three middle-aged men were old friends. They had been school-fellows, and when they were hardly out of their boyhood the war came on, and they enlisted in the same company, on the same day, and happened to march away elbow to elbow. Then came the great experience of a great war, and the years that followed their return from the South had come to each almost alike. These men might have been members of the same rustic household, they knew each other's history so well.

They were sitting on a low wooden bench at the left of the store door as you went in. People were coming and going on their Saturday night errands,—the post-office was in Barton's store,—but the friends talked on eagerly, without being interrupted, except by an occasional nod of recognition. They appeared to take no notice at all of the neighbors whom they saw oftenest. It was a most beautiful evening; the two great elms were almost half in leaf over the blacksmith's shop which stood across the wide road. Farther along were two small old-fashioned houses and the old white church, with its pretty belfry of four arched sides and a tiny dome at the top. The large cockerel on the vane was pointing a little south of west, and there was still light enough to make it shine bravely against the deep blue eastern sky. On the western side of the road, near the store, were the parsonage and the storekeeper's modern house, which had a French roof and some attempt at decoration, which the long-established Barlow people called gingerbread-work, and regarded with mingled pride and disdain. These buildings made the tiny village called Barlow Plains. They stood in the middle of a long narrow strip of level ground. They were islanded by green fields and pastures. There were hills beyond; the mountains themselves seemed very near. Scattered about on the hill slopes were farmhouses, which stood so far apart, with their clusters of out-buildings, that each looked lonely, and the pine woods above seemed to besiege them all. It was lighter on the uplands than it was in the valley, where the three men sat on their bench, with their backs to the store and the western sky.

"Well, here we be 'most into June, an' I 'ain't got a bush-bean above ground," lamented Henry Merrill.

"Your land's always late, ain't it? But you always catch up with the rest on us," Asa Brown consoled him. "I've often observed that your land, though early planted, was late to sprout. I view it there's a good week's difference betwixt me an' Stover an' your folks, but come first o' July we all even up."

"'T is just so," said John Stover, taking his pipe out of his mouth, as if he had a good deal more to say, and then replacing it, as if he had changed his mind.

"Made it extry hard having that long wet spell. Can't none on us take no day off this season," said Asa Brown; but nobody thought it worth his while to respond to such evident truth.

"Next Saturday 'll be the thirtieth o' May—that's Decoration Day, ain't it?—come round again. Lord! how the years slip by after you git to be forty-five an' along there!" said Asa again. "I s'pose some o' our folks'll go over to Alton to see the procession, same 's usual. I've got to git one o' them small flags to stick on our Joel's grave, an' Mis' Dexter always counts on havin' some for Harrison's lot. I calculate to get 'em somehow. I must make time to ride over, but I don't know where the time 's comin' from out o' next week. I wish the women folks would tend to them things. There's the spot where Eb Munson an' John Tighe lays in the poor-farm lot, an' I did mean certain to buy flags for 'em last year an' year before, but I went an' forgot it. I'd like to have folks that rode by notice 'em for once, if they was town paupers. Eb Munson was as darin' a man as ever stepped out to tuck o' drum."*

---

*The beating of a drum.

"So he was," said John Stover, taking his pipe with decision and knocking out the ashes. "Drink was his ruin; but I wan't one that could be harsh with Eb, no matter what he done. He worked hard long 's he could, too; but he wan't like a sound man, an' I think he took somethin' first not so much 'cause he loved it, but to kind of keep his strength up so 's he could work, an' then, all of a sudden, rum clinched with him an' threw him. Eb was talkin' 'long o' me one day when he was about half full, an' says he, right out, 'I wouldn't have fell to this state,' says he, 'if I'd had me a home an' a little fam'ly; but it don't make no difference to nobody, and it's the best comfort I seem to have, an' I ain't goin' to do without it. I'm ailin' all the time,' says he, 'an' if I keep middlin' full, I make out to hold my own an' to keep along o' my work.' I pitied Eb. I says to him, 'You ain't goin' to bring no disgrace on us old army boys, be you, Eb?' an' he says no, he wan't. I think if he'd lived to get one o' them big fat pensions, he'd had it easier. Eight dollars a month paid his board, while he'd pick up what cheap work he could, an' then he got so that decent folks didn't seem to want the bother of him, an' so he come on the town."

"There was somethin' else to it," said Henry Merrill soberly. "Drink come natural to him, 't was born in him, I expect, an' there wan't nobody that could turn the divil out same 's they did in Scriptur'.* His father an' his gran'father was drinkin' men; but they was kind-hearted an' good neighbors, an' never set out to wrong nobody. 'T was the custom to drink in their day; folks was colder an' lived poorer in early times, an' that's how most of 'em kept a-goin'. But what stove Eb all up was his disapp'intment with Marthy Peck—her forsakin' of him an' marryin' old John Down whilst Eb was off to war. I've always laid it up ag'inst her."

"So 've I," said Asa Brown. "She didn't use the poor fellow right. I guess she was full as well off, but it's one thing to show judgment, an' another thing to have heart."

There was a long pause; the subject was too familiar to need further comment.

"There ain't no public sperit here in Barlow," announced Asa Brown, with decision. "I don't s'pose we could ever get up anything

---

*Reference to the Bible, Matthew 8:16.

for Decoration Day. I've felt kind of 'shamed, but it always comes in a busy time; 't wan't no time to have it, anyway, right in late plantin'."

"'T ain't no use to look for public sperit 'less you've got some yourself," observed John Stover soberly; but something had pleased him in the discouraged suggestion. "Perhaps we could mark the day this year. It comes on a Saturday; that ain't nigh so bad as bein' in the middle of the week."

Nobody made any answer, and presently he went on,—

"There was a time along back when folks was too nigh the war-time to give much thought to the bigness of it. The best fellows was them that had stayed to home an' worked their trades an' laid up money; but I don't know 's it's so now."

"Yes, the fellows that stayed at home got all the fat places, an' when we come back we felt dreadful behind the times," grumbled Asa Brown. "I remember how 't was."

"They begun to call us heroes an' old stick-in-the-mud just about the same time," resumed Stover, with a chuckle. "We wa'n't no hand for strippin' woodland nor even tradin' hosses them first few years. I don' know why 't was we were so beat out. The best most on us could do was to sag right on to the old folks. Father he never wanted me to go to the war,—'t was partly his Quaker breed,*—an' he used to be dreadful mortified with the way I hung round down here to the store an' loafed round a-talkin' about when I was out South, an' arguin' with folks that didn't know nothin', about what the generals done. There! I see me now just as he see me then; but after I had my boy-strut out, I took holt o' the old farm 'long o' father, an' I've made it bounce. Look at them old meadows an' see the herd's grass that come off of 'em last year! I ain't ashamed o' my place now, if I did go to the war."

"It all looks a sight bigger to me now than it did then," said Henry Merrill. "Our goin' to the war, I refer to. We didn't sense it no more than other folks did. I used to be sick o' hearin' their stuff about patriotism and lovin' your country, an' them pieces o' poetry

*The Quakers, members of the Protestant group the Society of Friends, believed in passivism and objected to war and other forms of violence.

women folks wrote for the papers on the old flag, an' our fallen heroes, an' them things; they didn't seem to strike me in the right place; but I tell ye it kind o' starts me now every time I come on the flag sudden,—it does so. A spell ago—'long in the fall, I guess it was—I was over to Alton, an' there was a fire company paradin'. They'd got the prize at a fair, an' had just come home on the cars,* an' I heard the band; so I stepped to the front o' the store where me an' my woman was tradin', an' the company felt well, an' was comin' along the street 'most as good as troops. I see the old flag a-comin', kind of blowin' back, an' it went all over me. Somethin' worked round in my throat; I vow I come near cryin'. I was glad nobody see me."

"I'd go to war again in a minute," declared Stover, after an expressive pause; "but I expect we should know better what we was about. I don' know but we've got too many rooted opinions now to make us the best o' soldiers."

"Martin Tighe an' John Tighe was considerable older than the rest, and they done well," answered Henry Merrill quickly. "We three was the youngest of any, but we did think at the time we knew the most."

"Well, whatever you may say, that war give the country a great start," said Asa Brown. "I tell ye we just begin to see the scope on 't. There was my cousin, you know, Dan'l Evins, that stopped with us last winter; he was tellin' me that one o' his coastin' trips he was into the port o' Beaufort† lo'din' with yaller-pine lumber, an' he roved into an old buryin'-ground there is there, an' he see a stone that had on it some young Southern fellow's name that was killed in the war, an' under it was, 'He died for his country.' Dan'l knowed how I used to feel about them South Car'lina goings on, an' I did feel kind o' red an' ugly for a minute, an' then somethin' come over me, an' I says, 'Well, I don' know but what the poor chap did, Dan Evins, when you come to view it all round.'"

The other men made no answer.

---

*That is, by railroad.

†A harbor city in South Carolina, Beaufort was established in 1711; it was occupied by Union forces from 1861 until the end of the Civil War.

"Le's see what we can do this year. I don't care if we be a poor han'ful," urged Henry Merrill. "The young folks ought to have the good of it; I'd like to have my boys see somethin' different. Le's get together what men there is. How many 's left, anyhow? I know there was thirty-seven went from old Barlow, three-months"* men an' all."

"There can't be over eight now, countin' out Martin Tighe; he can't march," said Stover. "No, 't ain't worth while." But the others did not notice his disapproval.

"There's nine in all," announced Asa Brown, after pondering and counting two or three times on his fingers. "I can't make us no more. I never could carry figur's in my head."

"I make nine," said Merrill. "We'll have Martin ride, an' Jesse Dean too, if he will. He's awful lively on them canes o' his. An' there's Jo Wade with his crutch; he's amazin' spry for a short distance. But we can't let 'em go far afoot; they're decripped† men. We'll make 'em all put on what they've got left o' their uniforms, an' we'll scratch round an' have us a fife an' drum, an' make the best show we can."

"Why, Martin Tighe's boy, the next to the oldest, is an excellent hand to play the fife!" said John Stover, suddenly growing enthusiastic. "If you two are set on it, let's have a word with the minister to-morrow, an' see what he says. Perhaps he'll give out some kind of a notice. You have to have a good many bunches o' flowers. I guess we'd better call a meetin', some few on us, an' talk it over first o' the week. 'T wouldn't be no great of a range for us to take to march from the old buryin'-ground at the meetin'-house here up to the poor-farm an' round by Deacon Elwell's lane, so 's to notice them two stones he set up for his boys that was sunk on the man-o'-war. I expect they notice stones same 's if the folks laid there, don't they?"

He spoke wistfully. The others knew that Stover was thinking of the stone he had set up to the memory of his only brother, whose nameless grave had been made somewhere in the Wilderness.‡

---

*Soldiers who signed up to fight in the Civil War for a stint of three months.

†Colloquial for "decrepit."

‡Refers to the bloody Wilderness Campaign of the Civil War, staged in a heavily wooded section of central Virginia in May and June 1864.

"I don't know but what they'll be mad if we don't go by every house in town," he added anxiously, as they rose to go home. "'T is a terrible scattered population in Barlow to favor with a procession."

It was a mild starlit night. The three friends took their separate ways presently, leaving the Plains road and crossing the fields by foot-paths toward their farms.

II

THE WEEK WENT BY, and the next Saturday morning brought fair weather. It was a busy morning on the farms—like any other; but long before noon the teams of horses and oxen were seen going home from work in the fields, and everybody got ready in haste for the great event of the afternoon. It was so seldom that any occasion roused public interest in Barlow that there was an unexpected response, and the green before the old white meeting-house* was covered with country wagons and groups of people, whole families together, who had come on foot. The old soldiers were to meet in the church; at half past one the procession was to start, and on its return the minister was to make an address in the old burying-ground. John Stover had been first lieutenant in the war, so he was made captain of the day. A man from the next town had offered to drum for them, and Martin Tighe's proud boy was present with his fife. He had a great longing—strange enough in that peaceful, sheep-raising neighborhood—to go into the army; but he and his elder brother were the mainstay of their crippled father, and he could not be spared from the large household until a younger brother could take his place; so that all his fire and military zeal went for the present into martial tunes, and the fife was a safety-valve for his enthusiasm.

The army men were used to seeing each other; everybody knew everybody in the little country town of Barlow; but when one comrade after another appeared in what remained of his accoutrements, they felt the day to be greater than they had planned, and the simple ceremony proved more solemn than any one expected. They

---

*Church.

could make no use of their every-day jokes and friendly greetings. Their old blue coats and tarnished army caps looked faded and antiquated enough. One of the men had nothing left but his rusty canteen and rifle; but these he carried like sacred emblems. He had worn out all his army clothes long ago, because he was too poor when he was discharged to buy any others.

When the door of the church opened, the veterans were not abashed by the size and silence of the crowd. They came walking two by two down the steps, and took their places in line as if there were nobody looking on. Their brief evolutions were like a mystic rite. The two lame men refused to do anything but march as best they could; but poor Martin Tighe, more disabled than they, was brought out and lifted into Henry Merrill's best wagon, where he sat up, straight and soldierly, with his boy for driver. There was a little flag in the whip-socket before him, which flapped gayly in the breeze. It was such a long time since he had been seen out-of-doors that everybody found him a great object of interest, and paid him much attention. Even those who were tired of being asked to contribute to his support, who resented the fact of his having a helpless wife and great family; who always insisted that with his little pension and hopeless lameness, his fingerless left hand and failing sight, he could support himself and his household if he chose,—even those persons came forward now to greet him handsomely and with large approval. To be sure, he enjoyed the conversation of idlers, and his wife had a complaining way that was the same as begging, especially since her boys began to grow up and be of some use; and there were one or two near neighbors who never let them really want; so other people, who had cares enough of their own, could excuse themselves for forgetting him the year round, and even call him shiftless. But there were none to look askance at Martin Tighe on Decoration Day, as he sat in the wagon, with his bleached face like a captive's, and his thin, afflicted body. He stretched out his whole hand impartially to those who had remembered and those who had forgotten both his courage at Fredericksburg and his sorry need in Barlow.

Henry Merrill had secured the engine company's large flag in Alton, and now carried it proudly. There were eight men in line, two by two, and marching a good bit apart, to make their line the longer. The fife and drum struck up gallantly together, and the little procession moved away slowly along the country road. It gave an unwonted touch of color to the landscape,—the scarlet, the blue, between the new-ploughed fields and budding roadside thickets, between the wide dim ranges of the mountains, under the great white clouds of the spring sky. Such processions grow more pathetic year by year; it will not be so long now before wondering children will have seen the last. The aging faces of the men, the renewed comradeship, the quick beat of the hearts that remember, the tenderness of those who think upon old sorrows,—all these make the day a lovelier and a sadder festival. So men's hearts were stirred, they knew not why, when they heard the shrill fife and the incessant drum along the quiet Barlow road, and saw the handful of old soldiers marching by. Nobody thought of them as familiar men and neighbors alone,—they were a part of that army which had saved its country. They had taken their lives in their hands and gone out to fight for their country, plain John Stover and Jesse Dean and the rest. No matter if every other day in the year they counted for little or much, whether they were lame-footed and lagging, whether their farms were of poor soil or rich.

The little troop went in slender line along the road; the crowded country wagons and all the people who went afoot followed Martin Tighe's wagon as if it were a great gathering at a country funeral. The route was short, and the long, straggling line marched slowly; it could go no faster than the lame men could walk.

In one of the houses by the roadside an old woman sat by a window, in an old-fashioned black gown, and clean white cap with a prim border which bound her thin, sharp features closely. She had been for a long time looking out eagerly over the snowberry and cinnamon-rose bushes; her face was pressed close to the pane, and presently she caught sight of the great flag as it came down the road.

"Let me see 'em! I've got to see 'em go by!" she pleaded, trying to rise from her chair alone when she heard the fife, and the women helped her to the door, and held her so that she could stand and wait. She had been an old woman when the war began; she had sent sons and grandsons to the field; they were all gone now. As the men came by, she straightened her bent figure with all the vigor of youth. The fife and drum stopped suddenly; the colors lowered. She did not heed that, but her old eyes flashed and then filled with tears to see the flag going to salute the soldier's graves. "Thank ye, boys; thank ye!" she cried, in her quavering voice, and they all cheered her. The cheer went back along the straggling line for old Grandmother Dexter, standing there in her front door between the lilacs. It was one of the great moments of the day.

The few old people at the poor-house, too, were waiting to see the show. The keeper's young son, knowing that it was a day of festivity, and not understanding exactly why, had put his toy flag out of the gable window, and there it showed against the gray clapboards like a gay flower. It was the only bit of decoration along the veterans' way, and they stopped and saluted it before they broke ranks and went out to the field corner beyond the poor-farm barn to the bit of ground that held the paupers' unmarked graves. There was a solemn silence while Asa Brown went to the back of Tighe's wagon, where such light freight was carried, and brought two flags, and he and John Stover planted them straight in the green sod. They knew well enough where the right graves were, for these had been made in a corner by themselves, with unwonted sentiment. And so Eben Munson and John Tighe were honored like the rest, both by their flags and by great and unexpected nosegays of spring flowers, daffies* and flowering currant and red tulips, which lay on the graves already. John Stover and his comrade glanced at each other curiously while they stood singing, and then laid their own bunches of lilacs down and came away.

Then something happened that almost none of the people in the wagons understood. Martin Tighe's boy, who played the fife, had studied well his part, and on his poor short-winded instrument now sounded taps as well as he could. He had heard it done once in Alton at a soldier's funeral. The plaintive notes called sadly over the fields, and echoed back from the hills. The few veterans could not look at each other; their eyes brimmed up with tears; they could not have spoken. Nothing called back old army days like that. They had a sudden vision of the Virginian camp, the hillside dotted white with tents, the twinkling lights in other camps, and far away the glow of smouldering fires. They heard the

---

*Daffodils.

bugle call from post to post; they remembered the chilly winter night, the wind in the pines, the laughter of the men. Lights out! Martin Tighe's boy sounded it again sharply. It seemed as if poor Eb Munson and John Tighe must hear it too in their narrow graves.

The procession went on, and stopped here and there at the little graveyards on the farms, leaving their bright flags to flutter through summer and winter rains and snows, and to bleach in the wind and sunshine. When they returned to the church, the minister made an address about the war, and every one listened with new ears. Most of what he said was familiar enough to his listeners; they were used to reading those phrases about the results of the war, the glorious future of the South, in their weekly newspapers; but there never had been such a spirit of patriotism and loyalty waked in Barlow as was waked that day by the poor parade of the remnant of the Barlow soldiers. They sent flags to all the distant graves, and proud were those households who claimed kinship with valor, and could drive or walk away with their flags held up so that others could see that they, too, were of the elect.*

III

It is well that the days are long in the last of May, but John Stover had to hurry more than usual with his evening work, and then, having the longest distance to walk, he was much the latest comer to the Plains store, where his two triumphant friends were waiting for him impatiently on the bench. They also had made excuse of going to the post-office and doing an unnecessary errand for their wives, and were talking together so busily that they had gathered a group about them before the store. When they saw Stover coming, they rose hastily and crossed the road to meet him, as if they were a committee in special session. They leaned against the post-and-board fence, after they had shaken hands with each other solemnly.

---

*Reference to the Calvinist belief that God had selected specific human souls for salvation.

"Well, we've had a great day, ain't we, John?" asked Henry Merrill. "You did lead off splendid. We've done a grand thing, now, I tell you. All the folks say we've got to keep it up every year. Everybody had to have a talk about it as I went home. They say they had no idea we should make such a show. Lord! I wish we'd begun while there was more of us!"

"That han'some flag was the great feature," said Asa Brown generously. "I want to pay my part for hirin' it. An' then folks was glad to see poor old Martin made o' some consequence."

"There was half a dozen said to me that another year they was goin' to have flags out, and trim up their places somehow or 'nother. Folks has feelin' enough, but you've got to rouse it," said Merrill.

"I have thought o' joinin' the Grand Army* over to Alton time an' again, but it's a good ways to go, an' then the expense has been o' some consideration," Asa continued. "I don't know but two or three over there. You know, most o' the Alton men nat'rally went out in the rigiments t' other side o' the State line, an' they was in other battles, an' never camped nowheres nigh us. Seems to me we ought to have home feelin' enough to do what we can right here."

"The minister says to me this afternoon that he was goin' to arrange an' have some talks in the meetin'-house next winter, an' have some of us tell where we was in the South; an' one night 't will be about camp life, an' one about the long marches, an' then about the battles,—that would take some time,—an' tell all we could about the boys that was killed, an' their record, so they wouldn't be forgot. He said some of the folks must have the letters we wrote home from the front, an' we could make out quite a history of us. I call Elder Dallas a very smart man; he'd planned it all out a'ready, for the benefit o' the young folks, he said," announced Henry Merrill, in a tone of approval.

"I s'pose there ain't none of us but could add a little somethin'," answered John Stover modestly. "'T would re'lly learn the young

---

*Reference to the Grand Army of the Republic; established in April 1866 in Decatur, Illinois, it was the largest Union veterans rights organization in the United States.

folks a good deal. I should be scared numb to try an' speak from the pulpit. That ain't what the Elder means, is it? Now I was one that had a good chance to see somethin' o' Washin'ton. I shook hands with President Lincoln, an' I always think I'm worth lookin' at for that, if I ain't for nothin' else. 'T was that time I was just out o' hospit'l, an' able to crawl about some. I've often told you how 't was I met him, an' he stopped an' shook hands an' asked where I'd been at the front an' how I was gettin' along with my hurts. Well, we'll see how 't is when winter comes. I never thought I had no gift for public speakin', 'less 't was for drivin' cattle or pollin' the house town-meetin' days. Here! I've got somethin' in mind. You needn't speak about it if I tell it to ye," he added suddenly. "You know all them han'some flowers that was laid on to Eb Munson's grave an' Tighe's? I mistrusted you thought the same thing I did by the way you looked. They come from Marthy Down's front yard. My woman told me when we got home that she knew 'em in a minute; there wa'n't nobody in town had that kind o' red flowers but her. She must ha' kind o' harked back to the days when she was Marthy Peck. She must have come over with 'em after dark, or else dreadful early in the mornin'."

Henry Merrill cleared his throat. "There ain't nothin' half-way 'bout Mis' Down," he said. "I wouldn't ha' spoken 'bout this 'less you had led right on to it; but I overtook her when I was gittin' towards home this afternoon, an' I see by her looks she was worked up a good deal; but we talked about how well things had gone off, an' she wanted to know what expenses we'd been put to, an' I told her; and she said she'd give five dollars any day I'd stop in for it. An' then she spoke right out. 'I'm alone in the world,' says she, 'and I've got somethin' to do with, an' I'd like to have a plain stone put up to Eb Munson's grave, with the number of his rigiment on it, an' I'll pay the bill. 'T ain't out o' Mr. Down's money,' she says; ''t is mine, an' I want you to see to it.' I said I would, but we'd made a plot to git some o' them soldiers' headstones that's provided by the government. 'T was a shame it had been overlooked so long. 'No,' says she; 'I'm goin' to pay for Eb's myself.' An' I told her there wouldn't be no objection. Don't ary one o' you speak about it. 'T wouldn't be fair. She was real well-appearin'. I never felt to respect Marthy so before."

"We was kind o' hard on her sometimes, but folks couldn't help it. I've seen her pass Eb right by in the road an' never look at him when he first come home," said John Stover.

"If she hadn't felt bad, she wouldn't have cared one way or t' other," insisted Henry Merrill. "'T ain't for us to judge. Sometimes folks has to get along in years before they see things fair. Come; I must be goin' home. I'm tired as an old dog."

"It seemed kind o' natural to be steppin' out together again. Strange we three got through with so little damage, an' so many dropped round us," said Asa Brown. "I've never been one mite sorry I went out in old A Company. I was thinkin' when I was marchin' to-day, though, that we should all have to take to the wagons before long an' do our marchin' on wheels, so many of us felt kind o' stiff. There's one thing,—folks won't never say again that we can't show no public sperit here in old Barlow."

THE PASSING OF SISTER BARSETT

MRS. MERCY CRANE WAS of such firm persuasion that a house is meant to be lived in, that during many years she was never known to leave her own neat two-storied dwelling-place on the Ridge road. Yet being very fond of company, in pleasant weather she often sat in the side doorway looking out on her green yard, where the grass grew short and thick and was undisfigured even by a path toward the steps. All her faded green blinds were securely tied together and knotted on the inside by pieces of white tape; but now and then, when the sun was not too hot for her carpets, she opened one window at a time for a few hours, having pronounced views upon the necessity of light and air. Although Mrs. Crane was acknowledged by her best friends to be a peculiar person and very set in her ways, she was much respected, and one acquaintance vied with another in making up for her melancholy seclusion by bringing her all the news they could gather. She had been left alone many years before by the sudden death of her husband from sunstroke, and though she was by no means poor, she had, as some one said, "such a pretty way of taking a little present that you couldn't help being pleased when you gave her anything."

For a lover of society, such a life must have had its difficulties at times, except that the Ridge road was more traveled than any other in the township, and Mrs. Crane had invented a system of signals, to which she always resorted in case of wishing to speak to some one of her neighbors.

The afternoon was wearing late, one day toward the end of summer, and Mercy Crane sat in her doorway dressed in a favorite old-fashioned light calico and a small shoulder shawl figured with large palm leaves. She was making some tatting of a somewhat intricate pattern; she believed it to be the prettiest and most durable of trimmings, and having decorated her own wardrobe in the course of unlimited leisure, she was now making a few yards apiece for each of her more intimate friends, so that they might have something to remember her by. She kept glancing up the road as if she expected some one, but the time went slowly by, until at last a woman appeared to view, walking fast, and carrying a large bundle in a checked handkerchief.

Then Mercy Crane worked steadily for a short time without looking up, until the desired friend was crossing the grass between the dusty road and the steps. The visitor was out of breath, and did not respond to the polite greeting of her hostess until she had recovered herself to her satisfaction. Mrs. Crane made her the kind offer of a glass of water or a few peppermints, but was answered only by a shake of the head, so she resumed her work for a time until the silence should be broken.

"I have come from the house of mourning," said Sarah Ellen Dow at last, unexpectedly.

"You don't tell me that Sister Barsett"—

"She's left us this time, she's really gone," and the excited news-bringer burst into tears. The poor soul was completely overwrought; she looked tired and wan, as if she had spent her forces in sympathy as well as hard work. She felt in her great bundle for a pocket handkerchief, but was not successful in the search, and finally produced a faded gingham apron with long, narrow strings, with which she hastily dried her tears. The sad news appealed also to Mercy Crane, who looked across to the apple-trees, and could not see them for a dazzle of tears in her own eyes. The spectacle of Sarah Ellen Dow going home with her humble workaday possessions, from the house where she had gone in haste only a few days before to care for a sick person well known to them both, was a very sad sight.

"You sent word yesterday that you should be returnin' early this afternoon, and would stop. I presume I received the message as you gave it?" asked Mrs. Crane, who was tenacious in such matters; "but I do declare I never looked to hear she was gone."

"She's been failin' right along sence yisterday about this time," said the nurse. "She's taken no notice to speak of, an' been eatin' the vally o' nothin', I may say, sence I went there a-Tuesday. Her sisters both come back yisterday, an' of course I was expected to give up charge to them. They're used to sickness, an' both havin' such a name for bein' great housekeepers!"

Sarah Ellen spoke with bitterness, but Mrs. Crane was reminded instantly of her own affairs. "I feel condemned that I ain't begun my own fall cleanin' yet," she said, with an ostentatious sigh.

"Plenty o' time to worry about that," her friend hastened to console her.

"I do desire to have everything decent about my house," resumed Mrs. Crane. "There's nobody to do anything but me. If I was to be taken away sudden myself, I shouldn't want to have it said afterwards that there was wisps under my sofy or—There! I can't dwell on my own troubles with Sister Barsett's loss right before me. I can't seem to believe she's really passed away; she always was saying she should go in some o' these spells, but I deemed her to be troubled with narves."

Sarah Ellen Dow shook her head. "I'm all nerved up myself," she said brokenly. "I made light of her sickness when I went there first, I'd seen her what she called dreadful low so many times; but I saw her looks this morning, an' I begun to believe her at last. Them sisters o' hers is the master for unfeelin' hearts. Sister Barsett was a-layin' there yisterday, an' one of 'em was a-settin' right by her tellin' how difficult 't was for her to leave home, her niece was goin' to graduate to the high school, an' they was goin' to have a time in the evening, an' all the exercises promised to be extry interesting. Poor Sister Barsett knew what she said an' looked at her with contempt, an' then she give a glance at me an' closed up her eyes as if 't was for the last time. I know she felt it."

Sarah Ellen Dow was more and more excited by a sense of bitter grievance. Her rule of the afflicted household had evidently been interfered with; she was not accustomed to be ignored and set aside at such times. Her simple nature and uncommon ability found satisfaction in the exercise of authority, but she had now left her post feeling hurt and wronged, besides knowing something of the pain of honest affliction.

"If it hadn't been for esteemin' Sister Barsett as I always have done, I should have told 'em no, an' held to it, when they asked me to come back an' watch to-night. 'T ain't for none o' their sakes, but Sister Barsett was a good friend to me in her way." Sarah Ellen broke down once more, and felt in her bundle again hastily, but the handkerchief was again elusive, while a small object fell out upon the doorstep with a bounce.

"'T ain't nothin' but a little taste-cake I spared out o' the loaf I baked this mornin'," she explained, with a blush. "I was so shoved out that I seemed to want to turn my hand to somethin' useful an' feel I was still doin' for Sister Barsett. Try a little piece, won't you, Mis' Crane? I thought it seemed light an' good."

They shared the taste-cake with serious enjoyment, and pronounced it very good indeed when they had finished and shaken the crumbs out of their laps. "There's nobody but you shall come an' do for me at the last, if I can have my way about things," said Mercy Crane impulsively. She meant it for a tribute to Miss Dow's character and general ability, and as such it was meekly accepted.

"You're a younger person than I be, an' less wore," said Sarah Ellen, but she felt better now that she had rested, and her conversational powers seemed to be refreshed by her share of the little cake. "Doctor Bangs has behaved real pretty, I can say that," she continued presently in a mournful tone.

"Heretofore, in the sickness of Sister Barsett, I have always felt to hope certain that she would survive; she's recovered from a sight o' things in her day. She has been the first to have all the new diseases that's visited this region. I know she had the spinal mergeetis* months before there was any other case about," observed Mrs. Crane with satisfaction.

"An' the new throat troubles, all of 'em," agreed Sarah Ellen; "an' has made trial of all the best patent medicines,† an' could tell you their merits as no one else could in this vicinity. She never was one that depended on herbs alone, though she considered 'em extremely useful in some cases. Everybody has their herb, as we know, but I'm free to say that Sister Barsett sometimes done everything she could to kill herself with such rovin' ways o' dosin'. She must see it now she's gone an' can't stuff down no more invigorators." Sarah Ellen Dow burst out suddenly with this, as if she could no longer contain her honest opinion.

---

*Probably spinal meningitis.

†Patent medicine contained ingredients that, for the commercial benefit of the maker, were not publicly disclosed, unlike the widely known ingredients of herbal medicines.

"There, there! you're all worked up," answered placid Mercy Crane, looking more interested than ever.

"An' she was dreadful handy to talk religion to other folks, but I've come to a realizin' sense that religion is somethin' besides opinions. She an' Elder French has been mostly of one mind, but I don't know 's they've got hold of all the religion there is."

"Why, why, Sarah Ellen!" exclaimed Mrs. Crane, but there was still something in her tone that urged the speaker to further expression of her feelings. The good creature was much excited, her face was clouded with disapproval.

"I ain't forgettin' nothin' about their good points either," she went on in a more subdued tone, and suddenly stopped.

"Preachin' 'll be done away with soon or late,—preachin' o' Elder French's kind," announced Mercy Crane, after waiting to see if her guest did not mean to say anything more. "I should like to read 'em out that verse another fashion: 'Be ye doers o' the word, not preachers only,'* would hit it about right; but there, it's easy for all of us to talk. In my early days I used to like to get out to meetin' regular, because sure as I didn't I had bad luck all the week. I didn't feel pacified 'less I'd been half a day, but I was out all day the Sabbath before Mr. Barlow died as he did. So you mean to say that Sister Barsett's really gone?"

Mrs. Crane's tone changed to one of real concern, and her manner indicated that she had put the preceding conversation behind her with decision.

"She was herself to the last," instantly responded Miss Dow. "I see her put out a thumb an' finger from under the spread an' pinch up a fold of her sister Deckett's dress, to try an' see if 't was all wool. I thought 't wa'n't all wool, myself, an' I know it now by the way she looked. She was a very knowin' person about materials; we shall miss poor Mis' Barsett in many ways, she was always the one to consult with about matters o' dress."

"She passed away easy at the last, I hope?" asked Mrs. Crane with interest.

---

*Reference to the Bible, James 1:22 (KJV): "Be ye doers of the word, and not hearers only, deceiving your own selves."

"Why, I wa'n't there, if you'll believe it!" exclaimed Sarah Ellen, flushing, and looking at her friend for sympathy. "Sister Barsett revived up the first o' the afternoon, an' they sent for Elder French. She took notice of him, and he exhorted quite a spell, an' then he spoke o' there being need of air in the room, Mis' Deckett havin' closed every window, an' she asked me of all folks if I hadn't better step out; but Elder French come too, an' he was very reasonable, an' had a word with me about Mis' Deckett an' Mis' Peak an' the way they was workin' things. I told him right out how they never come near when the rest of us was havin' it so hard with her along in the spring, but now they thought she was re'lly goin' to die, they come settlin' down like a pair o' old crows in a field to pick for what they could get. I just made up my mind they should have all the care if they wanted it. It didn't seem as if there was anything more I could do for Sister Barsett, an' I set there in the kitchen within call an' waited, an' when I heard 'em sayin', 'There, she's gone, she's gone!' and Mis' Deckett a-weepin', I put on my bunnit and stepped myself out into the road. I felt to repent after I had gone but a rod,* but I was so worked up, an' I thought they'd call me back, an' then I was put out because they didn't, an' so here I be. I can't help it now." Sarah Ellen was crying again; she and Mrs. Crane could not look at each other.

"Well, you set an' rest," said Mrs. Crane kindly, and with the merest shadow of disapproval. "You set an' rest, an' by an' by, if you'd feel better, you could go back an' just make a little stop an' inquire about the arrangements. I wouldn't harbor no feelin's, if they be inconsiderate folks. Sister Barsett has often deplored their actions in my hearing an' wished she had sisters like other folks. With all her faults she was a useful person an' a good neighbor," mourned Mercy Crane sincerely. "She was one that always had somethin' interestin' to tell, an' if it wa'n't for her dyin' spells an' all that sort o' nonsense, she'd make a figger in the world, she would so. She walked with an air always, Mis' Barsett did; you'd ask who she was if you hadn't known, as she passed you by. How quick we forget the outs about anybody that's gone! but I always feel grateful to anybody that's friendly, situated as I be. I shall miss her runnin' over. I can seem to

---

*Unit of measurement—specifically, 16.5 feet.

see her now, coming over the rise in the road. But don't you get in a way of takin' things too hard, Sarah Ellen! You've worked yourself all to pieces since I saw you last; you're gettin' to be as lean as a meetin'-house fly. Now, you're comin' in to have a cup o' tea with me, an' then you'll feel better. I've got some new molasses gingerbread that I baked this mornin'."

"I do feel beat out, Mis' Crane," acknowledged the poor little soul, glad of a chance to speak, but touched by this unexpected mark of consideration. "If I could ha' done as I wanted to I should be feelin' well enough, but to be set aside an' ordered about, where I'd taken the lead in sickness so much, an' knew how to deal with Sister Barsett so well! She might be livin' now, perhaps"—

"Come; we'd better go in, 't is gettin' damp," and the mistress of the house rose so hurriedly as to seem bustling. "Don't dwell on Sister Barsett an' her foolish folks no more; I wouldn't, if I was you."

They went into the front room, which was dim with the twilight of the half-closed blinds and two great syringa bushes that grew against them. Sarah Ellen put down her bundle and bestowed herself in the large, cane-seated rocking-chair. Mrs. Crane directed her to stay there awhile and rest, and then come out into the kitchen when she got ready.

A cheerful clatter of dishes was heard at once upon Mrs. Crane's disappearance. "I hope she's goin' to make one o' her nice shortcakes, but I don't know's she'll think it quite worth while," thought the guest humbly. She desired to go out into the kitchen, but it was proper behavior to wait until she should be called. Mercy Crane was not a person with whom one could venture to take liberties. Presently Sarah Ellen began to feel better. She did not often find such a quiet place, or the quarter of an hour of idleness in which to enjoy it, and was glad to make the most of this opportunity. Just now she felt tired and lonely. She was a busy, unselfish, eager-minded creature by nature, but now, while grief was sometimes uppermost in her mind and sometimes a sense of wrong, every moment found her more peaceful, and the great excitement little by little faded away.

"What a person poor Sister Barsett was to dread growing old so she couldn't get about. I'm sure I shall miss her as much as anybody," said Mrs. Crane, suddenly opening the kitchen door, and letting in an unmistakable and delicious odor of short-cake that revived still more the drooping spirits of her guest. "An' a good deal of knowledge has died with her," she added, coming into the room and seeming to make it lighter.

"There, she knew a good deal, but she didn't know all, especially o' doctorin'," insisted Sarah Ellen from the rocking-chair, with an unexpected little laugh. "She used to lay down the law to me as if I had neither sense nor experience, but when it came to her bad spells she'd always send for me. It takes everybody to know everything, but Sister Barsett was of an opinion that her information was sufficient for the town. She was tellin' me the day I went there how she disliked to have old Mis' Doubleday come an' visit with her, an' remarked that she called Mis' Doubleday very officious. 'Went right down on her knees an' prayed,' says she. 'Anybody would have thought I was a heathen!' But I kind of pacified her feelin's, an' told her I supposed the old lady meant well."

"Did she give away any of her things?—Mis' Barsett, I mean," inquired Mrs. Crane.

"Not in my hearin'," replied Sarah Ellen Dow. "Except one day, the first of the week, she told her oldest sister, Mis' Deckett,—'t was that first day she rode over,—that she might have her green quilted petticoat; you see it was a rainy day, an' Mis' Deckett had complained o' feelin' thin. She went right up an' got it, and put it on an' wore it off, an' I'm sure I thought no more about it, until I heard Sister Barsett groanin' dreadful in the night. I got right up to see what the matter was, an' what do you think but she was wantin' that petticoat back, and not thinking any too well o' Nancy Deckett for takin' it when 't was offered. 'Nancy never showed no sense o' propriety,' says Sister Barsett; I just wish you'd heard her go on!

"If she had felt to remember me," continued Sarah Ellen, after they had laughed a little, "I'd full as soon have some of her nice crockery-ware. She told me once, years ago, when I was stoppin' to tea with her an' we were havin' it real friendly, that she should leave me her Britannia tea-set, but I ain't got it in writin', and I can't say she's ever referred to the matter since. It ain't as if I had a home o' my own to keep it in, but I should have thought a great deal of it for her sake," and the speaker's voice faltered. "I must say that with all her virtues she never was a first-class housekeeper, but I wouldn't say it to any but a friend. You never eat no preserves o' hers that wa'n't commencin' to work,* an' you know as well as I how little forethought she had about putting away her woolens. I sat behind her once in meetin' when I was stoppin' with the Tremletts and so occupied a seat in their pew, an' I see between ten an' a dozen moth millers† come workin' out o' her fitch-fur tippet.‡ They was flutterin' round her bonnet same 's 't was a lamp. I should be mortified to death to have such a thing happen to me."

"Every housekeeper has her weak point; I've got mine as much as anybody else," acknowledged Mercy Crane with spirit, "but you never see no moth millers come workin' out o' me in a public place."

"Ain't your oven beginning to get over-het?" anxiously inquired Sarah Ellen Dow, who was sitting more in the draught, and could not bear to have any accident happen to the supper. Mrs. Crane flew to a short-cake's rescue, and presently called her guest to the table.

The two women sat down to deep and brimming cups of tea. Sarah Ellen noticed with great gratification that her hostess had put on two of the best tea-cups and some citron-melon preserves. It was not an everyday supper. She was used to hard fare, poor, hard-working Sarah Ellen, and this handsome social attention did her good. Sister Crane rarely entertained a friend, and it would be a pleasure to speak of the tea-drinking for weeks to come.

"You've put yourself out quite a consid'able for me," she acknowledged. "How pretty these cups is! You oughtn't to use 'em so common as for me. I wish I had a home I could really call my own to ask you to, but 't ain't never been so I could. Sometimes I wonder what's goin' to become o' me when I get so I'm past work. Takin' care o' sick folks an' bein' in houses where there's a sight goin' on an' everybody in a hurry kind of wears on me now I'm most a-gittin' in years. I was wishin' the other day that I could get with some comfortable kind of a sick person, where I could live right along quiet as other folks do, but folks never sends for me 'less they're drove to it. I ain't laid up anything to really depend upon."

---

*Beginning to ferment.

†Moths whose wings release a powdery substance.

‡Cape made from the fur of a skunk.

The situation appealed to Mercy Crane, well to do as she was and not burdened with responsibilities. She stirred uneasily in her chair, but could not bring herself to the point of offering Sarah Ellen the home she coveted.

"Have some hot tea," she insisted, in a matter of fact tone, and Sarah Ellen's face, which had been lighted by a sudden eager hopefulness, grew dull and narrow again.

"Plenty, plenty, Mis' Crane," she said sadly, "'t is beautiful tea,—you always have good tea;" but she could not turn her thoughts from her own uncertain future. "None of our folks has ever lived to be a burden," she said presently, in a pathetic tone, putting down her cup. "My mother was thought to be doing well until four o'clock an' was dead at ten. My Aunt Nancy came to our house well at twelve o'clock an' died that afternoon; my father was sick but ten days. There was dear sister Betsy, she did go in consumption, but 't wa'n't an expensive sickness."

"I've thought sometimes about you, how you'd get past rovin' from house to house one o' these days. I guess your friends will stand by you." Mrs. Crane spoke with unwonted sympathy, and Sarah Ellen's heart leaped with joy.

"You're real kind," she said simply. "There's nobody I set so much by. But I shall miss Sister Barsett, when all 's said an' done. She's asked me many a time to stop with her when I wasn't doin' nothin'. We all have our failin's, but she was a friendly creatur'. I sha'n't want to see her laid away."

"Yes, I was thinkin' a few minutes ago that I shouldn't want to look out an' see the funeral go by. She's one o' the old neighbors. I s'pose I shall have to look, or I shouldn't feel right afterward," said Mrs. Crane mournfully. "If I hadn't got so kind of housebound," she added with touching frankness, "I'd just as soon go over with you an' offer to watch this night."

"'T would astonish Sister Barsett so I don't know but she'd return." Sarah Ellen's eyes danced with amusement; she could not resist her own joke, and Mercy Crane herself had to smile.

"Now I must be goin', or 't will be dark," said the guest, rising and sighing after she had eaten her last crumb of gingerbread. "Yes, thank ye, you're real good, I will come back if I find I ain't wanted. Look what a pretty sky there is!" and the two friends went to the side door and stood together in a moment of affectionate silence, looking out toward the sunset across the wide fields. The country was still with that deep rural stillness which seems to mean the absence of humanity. Only the thrushes were singing far away in the walnut woods beyond the orchard, and some crows were flying over and cawed once loudly, as if they were speaking to the women at the door.

Just as the friends were parting, after most grateful acknowledgments from Sarah Ellen Dow, some one came driving along the road in a hurry and stopped.

"Who's that with you, Mis' Crane?" called one of their near neighbors.

"It's Sarah Ellen Dow," answered Mrs. Crane. "What's the matter?"

"I thought so, but I couldn't rightly see. Come, they are in a peck o' trouble up to Sister Barsett's, wonderin' where you be," grumbled the man. "They can't do nothin' with her; she's drove off everybody an' keeps a-screechin' for you. Come, step along, Sarah Ellen, do!"

"Sister Barsett!" exclaimed both the women. Mercy Crane sank down upon the doorstep, but Sarah Ellen stepped out upon the grass all of a tremble, and went toward the wagon. "They said this afternoon that Sister Barsett was gone," she managed to say. "What did they mean?"

"Gone where?" asked the impatient neighbor. "I expect 't was one of her spells. She's come to; they say she wants somethin' hearty for her tea. Nobody can't take one step till you get there, neither."

Sarah Ellen was still dazed; she returned to the doorway, where Mercy Crane sat shaking with laughter. "I don't know but we might as well laugh as cry," she said in an aimless sort of way. "I know you too well to think you're going to repeat a single word. Well, I'll get my bonnet an' start; I expect I've got considerable to cope with, but I'm well rested. Good-night, Mis' Crane, I certain did have a beautiful tea, whatever the future may have in store."

She wore a solemn expression as she mounted into the wagon in haste and departed, but she was far out of sight when Mercy Crane stopped laughing and went into the house.

THE FLIGHT OF BETSEY LANE

I

One windy morning in May, three old women sat together near an open window in the shed chamber* of Byfleet Poor-house. The wind was from the northwest, but their window faced the southeast, and they were only visited by an occasional pleasant waft of fresh air. They were close together, knee to knee, picking over a bushel of beans, and commanding a view of the dandelion-starred, green yard below, and of the winding, sandy road that led to the village, two miles away. Some captive bees were scolding among the cobwebs of the rafters overhead, or thumping against the upper panes of glass; two calves were bawling from the barnyard, where some of the men were at work loading a dump-cart and shouting as if every one were deaf. There was a cheerful feeling of activity, and even an air of comfort, about the Byfleet Poor-house. Almost every one was possessed of a most interesting past, though there was less to be said about the future. The inmates were by no means distressed or unhappy; many of them retired to this shelter only for the winter season, and would go out presently, some to begin such work as they could still do, others to live in their own small houses; old age had impoverished most of them by limiting their power of endurance; but far from lamenting the fact that they were town charges, they rather liked the change and excitement of a winter residence on the poor-farm. There was a sharp-faced, hard-worked young widow with seven children, who was an exception to the general level of society, because she deplored the change in her fortunes. The older women regarded her with suspicion, and were apt to talk about her in moments like this, when they happened to sit together at their work.

The three bean-pickers were dressed alike in stout brown ginghams, checked by a white line, and all wore great faded aprons of blue drilling, with sufficient pockets convenient to the right hand. Miss Peggy Bond was a very small, belligerent-looking person, who wore a

*Room above a shed.

huge pair of steel-bowed spectacles, holding her sharp chin well up in air, as if to supplement an inadequate nose. She was more than half blind, but the spectacles seemed to face upward instead of square ahead, as if their wearer were always on the sharp lookout for birds. Miss Bond had suffered much personal damage from time to time, because she never took heed where she planted her feet, and so was always tripping and stubbing her bruised way through the world. She had fallen down hatchways and cellarways, and stepped composedly into deep ditches and pasture brooks; but she was proud of stating that she was upsighted, and so was her father before her. At the poorhouse, where an unusual malady was considered a distinction, upsightedness was looked upon as a most honorable infirmity. Plain rheumatism, such as afflicted Aunt Lavina Dow, whose twisted hands found even this light work difficult and tiresome,—plain rheumatism was something of every-day occurrence, and nobody cared to hear about it. Poor Peggy was a meek and friendly soul, who never put herself forward; she was just like other folks, as she always loved to say, but Mrs. Lavina Dow was a different sort of person altogether, of great dignity and, occasionally, almost aggressive behavior. The time had been when she could do a good day's work with anybody: but for many years now she had not left the town-farm, being too badly crippled to work; she had no relations or friends to visit, but from an innate love of authority she could not submit to being one of those who are forgotten by the world. Mrs. Dow was the hostess and social lawgiver here, where she remembered every inmate and every item of interest for nearly forty years, besides an immense amount of town history and biography for three or four generations back.

She was the dear friend of the third woman, Betsey Lane; together they led thought and opinion—chiefly opinion—and held sway, not only over Byfleet Poor-farm, but also the selectmen and all others in authority. Betsey Lane had spent most of her life as aid-in-general to the respected household of old General Thornton. She had been much trusted and valued, and, at the breaking up of that once large and flourishing family, she had been left in good circumstances, what with legacies and her own comfortable savings; but by sad misfortune and lavish generosity everything had been scattered, and after much illness, which ended in a stiffened arm and more uncertainty, the good soul had sensibly decided that it was easier for the whole town to support her than for a part of it. She had always hoped to see something of the world before she died; she came of an adventurous, seafaring stock, but had never made a longer journey than to the towns of Danby and Northville, thirty miles away.

They were all old women; but Betsey Lane, who was sixty-nine, and looked much older, was the youngest. Peggy Bond was far on in the seventies, and Mrs. Dow was at least ten years older. She made a great secret of her years; and as she sometimes spoke of events prior to the Revolution* with the assertion of having been an eye-witness, she naturally wore an air of vast antiquity. Her tales were an inexpressible delight to Betsey Lane, who felt younger by twenty years because her friend and comrade was so unconscious of chronological limitations.

The bushel basket of cranberry beans was within easy reach, and each of the pickers had filled her lap from it again and again. The shed chamber was not an unpleasant place in which to sit at work, with its traces of seed corn hanging from the brown cross-beams, its spare churns, and dusty loom, and rickety wool-wheels, and a few bits of old furniture. In one far corner was a wide board of dismal use and suggestion, and close beside it an old cradle. There was a battered chest of drawers where the keeper of the poor-house kept his garden-seeds, with the withered remains of three seed cucumbers ornamenting the top. Nothing beautiful could be discovered, nothing interesting, but there was something usable and homely about the place. It was the favorite and untroubled bower of the bean-pickers, to which they might retreat unmolested from the public apartments of this rustic institution.

Betsey Lane blew away the chaff from her handful of beans. The spring breeze blew the chaff back again, and sifted it over her face and shoulders. She rubbed it out of her eyes impatiently, and happened to notice old Peggy holding her own handful high, as if it were an oblation, and turning her queer, up-tilted head this way and that, to look at the beans sharply, as if she were first cousin to a hen.

"There, Miss Bond, 't is kind of botherin' work for you, ain't it?" Betsey inquired compassionately.

---

*The American Revolution (1775–1783).

"I feel to enjoy it, anything, that I can do my own way so," responded Peggy. "I like to do my part. Ain't that old Mis' Fales comin' up the road? It sounds like her step."

The others looked, but they were not farsighted, and for a moment Peggy had the advantage. Mrs. Fales was not a favorite.

"I hope she ain't comin' here to put up this spring. I guess she won't now, it's gettin' so late," said Betsey Lane. "She likes to go rovin' soon as the roads is settled."

"'T is Mis' Fales!" said Peggy Bond, listening with solemn anxiety. "There, do let's pray her by!"

"I guess she's headin' for her cousin's folks up Beech Hill way," said Betsey presently. "If she'd left her daughter's this mornin', she'd have got just about as far as this. I kind o' wish she had stepped in just to pass the time o' day, long 's she wa'n't going to make no stop."

There was a silence as to further speech in the shed chamber; and even the calves were quiet in the barnyard. The men had all gone away to the field where corn-planting was going on. The beans clicked steadily into the wooden measure at the pickers' feet. Betsey Lane began to sing a hymn, and the others joined in as best they might, like autumnal crickets; their voices were sharp and cracked, with now and then a few low notes of plaintive tone. Betsey herself could sing pretty well, but the others could only make a kind of accompaniment. Their voices ceased altogether at the higher notes.

"Oh my! I wish I had the means to go to the Centennial,"* mourned Betsey Lane, stopping so suddenly that the others had to go on croaking and shrilling without her for a moment before they could stop. "It seems to me as if I can't die happy 'less I do," she added; "I ain't never seen nothin' of the world, an' here I be."

"What if you was as old as I be?" suggested Mrs. Dow pompously. "You've got time enough yet, Betsey; don't you go an' despair. I knowed of a woman that went clean round the world four times when she was past eighty, an' enjoyed herself real well. Her

*The International Centennial Exhibition was held in Philadelphia in 1876 to celebrate the 100th anniversary of the U.S. Declaration of Independence.

folks followed the sea; she had three sons an' a daughter married,—all shipmasters, and she'd been with her own husband when they was young. She was left a widder early, and fetched up her family herself,—a real stirrin', smart woman. After they'd got married off, an' settled, an' was doing well, she come to be lonesome; and first she tried to stick it out alone, but she wa'n't one that could; an' she got a notion she hadn't nothin' before her but her last sickness, and she wa'n't a person that enjoyed havin' other folks do for her. So one on her boys—I guess 't was the oldest—said he was going to take her to sea; there was ample room, an' he was sailin' a good time o' year for the Cape o' Good Hope an' way up to some o' them tea-ports in the Chiny Seas. She was all high to go, but it made a sight o' talk at her age; an' the minister made it a subject o' prayer the last Sunday, and all the folks took a last leave; but she said to some she'd fetch 'em home something real pritty, and so did. An' then they come home t' other way, round the Horn, an' she done so well, an' was such a sight o' company, the other child'n was jealous, an' she promised she'd go a v'y'ge long o' each on 'em. She was as sprightly a person as ever I see; an' could speak well o' what she'd seen."

"Did she die to sea?" asked Peggy, with interest.

"No, she died to home between v'y'ges, or she'd gone to sea again. I was to her funeral. She liked her son George's ship the best; 't was the one she was going on to Callao.* They said the men aboard all called her 'gran'ma'am,' an' she kep' 'em mended up, an' would go below and tend to 'em if they was sick. She might 'a' been alive an' enjoyin' of herself a good many years but for the kick of a cow; 't was a new cow out of a drove, a dreadful unruly beast."

Mrs. Dow stopped for breath, and reached down for a new supply of beans; her empty apron was gray with soft chaff. Betsey Lane, still pondering on the Centennial, began to sing another verse of her hymn, and again the old women joined her. At this moment some strangers came driving round into the yard from the front of the house. The turf was soft, and our friends did not hear the horses' steps. Their voices

---

*Port in Peru.

cracked and quavered; it was a funny little concert, and a lady in an open carriage just below listened with sympathy and amusement.

II

"BETSEY! BETSEY! MISS LANE!" a voice called eagerly at the foot of the stairs that led up from the shed. "Betsey! There's a lady here wants to see you right away."

Betsey was dazed with excitement, like a country child who knows the rare pleasure of being called out of school. "Lor', I ain't fit to go down, be I?" she faltered, looking anxiously at her friends; but Peggy was gazing even nearer to the zenith than usual, in her excited effort to see down into the yard, and Mrs. Dow only nodded somewhat jealously, and said that she guessed 't was nobody would do her any harm. She rose ponderously, while Betsey hesitated, being, as they would have said, all of a twitter. "It is a lady, certain," Mrs. Dow assured her; " 't ain't often there's a lady comes here."

"While there was any of Mis' Gen'ral Thornton's folks left, I wa'n't without visits from the gentry," said Betsey Lane, turning back proudly at the head of the stairs, with a touch of old-world pride and sense of high station. Then she disappeared, and closed the door behind her at the stair-foot with a decision quite unwelcome to the friends above.

"She needn't 'a' been so dreadful 'fraid anybody was goin' to listen. I guess we've got folks to ride an' see us, or had once, if we hain't now," said Miss Peggy Bond, plaintively.

"I expect 't was only the wind shoved it to," said Aunt Lavina. "Betsey is one that gits flustered easier than some. I wish 't was somebody to take her off an' give her a kind of a good time; she's young to settle down 'long of old folks like us. Betsey's got a notion o' rovin' such as ain't my natur', but I should like to see her satisfied. She'd been a very understandin' person, if she had the advantages that some does."

" 'T is so," said Peggy Bond, tilting her chin high. "I suppose you can't hear nothin' they're saying? I feel my hearin' ain't up to whar it was. I can hear things close to me well as ever; but there, hearin' ain't everything; 't ain't as if we lived where there was more goin' on to hear. Seems to me them folks is stoppin' a good while."

"They surely be," agreed Lavina Dow.

"I expect it's somethin' particular. There ain't none of the Thornton folks left, except one o' the gran'darters, an' I've often heard Betsey remark that she should never see her more, for she lives to London. Strange how folks feels contented in them strayaway places off to the ends of the airth."

The flies and bees were buzzing against the hot window-panes; the handfuls of beans were clicking into the brown wooden measure. A bird came and perched on the window-sill, and then flitted away toward the blue sky. Below, in the yard, Betsey Lane stood talking with the lady. She had put her blue drilling apron over her head, and her face was shining with delight.

"Lor', dear," she said, for at least the third time, "I remember ye when I first see ye; an awful pritty baby you was, an' they all said you looked just like the old gen'ral. Be you goin' back to foreign parts right away?"

"Yes, I'm going back; you know that all my children are there. I wish I could take you with me for a visit," said the charming young guest. "I'm going to carry over some of the pictures and furniture from the old house; I didn't care half so much for them when I was younger as I do now. Perhaps next summer we shall all come over for a while. I should like to see my girls and boys playing under the pines."

"I wish you re'lly was livin' to the old place," said Betsey Lane. Her imagination was not swift; she needed time to think over all that was being told her, and she could not fancy the two strange houses across the sea. The old Thornton house was to her mind the most delightful and elegant in the world.

"Is there anything I can do for you?" asked Mrs. Strafford kindly,—"anything that I can do for you myself, before I go away? I shall be writing to you, and sending some pictures of the children, and you must let me know how you are getting on."

"Yes, there is one thing, darlin'. If you could stop in the village an' pick me out a pritty, little, small lookin'-glass, that I can keep for my own an' have to remember you by. 'T ain't that I want to set me above the rest o' the folks, but I was always used to havin' my own when I was to your grandma's. There's very nice folks here, some on 'em, and I'm better off than if I was able to keep house; but sence you ask me, that's the only thing I feel cropin' about.* What be you goin' right back for? ain't you goin' to see the great fair to Pheladelphy, that everybody talks about?"

"No," said Mrs. Strafford, laughing at this eager and almost convicting question. "No; I'm going back next week. If I were, I believe that I should take you with me. Good-by, dear old Betsey; you make me feel as if I were a little girl again; you look just the same."

For full five minutes the old woman stood out in the sunshine, dazed with delight, and majestic with a sense of her own consequence. She held something tight in her hand, without thinking what it might be; but just as the friendly mistress of the poor-farm came out to hear the news, she tucked the roll of money into the bosom of her brown gingham dress. "'T was my dear Mis' Katy Strafford," she turned to say proudly. "She come way over from London; she's been sick; they thought the voyage would do her good. She said most the first thing she had on her mind was to come an' find me, and see how I was, an' if I was comfortable; an' now she's goin' right back. She's got two splendid houses; an' said how she wished I was there to look after things,—she remembered I was always her gran'ma's right hand. Oh, it does so carry me back, to see her! Seems if all the rest on 'em must be there together to the old house. There, I must go right up an' tell Mis' Dow an' Peggy."

"Dinner's all ready; I was just goin' to blow the horn for the menfolks," said the keeper's wife. "They'll be right down. I expect you've got along smart with them beans,—all three of you together;" but Betsey's mind roved so high and so far at that moment that no achievements of bean-picking could lure it back.

III

THE LONG TABLE IN the great kitchen soon gathered its company of waifs and strays,—creatures of improvidence and misfortune, and the irreparable victims of old age. The dinner was satisfactory,

*Obscure dialectical expression that possibly means feeling a lack of, or a longing for, something.

and there was not much delay for conversation. Peggy Bond and Mrs. Dow and Betsey Lane always sat together at one end, with an air of putting the rest of the company below the salt.* Betsey was still flushed with excitement; in fact, she could not eat as much as usual, and she looked up from time to time expectantly, as if she were likely to be asked to speak of her guest; but everybody was hungry, and even Mrs. Dow broke in upon some attempted confidences by asking inopportunely for a second potato. There were nearly twenty at the table, counting the keeper and his wife and two children, noisy little persons who had come from school with the small flock belonging to the poor widow, who sat just opposite our friends. She finished her dinner before any one else, and pushed her chair back; she always helped with the housework,—a thin, sorry, bad-tempered-looking poor soul, whom grief had sharpened instead of softening. "I expect you feel too fine to set with common folks," she said enviously to Betsey.

"Here I be a-settin'," responded Betsey calmly. "I don' know 's I behave more unbecomin' than usual." Betsey prided herself upon her good and proper manners; but the rest of the company, who would have liked to hear the bit of morning news, were now defrauded of that pleasure. The wrong note had been struck; there was a silence after the clatter of knives and plates, and one by one the cheerful town charges disappeared. The bean-picking had been finished, and there was a call for any of the women who felt like planting corn; so Peggy Bond, who could follow the line of hills pretty fairly, and Betsey herself, who was still equal to anybody at that work, and Mrs. Dow, all went out to the field together. Aunt Lavina labored slowly up the yard, carrying a light splint-bottomed kitchen chair and her knitting-work, and sat near the stone wall on a gentle rise, where she could see the pond and the green country, and exchange a word with her friends as they came and went up and down the rows. Betsey vouchsafed a word now and then about Mrs. Strafford, but you would have thought that she had been suddenly elevated to Mrs. Strafford's own cares and the responsibilities attending them, and had little in common with her old

*English class-conscious expression referring to people of inferior social rank.

associates. Mrs. Dow and Peggy knew well that these high-feeling times never lasted long, and so they waited with as much patience as they could muster. They were by no means without that true tact which is only another word for unselfish sympathy.

The strip of corn land ran along the side of a great field; at the upper end of it was a field-corner thicket of young maples and walnut saplings, the children of a great nut-tree that marked the boundary. Once, when Betsey Lane found herself alone near this shelter at the end of her row, the other planters having lagged behind beyond the rising ground, she looked stealthily about, and then put her hand inside her gown, and for the first time took out the money that Mrs. Strafford had given her. She turned it over and over with an astonished look: there were new bank-bills for a hundred dollars. Betsey gave a funny little shrug of her shoulders, came out of the bushes, and took a step or two on the narrow edge of turf, as if she were going to dance; then she hastily tucked away her treasure, and stepped discreetly down into the soft harrowed and hoed land, and began to drop corn again, five kernels to a hill. She had seen the top of Peggy Bond's head over the knoll, and now Peggy herself came entirely into view, gazing upward to the skies, and stumbling more or less, but counting the corn by touch and twisting her head about anxiously to gain advantage over her uncertain vision. Betsey made a friendly, inarticulate little sound as they passed; she was thinking that somebody said once that Peggy's eyesight might be remedied if she could go to Boston to the hospital; but that was so remote and impossible an undertaking that no one had ever taken the first step. Betsey Lane's brown old face suddenly worked with excitement, but in a moment more she regained her usual firm expression, and spoke carelessly to Peggy as she turned and came alongside.

The high spring wind of the morning had quite fallen; it was a lovely May afternoon. The woods about the field to the northward were full of birds, and the young leaves scarcely hid the solemn shapes of a company of crows that patiently attended the corn-planting. Two of the men had finished their hoeing, and were busy with the construction of a scarecrow; they knelt in the furrows, chuckling, and looking over some forlorn, discarded garments. It was a time-honored custom to make the scarecrow resemble one of the poor-house family; and this year they intended to have Mrs. Lavina Dow protect the field in effigy; last year it was the counterfeit of Betsey Lane who stood on guard, with an easily recognized quilted hood and the remains of a valued shawl that one of the calves had found airing on a fence and chewed to pieces. Behind the men was the foundation for this rustic attempt at statuary,—an upright stake and bar in the form of a cross. This stood on the highest part of the field; and as the men knelt near it, and the quaint figures of the corn-planters went and came, the scene gave a curious suggestion of foreign life. It was not like New England; the presence of the rude cross appealed strangely to the imagination.

IV

LIFE FLOWED SO SMOOTHLY, for the most part, at the Byfleet Poor-farm, that nobody knew what to make, later in the summer, of a strange disappearance. All the elder inmates were familiar with illness and death, and the poor pomp of a town-pauper's funeral. The comings and goings and the various misfortunes of those who composed this strange family, related only through its disasters, hardly served for the excitement and talk of a single day. Now that the June days were at their longest, the old people were sure to wake earlier than ever; but one morning, to the astonishment of every one, Betsey Lane's bed was empty; the sheets and blankets, which were her own, and guarded with jealous care, were carefully folded and placed on a chair not too near the window, and Betsey had flown. Nobody had heard her go down the creaking stairs. The kitchen door was unlocked, and the old watch-dog lay on the step outside in the early sunshine, wagging his tail and looking wise, as if he were left on guard and meant to keep the fugitive's secret.

"Never knowed her to do nothin' afore 'thout talking it over a fortnight, and paradin' off when we could all see her," ventured a spiteful voice. "Guess we can wait till night to hear 'bout it."

Mrs. Dow looked sorrowful and shook her head. "Betsey had an aunt on her mother's side that went and drownded of herself; she was a pritty-appearing woman as ever you see."

"Perhaps she's gone to spend the day with Decker's folks," suggested Peggy Bond. "She always takes an extra early start; she was speakin' lately o' going up their way;" but Mrs. Dow shook her head with a most melancholy look. "I'm impressed that something 's befell her," she insisted. "I heard her a-groanin' in her sleep. I was wakeful the forepart o' the night,—'t is very unusual with me, too."

"'T wa'n't like Betsey not to leave us any word," said the other old friend, with more resentment than melancholy. They sat together almost in silence that morning in the shed chamber. Mrs. Dow was sorting and cutting rags, and Peggy braided them into long ropes, to be made into mats at a later date. If they had only known where Betsey Lane had gone, they might have talked about it until dinner-time at noon; but failing this new subject, they could take no interest in any of their old ones. Out in the field the corn was well up, and the men were hoeing. It was a hot morning in the shed chamber, and the woolen rags were dusty and hot to handle.

V

BYFLEET PEOPLE KNEW EACH other well, and when this mysteriously absent person did not return to the town-farm at the end of a week, public interest became much excited; and presently it was ascertained that Betsey Lane was neither making a visit to her friends the Deckers on Birch Hill, nor to any nearer acquaintances; in fact, she had disappeared altogether from her wonted haunts. Nobody remembered to have seen her pass, hers had been such an early flitting; and when somebody thought of her having gone away by train, he was laughed at for forgetting that the earliest morning train from South Byfleet, the nearest station, did not start until long after eight o'clock; and if Betsey had designed to be one of the passengers, she would have started along the road at seven, and been seen and known of all women. There was not a kitchen in that part of Byfleet that did not have windows toward the road. Conversation rarely left the level of the neighborhood gossip: to see Betsey Lane, in her best clothes, at that hour in the morning, would have been the signal for much exercise of imagination; but as day after day went by without news, the curiosity of those who knew her best turned slowly into fear, and at last Peggy Bond again gave utterance to the belief that Betsey had either gone out in the early morning and put an end to her life, or that she had gone to the Centennial. Some of the people at table were moved to loud laughter,—it was at supper-time on a Sunday night,—but others listened with great interest.

"She never'd put on her good clothes to drownd herself," said the widow. "She might have thought 't was good as takin' 'em with her, though. Old folks has wandered off an' got lost in the woods afore now."

Mrs. Dow and Peggy resented this impertinent remark, but deigned to take no notice of the speaker. "She wouldn't have wore her best clothes to the Centennial, would she?" mildly inquired Peggy, bobbing her head toward the ceiling. " 'T would be a shame to spoil your best things in such a place. An' I don't know of her havin' any money; there's the end o' that."

"You're bad as old Mis' Bland, that used to live neighbor to our folks," said one of the old men. "She was dreadful precise; an' she so begretched* to wear a good alapaca dress† that was left to her, that it hung in a press forty year, an' baited the moths at last."

"I often seen Mis' Bland a-goin' in to meetin' when I was a young girl," said Peggy Bond approvingly. "She was a good-appearin' woman, an' she left property."

"Wish she'd left it to me, then," said the poor soul opposite, glancing at her pathetic row of children: but it was not good manners at the farm to deplore one's situation, and Mrs. Dow and Peggy only frowned. "Where do you suppose Betsey can be?" said Mrs. Dow, for the twentieth time. "She didn't have no money. I know she ain't gone far, if it's so that she's yet alive. She's b'en real pinched all the spring."

---

*Begrudged.

†Dress of alpaca wool.

"Perhaps that lady that come one day give her some," the keeper's wife suggested mildly.

"Then Betsey would have told me," said Mrs. Dow, with injured dignity.

VI

ON THE MORNING OF her disappearance, Betsey rose even before the pewee and the English sparrow, and dressed herself quietly, though with trembling hands, and stole out of the kitchen door like a plunderless thief. The old dog licked her hand and looked at her anxiously; the tortoise-shell cat rubbed against her best gown, and trotted away up the yard, then she turned anxiously and came after the old woman, following faithfully until she had to be driven back. Betsey was used to long country excursions afoot. She dearly loved the early morning; and finding that there was no dew to trouble her, she began to follow pasture paths and short cuts across the fields, surprising here and there a flock of sleepy sheep, or a startled calf that rustled out from the bushes. The birds were pecking their breakfast from bush and turf; and hardly any of the wild inhabitants of that rural world were enough alarmed by her presence to do more than flutter away if they chanced to be in her path. She stepped along, light-footed and eager as a girl, dressed in her neat old straw bonnet and black gown, and carrying a few belongings in her best bundle-handkerchief, one that her only brother had brought home from the East Indies fifty years before. There was an old crow perched as sentinel on a small, dead pine-tree, where he could warn friends who were pulling up the sprouted corn in a field close by; but he only gave a contemptuous caw as the adventurer appeared, and she shook her bundle at him in revenge, and laughed to see him so clumsy as he tried to keep his footing on the twigs.

"Yes, I be," she assured him. "I'm a-goin' to Pheladelphy, to the Centennial, same 's other folks. I'd jest as soon tell ye 's not, old crow;" and Betsey laughed aloud in pleased content with herself and her daring, as she walked along. She had only two miles to go to the station at South Byfleet, and she felt for the money now and then, and found it safe enough. She took great pride in the success of her escape, and especially in the long concealment of her wealth. Not a night had passed since Mrs. Strafford's visit that she had not slept with the roll of money under her pillow by night, and buttoned safe inside her dress by day. She knew that everybody would offer advice and even commands about the spending or saving of it; and she brooked no interference.

The last mile of the foot-path to South Byfleet was along the railway track; and Betsey began to feel in haste, though it was still nearly two hours to train time. She looked anxiously forward and back along the rails every few minutes, for fear of being run over; and at last she caught sight of an engine that was apparently coming toward her, and took flight into the woods before she could gather courage to follow the path again. The freight train proved to be at a standstill, waiting at a turnout; and some of the men were straying about, eating their early breakfast comfortably in this time of leisure. As the old woman came up to them, she stopped too, for a moment of rest and conversation.

"Where be ye goin'?" she asked pleasantly; and they told her. It was to the town where she had to change cars and take the great through train; a point of geography which she had learned from evening talks between the men at the farm.

"What'll ye carry me there for?"

"We don't run no passenger cars," said one of the young fellows, laughing. "What makes you in such a hurry?"

"I'm startin' for Pheladelphy, an' it's a gre't ways to go."

"So 't is; but you're consid'able early, if you're makin' for the eight-forty train. See here! you haven't got a needle an' thread 'long of you in that bundle, have you? If you'll sew me on a couple o' buttons, I'll give ye a free ride. I'm in a sight o' distress, an' none o' the fellows is provided with as much as a bent pin."

"You poor boy! I'll have you seen to, in half a minute. I'm troubled with a stiff arm, but I'll do the best I can."

The obliging Betsey seated herself stiffly on the slope of the embankment, and found her thread and needle with utmost haste. Two of the train-men stood by and watched the careful stitches, and even offered her a place as spare brakeman, so that they might keep her near; and Betsey took the offer with considerable seriousness, only thinking it necessary to assure them that she was getting most too old to be out in all weathers. An express went by like an earthquake, and she was presently hoisted on board an empty box-car by two of her new and flattering acquaintances, and found herself before noon at the end of the first stage of her journey, without having spent a cent, and furnished with any amount of thrifty advice. One of the young men, being compassionate of her unprotected state as a traveler, advised her to find out the widow of an uncle of his in Philadelphia, saying despairingly that he couldn't tell her just how to find the house; but Miss Betsey Lane said that she had an English tongue in her head, and should be sure to find whatever she was looking for. This unexpected incident of the freight train was the reason why everybody about the South Byfleet station insisted that no such person had taken passage by the regular train that same morning, and why there were those who persuaded themselves that Miss Betsey Lane was probably lying at the bottom of the poor-farm pond.

VII

"Land sakes!" said Miss Betsey Lane, as she watched a Turkish person parading by in his red fez, "I call the Centennial somethin' like the day o' judgment! I wish I was goin' to stop a month, but I dare say 't would be the death o' my poor old bones."

She was leaning against the barrier of a patent pop-corn establishment, which had given her a sudden reminder of home, and of the winter nights when the sharp-kerneled little red and yellow ears were brought out, and Old Uncle Eph Flanders sat by the kitchen stove, and solemnly filled a great wooden chopping-tray for the refreshment of the company. She had wandered and loitered and looked until her eyes and head had grown numb and unreceptive; but it is only unimaginative persons who can be really astonished. The imagination can always outrun the possible and actual sights and sounds of the world; and this plain old body from Byfleet rarely found anything rich and splendid enough to surprise her. She saw the wonders of the West and the splendors of the East with equal calmness and satisfaction; she had always known that there was an amazing world outside the boundaries of Byfleet. There was a piece of paper in her pocket on which was marked, in her clumsy handwriting, "If Betsey Lane should meet with accident, notify the selectmen of Byfleet;" but having made this slight provision for the future, she had thrown herself boldly into the sea of strangers, and then had made the joyful discovery that friends were to be found at every turn.

There was something delightfully companionable about Betsey; she had a way of suddenly looking up over her big spectacles with a reassuring and expectant smile, as if you were going to speak to her, and you generally did. She must have found out where hundreds of people came from, and whom they had left at home, and what they thought of the great show, as she sat on a bench to rest, or leaned over the railings where free luncheons were afforded by the makers of hot waffles and molasses candy and fried potatoes; and there was not a night when she did not return to her lodgings with a pocket crammed with samples of spool cotton and nobody knows what. She had already collected small presents for almost everybody she knew at home, and she was such a pleasant, beaming old country body, so unmistakably appreciative and interested, that nobody ever thought of wishing that she would move on. Nearly all the busy people of the Exhibition called her either Aunty or Grandma at once, and made little pleasures for her as best they could. She was a delightful contrast to the indifferent, stupid crowd that drifted along, with eyes fixed at the same level, and seeing, even on that level, nothing for fifty feet at a time. "What be you making here, dear?" Betsey Lane would ask joyfully, and the most perfunctory guardian hastened to explain. She squandered money as she had never had the pleasure of doing before, and this hastened the day when she must return to Byfleet. She was always inquiring if there were any spectacle-sellers at hand, and received occasional directions; but it was a difficult place for her to find her way about in, and the very last day of her stay arrived before she found an exhibitor of the desired sort, an oculist and instrument-maker.

"I called to get some specs for a friend that's upsighted," she gravely informed the salesman, to his extreme amusement. "She's dreadful troubled, and jerks her head up like a hen a-drinkin'. She's got a blur a-growin' an' spreadin', an' sometimes she can see out to one side on 't, and more times she can't."

"Cataracts," said a middle-aged gentleman at her side; and Betsey Lane turned to regard him with approval and curiosity.

"'T is Miss Peggy Bond I was mentioning, of Byfleet Poor-farm," she explained. "I count on gettin' some glasses to relieve her trouble, if there's any to be found."

"Glasses won't do her any good," said the stranger. "Suppose you come and sit down on this bench, and tell me all about it. First, where is Byfleet?" and Betsey gave the directions at length.

"I thought so," said the surgeon. "How old is this friend of yours?"

Betsey cleared her throat decisively, and smoothed her gown over her knees as if it were an apron; then she turned to take a good look at her new acquaintance as they sat on the rustic bench together. "Who be you, sir, I should like to know?" she asked, in a friendly tone.

"My name 's Dunster."

"I take it you're a doctor," continued Betsey, as if they had overtaken each other walking from Byfleet to South Byfleet on a summer morning.

"I'm a doctor; part of one at least," said he. "I know more or less about eyes; and I spend my summers down on the shore at the mouth of your river; some day I'll come up and look at this person. How old is she?"

"Peggy Bond is one that never tells her age; 't ain't come quite up to where she'll begin to brag of it, you see," explained Betsey reluctantly; "but I know her to be nigh to seventy-six, one way or t' other. Her an' Mrs. Mary Ann Chick was same year's child'n, and Peggy knows I know it, an' two or three times when we've be'n in the buryin'-ground where Mary Ann lays an' has her dates right on her headstone, I couldn't bring Peggy to take no sort o' notice. I will say she makes, at times, a convenience of being upsighted. But there, I feel for her,—everybody does; it keeps her stubbin' an' trippin' against everything, beakin' and gazin' up the way she has to."

"Yes, yes," said the doctor, whose eyes were twinkling. "I'll come and look after her, with your town doctor, this summer,—some time in the last of July or first of August."

"You'll find occupation," said Betsey, not without an air of patronage. "Most of us to the Byfleet Farm has got our ails, now I tell ye. You ain't got no bitters that'll take a dozen years right off an ol' lady's shoulders?"

The busy man smiled pleasantly, and shook his head as he went away. "Dunster," said Betsey to herself, soberly committing the new name to her sound memory. "Yes, I mustn't forget to speak of him to the doctor, as he directed. I do' know now as Peggy would vally herself quite so much accordin' to, if she had her eyes fixed same as other folks. I expect there wouldn't been a smarter woman in town, though, if she'd had a proper chance. Now I've done what I set to do for her, I do believe, an' 't wa'n't glasses, neither. I'll git her a pritty little shawl with that money I laid aside. Peggy Bond ain't got a pritty shawl. I always wanted to have a real good time, an' now I'm havin' it."

VIII

Two or three days later, two pathetic figures might have been seen crossing the slopes of the poor-farm field, toward the low shores of Byfield pond. It was early in the morning, and the stubble of the lately mown grass was wet with rain and hindering to old feet. Peggy Bond was more blundering and liable to stray in the wrong direction than usual; it was one of the days when she could hardly see at all. Aunt Lavina Dow was unusually clumsy of movement, and stiff in the joints; she had not been so far from the house for three years. The morning breeze filled the gathers of her wide gingham skirt, and aggravated the size of her unwieldy figure. She supported herself with a stick, and trusted beside to the fragile support of Peggy's arm. They were talking together in whispers.

"Oh, my sakes!" exclaimed Peggy, moving her small head from side to side. "Hear you wheeze, Mis' Dow! This may be the death o' you; there, do go slow! You set here on the side-hill, an' le' me go try if I can see."

"It needs more eyesight than you've got," said Mrs. Dow, panting between the words. "Oh! to think how spry I was in my young days, an' here I be now, the full of a door, an' all my complaints so aggravated by my size. 'T is hard! 't is hard! but I'm a-doin' of all this for pore Betsey's sake. I know they've all laughed, but I look to see her ris' to the top o' the pond this day,—'t is just nine days since she departed; an' say what they may, I know she hove herself in. It run in her family; Betsey had an aunt that done just so, an' she ain't be'n like herself, a-broodin' an' hivin' away alone, an' nothin' to say to you an' me that was always sich good company all together. Somethin' sprung her mind, now I tell ye, Mis' Bond."

"I feel to hope we sha'n't find her, I must say," faltered Peggy. It was plain that Mrs. Dow was the captain of this doleful expedition. "I guess she ain't never thought o' drowndin' of herself, Mis' Dow; she's gone off a-visitin' way over to the other side o' South Byfleet; some thinks she's gone to the Centennial even now!"

"She hadn't no proper means, I tell ye," wheezed Mrs. Dow indignantly; "an' if you prefer that others should find her floatin' to the top this day, instid of us that's her best friends, you can step back to the house."

They walked on in aggrieved silence. Peggy Bond trembled with excitement, but her companion's firm grasp never wavered, and so they came to the narrow, gravelly margin and stood still. Peggy tried in vain to see the glittering water and the pond-lilies that starred it; she knew that they must be there; once, years ago, she had caught fleeting glimpses of them, and she never forgot what she had once seen. The clear blue sky overhead, the dark pine-woods beyond the pond, were all clearly pictured in her mind. "Can't you see nothin'?" she faltered; "I believe I'm wuss 'n upsighted this day. I'm going to be blind."

"No," said Lavina Dow solemnly; "no, there ain't nothin' whatever, Peggy. I hope to mercy she ain't"—

"Why, whoever 'd expected to find you 'way out here!" exclaimed a brisk and cheerful voice. There stood Betsey Lane herself, close behind them, having just emerged from a thicket of alders that grew close by. She was following the short way homeward from the railroad.

"Why, what's the matter, Mis' Dow? You ain't overdoin', be ye? an' Peggy 's all of a flutter. What in the name o' natur' ails ye?"

"There ain't nothin' the matter, as I knows on," responded the leader of this fruitless expedition. "We only thought we'd take a stroll this pleasant mornin'," she added, with sublime self-possession. "Where've you be'n, Betsey Lane?"

"To Pheladelphy, ma'am," said Betsey, looking quite young and gay, and wearing a townish and unfamiliar air that upheld her words. "All ought to go that can; why, you feel 's if you'd be'n all round the world. I guess I've got enough to think of and tell ye for the rest o' my days. I've always wanted to go somewheres. I wish you'd be'n there, I do so. I've talked with folks from Chiny an' the back o' Pennsylvany: and I see folks way from Australy that 'peared as well as anybody; an' I see how they made spool cotton, an' sights o' other things; an' I spoke with a doctor that lives down to the beach in the summer, an' he offered to come up 'long in the first of August, an' see what he can do for Peggy's eyesight. There was di'monds there as big as pigeon's eggs; an' I met with Mis' Abby Fletcher from South Byfleet depot; an' there was hogs there that weighed risin' thirteen hunderd"—

"I want to know," said Mrs. Lavina Dow and Peggy Bond, together.

"Well, 't was a great exper'ence for a person," added Lavina, turning ponderously, in spite of herself, to give a last wistful look at the smiling waters of the pond.

"I don't know how soon I be goin' to settle down," proclaimed the rustic sister of Sindbad. "What's for the good o' one's for the good of all. You just wait till we're setting together up in the old shed chamber! You know, my dear Mis' Katy Strafford give me a han'some present o' money that day she come to see me; and I'd be'n a-dreamin' by night an' day o' seein' that Centennial; and when I come to think on 't I felt sure somebody ought to go from this neighborhood, if 't was only for the good o' the rest; and I thought I'd better be the one. I wa'n't goin' to ask the selec'men neither. I've come back with one-thirty-five in money, and I see everything there, an' I fetched ye all a little somethin'; but I'm full o' dust now, an' pretty nigh beat out. I never see a place more friendly than Pheladelphy; but 't ain't natural to a Byfleet person to be always walkin' on a level. There, now, Peggy, you take my bundle-handkercher and the basket, and let Mis' Dow sag on to me. I'll git her along twice as easy."

With this the small elderly company set forth triumphant toward the poor-house, across the wide green field.

THE HILTONS' HOLIDAY

I

THERE WAS A BRIGHT, full moon in the clear sky, and the sunset was still shining faintly in the west. Dark woods stood all about the old Hilton farmhouse, save down the hill, westward, where lay the shadowy fields which John Hilton, and his father before him, had cleared and tilled with much toil,—the small fields to which they had given the industry and even affection of their honest lives.

John Hilton was sitting on the doorstep of his house. As he moved his head in and out of the shadows, turning now and then to speak to his wife, who sat just within the doorway, one could see his good face, rough and somewhat unkempt, as if he were indeed a creature of the shady woods and brown earth, instead of the noisy town. It was late in the long spring evening, and he had just come from the lower field as cheerful as a boy, proud of having finished the planting of his potatoes.

"I had to do my last row mostly by feelin'," he said to his wife. "I'm proper glad I pushed through, an' went back an' ended off after supper. 'T would have taken me a good part o' to-morrow mornin', an' broke my day."

"'T ain't no use for ye to work yourself all to pieces, John," answered the woman quickly. "I declare it does seem harder than ever that we couldn't have kep' our boy; he'd been comin' fourteen years old this fall, most a grown man, and he'd work right 'longside of ye now the whole time."

"'T was hard to lose him; I do seem to miss little John," said the father sadly. "I expect there was reasons why 't was best. I feel able an' smart to work; my father was a girt strong man* an' a monstrous worker afore me. 'T ain't that; but I was thinkin' by myself to-day what a sight o' company the boy would ha' been. You know, small 's he was, how I could trust to leave him anywheres with the team, and

*Great strong man.

how he'd beseech to go with me wherever I was goin'; always right in my tracks I used to tell 'em. Poor little John, for all he was so young he had a great deal o' judgment; he'd ha' made a likely man."

The mother sighed heavily as she sat within the shadow.

"But then there's the little girls, a sight o' help an' company," urged the father eagerly, as if it were wrong to dwell upon sorrow and loss. "Katy, she's most as good as a boy, except that she ain't very rugged. She's a real little farmer, she's helped me a sight this spring; an' you've got Susan Ellen, that makes a complete little housekeeper for ye as far as she's learnt. I don't see but we're better off than most folks, each on us having a workmate."

"That's so, John," acknowledged Mrs. Hilton wistfully, beginning to rock steadily in her straight, splint-bottomed chair. It was always a good sign when she rocked.

"Where be the little girls so late?" asked their father. "'T is gettin' long past eight o'clock. I don't know when we've all set up so late, but it's so kind o' summer-like an' pleasant. Why, where be they gone?"

"I've told ye; only over to Becker's folks," answered the mother. "I don't see myself what keeps 'em so late; they beseeched me after supper till I let 'em go. They're all in a dazzle with the new teacher; she asked 'em to come over. They say she's unusual smart with 'rethmetic, but she has a kind of a gorpen* look to me. She's goin' to give Katy some pieces for her doll, but I told Katy she ought to be ashamed wantin' dolls' pieces, big as she's gettin' to be. I don't know 's she ought, though; she ain't but nine this summer."

"Let her take her comfort," said the kindhearted man. "Them things draws her to the teacher, an' makes them acquainted. Katy's shy with new folks, more so 'n Susan Ellen, who's of the business kind. Katy's shy-feelin' and wishful."

"I don't know but she is," agreed the mother slowly. "Ain't it sing'lar how well acquainted you be with that one, an' I with Susan Ellen? 'T was always so from the first. I'm doubtful sometimes our Katy ain't one that'll be like to get married—anyways not about

---

*According to *The Oxford English Dictionary*, "gorpen" is a dialectical word possibly related to "gawping," which means "gaping" or "intrusively staring."

here. She lives right with herself, but Susan Ellen ain't nothin' when she's alone, she's always after company; all the boys is waitin' on her a'ready. I ain't afraid but she'll take her pick when the time comes. I expect to see Susan Ellen well settled,—she feels grown up now,—but Katy don't care one mite 'bout none o' them things. She wants to be rovin' out o' doors. I do believe she'd stand an' hark to a bird the whole forenoon."

"Perhaps she'll grow up to be a teacher," suggested John Hilton. "She takes to her book more 'n the other one. I should like one on 'em to be a teacher same 's my mother was. They're good girls as anybody's got."

"So they be," said the mother, with unusual gentleness, and the creak of her rocking-chair was heard, regular as the ticking of a clock. The night breeze stirred in the great woods, and the sound of a brook that went falling down the hillside grew louder and louder. Now and then one could hear the plaintive chirp of a bird. The moon glittered with whiteness like a winter moon, and shone upon the low-roofed house until its small window-panes gleamed like silver, and one could almost see the colors of a blooming bush of lilac that grew in a sheltered angle by the kitchen door. There was an incessant sound of frogs in the lowlands.

"Be you sound asleep, John?" asked the wife presently.

"I don't know but what I was a'most," said the tired man, starting a little. "I should laugh if I was to fall sound asleep right here on the step; 't is the bright night, I expect, makes my eyes feel heavy, an' 't is so peaceful. I was up an' dressed a little past four an' out to work. Well, well!" and he laughed sleepily and rubbed his eyes. "Where's the little girls? I'd better step along an' meet 'em."

"I wouldn't just yet; they'll get home all right, but 't is late for 'em certain. I don't want 'em keepin' Mis' Becker's folks up neither. There, le' 's wait a few minutes," urged Mrs. Hilton.

"I've be'n a-thinkin' all day I'd like to give the child'n some kind of a treat," said the father, wide awake now. "I hurried up my work 'cause I had it so in mind. They don't have the opportunities some do, an' I want 'em to know the world, an' not stay right here on the farm like a couple o' bushes."

"They're a sight better off not to be so full o' notions as some is," protested the mother suspiciously.

"Certain," answered the farmer; "but they're good, bright child'n, an' commencin' to take a sight o' notice. I want 'em to have all we can give 'em. I want 'em to see how other folks does things."

"Why, so do I,"—here the rocking-chair stopped ominously,—"but so long 's they're contented"—

"Contented ain't all in this world; hopper-toads may have that quality an' spend all their time a-blinkin'. I don't know 's bein' contented is all there is to look for in a child. Ambition 's somethin' to me."

"Now you've got your mind on to some plot or other." (The rocking-chair began to move again.) "Why can't you talk right out?"

"'T ain't nothin' special," answered the good man, a little ruffled; he was never prepared for his wife's mysterious powers of divination. "Well there, you do find things out the master! I only thought perhaps I'd take 'em to-morrow, an' go off somewhere if 't was a good day. I've been promisin' for a good while I'd take 'em to Topham Corners; they've never been there since they was very small."

"I believe you want a good time yourself. You ain't never got over bein' a boy." Mrs. Hilton seemed much amused. "There, go if you want to an' take 'em; they've got their summer hats an' new dresses. I don't know o' nothin' that stands in the way. I should sense it better if there was a circus or anythin' to go to. Why don't you wait an' let the girls pick 'em some strawberries or nice ros'berries, and then they could take an' sell 'em to the stores?"

John Hilton reflected deeply. "I should like to get me some good yellow-turnip seed to plant late. I ain't more 'n satisfied with what I've been gettin' o' late years o' Ira Speed. An' I'm goin' to provide me with a good hoe; mine 's gettin' wore out an' all shackly.* I can't seem to fix it good."

"Them 's excuses," observed Mrs. Hilton, with friendly tolerance. "You just cover up the hoe with somethin', if you get it—I would. Ira Speed 's so jealous he'll remember it of you this twenty year, your goin' an' buyin' a new hoe o' anybody but him."

---

*In poor condition.

"I've always thought 't was a free country," said John Hilton soberly. "I don't want to vex Ira neither; he favors us all he can in trade. 'T is difficult for him to spare a cent, but he's as honest as daylight."

At this moment there was a sudden sound of young voices, and a pair of young figures came out from the shadow of the woods into the moonlighted open space. An old cock crowed loudly from his perch in the shed, as if he were a herald of royalty. The little girls were hand in hand, and a brisk young dog capered about them as they came.

"Wa'n't it dark gittin' home through the woods this time o' night?" asked the mother hastily, and not without reproach.

"I don't love to have you gone so late; mother an' me was timid about ye, and you've kep' Mis' Becker's folks up, I expect," said their father regretfully. "I don't want to have it said that my little girls ain't got good manners."

"The teacher had a party," chirped Susan Ellen, the elder of the two children. "Goin' home from school she asked the Grover boys, an' Mary an' Sarah Speed. An' Mis' Becker was real pleasant to us: she passed round some cake, an' handed us sap sugar on one of her best plates, an' we played games an' sung some pieces too. Mis' Becker thought we did real well. I can pick out most of a tune on the cabinet organ; teacher says she'll give me lessons."

"I want to know, dear!" exclaimed John Hilton.

"Yes, an' we played Copenhagen,* an' took sides spellin', an' Katy beat everybody spellin' there was there."

Katy had not spoken; she was not so strong as her sister, and while Susan Ellen stood a step or two away addressing her eager little audience, Katy had seated herself close to her father on the doorstep. He put his arm around her shoulders, and drew her close to his side, where she stayed.

"Ain't you got nothin' to tell, daughter?" he asked, looking down fondly; and Katy gave a pleased little sigh for answer.

"Tell 'em what's goin' to be the last day o' school, and about our trimmin' the schoolhouse," she said; and Susan Ellen gave the programme in most spirited fashion.

---

*Formerly popular children's rope game.

"'T will be a great time," said the mother, when she had finished. "I don't see why folks wants to go trapesin' off to strange places when such things is happenin' right about 'em." But the children did not observe her mysterious air. "Come, you must step yourselves right to bed!"

They all went into the dark, warm house; the bright moon shone upon it steadily all night, and the lilac flowers were shaken by no breath of wind until the early dawn.

II

The Hiltons always waked early. So did their neighbors, the crows and song-sparrows and robins, the light-footed foxes and squirrels in the woods. When John Hilton waked, before five o'-clock, an hour later than usual because he had sat up so late, he opened the house door and came out into the yard, crossing the short green turf hurriedly as if the day were too far spent for any loitering. The magnitude of the plan for taking a whole day of pleasure confronted him seriously, but the weather was fair, and his wife, whose disapproval could not have been set aside, had accepted and even smiled upon the great project. It was inevitable now, that he and the children should go to Topham Corners. Mrs. Hilton had the pleasure of waking them, and telling the news.

In a few minutes they came frisking out to talk over the great plans. The cattle were already fed, and their father was milking. The only sign of high festivity was the wagon pulled out into the yard, with both seats put in as if it were Sunday; but Mr. Hilton still wore his every-day clothes, and Susan Ellen suffered instantly from disappointment.

"Ain't we goin', father?" she asked complainingly; but he nodded and smiled at her, even though the cow, impatient to get to pasture, kept whisking her rough tail across his face. He held his head down and spoke cheerfully, in spite of this vexation.

"Yes, sister, we're goin' certain', an' goin' to have a great time too." Susan Ellen thought that he seemed like a boy at that delightful moment, and felt new sympathy and pleasure at once. "You go an' help mother about breakfast an' them things; we want to get off quick 's we can. You coax mother now, both on ye, an' see if she won't go with us."

"She said she wouldn't be hired to," responded Susan Ellen. "She says it's goin' to be hot, an' she's laid out to go over an' see how her aunt Tamsen Brooks is this afternoon."

The father gave a little sigh; then he took heart again. The truth was that his wife made light of the contemplated pleasure, and, much as he usually valued her companionship and approval, he was sure that they should have a better time without her. It was impossible, however, not to feel guilty of disloyalty at the thought. Even though she might be completely unconscious of his best ideals, he only loved her and the ideals the more, and bent his energies to satisfying her indefinite expectations. His wife still kept much of that youthful beauty which Susan Ellen seemed likely to reproduce.

An hour later the best wagon was ready, and the great expedition set forth. The little dog sat apart, and barked as if it fell entirely upon him to voice the general excitement. Both seats were in the wagon, but the empty place testified to Mrs. Hilton's unyielding disposition. She had wondered why one broad seat would not do, but John Hilton meekly suggested that the wagon looked better with both. The little girls sat on the back seat dressed alike in their Sunday hats of straw with blue ribbons, and their little plaid shawls pinned neatly about their small shoulders. They wore gray thread gloves, and sat very straight. Susan Ellen was half a head the taller, but otherwise, from behind, they looked much alike. As for their father, he was in his Sunday best,—a plain black coat, and a winter hat of felt, which was heavy and rusty-looking for that warm early summer day. He had it in mind to buy a new straw hat at Topham, so that this with the turnip seed and the hoe made three important reasons for going.

"Remember an' lay off your shawls when you get there, an' carry them over your arms," said the mother, clucking like an excited hen to her chickens. "They'll do to keep the dust off your new dresses goin' an' comin'. An' when you eat your dinners don't get spots on you, an' don't point at folks as you ride by, an' stare, or they'll know you come from the country. An' John, you call into Cousin Ad'line Marlow's an' see how they all be, an' tell her I expect her over certain to stop awhile before hayin'. It always eases her phthisic* to git up here on the high land, an' I've got a new notion about doin' over her best-room carpet sence I see her that'll save rippin' one breadth. An' don't come home all wore out; an', John, don't you go an' buy me no kickshaws† to fetch home. I ain't a child, an' you ain't got no money to waste. I expect you'll go, like 's not, an' buy you some kind of a foolish boy's hat; do look an' see if it's reasonable good straw, an' won't splinter all off round the edge. An' you mind, John"—

"Yes, yes, hold on!" cried John impatiently; then he cast a last affectionate, reassuring look at her face, flushed with the hurry and responsibility of starting them off in proper shape. "I wish you was goin' too," he said, smiling. "I do so!" Then the old horse started, and they went out at the bars, and began the careful long descent of the hill. The young dog, tethered to the lilac-bush, was frantic with piteous appeals; the little girls piped their eager good-bys again and again, and their father turned many times to look back and wave his hand. As for their mother, she stood alone and watched them out of sight.

There was one place far out on the high-road where she could catch a last glimpse of the wagon, and she waited what seemed a very long time until it appeared and then was lost to sight again behind a low hill. "They're nothin' but a pack o' child'n together," she said aloud; and then felt lonelier than she expected. She even stooped and patted the unresigned little dog as she passed him, going into the house.

The occasion was so much more important than any one had foreseen that both the little girls were speechless. It seemed at first like going to church in new clothes, or to a funeral; they hardly knew how to behave at the beginning of a whole day of pleasure. They made grave bows at such persons of their acquaintance as happened to be straying in the road. Once or twice they stopped before a farmhouse, while their father talked an inconsiderately long time with some one about the crops and the weather, and even dwelt upon town business and the doings of the selectmen, which might be talked of at any time. The explanations that he gave of their

---

*Probably a reference to tuberculosis.

†Trifles, tidbits.

excursion seemed quite unnecessary. It was made entirely clear that he had a little business to do at Topham Corners, and thought he had better give the little girls a ride; they had been very steady at school, and he had finished planting, and could take the day as well as not. Soon, however, they all felt as if such an excursion were an every-day affair, and Susan Ellen began to ask eager questions, while Katy silently sat apart enjoying herself as she never had done before. She liked to see the strange houses, and the children who belonged to them; it was delightful to find flowers that she knew growing all along the road, no matter how far she went from home. Each small homestead looked its best and pleasantest, and shared the exquisite beauty that early summer made,—shared the luxury of greenness and floweriness that decked the rural world. There was an early peony or a late lilac in almost every dooryard.

It was seventeen miles to Topham. After a while they seemed very far from home, having left the hills far behind, and descended to a great level country with fewer tracts of woodland, and wider fields where the crops were much more forward. The houses were all painted, and the roads were smoother and wider. It had been so pleasant driving along that Katy dreaded going into the strange town when she first caught sight of it, though Susan Ellen kept asking with bold fretfulness if they were not almost there. They counted the steeples of four churches, and their father presently showed them the Topham Academy, where their grandmother once went to school, and told them that perhaps some day they would go there too. Katy's heart gave a strange leap; it was such a tremendous thing to think of, but instantly the suggestion was transformed for her into one of the certainties of life. She looked with solemn awe at the tall belfry, and the long rows of windows in the front of the academy, there where it stood high and white among the clustering trees. She hoped that they were going to drive by, but something forbade her taking the responsibility of saying so.

Soon the children found themselves among the crowded village houses. Their father turned to look at them with affectionate solicitude.

"Now sit up straight and appear pretty," he whispered to them. "We're among the best people now, an' I want folks to think well of you."

"I guess we're as good as they be," remarked Susan Ellen, looking at some innocent passers-by with dark suspicion, but Katy tried indeed to sit straight, and folded her hands prettily in her lap, and wished with all her heart to be pleasing for her father's sake. Just then an elderly woman saw the wagon and the sedate party it carried, and smiled so kindly that it seemed to Katy as if Topham Corners had welcomed and received them. She smiled back again as if this hospitable person were an old friend, and entirely forgot that the eyes of all Topham had been upon her.

"There, now we're coming to an elegant house that I want you to see; you'll never forget it," said John Hilton. "It's where Judge Masterson lives, the great lawyer; the handsomest house in the county, everybody says."

"Do you know him, father?" asked Susan Ellen.

"I do," answered John Hilton proudly. "Him and my mother went to school together in their young days, and were always called the two best scholars of their time. The judge called to see her once; he stopped to our house to see her when I was a boy. An' then, some years ago—you've heard me tell how I was on the jury, an' when he heard my name spoken he looked at me sharp, and asked if I wa'n't the son of Catharine Winn, an' spoke most beautiful of your grandmother, an' how well he remembered their young days together."

"I like to hear about that," said Katy.

"She had it pretty hard, I'm afraid, up on the old farm. She was keepin' school in our district when father married her—that's the main reason I backed 'em down when they wanted to tear the old schoolhouse all to pieces," confided John Hilton, turning eagerly. "They all say she lived longer up here on the hill than she could anywhere, but she never had her health. I wa'n't but a boy when she died. Father an' me lived alone afterward till the time your mother come; 't was a good while, too; I wa'n't married so young as some. 'T was lonesome, I tell you; father was plumb discouraged losin' of his wife, an' her long sickness an' all set him back, an' we'd work all day on the land an' never say a word. I s'pose 't is bein' so lonesome early in life that makes me so pleased to have some nice girls growin' up round me now."

There was a tone in her father's voice that drew Katy's heart toward him with new affection. She dimly understood, but Susan

Ellen was less interested. They had often heard this story before, but to one child it was always new and to the other old. Susan Ellen was apt to think it tiresome to hear about her grandmother, who, being dead, was hardly worth talking about.

"There's Judge Masterson's place," said their father in an everyday manner, as they turned a corner, and came into full view of the beautiful old white house standing behind its green trees and terraces and lawns. The children had never imagined anything so stately and fine, and even Susan Ellen exclaimed with pleasure. At that moment they saw an old gentleman, who carried himself with great dignity, coming slowly down the wide box-bordered* path toward the gate.

"There he is now, there's the judge!" whispered John Hilton excitedly, reining his horse quickly to the green roadside. "He's goin' down-town to his office; we can wait right here an' see him. I can't expect him to remember me; it's been a good many years. Now you are goin' to see the great Judge Masterson!"

There was a quiver of expectation in their hearts. The judge stopped at his gate, hesitating a moment before he lifted the latch, and glanced up the street at the country wagon with its two prim little girls on the back seat, and the eager man who drove. They seemed to be waiting for something; the old horse was nibbling at the fresh roadside grass. The judge was used to being looked at with interest, and responded now with a smile as he came out to the sidewalk, and unexpectedly turned their way. Then he suddenly lifted his hat with grave politeness, and came directly toward them.

"Good-morning, Mr. Hilton," he said. "I am very glad to see you, sir;" and Mr. Hilton, the little girls' own father, took off his hat with equal courtesy, and bent forward to shake hands.

Susan Ellen cowered and wished herself away, but little Katy sat straighter than ever, with joy in her father's pride and pleasure shining in her pale, flower-like little face.

"These are your daughters, I am sure," said the old gentleman kindly, taking Susan Ellen's limp and reluctant hand; but when he looked at Katy, his face brightened. "How she recalls your mother!" he

---

*Bordered by a hedge formed of the evergreen shrub called "box."

said with great feeling. "I am glad to see this dear child. You must come to see me with your father, my dear," he added, still looking at her. "Bring both the little girls, and let them run about the old garden; the cherries are just getting ripe," said Judge Masterson hospitably. "Perhaps you will have time to stop this afternoon as you go home?"

"I should call it a great pleasure if you would come and see us again some time. You may be driving our way, sir," said John Hilton.

"Not very often in these days," answered the old judge. "I thank you for the kind invitation. I should like to see the fine view again from your hill westward. Can I serve you in any way while you are in town? Good-by, my little friends!"

Then they parted, but not before Katy, the shy Katy, whose hand the judge still held unconsciously while he spoke, had reached forward as he said good-by, and lifted her face to kiss him. She could not have told why, except that she felt drawn to something in the serious, worn face. For the first time in her life the child had felt the charm of manners; perhaps she owned a kinship between that which made him what he was, and the spark of nobleness and purity in her own simple soul. She turned again and again to look back at him as they drove away.

"Now you have seen one of the first gentlemen in the country," said their father. "It was worth comin' twice as far"—but he did not say any more, nor turn as usual to look in the children's faces.

In the chief business street of Topham a great many country wagons like the Hiltons' were fastened to the posts, and there seemed to our holiday-makers to be a great deal of noise and excitement.

"Now I've got to do my errands, and we can let the horse rest and feed," said John Hilton. "I'll slip his headstall* right off, an' put on his halter. I'm goin' to buy him a real good treat o' oats. First we'll go an' buy me my straw hat; I feel as if this one looked a little past to wear in Topham. We'll buy the things we want, an' then we'll walk all along the street, so you can look in the windows an' see the han'some things, same's your mother likes to. What was it mother told you about your shawls?"

---

*The part of the bridle that circled the horse's head.

"To take 'em off an' carry 'em over our arms," piped Susan Ellen, without comment, but in the interest of alighting and finding themselves afoot upon the pavement the shawls were forgotten. The children stood at the doorway of a shop while their father went inside, and they tried to see what the Topham shapes of bonnets were like, as their mother had advised them; but everything was exciting and confusing, and they could arrive at no decision. When Mr. Hilton came out with a hat in his hand to be seen in a better light, Katy whispered that she wished he would buy a shiny one like Judge Masterson's; but her father only smiled and shook his head, and said that they were plain folks, he and Katy. There were dry-goods for sale in the same shop, and a young clerk who was measuring linen kindly pulled off some pretty labels with gilded edges and gay pictures, and gave them to the little girls, to their exceeding joy. He may have had small sisters at home, this friendly lad, for he took pains to find two pretty blue boxes besides, and was rewarded by their beaming gratitude.

It was a famous day; they even became used to seeing so many people pass. The village was full of its morning activity, and Susan Ellen gained a new respect for her father, and an increased sense of her own consequence, because even in Topham several persons knew him and called him familiarly by name. The meeting with an old man who had once been a neighbor seemed to give Mr. Hilton the greatest pleasure. The old man called to them from a house doorway as they were passing, and they all went in. The children seated themselves wearily on the wooden step, but their father shook his old friend eagerly by the hand, and declared that he was delighted to see him so well and enjoying the fine weather.

"Oh, yes," said the old man, in a feeble, quavering voice, "I'm astonishin' well for my age. I don't complain, John, I don't complain."

They talked long together of people whom they had known in the past, and Katy, being a little tired, was glad to rest, and sat still with her hands folded, looking about the front yard. There were some kinds of flowers that she never had seen before.

"This is the one that looks like my mother," her father said, and touched Katy's shoulder to remind her to stand up and let herself be seen. "Judge Masterson saw the resemblance; we met him at his gate this morning."

"Yes, she certain does look like your mother, John," said the old man, looking pleasantly at Katy, who found that she liked him better than at first. "She does, certain; the best of young folks is, they remind us of the old ones. 'T is nateral to cling to life, folks say, but for me, I git impatient at times. Most everybody 's gone now, an' I want to be goin'. 'T is somethin' before me, an' I want to have it over with. I want to be there 'long o' the rest o' the folks. I expect to last quite a while though; I may see ye couple o' times more, John."

John Hilton responded cheerfully, and the children were urged to pick some flowers. The old man awed them with his impatience to be gone. There was such a townful of people about him, and he seemed as lonely as if he were the last survivor of a former world. Until that moment they had felt as if everything were just beginning.

"Now I want to buy somethin' pretty for your mother," said Mr. Hilton, as they went soberly away down the street, the children keeping fast hold of his hands. "By now the old horse will have eat his dinner and had a good rest, so pretty soon we can jog along home. I'm goin' to take you round by the academy, and the old North Meetinghouse where Dr. Barstow used to preach. Can't you think o' somethin' that your mother'd want?" he asked suddenly, confronted by a man's difficulty of choice.

"She was talkin' about wantin' a new pepper-box, one day; the top o' the old one won't stay on," suggested Susan Ellen, with delightful readiness. "Can't we have some candy, father?"

"Yes, ma'am," said John Hilton, smiling and swinging her hand to and fro as they walked. "I feel as if some would be good myself. What's all this?" They were passing a photographer's doorway with its enticing array of portraits. "I do declare!" he exclaimed excitedly, "I'm goin' to have our pictures taken; 't will please your mother more 'n a little."

This was, perhaps, the greatest triumph of the day, except the delightful meeting with the judge; they sat in a row, with the father in the middle, and there was no doubt as to the excellence of the likeness. The best hats had to be taken off because they cast a shadow, but they were not missed, as their owners had feared. Both Susan Ellen and Katy looked their brightest and best; their eager young faces would forever shine there; the joy of the holiday was mirrored in the little picture. They did not know why their father was so pleased with it; they would not know until age had dowered them with the riches of association and remembrance.

Just at nightfall the Hiltons reached home again, tired out and happy. Katy had climbed over into the front seat beside her father, because that was always her place when they went to church on Sundays. It was a cool evening, there was a fresh sea wind that brought a light mist with it, and the sky was fast growing cloudy. Somehow the children looked different; it seemed to their mother as if they had grown older and taller since they went away in the morning, and as if they belonged to the town now as much as to the country. The greatness of their day's experience had left her far behind; the day had been silent and lonely without them, and she had had their supper ready, and been watching anxiously, ever since five o'clock. As for the children themselves they had little to say at first—they had eaten their luncheon early on the way to Topham. Susan Ellen was childishly cross, but Katy was pathetic and wan. They could hardly wait to show the picture, and their mother was as much pleased as everybody had expected.

"There, what did make you wear your shawls?" she exclaimed a moment afterward, reproachfully. "You ain't been an' wore 'em all day long? I wanted folks to see how pretty your new dresses was, if I did make 'em. Well, well! I wish more 'n ever now I'd gone an' seen to ye!"

"An' here's the pepper-box!" said Katy, in a pleased, unconscious tone.

"That really is what I call beautiful," said Mrs. Hilton, after a long and doubtful look. "Our other one was only tin. I never did look so high as a chiny one with flowers, but I can get us another any time for every day. That's a proper hat, as good as you could have got, John. Where's your new hoe?" she asked as he came toward her from the barn, smiling with satisfaction.

"I declare to Moses if I didn't forget all about it," meekly acknowledged the leader of the great excursion. "That an' my yellow turnip seed, too; they went clean out o' my head, there was so many other things to think of. But 't ain't no sort o' matter; I can get a hoe just as well to Ira Speed's."

His wife could not help laughing. "You an' the little girls have had a great time. They was full o' wonder to me about everything, and I expect they'll talk about it for a week. I guess we was right about havin' 'em see somethin' more o' the world."

"Yes," answered John Hilton, with humility, "yes, we did have a beautiful day. I didn't expect so much. They looked as nice as anybody, and appeared so modest an' pretty. The little girls will remember it perhaps by an' by. I guess they won't never forget this day they had 'long o' father."

It was evening again, the frogs were piping in the lower meadows, and in the woods, higher up the great hill, a little owl began to hoot. The sea air, salt and heavy, was blowing in over the country at the end of the hot bright day. A lamp was lighted in the house, the happy children were talking together, and supper was waiting. The father and mother lingered for a moment outside and looked down over the shadowy fields; then they went in, without speaking. The great day was over, and they shut the door.

THE GUESTS OF MRS. TIMMS

I

MRS. PERSIS FLAGG STOOD in her front doorway taking leave of Miss Cynthia Pickett, who had been making a long call. They were not intimate friends. Miss Pickett always came formally to the front door and rang when she paid her visits, but, the week before, they had met at the county conference,* and happened to be sent to the same house for entertainment, and so had deepened and renewed the pleasures of acquaintance.

It was an afternoon in early June; the syringa-bushes were tall and green on each side of the stone doorsteps, and were covered with their lovely white and golden flowers. Miss Pickett broke off the nearest twig, and held it before her prim face as she talked. She had a pretty childlike smile that came and went suddenly, but her face was not one that bore the marks of many pleasures. Mrs. Flagg was a tall, commanding sort of person, with an air of satisfaction and authority.

"Oh, yes, gather all you want," she said stiffly, as Miss Pickett took the syringa without having asked beforehand; but she had an amiable expression, and just now her large countenance was lighted up by pleasant anticipation.

"We can tell early what sort of a day it's goin' to be," she said eagerly. "There ain't a cloud in the sky now. I'll stop for you as I come along, or if there should be anything unforeseen to detain me, I'll send you word. I don't expect you'd want to go if it wa'n't so that I could?"

"Oh my sakes, no!" answered Miss Pickett discreetly, with a timid flush. "You feel certain that Mis' Timms won't be put out? I shouldn't feel free to go unless I went 'long o' you."

"Why, nothin' could be plainer than her words," said Mrs. Flagg in a tone of reproval. "You saw how she urged me, an' had

*Formal gathering of people from local churches.

over all that talk about how we used to see each other often when we both lived to Longport, and told how she'd been thinkin' of writin', and askin' if it wa'n't so I should be able to come over and stop three or four days as soon as settled weather come, because she couldn't make no fire in her best chamber on account of the chimbley smokin' if the wind wa'n't just right. You see how she felt toward me, kissin' of me comin' and goin'? Why, she even asked me who I employed to do over my bonnet, Miss Pickett, just as interested as if she was a sister; an' she remarked she should look for us any pleasant day after we all got home, an' were settled after the conference."

Miss Pickett smiled, but did not speak, as if she expected more arguments still.

"An' she seemed just about as much gratified to meet with you again. She seemed to desire to meet you again very particular," continued Mrs. Flagg. "She really urged us to come together an' have a real good day talkin' over old times—there, don't le' 's go all over it again! I've always heard she'd made that old house of her aunt Bascoms' where she lives look real handsome. I once heard her best parlor carpet described as being an elegant carpet, different from any there was round here. Why, nobody couldn't be more cordial, Miss Pickett; you ain't goin' to give out just at the last?"

"Oh, no!" answered the visitor hastily; "no, 'm! I want to go full as much as you do, Mis' Flagg, but you see I never was so well acquainted with Mis' Cap'n Timms, an' I always seem to dread putting myself for'ard. She certain was very urgent, an' she said plain enough to come any day next week, an' here 't is Wednesday, though of course she wouldn't look for us either Monday or Tuesday. 'T will be a real pleasant occasion, an' now we've been to the conference it don't seem near so much effort to start."

"Why, I don't think nothin' of it," said Mrs. Flagg proudly. "We shall have a grand good time, goin' together an' all, I feel sure."

Miss Pickett still played with her syringa flower, tapping her thin cheek, and twirling the stem with her fingers. She looked as if she were going to say something more, but after a moment's hesitation she turned away.

"Good-afternoon, Mis' Flagg," she said formally, looking up with a quick little smile; "I enjoyed my call; I hope I ain't kep' you too late; I don't know but what it's 'most tea-time. Well, I shall look for you in the mornin'."

"Good-afternoon, Miss Pickett; I'm glad I was in when you came. Call again, won't you?" said Mrs. Flagg. "Yes; you may expect me in good season," and so they parted. Miss Pickett went out at the neat clicking gate in the white fence, and Mrs. Flagg a moment later looked out of her sitting-room window to see if the gate were latched, and felt the least bit disappointed to find that it was. She sometimes went out after the departure of a guest, and fastened the gate herself with a loud, rebuking sound. Both of these Woodville women lived alone, and were very precise in their way of doing things.

II

THE NEXT MORNING DAWNED clear and bright, and Miss Pickett rose even earlier than usual. She found it most difficult to decide which of her dresses would be best to wear. Summer was still so young that the day had all the freshness of spring, but when the two friends walked away together along the shady street, with a chorus of golden robins singing high overhead in the elms, Miss Pickett decided that she had made a wise choice of her second-best black silk gown, which she had just turned again and freshened. It was neither too warm for the season nor too cool, nor did it look overdressed. She wore her large cameo pin, and this, with a long watch-chain, gave an air of proper mural decoration. She was a straight, flat little person, as if, when not in use, she kept herself, silk dress and all, between the leaves of a book. She carried a noticeable parasol with a fringe, and a small shawl, with a pretty border, neatly folded over her left arm. Mrs. Flagg always dressed in black cashmere, and looked, to hasty observers, much the same one day as another; but her companion recognized the fact that this was the best black cashmere of all, and for a moment quailed at the thought that Mrs. Flagg was paying such extreme deference to their prospective hostess. The visit turned for a moment into an unexpectedly solemn formality, and pleasure seemed to wane before Cynthia Pickett's eyes, yet with great courage she never slackened a single step. Mrs. Flagg carried a somewhat worn black leather handbag, which Miss Pickett regretted; it did not give the visit that casual and unpremeditated air which she felt to be more elegant.

"Sha'n't I carry your bag for you?" she asked timidly. Mrs. Flagg was the older and more important person.

"Oh, dear me, no," answered Mrs. Flagg. "My pocket 's so remote, in case I should desire to sneeze or anything, that I thought 't would be convenient for carrying my handkerchief and pocketbook; an' then I just tucked in a couple o' glasses o' my crab-apple jelly for Mis' Timms. She used to be a great hand for preserves of every sort, an' I thought 't would be a kind of an attention, an' give rise to conversation. I know she used to make excellent drop-cakes when we was both residin' to Longport; folks used to say she never would give the right receipt, but if I get a real good chance, I mean to ask her. Or why can't you, if I start talkin' about receipts—why can't you say, sort of innocent, that I have always spoken frequently of her drop-cakes, an' ask for the rule? She would be very sensible to the compliment, and could pass it off if she didn't feel to indulge us. There, I do so wish you would!"

"Yes, 'm," said Miss Pickett doubtfully; "I'll try to make the opportunity. I'm very partial to drop-cakes. Was they flour or rye, Mis' Flagg?"

"They was flour, dear," replied Mrs. Flagg approvingly; "crisp an' light as any you ever see."

"I wish I had thought to carry somethin' to make it pleasant," said Miss Pickett, after they had walked a little farther; "but there, I don't know 's 't would look just right, this first visit, to offer anything to such a person as Mis' Timms. In case I ever go over to Baxter again I won't forget to make her some little present, as nice as I've got. 'T was certain very polite of her to urge me to come with you. I did feel very doubtful at first. I didn't know but she thought it behooved her, because I was in your company at the conference, and she wanted to save my feelin's, and yet expected I would decline. I never was well acquainted with her; our folks wasn't well off when I first knew her; 't was before uncle Cap'n Dyer passed away an' remembered mother an' me in his will. We couldn't make no han'some companies in them days, so we didn't go to none, an' kep' to ourselves; but in my grandmother's time, mother always said, the families was very friendly. I shouldn't feel like goin' over to pass the day with Mis' Timms if I didn't mean to ask her to return the visit. Some don't think o' these things, but mother was very set about not bein' done for when she couldn't make no return."

"'When it rains porridge hold up your dish,' " said Mrs. Flagg; but Miss Pickett made no response beyond a feeble "Yes, 'm," which somehow got caught in her pale-green bonnet-strings.

"There, 't ain't no use to fuss too much over all them things," proclaimed Mrs. Flagg, walking along at a good pace with a fine sway of her skirts, and carrying her head high. "Folks walks right by an' forgits all about you; folks can't always be going through with just so much. You'd had a good deal better time, you an' your ma, if you'd been freer in your ways; now don't you s'pose you would? 'T ain't what you give folks to eat so much as 't is makin' 'em feel welcome. Now, there's Mis' Timms; when we was to Longport she was dreadful methodical. She wouldn't let Cap'n Timms fetch nobody home to dinner without lettin' of her know, same's other cap'ns' wives had to submit to. I was thinkin', when she was so cordial over to Danby, how she'd softened with time. Years do learn folks somethin'! She did seem very pleasant an' desirous. There, I am so glad we got started; if she'd gone an' got up a real good dinner to-day, an' then not had us come till to-morrow, 't would have been real too bad. Where anybody lives alone such a thing is very tryin'."

"Oh, so 't is!" said Miss Pickett. "There, I'd like to tell you what I went through with year before last. They come an' asked me one Saturday night to entertain the minister, that time we was having candidates"—

"I guess we'd better step along faster," said Mrs. Flagg suddenly. "Why, Miss Pickett, there's the stage comin' now! It's dreadful prompt, seems to me. Quick! there's folks awaitin', an' I sha'n't get to Baxter in no state to visit Mis' Cap'n Timms if I have to ride all the way there backward!"

III

The stage was not full inside. The group before the store proved to be made up of spectators, except one man, who climbed at once to a vacant seat by the driver. Inside there was only one person, after two passengers got out, and she preferred to sit with her back to the horses, so that Mrs. Flagg and Miss Pickett settled themselves comfortably in the coveted corners of the back seat. At first they took no notice of their companion, and spoke to each other in low tones, but presently something attracted the attention of all three and engaged them in conversation.

"I never was over this road before," said the stranger. "I s'pose you ladies are well acquainted all along."

"We have often traveled it in past years. We was over this part of it last week goin' and comin' from the county conference," said Mrs. Flagg in a dignified manner.

"What persuasion?" inquired the fellow-traveler, with interest.

"Orthodox," said Miss Pickett quickly, before Mrs. Flagg could speak. "It was a very interestin' occasion; this other lady an' me stayed through all the meetin's."

"I ain't Orthodox," announced the stranger, waiving any interest in personalities. "I was brought up amongst the Freewill Baptists."*

"We're well acquainted with several of that denomination in our place," said Mrs. Flagg, not without an air of patronage.

"They've never built 'em no church; there ain't but a scattered few."

"They prevail where I come from," said the traveler. "I'm goin' now to visit with a Freewill lady. We was to a conference together once, same 's you an' your friend, but 't was a state conference. She asked me to come some time an' make her a good visit, and I'm on my way now. I didn't seem to have nothin' to keep me to home."

"We're all goin' visitin' to-day, ain't we?" said Mrs. Flagg sociably; but no one carried on the conversation.

---

*Protestant denomination founded in New England during the late eighteenth century in reaction to the elitism of Calvinism; Freewill Baptists held that all people could experience God's grace if they exercised their God-given free will.

The day was growing very warm; there was dust in the sandy road, but the fields of grass and young growing crops looked fresh and fair. There was a light haze over the hills, and birds were thick in the air. When the stage-horses stopped to walk, you could hear the crows caw, and the bobolinks singing, in the meadows. All the farmers were busy in their fields.

"It don't seem but little ways to Baxter, does it?" said Miss Pickett, after a while. "I felt we should pass a good deal o' time on the road, but we must be pretty near half-way there a'ready."

"Why, more 'n half!" exclaimed Mrs. Flagg. "Yes; there's Beckett's Corner right ahead, an the old Beckett house. I haven't been on this part of the road for so long that I feel kind of strange. I used to visit over here when I was a girl. There's a nephew's widow owns the place now. Old Miss Susan Beckett willed it to him, an' he died; but she resides there an' carries on the farm, an unusual smart woman, everybody says. Ain't it pleasant here, right out among the farms!"

"Mis' Beckett's place, did you observe?" said the stranger, leaning forward to listen to what her companions said. "I expect that's where I'm goin'—Mis' Ezra Beckett's?"

"That's the one," said Miss Pickett and Mrs. Flagg together, and they both looked out eagerly as the coach drew up to the front door of a large old yellow house that stood close upon the green turf of the roadside.

The passenger looked pleased and eager, and made haste to leave the stage with her many bundles and bags. While she stood impatiently tapping at the brass knocker, the stage-driver landed a large trunk, and dragged it toward the door across the grass. Just then a busy-looking middle-aged woman made her appearance, with floury hands and a look as if she were prepared to be somewhat on the defensive.

"Why, how do you do, Mis' Beckett?" exclaimed the guest. "Well, here I be at last. I didn't know 's you thought I was ever comin'. Why, I do declare, I believe you don't recognize me, Mis' Beckett."

"I believe I don't," said the self-possessed hostess. "Ain't you made some mistake, ma'am?"

"Why, don't you recollect we was together that time to the state conference, an' you said you should be pleased to have me come an' make you a visit some time, an' I said I would certain. There, I expect I look more natural to you now."

Mrs. Beckett appeared to be making the best possible effort, and gave a bewildered glance, first at her unexpected visitor, and then at the trunk. The stage-driver, who watched this encounter with evident delight, turned away with reluctance. "I can't wait all day to see how they settle it," he said, and mounted briskly to the box, and the stage rolled on.

"He might have waited just a minute to see," said Miss Pickett indignantly, but Mrs. Flagg's head and shoulders were already far out of the stage window—the house was on her side. "She ain't got in yet," she told Miss Pickett triumphantly. "I could see 'em quite a spell. With that trunk, too! I do declare, how inconsiderate some folks is!"

"'T was pushin' an acquaintance most too far, wa'n't it?" agreed Miss Pickett. "There, 't will be somethin' laughable to tell Mis' Timms. I never see anything more divertin'. I shall kind of pity that woman if we have to stop an' git her as we go back this afternoon."

"Oh, don't let's forgit to watch for her," exclaimed Mrs. Flagg, beginning to brush off the dust of travel. "There, I feel an excellent appetite, don't you? And we ain't got more 'n three or four miles to go, if we have that. I wonder what Mis' Timms is likely to give us for dinner; she spoke of makin' a good many chicken-pies, an' I happened to remark how partial I was to 'em. She felt above most of the things we had provided for us over to the conference. I know she was always counted the best o' cooks when I knew her so well to Longport. Now, don't you forget, if there's a suitable opportunity, to inquire about the drop-cakes;" and Miss Pickett, a little less doubtful than before, renewed her promise.

IV

"My gracious, won't Mis' Timms be pleased to see us! It's just exactly the day to have company. And ain't Baxter a sweet pretty place?" said Mrs. Flagg, as they walked up the main street. "Cynthy Pickett, now ain't you proper glad you come? I felt sort o' calm about it part o' the time yesterday, but I ain't felt so like a girl for a good while. I do believe I'm goin' to have a splendid time."

Miss Pickett glowed with equal pleasure as she paced along. She was less expansive and enthusiastic than her companion, but now that they were fairly in Baxter, she lent herself generously to the occasion. The social distinction of going away to spend a day in company with Mrs. Flagg was by no means small. She arranged the folds of her shawl more carefully over her arm so as to show the pretty palm-leaf border, and then looked up with great approval to the row of great maples that shaded the broad sidewalk. "I wonder if we can't contrive to make time to go an' see old Miss Nancy Fell?" she ventured to ask Mrs. Flagg. "There ain't a great deal o' time before the stage goes at four o'clock; 't will pass quickly, but I should hate to have her feel hurt. If she was one we had visited often at home, I shouldn't care so much, but such folks feel any little slight. She was a member of our church; I think a good deal of that."

"Well, I hardly know what to say," faltered Mrs. Flagg coldly. "We might just look in a minute; I shouldn't want her to feel hurt."

"She was one that always did her part, too," said Miss Pickett, more boldly. "Mr. Cronin used to say that she was more generous with her little than many was with their much.* If she hadn't lived in a poor part of the town, and so been occupied with a different kind of people from us, 't would have made a difference. They say she's got a comfortable little home over here, an' keeps house for a nephew. You know she was to our meeting one Sunday last winter, and 'peared dreadful glad to get back; folks seemed glad to see her, too. I don't know as you were out."

"She always wore a friendly look," said Mrs. Flagg indulgently. "There, now, there's Mis' Timms's residence; it's handsome, ain't it, with them big spruce-trees? I expect she may be at the window now, an' see us as we come along. Is my bonnet or straight, an' everything? The blinds looks open in the room this way; I guess she's to home fast enough."

The friends quickened their steps, and with shining eyes and beating hearts hastened forward. The slightest mists of uncertainty were now cleared away; they gazed at the house with deepest pleasure; the visit was about to begin.

---

*Reference to the Bible: Mark 12:42–44 and Luke 21:1–4.

They opened the front gate and went up the short walk, noticing the pretty herringbone pattern of the bricks, and as they stood on the high steps Cynthia Pickett wondered whether she ought not to have worn her best dress, even though there was lace at the neck and sleeves, and she usually kept it for the most formal of tea-parties and exceptional parish festivals. In her heart she commended Mrs. Flagg for that familiarity with the ways of a wider social world which had led her to wear the very best among her black cashmeres.

"She's a good while coming to the door," whispered Mrs. Flagg presently. "Either she didn't see us, or else she's slipped upstairs to make some change, an' is just goin' to let us ring again. I've done it myself sometimes. I'm glad we come right over after her urgin' us so; it seems more cordial than to keep her expectin' us. I expect she'll urge us terribly to remain with her over-night."

"Oh, I ain't prepared," began Miss Pickett, but she looked pleased. At that moment there was a slow withdrawal of the bolt inside, and a key was turned, the front door opened, and Mrs. Timms stood before them with a smile. Nobody stopped to think at that moment what kind of smile it was.

"Why, if it ain't Mis' Flagg," she exclaimed politely, "an' Miss Pickett too! I am surprised!"

The front entry behind her looked well furnished, but not exactly hospitable; the stairs with their brass rods looked so clean and bright that it did not seem as if anybody had ever gone up or come down. A cat came purring out, but Mrs. Timms pushed her back with a determined foot, and hastily closed the sitting-room door. Then Miss Pickett let Mrs. Flagg precede her, as was becoming, and they went into a darkened parlor, and found their way to some chairs, and seated themselves solemnly.

" 'T is a beautiful day, ain't it?" said Mrs. Flagg, speaking first. "I don't know 's I ever enjoyed the ride more. We've been having a good deal of rain since we saw you at the conference, and the country looks beautiful."

"Did you leave Woodville this morning? I thought I hadn't heard you was in town," replied Mrs. Timms formally. She was seated just a little too far away to make things seem exactly pleasant. The darkness of the best room seemed to retreat somewhat, and Miss Pickett looked over by the door, where there was a pale gleam from the sidelights in the hall, to try to see the pattern of the carpet; but her effort failed.

"Yes, 'm," replied Mrs. Flagg to the question. "We left Woodville about half past eight, but it is quite a ways from where we live to where you take the stage. The stage does come slow, but you don't seem to mind it such a beautiful day."

"Why, you must have come right to see me first!" said Mrs. Timms, warming a little as the visit went on. "I hope you're going to make some stop in town. I'm sure it was very polite of you to come right an' see me; well, it's very pleasant, I declare. I wish you'd been in Baxter last Sabbath; our minister did give us an elegant sermon on faith an' works. He spoke of the conference, and gave his views on some o' the questions that came up, at Friday evenin' meetin'; but I felt tired after getting home, an' so I wasn't out. We feel very much favored to have such a man amon'st us. He's building up the parish very considerable. I understand the pew-rents come to thirty-six dollars more this quarter than they did last."

"We also feel grateful in Woodville for our pastor's efforts," said Miss Pickett; but Mrs. Timms turned her head away sharply, as if the speech had been untimely, and trembling Miss Pickett had interrupted.

"They're thinking here of raisin' Mr. Barlow's salary another year," the hostess added; "a good many of the old parishioners have died off, but every one feels to do what they can. Is there much interest among the young people in Woodville, Mis' Flagg?"

"Considerable at this time, ma'am," answered Mrs. Flagg, without enthusiasm, and she listened with unusual silence to the subsequent fluent remarks of Mrs. Timms.

The parlor seemed to be undergoing the slow processes of a winter dawn. After a while the three women could begin to see one another's faces, which aided them somewhat in carrying on a serious and impersonal conversation. There were a good many subjects to be touched upon, and Mrs. Timms said everything that she should have said, except to invite her visitors to walk upstairs and take off their bonnets. Mrs. Flagg sat her parlor-chair as if it were a throne, and carried her banner of self-possession as high as she knew how, but toward the end of the call even she began to feel hurried.

"Won't you ladies take a glass of wine an' a piece of cake after your ride?" inquired Mrs. Timms, with an air of hospitality that almost concealed the fact that neither cake nor wine was anywhere to be seen; but the ladies bowed and declined with particular elegance. Altogether it was a visit of extreme propriety on both sides, and Mrs. Timms was very pressing in her invitation that her guests should stay longer.

"Thank you, but we ought to be going," answered Mrs. Flagg, with a little show of ostentation, and looking over her shoulder to be sure that Miss Pickett had risen too. "We've got some little ways to go," she added with dignity. "We should be pleased to have you call an' see us in case you have occasion to come to Woodville," and Miss Pickett faintly seconded the invitation. It was in her heart to add, "Come any day next week," but her courage did not rise so high as to make the words audible. She looked as if she were ready to cry; her usual smile had burnt itself out into gray ashes; there was a white, appealing look about her mouth. As they emerged from the dim parlor and stood at the open front door, the bright June day, the golden-green trees, almost blinded their eyes. Mrs. Timms was more smiling and cordial than ever.

"There, I ought to have thought to offer you fans; I am afraid you was warm after walking," she exclaimed, as if to leave no stone of courtesy unturned. "I have so enjoyed meeting you again, I wish it was so you could stop longer. Why, Mis' Flagg, we haven't said one word about old times when we lived to Longport. I've had news from there, too, since I saw you; my brother's daughter-in-law was here to pass the Sabbath after I returned."

Mrs. Flagg did not turn back to ask any questions as she stepped stiffly away down the brick walk. Miss Pickett followed her, raising the fringed parasol; they both made ceremonious little bows as they shut the high white gate behind them. "Good-by," said Mrs. Timms finally, as she stood in the door with her set smile; and as they departed she came out and began to fasten up a rosebush that climbed a narrow white ladder by the steps.

"Oh, my goodness alive!" exclaimed Mrs. Flagg, after they had gone some distance in aggrieved silence, "if I haven't gone and forgotten my bag! I ain't goin' back, whatever happens. I expect she'll trip over it in that dark room and break her neck!"

"I brought it; I noticed you'd forgotten it," said Miss Pickett timidly, as if she hated to deprive her companion of even that slight consolation.

"There, I'll tell you what we'd better do," said Mrs. Flagg gallantly; "we'll go right over an' see poor old Miss Nancy Fell; 't will please her about to death. We can say we felt like goin' somewhere to-day, an' 't was a good many years since either one of us had seen Baxter, so we come just for the ride, an' to make a few calls. She'll like to hear all about the conference; Miss Fell was always one that took a real interest in religious matters."

Miss Pickett brightened, and they quickened their step. It was nearly twelve o'clock, they had breakfasted early, and now felt as if they had eaten nothing since they were grown up. An awful feeling of tiredness and uncertainty settled down upon their once buoyant spirits.

"I can forgive a person," said Mrs. Flagg, once, as if she were speaking to herself; "I can forgive a person, but when I'm done with 'em, I'm done."

V

"I DO DECLARE, 'T was like a scene in Scriptur' to see that poor good-hearted Nancy Fell run down her walk to open the gate for us!" said Mrs. Persis Flagg later that afternoon, when she and Miss Pickett were going home in the stage. Miss Pickett nodded her head approvingly.

"I had a good sight better time with her than I should have had at the other place," she said with fearless honesty. "If I'd been Mis' Cap'n Timms, I'd made some apology or just passed us the compliment. If it wa'n't convenient, why couldn't she just tell us so after all her urgin' and sayin' how she should expect us?"

"I thought then she'd altered from what she used to be," said Mrs. Flagg. "She seemed real sincere an' open away from home. If she wa'n't prepared to-day, 't was easy enough to say so; we was reasonable folks, an' should have gone away with none but friendly feelin's. We did have a grand good time with Nancy. She was as happy to see us as if we'd been queens."

" 'T was a real nice little dinner," said Miss Pickett gratefully. "I thought I was goin' to faint away just before we got to the house, and I didn't know how I should hold out if she undertook to do anything extra, and keep us a-waitin'; but there, she just made us welcome, simple-hearted, to what she had. I never tasted such dandelion greens; an' that nice little piece o' pork and new biscuit, why, they was just splendid. She must have an excellent good cellar, if 't is such a small house. Her potatoes was truly remarkable for this time o' year. I myself don't deem it necessary to cook potatoes when I'm goin' to have dandelion greens. Now, didn't it put you in mind of that verse in the Bible that says, 'Better is a dinner of herbs where love is'?* An' how desirous she'd been to see somebody that could tell her some particulars about the conference!"

"She'll enjoy tellin' folks about our comin' over to see her. Yes, I'm glad we went; 't will be of advantage every way, an' our bein' of the same church an' all, to Woodville. If Mis' Timms hears of our bein' there, she'll see we had reason, an' knew of a place to go. Well, I needn't have brought this old bag!"

Miss Pickett gave her companion a quick resentful glance, which was followed by one of triumph directed at the dust that was collecting on the shoulders of the best black cashmere; then she looked at the bag on the front seat, and suddenly felt illuminated with the suspicion that Mrs. Flagg had secretly made preparations to pass the night in Baxter. The bag looked plump, as if it held much more than the pocket-book and the jelly.

Mrs. Flagg looked up with unusual humility. "I did think about that jelly," she said, as if Miss Pickett had openly reproached her. "I was afraid it might look as if I was tryin' to pay Nancy for her kindness."

"Well, I don't know," said Cynthia; "I guess she'd been pleased. She'd thought you just brought her over a little present: but I do' know as 't would been any good to her after all; she'd thought so much of it, comin' from you, that she'd kep' it till 't was all candied." But Mrs. Flagg didn't look exactly pleased by this unexpected

*Based on the Bible, Proverbs 15:17 (KJV): "Better is a dinner of herbs where love is, than a stalled ox and hatred therewith."

compliment, and her fellow-traveler colored with confusion and a sudden feeling that she had shown undue forwardness.

Presently they remembered the Beckett house, to their great relief, and, as they approached, Mrs. Flagg reached over and moved her hand-bag from the front seat to make room for another passenger. But nobody came out to stop the stage, and they saw the unexpected guest sitting by one of the front windows comfortably swaying a palm-leaf fan, and rocking to and fro in calm content. They shrank back into their corners, and tried not to be seen. Mrs. Flagg's face grew very red.

"She got in, didn't she?" said Miss Pickett, snipping her words angrily, as if her lips were scissors. Then she heard a call, and bent forward to see Mrs. Beckett herself appear in the front doorway, very smiling and eager to stop the stage.

The driver was only too ready to stop his horses. "Got a passenger for me to carry back, ain't ye?" said he facetiously. "Them's the kind I like; carry both ways, make somethin' on a double trip," and he gave Mrs. Flagg and Miss Pickett a friendly wink as he stepped down over the wheel. Then he hurried toward the house, evidently in a hurry to put the baggage on; but the expected passenger still sat rocking and fanning at the window.

"No, sir; I ain't got any passengers," exclaimed Mrs. Beckett, advancing a step or two to meet him, and speaking very loud in her pleasant excitement. "This lady that come this morning wants her large trunk with her summer things that she left to the depot in Woodville. She's very desirous to git into it, so don't you go an' forgit; ain't you got a book or somethin', Mr. Ma'sh? Don't you forgit to make a note of it; here's her check, an' we've kep' the number in case you should mislay it or anything. There's things in the trunk she needs; you know how you overlooked stoppin' to the milliner's for my bunnit last week."

"Other folks disremembers things as well's me," grumbled Mr. Marsh. He turned to give the passengers another wink more familiar than the first, but they wore an offended air, and were looking the other way. The horses had backed a few steps, and the guest at the front window had ceased the steady motion of her fan to make them a handsome bow, and been puzzled at the lofty manner of their acknowledgment.

"Go 'long with your foolish jokes, John Ma'sh!" Mrs. Beckett said cheerfully, as she turned away. She was a comfortable, hearty person, whose appearance adjusted the beauties of hospitality. The driver climbed to his seat, chuckling, and drove away with the dust flying after the wheels.

"Now, she's a friendly sort of a woman, that Mis' Beckett," said Mrs. Flagg unexpectedly, after a few moments of silence, when she and her friend had been unable to look at each other. "I really ought to call over an' see her some o' these days, knowing her husband's folks as well as I used to, an' visitin' of 'em when I was a girl." But Miss Pickett made no answer.

"I expect it was all for the best, that woman's comin'," suggested Mrs. Flagg again hopefully. "She looked like a willing person who would take right hold. I guess Mis' Beckett knows what she's about, and must have had her reasons. Perhaps she thought she'd chance it for a couple o' weeks anyway, after the lady 'd come so fur, an' bein' one o' her own denomination. Hayin'-time 'll be here before we know it. I think myself, gen'rally speakin', 't is just as well to let anybody know you're comin'."

"Them seemed to be Mis' Cap'n Timms's views," said Miss Pickett in a low tone; but the stage rattled a good deal, and Mrs. Flagg looked up inquiringly, as if she had not heard.

NON-FICTION

CONTENTS

THE WHITE ROSE ROAD

BEING A NEW ENGLANDER,* it is natural that I should first speak about the weather. Only the middle of June, the green fields, and blue sky, and bright sun, with a touch of northern mountain wind blowing straight toward the sea, could make such a day, and that is all one can say about it. We were driving seaward through a part of the country which has been least changed in the last thirty years,—among farms which have been won from swampy lowland, and rocky, stump-buttressed hillsides: where the forests wall in the fields, and send their outposts year by year farther into the pastures. There is a year or two in the history of these pastures before they have arrived at the dignity of being called woodland, and yet are too much shaded and overgrown by young trees to give proper pasturage, when they made delightful harbors for the small wild creatures which yet remain, and for wild flowers and berries. Here you send an astonished rabbit scurrying to his burrow, and there you startle yourself with a partridge, who seems to get the best of the encounter. Sometimes you see a hen partridge and her brood of chickens crossing your path with an air of comfortable door-yard security. As you drive along the narrow, grassy road, you see many charming sights and delightful nooks on either hand, where the young trees spring out of a close-cropped turf that carpets the ground like velvet. Toward the east and the quaint fishing village of Ogunquit† I find the most delightful woodland roads. There is little left of the large timber which once filled the region, but much young growth, and there are hundreds of acres of cleared land and pasture-ground where the forests are springing fast and covering the country once more, as if they had no idea of losing in their war with civilization and the intruding white settler. The pine woods and the Indians

*This is an autobiographical nonfiction sketch, and Jewett is referring to herself; the sketch grew out of Jewett's excursion to Orris Falls near South Berwick.

†In her short stories Jewett frequently used fictional names for towns and other geographical landmarks; this place name and others in this sketch are real.

seem to be next of kin, and the former owners of this corner of New England are the only proper figures to paint into such landscapes. The twilight under tall pines seems to be untenanted and to lack something, at first sight, as if one opened the door of an empty house. A farmer passing through with his axe is but an intruder, and children straying home from school give one a feeling of solicitude at their unprotectedness. The pine woods are the red man's house, and it may be hazardous even yet for the gray farmhouses to stand so near the eaves of the forest. I have noticed a distrust of the deep woods, among elderly people, which was something more than a fear of losing their way. It was a feeling of defenselessness against some unrecognized but malicious influence.

Driving through the long woodland way, shaded and chilly when you are out of the sun; across the Great Works River and its pretty elm-grown intervale; across the short bridges of brown brooks; delayed now and then by the sight of ripe strawberries in sunny spots by the roadside, one comes to a higher open country, where farm joins farm, and the cleared fields lie all along the highway, while the woods are pushed back a good distance on either hand. The wooded hills, bleak here and there with granite ledges, rise beyond. The houses are beside the road, with green door-yards and large barns, almost empty now, and with wide doors standing open, as if they were already expecting the hay crop to be brought in. The tall green grass is waving in the fields as the wind goes over, and there is a fragrance of whiteweed and ripe strawberries and clover blowing through the sunshiny barns, with their lean sides and their festoons of brown, dusty cobwebs; dull, comfortable creatures they appear to imaginative eyes, waiting hungrily for their yearly meal. The eave-swallows are teasing their sleepy shapes, like the birds which flit about great beasts; gay, movable, irreverent, almost derisive, those barn swallows fly to and fro in the still, clear air.

The noise of our wheels brings fewer faces to the windows than usual, and we lose the pleasure of seeing some of our friends who are apt to be looking out, and to whom we like to say good-day. Some funeral must be taking place, or perhaps the women may have gone out into the fields. It is hoeing-time and strawberry-time, and already we have seen some of the younger women at work among the corn and potatoes. One sight will be charming to remember. On a green hillside sloping to the west, near one of the houses, a thin little girl was working away lustily with a big hoe on a patch of land perhaps fifty feet by twenty. There were all sorts of things growing there, as if a child's fancy had made the choice,—straight rows of turnips and carrots and beets, a little of everything, one might say; but the only touch of color was from a long border of useful sage in full bloom of dull blue, on the upper side. I am sure this was called Katy's or Becky's *piece* by the elder members of the family. One can imagine how the young creature had planned it in the spring, and persuaded the men to plough and harrow it, and since then had stoutly done all the work herself, and meant to send the harvest of the piece to market, and pocket her honest gains, as they came in, for some great end. She was as thin as a grasshopper, this busy little gardener, and hardly turned to give us a glance, as we drove slowly up the hill close by. The sun will brown and dry her like a spear of grass on that hot slope, but a spark of fine spirit is in the small body, and I wish her a famous crop. I hate to say that the piece looked backward, all except the sage, and that it was a heavy bit of land for the clumsy hoe to pick at. The only puzzle is, what she proposes to do with so long a row of sage. Yet there may be a large family with a downfall of measles yet ahead, and she does not mean to be caught without sage-tea.

Along this road every one of the old farmhouses has at least one tall bush of white roses* by the door,—a most lovely sight, with buds and blossoms, and unvexed green leaves. I wish that I knew the history of them, and whence the first bush was brought. Perhaps from England itself, like a red rose that I know in Kittery, and the new shoots from the root were given to one neighbor after another all through the district. The bushes are slender, but they grow tall without climbing against the wall, and sway to and fro in the wind with a grace of youth and an inexpressible charm of beauty. How many lovers must have picked them on Sunday evenings, in all the bygone years, and carried them along the roads or by the pasture footpaths, hiding them clumsily under their Sunday coats if they caught sight of any one coming. Here, too, where the sea wind nips many a

---

*Possibly the rose variety *Alba maxima*.

young life before its prime, how often the white roses have been put into paler hands, and withered there!

In spite of the serene and placid look of the old houses, one who has always known them cannot help thinking of the sorrows of these farms and their almost undiverted toil. Near the little gardener's plot, we turned from the main road and drove through lately cleared woodland up to an old farmhouse, high on a ledgy hill, whence there is a fine view of the country seaward and mountainward. There were few of the once large household left there: only the old farmer, who was crippled by war wounds,* active, cheerful man that he was once, and two young orphan children. There has been much hard work spent on the place. Every generation has toiled from youth to age without being able to make much beyond a living. The dollars that can be saved are but few, and sickness and death have often brought their bitter cost. The mistress of the farm was helpless for many years; through all the summers and winters she sat in her pillowed rocking-chair in the plain room. She could watch the seldom-visited lane, and beyond it, a little way across the fields, were the woods; besides these, only the clouds in the sky. She could not lift her food to her mouth; she could not be her husband's working partner. She never went into another woman's house to see her works and ways, but sat there, aching and tired, vexed by flies and by heat, and isolated in long storms. Yet the whole countryside neighbored her with true affection. Her spirit grew stronger as her body grew weaker, and the doctors, who grieved because they could do so little with their skill, were never confronted by that malady of the spirit, a desire for ease and laziness, which makes the soundest of bodies useless and complaining. The thought of her blooms in one's mind like the whitest of flowers; it makes one braver and more thankful to remember the simple faith and patience with which she bore her pain and trouble. How often she must have said, "I wish I could do something for you in return," when she was doing a thousand times more than if, like her neighbors, she followed the simple round of daily life! She was doing constant kindness by her example; but nobody can tell the woe of her long days and nights,

*That is, from the Civil War.

the solitude of her spirit, as she was being lifted by such hard ways to the knowledge of higher truth and experience. Think of her pain when, one after another, her children fell ill and died, and she could not tend them! And now, in the same worn chair where she lived and slept sat her husband, helpless too, thinking of her, and missing her more than if she had been sometimes away from home, like other women. Even a stranger would miss her in the house.

There sat the old farmer looking down the lane in his turn, bearing his afflictions with a patient sternness that may have been born of watching his wife's serenity. There was a half-withered rose lying within his reach. Some days nobody came up the lane, and the wild birds that ventured near the house and the clouds that blew over were his only entertainment. He had a fine face, of the older New England type, clean-shaven and strong-featured,—a type that is fast passing away. He might have been a Cumberland dalesman,* such were his dignity, and self-possession, and English soberness of manner. His large frame was built for hard work, for lifting great weights and pushing his plough through new-cleared land. We felt at home together, and each knew many things that the other did of earlier days, and of losses that had come with time. I remembered coming to the old house often in my childhood; it was in this very farm lane that I first saw anemones, and learned what to call them. After we drove away, this crippled man must have thought a long time about my elders and betters, as if he were reading their story out of a book. I suppose he has hauled many a stick of timber pine down for ship-yards, and gone through the village so early in the winter morning that I, waking in my warm bed, only heard the sleds creak through the frozen snow as the slow oxen plodded by.

Near the house a trout brook comes plashing over the ledges. At one place there is a most exquisite waterfall, to which neither painter's brush nor writer's pen can do justice. The sunlight falls through flickering leaves into the deep glen, and makes the foam whiter and the brook more golden-brown. You can hear the merry noise of it all night, all day, in the house. A little way above the farmstead it comes through marshy ground, which I fear has been the cause of

*Someone from the north of England.

much illness and sorrow to the poor, troubled family. I had a thrill of pain, as it seemed to me that the brook was mocking at all that trouble with all its wild carelessness and loud laughter, as it hurried away down the glen.

When we had said good-by and were turning the horses away, there suddenly appeared in a footpath that led down from one of the green hills the young grandchild, just coming home from school. She was as quick as a bird, and as shy in her little pink gown, and balanced herself on one foot, like a flower. The brother was the elder of the two orphans; he was the old man's delight and dependence by day, while his hired man was afield. The sober country boy had learned to wait and tend, and the young people were indeed a joy in that lonely household. There was no sign that they ever played like other children,—no truckle-cart* in the yard, no doll, no bits of broken crockery in order on a rock. They had learned a fashion of life from their elders, and already could lift and carry their share of the burdens of life.

It was a country of wild flowers; the last of the columbines were clinging to the hillsides; down in the small, fenced meadows belonging to the farm were meadow rue just coming in flower, and red and white clover; the golden buttercups were thicker than the grass, while many mulleins were standing straight and slender among the pine stumps, with their first blossoms atop. Rudbeckias had found their way in, and appeared more than ever like bold foreigners. Their names should be translated into country speech, and the children ought to call them "rudebeckies," by way of relating them to bouncing-bets and sweet-williams. The pasture grass was green and thick after the plentiful rains, and the busy cattle took little notice of us as they browsed steadily and tinkled their pleasant bells. Looking off, the smooth, round back of Great Hill caught the sunlight with its fields of young grain, and all the long, wooded slopes and valleys were fresh and fair in the June weather, away toward the blue New Hampshire hills on the northern horizon. Seaward stood Agamenticus, dark with its pitch pines, and the far sea itself, blue and calm, ruled the uneven country with its unchangeable line.

---

*Child's cart with wheels.

Out on the white rose road again, we saw more of the rose-trees than ever, and now and then a carefully tended flower garden, always delightful to see and think about. These are not made by merely looking through a florist's catalogue, and ordering this or that new seedling and a proper selection of bulbs or shrubs; everything in a country garden has its history and personal association. The old bushes, the perennials, are apt to have most tender relationship with the hands that planted them long ago. There is a constant exchange of such treasures between the neighbors, and in the spring, slips and cuttings may be seen rooting on the window ledges, while the house plants give endless work all winter long, since they need careful protection against frost in long nights of the severe weather. A flower-loving woman brings back from every one of her infrequent journeys some treasure of flower-seeds or a huge miscellaneous nosegay. Time to work in the little plot of pleasure-ground is hardly won by the busy mistress of the farmhouse. The most appealing collection of flowering plants and vines that I ever saw was in Virginia, once, above the exquisite valley spanned by the Natural Bridge, a valley far too little known or praised.* I had noticed an old log house, as I learned to know the outlook from the picturesque hotel, and was sure that it must give a charming view from its perch on the summit of a hill.

One day I went there,—one April day, when the whole landscape was full of color from the budding trees,—and before I could look at the view, I caught sight of some rare vines, already in leaf, about the dilapidated walls of the cabin. Then across the low paling I saw the brilliant colors of tulips and daffodils. There were many rose-bushes; in fact, the whole top of the hill was a flower garden, once well cared for and carefully ordered. It was all the work of an old woman of Scotch-Irish descent, who had been busy with the cares of life, and a very hard worker; yet I was told that to gratify her love for flowers she would often go afoot many miles over those rough Virginia roads, with a root or cutting from her own garden, to barter for a new rose or a brighter blossom of some sort, with which she would return in triumph. I fancied that sometimes she had to go by

*The Shenandoah Valley in Virginia.

night on these charming quests. I could see her business-like, small figure setting forth down the steep path, when she had a good conscience toward her housekeeping and the children were in order to be left. I am sure that her friends thought of her when they were away from home and could bring her an offering of something rare. Alas, she had grown too old and feeble to care for her dear blossoms any longer, and had been forced to go to live with a married son. I dare say that she was thinking of her garden that very day, and wondering if this plant or that were not in bloom, and perhaps had a heartache at the thought that her tenants, the careless colored children, might tread the young shoots of peony and rose, and make havoc in the herb-bed. It was an uncommon collection, made by years of patient toil and self-sacrifice.

I thought of that deserted Southern garden as I followed my own New England road. The flower-plots were in gay bloom all along the way; almost every house had some flowers before it, sometimes carefully fenced about by stakes and barrel staves from the miscreant hens and chickens which lurked everywhere, and liked a good scratch and fluffing in soft earth this year as well as any other. The world seemed full of young life. There were calves tethered in pleasant shady spots, and puppies and kittens adventuring from the door-ways. The trees were full of birds: bobolinks, and cat-birds, and yellow-hammers, and golden robins,* and sometimes a thrush, for the afternoon was wearing late. We passed the spring which once marked the boundary where three towns met,—Berwick, York, and Wells,—a famous spot in the early settlement of the country, but many of its old traditions are now forgotten. One of the omnipresent regicides of Charles the First† is believed to have hidden himself for a long time under a great rock close by. The story runs that he made his miserable home in this den for several years, but I believe that there is no record that more than three of the regicides escaped, to this country, and their wanderings are otherwise accounted for. There is a firm belief that one of them came to York,

---

*Baltimore orioles (in recent years this species has been called the northern oriole).

†Three of the English revolutionaries who helped to overthrow King Charles I in 1649 escaped to New England after the 1660 Restoration of the monarchy.

and was the ancestor of many persons now living there, but I do not know whether he can have been the hero of the Baker's Spring hermitage beside. We stopped to drink some of the delicious water, which never fails to flow cold and clear under the shade of a great oak, and were amused with the sight of a flock of gay little country children who passed by in deep conversation. What could such atoms of humanity be talking about? "Old times," said John, the master of horse, with instant decision.

We met now and then a man or woman, who stopped to give us hospitable greeting; but there was no staying for visits, lest the daylight might fail us. It was delightful to find this old-established neighborhood so thriving and populous, for a few days before I had driven over three miles of road, and passed only one house that was tenanted, and six cellars or crumbling chimneys where good farmhouses had been, the lilacs blooming in solitude, and the fields, cleared with so much difficulty a century or two ago, all going back to the original woodland from which they were won. What would the old farmers say to see the fate of their worthy bequest to the younger generation? They would wag their heads sorrowfully, with sad foreboding.

After we had passed more woodland and a well-known quarry, where, for a wonder, the derrick was not creaking and not a single hammer was clinking at the stone wedges, we did not see any one hoeing in the fields, as we had seen so many on the white rose road, the other side of the hills. Presently we met two or three people walking sedately, clad in their best clothes. There was a subdued air of public excitement and concern, and one of us remembered that there had been a death in the neighborhood; this was the day of the funeral. The man had been known to us in former years. We had an instinct to hide our unsympathetic pleasuring, but there was nothing to be done except to follow our homeward road straight by the house.

The occasion was nearly ended by this time: the borrowed chairs were being set out in the yard in little groups; even the funeral supper had been eaten, and the brothers and sisters and near relatives of the departed man were just going home. The new grave showed plainly out in the green field near by. He had belonged to one of the ancient families of the region, long settled on this old farm by the narrow river; they had given their name to a bridge, and the bridge had christened the meeting-house which stood close by. We were much struck by the solemn figure of the mother, a very old woman, as she walked toward her old home with some of her remaining children. I had not thought to see her again, knowing her great age and infirmity. She was like a presence out of the last century, tall and still erect, dark-eyed and of striking features, and a firm look not modern, but as if her mind were still set upon an earlier and simpler scheme of life. An air of dominion cloaked her finely. She had long been queen of her surroundings and law-giver to her great family. Royalty is a quality, one of Nature's gifts, and there one might behold it as truly as if Victoria Regina Imperatrix* had passed by. The natural instincts common to humanity were there undisguised, unconcealed, simply accepted. We had seen a royal progress; she was the central figure of that rural society; as you looked at the little group, you could see her only. Now that she came abroad so rarely, her presence was not without deep significance, and so she took her homeward way with a primitive kind of majesty.

It was evident that the neighborhood was in great excitement and quite thrown out of its usual placidity. An acquaintance came from a small house farther down the road, and we stopped for a word with him. We spoke of the funeral, and were told something of the man who had died. "Yes, and there 's a man layin' very sick here," said our friend in an excited whisper. "*He* won't last but a day or two. There's another man buried yesterday that was struck by lightnin', comin' acrost a field when that great shower begun. The lightnin' stove through his hat and run down all over him, and ploughed a spot in the ground." There was a knot of people about the door; the minister of that scattered parish stood among them, and they all looked at us eagerly, as if we too might be carrying news of a fresh disaster through the countryside.

Somehow the melancholy tales did not touch our sympathies as they ought, and we could not see the pathetic side of them as at another time, the day was so full of cheer and the sky and earth so glorious. The very fields looked busy with their early summer

*That is, Queen Victoria.

growth, the horses began to think of the clack of the oat-bin cover, and we were hurried along between the silvery willows and the rustling alders, taking time to gather a handful of stray-away conserve roses by the roadside; and where the highway made a long bend eastward among the farms, two of us left the carriage, and followed a footpath along the green river bank and through the pastures, coming out to the road again only a minute later than the horses. I believe that it is an old Indian trail followed from the salmon falls farther down the river, where the up-country Indians came to dry the plentiful fish for their winter supplies. I have traced the greater part of this deep-worn footpath, which goes straight as an arrow across the country, the first day's trail being from the falls (where Mason's settlers came in 1627, and built their Great Works of a saw-mill with a gang of saws, and presently a grist mill beside) to Emery's Bridge. I should like to follow the old footpath still farther. I found part of it by accident a long time ago. Once, as you came close to the river, you were sure to find fishermen scattered along,—sometimes I myself have been discovered; but it is not much use to go fishing any more. If some public-spirited person would kindly be the Frank Buckland* of New England, and try to have the laws enforced that protect the inland fisheries, he would do his country great service. Years ago, there were so many salmon that, as an enthusiastic old friend once assured me, "you could walk across on them below the falls;" but now they are unknown, simply because certain substances which would enrich the farms are thrown from factories and tanneries into our clear New England streams. Good river fish are growing very scarce. The smelts, and bass, and shad have all left this upper branch of the Piscataqua, as the salmon left it long ago, and the supply of one necessary sort of good cheap food is lost to a growing community, for the lack of a little thought and care in the factory companies and saw-mills, and the building in some cases of fish-ways over the dams. I think that the need of preaching against this bad economy is very great. The sight of a proud lad with a string of undersized trout will scatter half the idlers

---

*Buckland (1826–1860) was a conservationist in Great Britain who specialized in protecting fish.

in town into the pastures next day, but everybody patiently accepts the depopulation of a fine clear river, where the tide comes fresh from the sea to be tainted by the spoiled stream, which started from its mountain sources as pure as heart could wish. Man has done his best to ruin the world he lives in, one is tempted to say at impulsive first thought; but after all, as I mounted the last hill before reaching the village, the houses took on a new look of comfort and pleasantness; the fields that I knew so well were a fresher green than before, the sun was down, and the provocations of the day seemed very slight compared to the satisfaction. I believed that with a little more time we should grow wiser about our fish and other things beside.

It will be good to remember the white rose road and its quietness in many a busy town day to come. As I think of these slight sketches, I wonder if they will have to others a tinge of sadness; but I have seldom spent an afternoon so full of pleasure and fresh and delighted consciousness of the possibilities of rural life.

FOR THE COMPANION

LOOKING BACK ON GIRLHOOD

First Paper

In giving this brief account of my childhood, or, to speak exactly, of the surroundings which have affected the course of my work as a writer, my first thought flies back to those who taught me to observe, and to know the deep pleasures of simple things, and to be interested in the lives of people about me.

With its high hills and pine forests, and all its ponds and brooks and distant mountain views, there are few such delightful country towns in New England as the one where I was born. Being one of the oldest colonial settlements, it is full of interesting traditions and relics of the early inhabitants, both Indians and Englishmen. Two large rivers* join just below the village at the head of tide-water, and these, with the great inflow from the sea, make a magnificent stream, bordered on its seaward course now by high-wooded banks of dark pines and hemlocks, and again by lovely green fields that slope gently to long lines of willows at the water's edge.

There is never-ending pleasure in making one's self familiar with such a region. One may travel at home in a most literal sense, and be always learning history, geography, botany, or biography—whatever one chooses.

I have had a good deal of journeying in my life, and taken great delight in it, but I have never taken greater delight than in my rides and drives and tramps and voyages within the borders of my native town. There is always something fresh, something to be traced or discovered, something particularly to be remembered. One grows rich in memories and associations.

*The Salmon Falls River and the Great Works River.

I believe that we should know our native towns much better than most of us do, and never let ourselves be strangers at home. Particularly when one's native place is so really interesting as my own!

Above tide-water the two rivers are barred by successive falls. You hear the noise of them by night in the village like the sound of the sea, and this fine water power so near the coast, beside a great salmon fishery famous among the Indians, brought the first English settlers to the town in 1627. I know some families who still live upon the lands which their ancestors bought from the Indians, and their single deed bears the queer barbaric signatures.

There are many things to remind one of these early settlers beside the old farms upon which they and their descendants have lived for six or seven generations. One is a quaint fashion of speech which survives among the long-established neighborhoods, in words and phrases common in England in the sixteenth and seventeenth centuries.

One curious thing is the pronunciation of the name of the town: Berwick by the elder people has always been called *Barvik*, after the fashion of Danes and Northmen; never *Berrik*, as the word has so long been pronounced in modern England.

The descendants of the first comers to the town have often been distinguished in the affairs of their time. No village of its size in New England could boast, particularly in the early part of the present century, of a larger number of men and women who kept themselves more closely in touch with "the best that has been thought and said in the world."*

As I write this, I keep in mind the truth that I have no inheritance from the ancient worth and dignity of Berwick—or what is now North Berwick—in Maine. My own people are comparatively late comers. I was born in a pleasant old colonial house built near 1750, and bought by my grandfather sixty or seventy years ago, when he brought his household up the river to Berwick from Portsmouth.

He was a sea-captain, and had run away to sea in his boyhood and led a most adventurous life, but was quite ready to forsake seafaring

---

*Reference to Matthew Arnold's preface to his book *Literature and Dogma* (1873).

in his early manhood, and at last joined a group of acquaintances who were engaged in the flourishing West India trade of that time.

For many years he kept and extended his interests in shipping, building ships and buying large quantities of timber from the northward and eastward, and sending it down the river and so to sea.

This business was still in existence in my early childhood, and the manner of its conduct was primitive enough, the barter system still prevailing by force of necessity. Those who brought the huge sticks of oak and pine timber for masts and plank were rarely paid in money, which was of comparatively little use in remote and sparsely settled districts. When the sleds and long trains of yoked oxen returned from the river wharves to the stores, they took a lighter load in exchange of flour and rice and barrels of molasses, of sugar and salt and cotton cloth and raisins and spices and tea and coffee; in fact, all the household necessities and luxuries that the northern farms could not supply.

They liked to have a little money with which to pay their taxes and their parish dues, if they were so fortunate as to be parishioners, but they needed very little money besides.

So I came in contact with the up-country people as well as with the sailors and shipmasters of the other side of the business. I used to linger about the busy country stores, and listen to the graphic country talk. I heard the greetings of old friends, and their minute details of neighborhood affairs, their delightful jokes and Munchausen-like reports* of tracts of timber-pines ever so many feet through at the butt.

When the great teams came in sight at the head of the village street, I ran to meet them over the creaking snow, if possible to mount and ride into town in triumph; but it was not many years before I began to feel sorry at the sight of every huge lopped stem of oak or pine that came trailing along after the slow-stepping, frosted oxen. Such trees are unreplaceable. I only know of one small group now in all this part of the country of those great timber pines.

---

*That is, exaggerated reports; a reference to Rudolph Erich Raspe's 1785 book *The Surprising Adventures of Baron Munchausen,* which chronicled the exaggerated adventures of that book's protagonist, who was based on an actual person.

My young ears were quick to hear the news of a ship's having come into port, and I delighted in the elderly captains, with their sea-tanned faces, who came to report upon their voyages, dining cheerfully and heartily with my grandfather, who listened eagerly to their exciting tales of great storms on the Atlantic, and winds that blew them north-about, and good bargains in Havana, or Barbadoes, or Havre.*

I listened as eagerly as any one; this is the charming way in which I was taught something of a fashion of life already on the wane, and of that subsistence upon sea and forest bounties which is now almost a forgotten thing in my part of New England.

Much freight still came and went by the river gundelows and packets long after the railroad had made such changes, and every village along its line lost its old feeling of self-sufficiency.

In my home the greater part of the minor furnishings had come over in the ships from Bristol and Havre. My grandfather seemed to be a citizen of the whole geography. I was always listening to stories of three wars from older people—the siege of Louisburg,† the Revolution, in which my father's ancestors had been honest but mistaken Tories, and in which my mother's, the Gilmans of Exeter, had taken a nobler part.

As for the War of 1812, "the last war," as everybody called it, it was a thing of yesterday in the town. One of the famous privateer‡ crews was gathered along our own river shore, and one member of the crew, in his old age, had been my father's patient.

The Berwick people were great patriots, and were naturally proud of the famous Sullivans, who were born in the upper part of the town, and came to be governors and judge and general.

I often heard about Lafayette,§ who had made an ever-to-be-remembered visit in order to see again some old friends who lived

---

*Le Havre is a port town in northern France.

†The 1745 siege of the French-occupied fortress at Louisbourg, Cape Breton Island, Nova Scotia, by British-allied New England forces.

‡Privately owned ship hired by one government to interrupt the shipping commerce of an enemy.

§The Marquis de Lafayette, French political leader and general, visited friends in South Berwick, Maine, in 1825.

in the town. The name of a famous Colonel Hamilton, the leader in the last century of the West India trade, and the histories of the old Berwick houses of Chadbourn and Lord* were delightfully familiar, and one of the traditions of the latter family is more than good enough to be told again.

There was a Berwick lad who went out on one of the privateers that sailed from Portsmouth in the Revolution. The vessel was taken by a British frigate, and the crew put in irons. One day one of the English midshipmen stood near these prisoners as they took their airing on deck, and spoke contemptuously about "the rebels."

Young Lord heard what he said, and turned himself about to say boldly, "If it were not for your rank, sir, I would make you take that back!"

"No matter about my rank," said the gallant middy. "If you can whip me, you are welcome to."

So they had a "capital good fight," standing over a tea-chest, as proud tradition tells, and the Berwick sailor was the better fighter of the two, and won.

The Englishman shook hands, and asked his name and promised not to forget him—which was certainly most handsome behavior.

When they reached an English port all the prisoners but one were sent away under guard to join the other American prisoners of war; but the admiral sent for a young man named Nathan Lord, and told him that his Grace the Duke of Clarence, son of his Majesty the King,[12] begged for his pardon, and had left a five-pound note at his disposal.

This was not the first or last Berwick lad who proved himself of good courage in a fight, but there never was another to whip a future King of England, and moreover to be liked the better for it by that fine gentleman.

My grandfather died in my eleventh year, and presently the Civil War began.

From that time the simple village life was at an end. Its provincial character was fading out; shipping was at a disadvantage, and

---

*Jewett further discussed these South Berwick families in her nonfiction sketch "The Old Town of Berwick" (1894).

there were no more bronzed sea-captains coming to dine and talk about their voyages, no more bags of filberts or oranges for the children, or great red jars of olives; but in these childish years I had come in contact with many delightful men and women of real individuality and breadth of character, who had fought the battle of life to good advantage, and sometimes against great odds.

In these days I was given to long, childish illnesses, and it must be honestly confessed, to instant drooping if ever I were shut up in school. I had apparently not the slightest desire for learning, but my father was always ready to let me be his companion in long drives about the country.

In my grandfather's business household, my father, unconscious of tonnage and timber measurements, of the markets of the Windward Islands* or the Mediterranean ports, had taken to his book, as old people said, and gone to college and begun that devotion to the study of medicine which only ended with his life.

I have tried already to give some idea of my father's character in my story of "The Country Doctor,"† but all that is inadequate to the gifts and character of the man himself. He gave me my first and best knowledge of books by his own delight and dependence upon them, and ruled my early attempts at writing by the severity and simplicity of his own good taste.

"Don't try to write *about* people and things, tell them just as they are!"

How often my young ears heard these words without comprehending them! But while I was too young and thoughtless to share in an enthusiasm for Sterne or Fielding, and Smollett or Don Quixote, my mother and grandmother were leading me into the pleasant ways of "Pride and Prejudice," and "The Scenes of Clerical Life," and the delightful stories of Mrs. Oliphant.[13]

The old house was well provided with leather-bound books of a deeply serious nature, but in my youthful appetite for knowledge, I could even in the driest find something vital, and in the more entertaining I was completely lost.

---

*Southern part of the Lesser Antilles in the West Indies.

†Jewett's 1884 novel *A Country Doctor*.

My father had inherited from his father an amazing knowledge of human nature, and from his mother's French ancestry, that peculiarly French trait, called *gaieté de cœur.** Through all the heavy responsibilities and anxieties of his busy professional life, this kept him young at heart and cheerful. His visits to his patients were often made perfectly delightful and refreshing to them by his kind heart, and the charm of his personality.

I knew many of the patients whom he used to visit in lonely inland farms, or on the seacoast in York and Wells. I used to follow him about silently, like an undemanding little dog, content to follow at his heels.

I had no consciousness of watching or listening, or indeed of any special interest in the country interiors. In fact, when the time came that my own world of imagination was more real to me than any other, I was sometimes perplexed at my father's directing my attention to certain points of interest in the character or surroundings of our acquaintances.

I cannot help believing that he recognized, long before I did myself, in what direction the current of purpose in my life was setting. Now, as I write my sketches of country life, I remember again and again the wise things he said, and the sights he made me see. He was only impatient with affectation and insincerity.

I may have inherited something of my father's and grandfather's knowledge of human nature, but my father never lost a chance of trying to teach me to observe. I owe a great deal to his patience with a heedless little girl given far more to dreams than to accuracy, and with perhaps too little natural sympathy for the dreams of others.

The quiet village life, the dull routine of farming or mill life, early became interesting to me. I was taught to find everything that an imaginative child could ask, in the simple scenes close at hand.

I say these things eagerly, because I long to impress upon every boy and girl this truth: that it is not one's surroundings that can help or hinder—it is having a growing purpose in one's life to make the most of whatever is in one's reach.

---

*French phrase (literally, "gaiety of the heart") that refers to the French cultural attitude of lightheartedness.

If you have but a few good books, learn those to the very heart of them. Don't for one moment believe that if you had different surroundings and opportunities you would find the upward path any easier to climb. One condition is like another, if you have not the determination and the power to grow in yourself.

I was still a child when I began to write down the things I was thinking about, but at first I always made rhymes and found prose so difficult that a school composition was a terror to me, and I do not remember ever writing one that was worth anything. But in course of time rhymes themselves became difficult and prose more and more enticing, and I began my work in life, most happy in finding that I was to write of those country characters and rural landscapes to which I myself belonged, and which I had been taught to love with all my heart.

I was between nineteen and twenty when my first sketch was accepted by Mr. Howells for the *Atlantic.** I already counted myself as by no means a new contributor to one or two other magazines—*Young Folks* and *The Riverside*—but I had no literary friends "at court."

I was very shy about speaking of my work at home, and even sent it to the magazine under an assumed name, and then was timid about asking the post-mistress for those mysterious and exciting editorial letters which she announced upon the post-office list as if I were a stranger in the town.

---

*William Dean Howells (1837–1920), editor of the *Atlantic Monthly*, accepted numerous stories by Jewett for publication in that periodical.

ENDNOTES

The Country of the Pointed Firs

1. (p. 7) *the coast town of Dunnet:* In a December 19, 1897, letter sent to one of her Maine readers (reprinted in *Sarah Orne Jewett Letters*, edited by Richard Cary, p. 116; see "For Further Reading"), Sarah Orne Jewett confessed that the town of Dunnet Landing was entirely fictional. "I cannot tell you just where Dunnet Landing is except that it must be somewhere 'along shore' between the regions of Tenants Harbor and Boothbay, or it might be farther to the eastward in a country that I know less well. It is not any real 'landing' or real 'harbor.' "

2. (p. 18) *the Countess of Carberry:* Frances, countess of Carbery, was known in England and in New England into the nineteenth century as the epitome of religious devotion. She was the second wife of Richard Vaughan, earl of Carbery (c.1600–1686). After her death in 1650, she was immortalized by the writer Jeremy Taylor (1613–1667).

3. (p. 22) *Parry's Discoveries:* Located north of Melville Sound and Banks Island in the Arctic Ocean, the Parry Islands (today part of the Queen Elizabeth Islands in Canada's Northwest Territories) were named after English explorer William Edward Parry (1790–1855), who visited the area three times searching the Arctic archipelago for the Northwest Passage.

The Queen's Twin

4. (p. 119) *the Northmen's children:* Here Jewett reflected a widely held nineteenth-century notion of the superiority of northern European peoples.

A Dunnet Shepherdess

5. (p. 139) *I was reminded of Medea's anointing Jason before the great episode of the iron bulls:* This is a reference to the Greek myth of Jason and the Golden Fleece, in which King Aeetes agreed to surrender the Golden Fleece to Jason if the latter could yoke two fire-breathing bulls with iron-tipped horns. To accomplish that task, Jason obtained a magic ointment from the King's daughter Medea.

William's Wedding

6. (p. 188) *Medea could not have been more conscious of high ultimate purposes:* In the Greek myth of Jason and the Golden Fleece, King Aeetes agreed to surrender the Golden Fleece to Jason if the latter could yoke two fire-breathing bulls. To accomplish that task, Jason obtained a magic ointment from the King's daughter Medea.

A White Heron

7. (p. 201) *The little white heron, it is:* The ornithologist in the story was referring to the snowy egret. In the nineteenth century, snowy egret feathers were much sought after as decoration for women's hats. Overhunting nearly led to the extirpation of the species.

The Dulham Ladies

8. (p. 207) *Miss Dobin and Miss Lucinda Dobin:* In nineteenth-century New England society, an older unmarried sister was addressed by the term "Miss" along with her last name, while the younger unmarried sister was referred to by "Miss" plus her first (and sometimes her last) name.

9. (p. 208) *"Of course, those were the days of small-clothes and long silk stockings!":* In the eighteenth and early nineteenth centuries, *small-clothes* were men's pants that extended down to the knees, while *silk stockings* were worn up to the knees.

The Courting of Sister Wisby

10. (p. 222) *a black reviewer croaked at Keats:* A reference to the fallacious notion, memorably advanced by English poet Percy Bysshe Shelley (1792–1822) in his poem "Adonis," that English poet John Keats (1795–1821) died at a young age after suffering negative criticism from literary critics. Keats in fact died from tuberculosis.

Decoration Day

11. (p. 267) *the thirtieth of May:* Decoration Day was a holiday historically celebrated on May 30 each year to commemorate the dead from the Civil War (1861–1865) through the decoration of soldiers' graves. This holiday, later renamed Memorial Day, evolved to include the commemoration of deceased American veterans from all wars.

Looking Back on Girlhood

12. (p. 365) *Nathan Lord, . . . his Grace the Duke of Clarence, son of his Majesty the King:* Nathan Lord (1758–1807) fought for the American Revolutionary cause as a privateer. The Duke of Clarence was Prince William Henry (1765–1837); the third son of King George III, he later became King William IV.

13. (p. 366) *"The Scenes of Clerical Life," and the delightful stories of Mrs. Oliphant: Scenes of a Clerical Life* is a collection of three stories by George Eliot. Margaret Oliphant (1828–1897) was a Scottish author.

INSPIRED BY SARAH ORNE JEWETT

Sarah Orne Jewett was a genius in her use of the "local color" writing style. This literary approach—mostly used in short stories and nonfiction sketches—was immensely popular during the four decades after the end of the Civil War. With varying degrees of commercial and aesthetic success, local colorists described the lives and folkways of people whose cultural identities were unique to a particular region, as well as the landscapes associated with those localities. Jewett's style was influenced by several authors whose works she read during her teenage years, including Louisa May Alcott and Harriet Beecher Stowe. In the mid-1860s, Jewett read Stowe's 1862 book *The Pearl of Orr's Island*, which inspired the aspiring author to portray in her writings the everyday life and customs of the inhabitants of the Maine coast, where she grew up. In turn, Jewett's mastery of the local color style was to strongly influence another American author, Willa Cather.

Cather, whose masterpieces *O Pioneers!* (1913) and *My Ántonia* (1918) brilliantly evoke life on the American prairie, greatly admired the author of *The Country of the Pointed Firs*. Jewett's influence, in fact, was crucial in shaping Cather's career. In her critical study *Sarah Orne Jewett* (1980; see "For Further Reading"), Josephine Donovan notes that Cather "despaired of ever writing about Nebraska before she met Jewett." The two authors developed a friendship and corresponded in the last year of Jewett's life, during which time Jewett—who had read Cather's early stories—encouraged the young author to write about the Nebraska pioneers she knew during her youth. Jewett advised Cather regarding the latter author's approach to her work. According to Cather, Jewett said: "Write it as it is, don't try to make it like this or that. You can't do it in anybody else's way—you will have to make a way of your own" (from an interview with Cather in the *Philadelphia Record*, August 9, 1913).

Born in Virginia and raised in Nebraska from age eight, Cather depicted the lives of immigrants in Nebraska with the same heightened level of honesty and sensitivity that Jewett brought to her stories about life in coastal Maine. *O Pioneers!*, Cather's second novel, describes the hardships and moral fortitude of the women who helped establish farms and communities on the Nebraska frontier. The story centers on the courageous Swedish settler Alexandra Bergson, who transforms her father's windswept land into a prospering farm. *My Ántonia*, Cather's fourth novel and often considered her finest work, takes the form of a memoir about the Bohemian immigrant Ántonia Shimerda, as told by her childhood friend Jim Burden. Many hardships befall Ántonia in her early life, including her father's suicide, the back-breaking farm labor of her teenage years, and the desertion of her fiancé, who left her to raise their child alone. After twenty years of separation, Jim travels back to Nebraska to find Ántonia married to another Bohemian and, after years of adversity, at last satisfied with her lot.

In an interview published in the May 1921 issue of *Bookman* magazine, Cather describes how *O Pioneers!*, her first successful work, grew out of advice from her mentor:

> In "Alexander's Bridge" I was still more preoccupied with trying to write well than with anything else. It takes a great deal of experience to become natural. People grow in honesty as they grow in anything else. A painter or writer must learn to distinguish what is his *own* from that which he admires. I never abandoned trying to make a compromise between the kind of matter that my experience had given me and the manner of writing which I admired, until I began my second novel, "O Pioneers!" And from the first chapter, I decided not to "write" at all—simply to give myself up to the pleasure of recapturing in memory people and places I had believed forgotten. This was what my friend Sarah Orne Jewett had advised me to do. She said to me that if my life had lain in a part of the world that was without a literature, and I couldn't tell about it truthfully in the form

> I most admired, I'd have to make a kind of writing that would tell it, no matter what I lost in the process.

In her book, Donovan points out that Cather and Jewett shared an approach common to local color writing: "Both were more interested in character than in plot, both preferred emotional drama to drama of incident, both were concerned with the character of the locale, both used a spare, simple prose style." In appreciation of Jewett's influence on her work, Cather dedicated *O Pioneers!* to her mentor. The inscription reads, "To the memory of Sarah Orne Jewett, in whose beautiful and delicate work there is the perfection that endures." In the *Philadelphia Record* article, Cather noted that she had talked with Jewett about several of the characters in *O Pioneers!*, and in her dedication to her mentor in that novel Cather said that she "tried to tell the story of the people as truthfully and simply as if I were telling it to her [Jewett] by word of mouth."

Edith Wharton, known for her portraits of the social life of moneyed New Yorkers, wrote her novella *Ethan Frome* (1911)—her single piece of writing about New England—as a deliberate argument against Jewett's sympathetic view of country life. With psychological accuracy the novel tells the tragic story of Ethan, a poor rural farmer, his malevolent wife Zeena, and Zeena's cousin Mattie, with whom Ethan falls in love. In her autobiography, *A Backward Glance* (1934), Wharton recalled her desire to respond to Jewett's optimism, which Wharton viewed as naive: "For years I wanted to draw life as it really was in the derelict mountain villages of New England, a life even in my own time, and a thousandfold more a generation earlier, utterly unlike that seen through the rose-colored spectacles of my predecessors, Mary Wilkins and Sarah Orne Jewett."

COMMENTS & QUESTIONS

In this section, we aim to provide the reader with an array of perspectives on the texts, as well as questions that challenge those perspectives. The commentary has been culled from sources as diverse as reviews contemporaneous with the works, letters written by the author, literary criticism of later generations, and appreciations written throughout the works' history. Following the commentary, a series of questions seeks to examine Sarah Orne Jewett's The Country of the Pointed Firs and Selected Short Fiction *from a variety of perspectives and to bring about a richer understanding of these enduring works.*

Comments

WILLIAM DEAN HOWELLS

Miss Jewett here gives proof of such powers of observation and characterization as we hope will some day be turned to the advantage of all of us in fiction. Meanwhile we are glad of these studies, so refined, so simple, so exquisitely imbued with a true feeling for the ideal within the real.

—from a review of *Deephaven* in the *Atlantic Monthly* (June 1877)

HORACE E. SCUDDER

It is situations rather than dramatic action with which Miss Jewett concerns herself, and situations especially which illustrate character. Thus, in the volume before us, "A Native of Winby" sets forth the return to his old village home of a man who has won fame; his appearance, large as life, in the little schoolhouse which knew his boyish inconspicuousness; and his encounter with a woman who, as a girl, had known the boy. It is indicative of the reserve of Miss Jewett, her nice sense of the limits of her art, that she does not resort to any conventional device of rounding out her story, and Mr. Laneway does not pair off with Abby Hender as an effective conclusion. Miss Jewett cares more for the real interest of the situation, for the working of such a nature as Mr. Laneway's in this half-egotistic, half-shamefaced return. "Decoration Day," again, as a story, could be told in a few lines, but as a reflection of a half-buried patriotic emotion it is of moving power. "The Passing of Sister Barsett" has a witty climax, but, after all, it is the inimitable humor and pathos of the conversation between the two women which make the story a patch of New England life; and if there had been no witty turn, the reader still would have had his half-hour's worth. "The Flight of Betsey Lane" is the most complete story in the book, but it is a tale of adventure illustrative of character, and never does the reader lose his interest in the quaint figure who has the delightful escapade from any strong attraction to the issue of the story. . . .

It is scarcely expected that Miss Jewett will ever attain the constructive power which holds in the grasp a variety of complex activities and controls their energy, directing it to some conclusive end; but her imagination is strong to conceive a genuine situation, to illustrate it through varied character, to illuminate it with humor and dewy pathos; and as she extends the range of her characters, so she is likely to display even more invention in the choice of situations which shall give opportunity to those delightful characters who spring at her bidding from no one class, and even from no one nation.

—from the *Atlantic Monthly* (January 1894)

ALICE BROWN

The Country of the Pointed Firs is the flower of a sweet, sane knowledge of life, and an art so elusive that it smiles up at you while you pull aside the petals, vainly probing its heart. The title is exacting, prophetic; a little bit of genius of which the book has to be worthy or come very "tardy off." And the book is worthy. Here is the idyllic atmosphere of country life, unbroken by one jarring note; even the attendant sadness and pathos of being are resolved into that larger harmony destined to elude our fustian words. It is a book made to defy the praise ordinarily given to details; it must be regarded *au large.* For it takes hold of the very centre of things. . . . It is the acme of Miss Jewett's fine achievement, blending the humanity of the "Native of Winby" and the fragrance of the "White Heron." No such beautiful and perfect work has been done for many years; perhaps no such beautiful work has ever been done in America.

—from the *Book Buyer* (October 1897)

JULIA R. TUTWILER

Reading *The Country of the Pointed Firs* is like opening one's grandmother's chest of spotless, lavendered linen, or spending a day in a deep forest glade within sight and sound of clear, softly flowing water, the sky blue above the pines and the air shot through and through with Indian summer sunshine.

—from *Gunton's Magazine* (November 1903)

HENRY JAMES

To speak in a mere parenthesis of Miss Jewett, mistress of an art of fiction all her own, even though of a minor compass, and surpassed only by Hawthorne as producer of the most finished and penetrating of the numerous 'short stories' that have the domestic life of New England for their general and their doubtless somewhat lean subject, is to do myself, I feel, the violence of suppressing a chapter of appreciation that I should long since somewhere have found space for. Her admirable gift, that artistic sensibility in her which rivaled the rare personal, that sense for the finest kind of truthful rendering, the sober and tender note, the temperately touched, whether in the ironic or the pathetic, would have deserved some more pointed commemoration than I judge her beautiful little quantum of achievement, her free and high, yet all so generously subdued character, a sort of elegance of humility or fine flame of modesty, with her remarkably distinguished outward stamp, to have called forth before the premature and overdarkened close of her young course of production.

—from the *Atlantic Monthly* (July 1915)

EDWARD GARNETT

By what special excellence, the curious reader will ask, is the province of Miss Jewett's art marked out as a country set apart from its neighbours? By a peculiar spirituality which her work exhales, a spirituality which is inseparable from her unerring perception of her country-people's native outlook and instinctive attitude of life. It is by this exquisite spiritual gravity interpenetrating with the finest sense of humour, intensely, even maliciously discriminating, that Miss Jewett seems to speak for the feminine soul of the New England race. . . .

I have spoken of Miss Jewett's art as coming second only to Hawthorne's in its spiritual interpretation of the New England character. In originality of vision, and in intense and passionate creative force she is, of course, not to be compared with him. The range of her insight is undeniably restricted. Nevertheless, it makes the cosmopolitan appeal, that all art of high quality makes, and her work at its best, no less than Hawthorne's conveys to us a mysterious sense of her country people's mental and moral life, seen as a whole in relation to their environment and to their past, and reveals it as the natural growth of the very definite history of the many Puritan generations that have gone before them. In stories such as "Decoration Day," "The Hilton's Holiday," "A Dunnet Shepherdess," and in scenes in "The Country of the Pointed Firs," such as "The Bowden Reunion," and "Shellheap Island," her art attains to that highest perfection of literature when the fleeting passage of life presented is felt in its invisible relations to immense reaches of life around it, in which, as in an ocean, it blends, merges, and is lost. . . .

Now this rare poetic breath that emanates from Miss Jewett's homely realism is her artistic reward for caring above all things for the essential spiritual reality of her scenes, and for departing not a hair's-breadth from its prosaic actualities. A word wrong, a note untrue, the slightest straining after effect, and the natural atmosphere of scene and place would be destroyed, and the whole illusion of the life presented would be shattered.

—from *Friday Nights* (1922)

MARTHA HALE SHACKFORD

Miss Jewett's stories are always stories of character. Plots hardly exist in her work; she has little interest in creating suspense or in weaving together threads of varied interests. She presents people through mild desultory action, in situations seldom dramatically striking. The people interpreted live simple, inconspicuous lives, without great tragedy attending them, but made significant through the little things which, by reiterated irritation and pain, tax the spirit of endurance and shape character. The wisdom won from slow pondering of life is found on the lips of her men and women. And these persons speak the very thoughts and the very language of their region; thoughts expressed in a shrewd, picturesque, colloquial fashion, in a dialect directly true to life, not a romantic make-believe. But the best part, perhaps, of her delineation of these people is in her record of their silences. Miss Jewett has interpreted the impulse to reticence, has accounted for the temperament of these watchful, guarded folk who imitate the granite impenetrability of their natural surroundings. Also she has shown the extraordinary sense of justice to be noted in this district. So bound up with nature are these people that they feel accountable for nature's doings; they must help atone for nature's ravages and aberrations. But like the ocean's ebb and flow, the method of giving aid and comfort is somewhat indirect, oblique, attaining its end with the seventh wave.

Miss Jewett's most successful and probably her most representative work is *The Country of the Pointed Firs*, a series of chapters linked together loosely enough by the fact that one person records her experiences in a typical Maine village, on the edge of the sea, a village that reaches back to the land overgrown with the spruce trees that, in sharp spires, stand out against the blue sky. It is really a group of character sketches, not a story, and the chief character is Mrs. Todd, a woman with a tragic past, fighting for her daily bread, yet brisk, hopeful, romantic to the last degree. Skilled in the lore of healing herbs, she seems like one of the Fates, endowed with portentous wisdom, stooping to pick sprigs of fragrant pennyroyal, in a sunshiny green pasture. Slowly, and with most delicate humor, Miss Jewett makes clear Mrs. Todd's endless curiosity, high-mindedness, and shrewd, inexhaustible kindness. . . .

The book is sheer reality both in setting and in character study. The scattered bits of description give one the very look of green pastures, the scent of aromatic herbs, the fragrance of sun-smitten spruce trees, the sting of the cool salt air, and the milder aspects of blue, sunshiny, safe harbors.

—from *Sewanee Review* (January 1922)

WILLA CATHER

If I were asked to name three American books which have the possibility of a long, long life, I would say at once, *The Scarlet Letter*, *Huckleberry Finn*, and *The Country of the Pointed Firs*. I can think of no others that confront time and change so serenely.

—from her preface to *The Best Stories of Sarah Orne Jewett* (1925)

Questions

1. Why should a New Yorker, say, or a Houstonian or a Londoner care about Sarah Orne Jewett's fiction? Does it transcend its colorful local setting?
2. From the fiction in this edition, what do you think is Sarah Orne Jewett's attitude toward men? Is she simply not interested in men? Or is she against them for some reason?
3. What traits held in common by the denizens of Dunnet Landing separate them from other people, Americans or otherwise? How is Dunnet Landing's "group" different from any other?
4. Would you like to have lived in Dunnet Landing? Why, or why not?

FOR FURTHER READING

Letters

Cary, Richard, ed. *Sarah Orne Jewett Letters.* Enlarged and revised edition. Waterville, ME: Colby College Press, 1967.

Fields, Annie, ed. *Letters of Sarah Orne Jewett.* Boston: Houghton Mifflin, 1911.

Biographies

Blanchard, Paula. *Sarah Orne Jewett: Her World and Her Work.* Radcliffe Biography Series. Reading, MA: Addison-Wesley, 1994.

Silverthorne, Elizabeth. *Sarah Orne Jewett: A Writer's Life.* Woodstock, NY: Overlook Press, 1993.

Critical Studies

Cary, Richard, ed. *Appreciation of Sarah Orne Jewett: 29 Interpretive Essays.* Waterville, ME: Colby College Press, 1973.

Cary, Richard. *Sarah Orne Jewett.* Twayne's United States Authors Series, no. 19. New York: Twayne Publishers, 1962.

Donovan, Josephine. *Sarah Orne Jewett.* Modern Literature Series. New York: F. Ungar, 1980.

Nagel, Gwen L., ed. *Critical Essays on Sarah Orne Jewett.* Boston: G. K. Hall, 1984.

Roman, Margaret. *Sarah Orne Jewett: Reconstructing Gender.* Tuscaloosa: University of Alabama Press, 1992.

Sherman, Sarah Way. *Sarah Orne Jewett: An American Persephone.* Hanover, NH: University Press of New England, 1989.

Thorp, Margaret Farrand. *Sarah Orne Jewett.* University of Minnesota Pamphlets on American Writers, no. 61. Minneapolis: University of Minnesota Press, 1966.

Toth, Emily, ed. *Regionalism and the Female Imagination: A Collection of Essays.* New York: Human Sciences Press, 1985.

Westbrook, Perry D. *Acres of Flint: Sarah Orne Jewett and Her Contemporaries.* Metuchen, NJ: Scarecrow Press, 1981.

Other Works Cited in the Introduction and Notes

Brooks, Van Wyck. *New England: Indian Summer, 1865–1915.* New York: E. P. Dutton, 1940.

Cassidy, Frederic Gomes, and Joan Houston Hall, eds. *Dictionary of American Regional English.* Cambridge, MA: Belknap Press, 1985–.

Cather, Willa. "Preface." *The Best Stories of Sarah Orne Jewett.* Vol. 1. Boston: Houghton Mifflin, 1925.

Chapman, Edward M. "The New England of Sarah Orne Jewett." *Yale Review* 3 (October 1913), pp. 157–172.

Howard, Leon, Louis B. Wright, and Carl Bode, eds. *American Heritage: An Anthology and Interpretive Survey of Our Literature.* Vol. 2. Boston: Heath, 1955.

Howe, M. A. De Wolfe. "Sarah Orne Jewett." *Atlantic Monthly* 104 (August 1909), pp. 280–281.

Matthiessen, Francis Otto. *Sarah Orne Jewett.* Boston and New York: Houghton Mifflin, 1929.

Scudder, Horace E. "Miss Jewett." *Atlantic Monthly* 73 (January 1894), pp. 130–133.

Simpson, J. A., and E. S. C. Weiner, eds. *The Oxford English Dictionary.* Second edition. New York: Oxford University Press, 1989.

Spiller, Robert E., et al., eds. *Literary History of the United States.* Vol. 2. New York: Macmillan, 1948.

Thompson, Charles Miner. "The Art of Miss Jewett." *Atlantic Monthly* 94 (October 1904), pp. 485–497.

Original Publication of the Works in This Edition

Jewett's works that appear in this edition are listed below, annotated to show their first publication in a periodical and their first appearance in book form during Jewett's lifetime.

The Country of the Pointed Firs

"The Country of the Pointed Firs." *Atlantic Monthly* 77 (January 1896).
"The Country of the Pointed Firs." *Atlantic Monthly* 77 (March 1896).
"The Country of the Pointed Firs." *Atlantic Monthly* 78 (July 1896).
"The Country of the Pointed Firs." *Atlantic Monthly* 78 (September 1896).
The Country of the Pointed Firs. Boston and New York: Houghton Mifflin, 1896.

Four Dunnet Landing Stories

"A Dunnet Shepherdess." *Atlantic Monthly* 84 (December 1899); *The Queen's Twin, and Other Stories*, Boston: Houghton Mifflin, 1899.
"The Foreigner." *Atlantic Monthly* 86 (August 1900).
"The Queen's Twin." *Atlantic Monthly* 83 (February 1899); *The Queen's Twin, and Other Stories*, Boston: Houghton Mifflin, 1899.
"William's Wedding." *Atlantic Monthly* 106 (August 1910).

Other Stories and Sketches

"The Courting of Sister Wisby." *Atlantic Monthly* 59 (May 1887); *The King of Folly Island, and Other People*, Boston: Houghton Mifflin, 1888.
"Decoration Day." *Harper's New Monthly Magazine* 85 (June 1892); *A Native of Winby, and Other Tales*, Boston and New York: Houghton Mifflin, 1893.
"The Dulham Ladies." *Atlantic Monthly* 57 (April 1886); *A White Heron, and Other Stories*, Boston and New York: Houghton Mifflin, 1886.

"The Flight of Betsey Lane." *Scribner's Magazine* 14 (August 1893); *A Native of Winby, and Other Tales*, Boston and New York: Houghton Mifflin, 1893.

"The Guests of Mrs. Timms." *The Century* 47 (February 1894); *The Life of Nancy*, Boston and New York: Houghton Mifflin, 1895.

"The Hiltons' Holiday." *The Century* 46 (September 1893); *The Life of Nancy*, Boston and New York: Houghton Mifflin, 1895.

"Looking Back on Girlhood." *Youth's Companion* 65 (January 7, 1892), pp. 5–6.

"A Native of Winby." *Atlantic Monthly* 67 (May 1891); *A Native of Winby, and Other Tales*, Boston and New York: Houghton Mifflin, 1893.

"The Passing of Sister Barsett." *Cosmopolitan* 13 (May 1892); *A Native of Winby, and Other Tales*, Boston and New York: Houghton Mifflin, 1893.

"A White Heron." *A White Heron, and Other Stories.* Boston and New York: Houghton Mifflin, 1886.

"The White Rose Road." *Atlantic Monthly* 64 (September 1889); *Strangers and Wayfarers*, Boston and New York: Houghton Mifflin, 1890.

"A Winter Courtship." *Atlantic Monthly* 63 (February 1889); *Strangers and Wayfarers*, Boston and New York: Houghton Mifflin, 1890.